CHAOS
CHOREOGRAPHY

AN INCRYPTID NOVEL

SEANAN McGUIRE

DAW BOOKS, INC.

DONALD A. WOLLHEIM, FOUNDER

375 Hudson Street, New York, NY 10014

ELIZABETH R. WOLLHEIM
SHEILA E. GILBERT
PUBLISHERS

www.dawbooks.com

For Will, who has felt the sting of
reality television and lived to tell the tale.

Price Family Tree

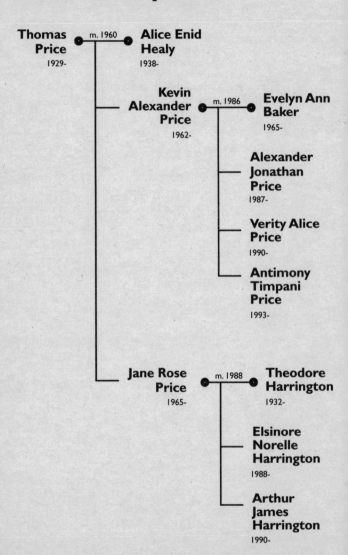

Thomas Price 1929–
m. 1960
Alice Enid Healy 1938–

Kevin Alexander Price 1962–
m. 1986
Evelyn Ann Baker 1965–

Alexander Jonathan Price 1987–

Verity Alice Price 1990–

Antimony Timpani Price 1993–

Jane Rose Price 1965–
m. 1988
Theodore Harrington 1932–

Elsinore Norelle Harrington 1988–

Arthur James Harrington 1990–

Baker Family Tree

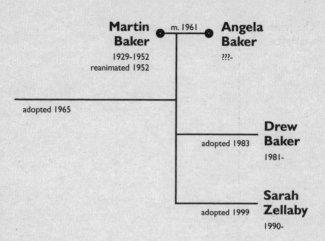

Martin Baker
1929-1952
reanimated 1952

m. 1961

Angela Baker
???-

adopted 1965

adopted 1983 **Drew Baker**
1981-

adopted 1999 **Sarah Zellaby**
1990-

Dance or Die
Dramatis Personae:

The Judges:
  Adrian Crier, executive producer
  Lindy O'Toole, ballroom expert
  Clint Goldfein, choreographer

Our Host:
  Brenna Kelly

The Dancers:
  Season 1: Reggie (hip-hop, winner), Jessica (contemporary), Poppy (ballroom), and Chaz (jazz).
  Season 2: Lyra (jazz, winner), Valerie (ballroom), Anders (tap), and Pax (contemporary).
  Season 3: Mac (ballet, winner), Emily (contemporary), Malena (ballroom), and Troy (hip-hop).
  Season 4: Lo (ballroom, winner), Ivan (ballroom), Will (contemporary), and Raisa (hip-hop).
  Season 5: Graham (contemporary, winner), Danny (ballroom), Leanne (contemporary), and Bobbi (jazz).

Dancer, noun:

1. A person who dances.

Destiny, noun:

1. The inevitable or irresistible course of events.

2. The inescapable future.

3. See also "screwed."

Prologue

"Children know who they're meant to become. It's on us to see to it that they live long enough to get there."
— Enid Healy

*The **Dance or Die** stage, live finale, Los Angeles, California*

Three years ago

"WHEN WE TOOK THE STAGE at the start of this season, twenty dancers stood before you, ready to dazzle you with their talent, strength, and personalities. We're down to two, America: the two dancers you have voted all the way to the end." The show's host, Brenna Kelly, towered over the remaining contestants. She was taller than either of them in her stocking feet, and her fondness for sky-high heels when on stage meant that she currently had almost six inches on Lyra and eight inches on Valerie.

The girls clung to each other's hands, heads bowed, as the lights and glitter swirled around them. Standing at the center of the stage was so bright it felt like standing on the sun. Valerie's thighs ached so badly she was almost shaking. The live finale had opened with the top four doing a complicated jazz number, and had continued from there, never letting up, never relenting. She'd been allowed to rest when the eliminated dancers returned to the stage to perform the judges' favorite routines from the season, but even then, she'd been changing costumes, doing warm-up exercises, doing whatever it took to stay limber and ready to go. She couldn't afford to miss a beat. Not now, not even with the votes already cast and the outcome already determined.

The show was called *Dance or Die*. If she didn't win, there was a good chance that Valerie Pryor—dancer, redhead, innocent human with no connection to the cryptozoological world—was going to die, or at least cease to exist as more than a dead link on the show's Wikipedia page. She'd been created as a mask, intended to prove that the woman who wore her was good enough to leave the family business and forge her own future, complicated and difficult as it might be. Valerie had fought her way through auditions, grueling rehearsals, backstage drama, and she'd done it all to stand right where she was, breathing in this moment.

She was grateful for the lights, even as they blinded her. Their glare meant she couldn't see the audience. Week after week, her fellow contestants had pointed out people in the crowd, mothers and fathers and siblings and lovers. She never had. When the judges asked if she had anyone there to cheer her on, she'd only ever shrugged and said her family didn't support her dancing. The lie ached. Her family supported her more than she could ever have asked. Without their support, she wouldn't have been allowed to craft her Valerie persona and audition in the first place . . . but supporting her career didn't mean they could risk being seen on camera. Every week she'd danced for the families of strangers. She'd never danced for her own.

Lyra's hand was sweaty, her fingers like twigs that clutched and bore down on Valerie's palm until it hurt. Valerie didn't snatch her hand away. That would have looked bad, and petty, and the camera wouldn't miss a second of it. The camera would make sure everyone knew she was a sore loser, and any chance she might have had at a career would be damaged past repair.

Brenna stopped talking. The clip reel music started. A hush fell over the crowd, and Valerie and Lyra obediently turned to watch their season's highlights play out on the jumbo flat-screen monitors. It was eerie. Valerie knew she was the girl with the red hair and the coquettish smile—she'd been living the part long enough to recognize her reflection—but it still felt like watching a stranger, someone who happened to share her footwork and her tendency to fling her left hand dramatically forward. She could see her flaws more easily when they were coming through a stranger. She could also see her merits. And she was *good*. Really, really good.

Please, she thought, as the clip reel wound to an end and the audience erupted in cheers (which were only *slightly* orchestrated by the show's producers; this was reality television, after all). *Please let me win, please let me keep being Valerie, please let this be my life from now on. Please let me be the first one in my generation to get out. Please.*

"The time is here: we've kept you waiting long enough. Are you nervous, my darling girls?" Brenna cast a sincere smile toward both Valerie and Lyra. "You've both been amazing. No matter what this envelope says, you're both winners to me."

Valerie forced a smile. She'd never felt so small, or so certain that everything was about to change. One way or the other, everything was about to change.

"All right. Here we go. The votes are in, and America's Dancer of Choice is . . ."

Please, thought Valerie, and closed her eyes.

". . . Lyra!"

The crowd went wild. Lyra's hand was pulled from Valerie's as she covered her mouth and began to sob. Valerie turned to hug her, feeling like her entire body—her body, which had always listened so well to her commands, carrying her through so much—had gone numb.

"Congratulations," she whispered. She wasn't sure Lyra heard her. The other woman was too busy grinning through her tears, and being handed a bouquet of red roses bigger around than her chest, and then one of the stagehands was there, helping Valerie back, out of the spotlight, out of the way.

Valerie Pryor closed her eyes. Verity Price opened them. It had been fun to be someone else for a little while. She'd even allowed herself to hope it might be forever. But nothing was forever, was it? Valerie Pryor was just a mask she'd been wearing, and now . . .

Now she had work to do.

One

"If at first you don't succeed, try again with a bigger gun."

—Alice Healy

The bank of the main civic reservoir, in the middle of the night, Portland, Oregon

Now

TOO MANY EYES TO COUNT watched us from the surface of the reservoir. Every time I swept my flashlight across the water, I found another two or three dozen pairs glowing in the darkness. All of them were focused on the flashlight, which meant all of them were focused on us. Way to make a girl feel loved.

"Forgive me for stating the obvious, but we're outnumbered," murmured Dominic. He wasn't holding a flashlight. His hands were empty, for now. If something moved, so would he, and given how many knives he could conceal in his leather duster—which may have been cool fifteen years ago; now it was just a weird, if practical, affectation—he wouldn't have any trouble fighting it off.

"Yup," I agreed, continuing to play my flashlight across the water. Eyes, eyes, eyes. Everywhere eyes. I ran down the checklist in the back of my head, trying to find something they could belong to that *wasn't* a sudden and inexplicable infestation of swamp hags. Swamp hags don't belong in city reservoirs. Adults don't move between territories very often, and the size of the eyes I was seeing implied an infestation of adolescents. Which made no sense at all. They would've had to be carried here, and who the hell thought *that* was a good idea? Why—

A bullfrog's sonorous croak split the air. I blinked twice before I burst out laughing, earning myself a side-long look from Dominic.

"What is so funny?" he asked.

"We're here because Artie heard a rumor about 'something weird at the reservoir,' right?" A nod. "And we both assumed the eyes were the weird thing, hence your comment about us being outnumbered." Another nod. I grinned. "The only thing that's wrong here is how many frogs are swimming in the drinking water. Some-body should probably tell the city."

"Frogs."

"Yup. Frogs." I picked up a rock and lobbed it toward a cluster of eyes. The cluster scattered. Several plump bull-frog bodies were briefly visible in the flashlight beam. The rest of the eyes didn't budge. I lowered my flashlight. "They get hypnotized by the light—hence the staring. They're an invasive species, but they're not our problem."

Something splashed a little farther out in the reser-voir.

"Ah, Verity," said Dominic.

"People introduced them all over the country, some-times by mistake, sometimes on purpose, and sometimes because they were trying to feed the family manticore," I said. "Manticore are surprisingly chill about eating am-phibians. You'd think the whole 'cold blood' thing would be a problem, but you'd be wrong."

"Verity, I must insist," said Dominic.

"Insist on what?" I turned to face him, the beam of my flashlight striking his chest and illuminating his face. He had his serious expression on, the one that implied an asteroid was about to smack into the planet and wipe out all human life, thus sparing him the indignity of put-ting up with it for one minute more. It used to piss me off when he made that face. These days I find it funny as hell. Nobody fights harder for the survival of the people around him than Dominic, and it's not his fault he sounds like a stuffed shirt half the time.

He is a man of many excellent qualities, which is why I married him.

"I must insist you look back at the water." He was starting to sound faintly strangled. That wasn't normal. It probably wasn't good. I turned my flashlight back toward the reservoir.

The light gleamed off the scales of a long, slender column that stretched from the water to some unseen higher point. Mouth suddenly dry, I played the light upward, confirming that a) the column was a neck, and b) the neck belonged to something carnivorous in the long-necked plesiosaur family.

"Oh," I said. "Well. Will you look at that?"

Like the frogs, the plesiosaur seemed fascinated by my light. Unlike the frogs, the plesiosaur had a head at least two feet long, and a mouth that bristled with sharp, flesh-ripping teeth. I'd been a lot happier when it was just frogs.

"That is a dinosaur," said Dominic. "I . . . I admit, I was not expecting a dinosaur."

"Technically it's not a dinosaur, it's a plesiosaur," I said. "I think. Probably. I don't feel like getting closer so I can find out, do you?" Plesiosaurs, and things like them, are the purview of my brother Alex, who likes reptiles and amphibians and other creatures he can't reasonably have a conversation with. Unfortunately, Alex was in Ohio, and had not accompanied us on the night's adventure. I'm the urban cryptid girl. My job involves talking to things that can talk *back*, and as far as I knew, plesiosaurs didn't fall under that umbrella.

Maybe I was being hasty. I cleared my throat, pasted on my most reasonable-looking smile, and called, "Hello, the plesiosaur! Would you like to have a nice chat about what you're doing in our reservoir?"

My name is Verity Price; I'm a cryptozoologist. That means that sometimes my life includes shouting at extinct genera of reptiles. My life is weird.

The plesiosaur cocked its head, looking for all the world like an enormous iguana. For a moment, I thought maybe this was going to work out for the best. The plesiosaur would reveal a heretofore unsuspected intelligence, and explain in small, pleasant words how it had wound up in the Portland reservoir, and how I could get it out before the authorities noticed.

Then the plesiosaur opened its mouth, made a horrifying keening noise, and darted toward us, moving fast enough to constitute a clear and present danger. I yelped, jumping out of the way. Dominic was a dark blur against the bushes as he raced for safety. The plesiosaur's jaws snapped shut where I'd been standing only a moment before.

"Not friendly," I said, in case Dominic had somehow managed to miss the memo.

"Oh *really*? Whatever gave you that idea?"

"There's no need for sarcasm," I called. In the distance, Dominic snorted.

The plesiosaur pulled back for another strike. I braced myself to jump again. The thing couldn't stay in the reservoir, that was for sure, and I didn't want to leave when there was a chance it might eat a jogger or something, but I wasn't ready to kill it, either. There'd been no reports of it hurting anyone. There hadn't even been any conclusive sightings, prior to me and my flashlight. It was just an innocent prehistoric reptile, doing what came naturally for innocent prehistoric reptiles.

The head snapped forward again. I jumped backward this time, using my momentum to turn the motion into a handspring. It was showy and pointless, but a girl's got to stay in practice somehow, and besides, it wasn't like we were in a lot of danger as long as we didn't hold still. The plesiosaur was cranky and snappy, but it couldn't leave the water. Well. I didn't *think* it could leave the water. It probably couldn't leave the water.

I decided to stay a little farther back from the water.

"Is there a plan? Or are you just going to keep jumping about like a startled cat?" Dominic's voice came from behind me. He must have gotten through the bushes and worked his way around to avoid the plesiosaur.

"Those bushes are like half blackberry bramble," I said.

"I'm aware," said Dominic.

"I have a plan," I said, tensing as the plesiosaur pulled back. "I'm going to wear it out, and when it submerges, I'm going to find out who thought it was okay to store their giant lizard in the city reservoir, and we're going to have a little talk."

"There will still be a plesiosaur in the reservoir," said Dominic.

Sometimes he was so practical it made me want to scream. "That's why God invented U-Haul rentals," I said. The plesiosaur lunged. I leaped. From the blackberry bushes, Dominic swore. I allowed myself to smile. He was learning the dangers of questioning me.

Not that he had much left to learn. Dominic and I met in New York, where I'd been spending a year working as a professional ballroom dancer and he was doing the prep work for a purge by the Covenant of St. George. Naturally, we hit it off right away. He hit me with a snare, and then I hit him with my stunning wit and cheerful willingness to shoot him until he stopped squirming. It wasn't your classic Hollywood meet-cute—more of a standoff with the cryptid population of Manhattan hanging in the balance—but we'd been able to make things work. Mostly because he was a nice guy, under all that Covenant brainwashing, and he had the common sense to find me mad cute, which meant he was also a *smart* guy.

"Please tell me you're not planning to put the dinosaur in the back of a U-Haul." There was a pleading note in Dominic's tone, like he couldn't believe those words had left his mouth in that order. "The company is still angry with us over the *last* U-Haul you rented."

"I am a constant source of enlightenment and delight, and it's a plesiosaur!" I chirped, and jumped again.

Two things happened then: three flashlights clicked

on at the edge of the path along the reservoir, and a voice shouted, "Hey! What are you doing over there?"

"Oh, great, civilians," I muttered.

Most people don't believe in monsters. Sure, the general public enjoys a good scare. Somebody makes a movie about a cursed videotape or a haunted doll, and they're right in the front row, shoveling down popcorn and screaming happy screams when somebody's guts hit the floor. That's not the same as believing. Some things we have to hide from science, waiting for the day when people will be ready to deal with the idea of talking mice or fish with fur. Other things science hides from itself, because no one really wants the night to be dark and filled with monsters. That era has passed.

The trouble is, nobody gave the monsters—better described as "predatory cryptids," since "monster" is sort of insulting—the memo. They exist, and when given the opportunity, they happily eat people who don't believe in them. This brought me back to the civilians running down the path in our direction, heedless of the fact that at the end of their jog, they were going to be facing a lot of teeth.

"Dominic," I hissed.

"I'm on it," he said. The bushes rustled, and he appeared a few yards down the path, running toward the flashlights.

"I married Batman," I said fondly. The plesiosaur struck. I yelped, barely jumping out of the way in time.

"Stop harassing Nemo!" wailed an unfamiliar voice.

The plesiosaur turned toward it, neck stretching into a curve I could only describe as curious. Really tame snakes sometimes assumed that position. So did snakes that were thinking about turning something into a new source of protein. I gave serious, if rapid, thought to launching myself at the plesiosaur. I wasn't wearing anything I couldn't get wet, and it might keep somebody from being eaten.

Then the words sunk in. "Wait. Nemo?" I turned to look in the same direction as the plesiosaur. "You *named* it?"

The owners of the flashlights kept running. Dominic grabbed one by the shoulders, hauling the figure to a halt, but the other two got past him, becoming visible. Both were in their early twenties, at best; they might have been in their teens. One was faster than the other. He reached me first, and shoved me hard enough that I actually stumbled. His companion ran for the edge of the reservoir, where the plesiosaur was bowing its head to meet her.

"What do you think you're doing?" he demanded, going in to shove me again.

Right. I'd been startled before, but no way was he putting his hands on me a second time. I grabbed his wrist, spinning hard to the side and twisting as I went, until I wound up behind him with his arm bent at an angle that wasn't *quite* going to dislocate his shoulder. Well, probably not. If he moved, all bets were off.

He made a guttural keening noise, surprisingly low for the amount of pain he was almost certainly in. His companion turned from the act of stroking the plesiosaur's nose, her eyes gone wide with shock. He'd dropped his flashlight when I grabbed him. It was spinning, illuminating different parts of the scene.

"Hi," I said brightly, giving the girl my best camera-ready smile. "Who feels like explaining what the hell is going on? I'll give you a hint: it's probably not your friend here. He's sort of got other things to worry about." I gave his arm another squeeze. He moaned again.

"What are you doing?" The girl stepped forward, putting herself between me and the plesiosaur. "Let Charlie go! He didn't do anything to you!"

"Uh, wrong," I said. "He shoved me. Didn't anybody ever teach him that it's rude to lay hands on a lady?"

Dominic came walking down the path, dragging another young woman by the arm. She had long brown hair, and looked like the sort of girl I was used to finding on my sister's roller derby team. Too bad she *wasn't* on my sister's roller derby team. Antimony would have known about the plesiosaur if that had been the case, and we wouldn't be standing here now.

"Please, we're not hurting anything," said the second girl. "We didn't expect to see your flashlights, and we sort of panicked. Please, let us go."

"Were you expecting to see the plesiosaur?" I asked.

"Nemo's not a dino—" protested the first girl. Then she caught herself, and blinked, and said, "Um, yes. He's ours."

"I'm sorry. Maybe I got something in my ear when your friend here shoved me," I said. "Did you just say the plesiosaur was *yours*?"

Dominic released the second girl, who rocked back and forth for a moment, torn between rushing to defend her prehistoric reptile and going to the aid of her much more modern, if not much more evolved, companion. In the end, the plesiosaur won, and she fled to stand next to the other girl, blocking "Nemo" from our deadly attentions.

"Yes," snapped the first girl. "Nemo's ours, and he's never hurt anybody, and no one would believe you anyway, so you should just go. You hear me? Get out of here and go."

"Since we weren't doing anything but being near the reservoir when Nemo decided to pop his head *out* and start trying to bite my head *off*, I think you may be wrong about whether he's ever hurt anybody," I said. It was hard to sound gentle while I had their friend in an armlock. I leaned forward, murmuring in his ear, "Are you going to shove me again?"

"No, I swear," he whimpered.

I let him go. He ran to his friends, cradling his arm and staring at me fearfully.

"You must have done something," said the first girl. "Nemo wouldn't hurt a fly."

"Nemo has a fifteen-foot neck, which means he's a pretty big boy," I said. "Have you been dumping tadpoles in the reservoir to feed him?" They didn't answer me. They didn't need to. Their guilty expressions were answer enough. "There are a lot of frogs in there, so I'm going to wager that Nemo doesn't eat frogs. They probably taste funny. So he ate all the fish in the reservoir — alas for the free-range goldfish population — and then he probably moved on to small mammals. There sure were a lot of missing pet fliers up at the mouth of the trail, did you notice?"

No missing kid fliers. Not yet. That was a small blessing. Things like Nemo were miracles of endurance and evolution, but they couldn't be allowed to go around eating children.

The newcomers blanched. The second girl looked faintly sick. She must have been an animal lover, not just a plesiosaur fan.

The first girl leaned up to wrap her arms around Nemo's head. The plesiosaur endured her affections surprisingly well for a prehistoric reptile. "I don't care," she said. "He's not hurting anything, and we're not going to let you hurt him."

I sighed. "We're not going to hurt him. But we might be able to help you save him. Or did you think you could keep him in the reservoir forever?"

The trio exchanged glances. Finally, the first girl asked, "Save him how?"

Girl #1's name was Kim; girl #2 was Angie. The boy was Charlie. All three were students at the local community college, and had gone on an archaeological dig in Kansas the summer before. They'd fallen through a false floor in one of the caverns, and into a moist, warm chamber, where there'd been a nest mounded with leathery, football-sized eggs. Being scientists, they had naturally been fascinated, and being primates, they had naturally dealt with this fascination by stealing an egg from the edge of the nest.

"We thought it would be an old fossil with a remarkably well-preserved eggshell, but when we put it through the X-ray, we realized it was alive," said Kim, stroking

Nemo's snout, as if to reassure herself that it was okay to tell us this. "So we smuggled it home in one of the specimen cases, and at the end of the summer, it hatched into Nemo here. My beautiful boy."

The plesiosaur nuzzled her cheek. Kim laughed. Angie gave her a look that made it clear that Nemo wasn't the only one who wanted to be nuzzling her. Kim didn't notice. I felt like I was seeing their entire relationship in microcosm, and I didn't want anything to do with it.

"When did you decide to put your pet in the reservoir?" I asked.

All three of them looked guilty. It was like I'd flipped a switch. Charlie spoke, saying, "It was my idea. Nemo was growing so fast, and we were afraid somebody was going to find him at the school. But nobody comes up to the reservoir."

"Nobody except joggers, and teenagers, and homeless people looking for a place to camp, and birders, and whatever the 'I like to look at butterflies' equivalent of birders is . . ." I let my voice trail off, looking at the trio. They seemed to be grasping the seriousness of their situation.

"Oh," said Kim, in a small voice.

"Yeah, 'oh.' You're lucky no one's been eaten yet. Which, let me tell you, is not a situation that's going to last. Between the way Nemo went for me, and the fact that *someone* is eventually going to tell the city about the reservoir being full of frogs, it's only a matter of time." I folded my arms. "We don't even know how big he's going to get. You really want to see your pet on the news, being gunned down by a SWAT team? Because that's what's going to happen."

"We didn't know what else to do," protested Kim. "You startled him, he's never been aggressive with any of us, he wouldn't really . . . wouldn't really *eat* people."

"And it's not like we can move him," added Charlie. "We brought him here in the back of a pickup truck. He's bigger than my pickup truck now. We couldn't move him even if we had a place to move him to."

"The reservoir is fresh water," I said. "Can he handle saltwater, or is he purely a lake monster?"

I used the word "monster" on purpose, and was pleased to see all three of them flinch, Kim most of all. "He doesn't like saltwater," said Kim stiffly. "It tickles his nose. But he can handle it if he has to."

"What's his temperature range?"

"Good." Kim continued to rub Nemo's snout as she spoke, apparently calming both of them. "He doesn't seem to mind the cold much, although it slows him down some. I'm sorry, but who *are* you people? Why are you asking us all these questions?"

"We're cryptozoologists, and we're here to solve your problem," I said, and smiled.

They didn't smile back.

Six phone calls later—including one to Uncle Mike, who wasn't thrilled about being woken up in the wee hours of the morning just so I could talk to Aunt Lea—we had the solution.

"My dad's coming over with an old dump truck that can be filled with water," I said, tucking my phone into my pocket. "Kim, you'll ride with Nemo. Dad's going to take you upriver to an isolated spot where you should be good for a week or so while we get some old friends of ours to turn around and come back to Portland. The Campbell Family Carnival has a tank large enough for an adult plesiosaur. They'll be able to transport him—and you, we're not leaving you out of this—to the Cascades, where you can find him a suitable lake. Something deep and full of fish and not popular with boaters."

"Why are you doing this?" asked Angie. "What's in it for you?"

"One more plesiosaur in the world," I said. "That's pretty cool. Can I get a picture? My brother's gonna be *pissed* that he missed this."

"Sure," said Kim, looking bewildered.

"Awesome." I pulled my phone out again. "Dominic, hit the lights?"

He sighed and pulled out his flashlight, shining it on us as I backed up and held out my phone. "Say Cretaceous," I said, and snapped the selfie.

All in all, not the worst night.

Two

"Love what you do. Even if it's not what you thought you'd be doing when you were a kid, love what you do. Eventually, it's going to kill you, and it would be a real pity if you died doing something you hate."

—Evelyn Baker

A small survivalist compound about an hour's drive east of Portland, Oregon

THE SUN WAS DOWN and the house was dark when we pulled up to the gate. Dad was going to be out a lot later than we were: he was transporting Nemo the plesiosaur, Nemo's human friends, and a few hundred gallons of water upriver, and that took time. We'd be lucky to see him before lunch.

Dominic politely averted his eyes while I punched in the current security code. He's family now—he's even planning to change his last name to "Price," since it's not like he can go around using "De Luca" without attracting Covenant attention—but that doesn't mean he's been cleared to have full access to the house. My argument with the parents is ongoing. If Dominic is going to be living with us, he needs to be able to get into the bugout room, almost as much as he needs to be able to go to the grocery store without an escort.

Dominic says he's willing to wait until he earns their trust. I say they're punishing him, and by extension, me, for getting married by an Elvis impersonator in Las Vegas, rather than having a fancy ceremony for everyone in the family to attend and pass judgment on.

My parents have no respect for the classics.

(To be fair, they're correct in assuming that Dominic and I got married the way we did in order to make it harder for them to reject him out of hand. We also did it because we really wanted to get married, and we were passing through Vegas on the way to Portland anyway, so why not? No Las Vegas wedding is complete without a chupacabra dressed as Elvis asking if you're planning to love, honor, obey, and finish eating your banana sandwich.)

We slipped through the front door and crossed the living room to the kitchen, where not a creature was stirring, not even a mouse. At this hour of the morning, most of the Aeslin were asleep, and the ones that weren't would be preparing the temples for the day ahead. Our family colony of polytheistic mice kept a very strict calendar of religious observances, one that included every day of the year, as well as a few days they had shoehorned in there, just to get a bit of extra worshipping in. It must have been exhausting, being an Aeslin mouse.

Once the kitchen door was closed, I sighed, sagged against the counter, and asked, "What are your feelings on breakfast? We need to eat something before we go to bed, or we're going to wake up gnawing on each other."

"Waffles," said Dominic, opening the freezer and producing a familiar yellow Eggo box. "No effort. No cleanup. Good delivery mechanism for peanut butter."

"Sold." I took the box and peered inside. There were four waffles remaining. Miraculously, that was also the number of slots on our family-sized toaster. I dropped them in. "We need something else. This is insufficient waffles."

"Oh, no. This is not your territory." Dominic's hands closed on my shoulders, pulling me back before I could start investigating the contents of the fridge. "Go sit down. I will figure out breakfast."

"But I want to help," I protested.

"The last time you scavenged for breakfast, we wound up with leftover pizza omelets." Dominic pushed me toward the table. "That's not a meal. That's a punishment for bad behavior. I'll make something intended to be eaten by humans, and I'll bring it to you, and then we can go to bed."

"Fine." I grabbed a laptop off the counter and sulked away. Dominic watched me go, shaking his head fondly. He knew I hadn't really wanted to win; I knew he enjoyed the fight. Of such little understandings are a solid relationship built.

I dropped my butt into a seat and opened the laptop. Each of us in the family has our own computer—how else could we have ever felt comfortable looking at porn?—but there are always a few loaner machines floating around, courtesy of Antimony's constant equipment upgrades and Artie's equally constant glee at nuking their contents and turning them into helpful shells. We don't use the spares for anything secure. They're still extremely convenient when, say, I want to check my email without going upstairs to my bedroom.

(Not that my bedroom was particularly livable at the moment. We were in the process of prepping the guesthouse out back for me and Dominic. It meant we wouldn't be as well-equipped for actual guests, but I didn't care if it meant having a bathroom we wouldn't need to share with my younger sister. Half my things were in boxes, and the remaining half were strewn across the room like there'd been some sort of localized explosion. It was all going to be worth it when we didn't have to cram ourselves into a twin bed every night. I loved the man, but I was starting to feel like one of us needed to remove an arm before either of us would be able to sleep comfortably.)

Dominic muttered and rattled around the kitchen while the laptop loaded my settings. When it was done, I pulled up my email, skimming the subject lines to see if anything needed my immediate attention. Nothing did.

The thing about being in the family business is that you never really strike out as an independent contractor: you're always going to be running things through the central clearing house that is your older relatives. I'd been able to find problems that needed fixing without their help while I was in New York, but I wasn't in New York anymore. I was back in Portland, back in the place where people remembered me as a three-foot-tall moppet running to her ballet recital, and when they had problems, they took them to my dad or my Aunt Jane. Not to me.

I sighed and clicked over to Valerie's email. Valerie was my mundane alter ego, a redheaded Latin ballroom specialist who never had to worry about getting blood out of sequins or whether it was appropriate to go clubbing after beating the crap out of a ghoul. Valerie was half my imaginary friend and half my imaginary self. She slept in when she wanted to. She danced every day. Most importantly, she lived her life on her terms, with no one telling her who she had to be or what she had to love.

There was a time when all I wanted was to find a way to *become* Valerie, even if it meant leaving Verity behind. I would've missed my family, but I had every faith we'd have been able to find a way to be together, even once I was no longer considered a Price. I would have been dancing. For me, on some level, that would have been enough . . . at least for a while.

It could never have been enough forever, which was why when the choice was actually put in front of me—be a cryptozoologist, and *help* people, or be a professional dancer, and never do the work I'd been raised to do ever again—I'd made the only choice I really could. I'd put Valerie aside and become Verity for good.

That didn't mean I'd deleted Valerie's email account. For one thing, Valerie had been a beloved contestant on *Dance or Die*, one of the few reality competitions completely based on skill, instead of relying on how much drama the contestants could stir up to amuse the producers. If she'd disappeared completely, it would have been a scandal and something for people to investigate. The official story was that she was taking a year off from teaching dance in Manhattan while she put her head back together. I maintained her Facebook fan page and answered her email. Eventually, it would all taper off, more than it already had, and Valerie would be able to rest in peace.

That was the idea, anyway. I skimmed the subject lines in her inbox, opening the messages that looked interesting. Most were reports from the fan page. A few pieces of spam, as always, had managed to slither past the filters. One of my old dance buddies was asking whether there was any chance I'd be attending a competition in Kansas, since he needed a partner, his having decided to get pregnant. Another dancer I used to compete with wanted to know if it was true that I'd snapped my leg like a twig doing one of my, quote, "stupid jumps." And the producers of *Dance or Die* wanted to know about my availability.

Wait. What?

I opened the email again, forcing myself to read slowly this time. The producers of *Dance or Die* were interested in knowing whether I was in "fighting shape" and available for a project to begin in six weeks, and last up to two months after that.

"Two months," I muttered. "That's the length of a competition season."

"What?" asked Dominic.

"Uh." I twisted to look at him. He was frying something on the stove; I sniffed the air. Bacon. He was making me bacon. My aggravating, wonderful, ex-Covenant husband, who had no real idea what the dance part of my life entailed, was making me bacon.

"I need to set the alarm when we go to bed," I said. "I need to make a phone call."

The *Dance or Die* production offices were located in Burbank, California, which meant we were at least in the same time zone, even if Southern California should really be considered a whole other world. They opened at nine. The alarm went off at eight fifty-five, almost three hours after Dominic and I had finally crawled into bed.

Dominic made an unhappy noise and attempted to burrow deeper into his pillow, lacing his hands together behind his head like he could somehow convince the noise that he'd already surrendered and no longer needed to be tormented. I leaned over him to slap the alarm off, only to find myself facing a veritable sea of mice. They covered the floor beside the bed, looking up at me with wide and hopeful eyes.

"What?" I hissed. Realizing my mistake, I hurriedly added, "And do *not* hail me, Dominic is trying to sleep."

"Failing," came Dominic's woeful comment, voice muffled by his pillow.

The mice looked somewhat deflated. A small voice from the back of the crowd peeped a soft "Hail," and was shushed by the mice around it. I raised an eyebrow. The leader of this merry band—identifiable by the fact that it was wearing a fancy cloak made of braided doll hair—stepped forward, motioning for the rest to be quiet.

"Hail to Verity, the Arboreal Priestess, bride to the God of Hard Choices in Dark Places," it squeaked. "To-day begins the great feast of Dammit, Enid, Where Is That Girl, I Know She Tells You When She's Sneaking Out. We have come to beg a re-creation."

I was still partially asleep, and it took me a moment to remember which holiday they were talking about. "Wait—isn't this the one where Grandma Alice got lost in the woods for almost a whole day, and then wound up at Grandpa Thomas' house for the first time?"

The mice nodded vigorously, and this time there were multiple soft, forbidden "hails" from the center of the crowd.

"Sorry, guys." I shook my head. "I normally like a good romp around the woods as much as the next girl, but I have some work I need to do today. Work that can't be done from a tree. Go ask Antimony, I'm sure she'd be happy to."

"The Precise Priestess said, upon your return home, 'Oh, Thank God, At Least With Barbie Back In The House, I Won't Have To Do Every Single Ritual,'" said the lead mouse, fanning out its whiskers. "Was she so wrong?"

Aeslin mice have an eidetic memory for everything they see and hear, and it's against their religion to misquote their gods—i.e., us. Which meant Antimony was definitely at the end of her patience. Also that she had definitely called me "Barbie." I wasn't sure how to feel about that. "She wasn't wrong, no, but I can't do it today," I said. "I have to make some phone calls, and you know the cell service in the woods sucks. It's important. Sorry. I'll do the next one." None of the rituals were actually *dangerous* for the humans the mice recruited to act them out. Sometimes slimy, and occasionally embarrassing, but the mice would never hurt us. They loved us too much for that.

"As you say, Priestess," said the head priest, ears drooping.

I sighed. The jury's still out on whether the Aeslin mice guilt trip us intentionally, or whether they're just really, really good at it, but the fact remains that every time we say "no," they react like the world is ending—and there's only one way to fix it. "Meet me in the kitchen in an hour," I said. "Cheese and cake will be provided."

The priest looked back to me, suddenly hopeful. "May we cheer, Priestess?"

"Yes, yes, let them cheer," muttered Dominic, not pulling his head out of the pillow. "It's not like I was going to get any more sleep this morning. What's a little cheering after a dinosaur and an alarm clock?"

"It wasn't a dinosaur," I said automatically, before telling the mice, "You can cheer."

The racket that went up was better than a cup of coffee for clearing my head. I blinked.

"Whoa. Um, okay. And on that note, I invoke Bedroom Privileges. Get out."

"Yes, Priestess!" squeaked the mouse priest, now in much better spirits. The crowd dispersed with remarkable speed, vanishing under furniture and through the holes cut into the baseboards.

(If we ever tried to sell the property—which we wouldn't; Dad would burn the place to the ground before he let it leave the family—we'd have some explaining to do when the realtor saw the tiny, geometrically perfect mouse holes cut into every interior wall. In the case of long walls, like hallways or the living room, there were multiple holes, at least one every six feet. Of course, that was nothing compared to the explaining we'd have to do if the realtors decided to look inside one of those walls, and found the intricate network of stairways, portrait galleries, and rooms the Aeslin had built there, working around the insulation and wiring. Some houses have a mouse problem. We have a mouse utopia.)

Dominic left his face buried in his pillow. I planted a kiss at the back of his neck and slid off the bed, heading for the desk on the other side of the room. Getting there required me to weave around piles of boxes, which reinforced my determination to be completely moved out of this room by the end of the week. After spending a year in someone else's apartment, followed by six months in a U-Haul, I was ready to stop living out of boxes.

The power strip on the desk was connected to four phones: mine, Dominic's, and two burners. I picked up one of the burners, checked its charge, and took a deep breath before unlocking the screen and keying in the number for the production offices.

I didn't want to sit on the bed while I made the call, so I sat on the desk, crossing my legs and trying to focus on thoughts of serenity and calm.

The phone rang once; twice; three times, and I was starting to think I was calling too early in the day when there was a click and a generically pleasant female voice said, "Adrian Crier Productions, how may I direct your call?"

I took a deep breath. When I spoke, my voice was light, breezy, and half an octave higher than it usually was: the voice of a woman whose greatest concern was figuring out how she was going to pay for a new tango costume. "Hi, this is Valerie Pryor, I got a message saying you wanted to speak with me?"

"Miss Pryor!" Suddenly, the woman on the other end of the phone sounded like she was actually invested in talking to me. That was . . . odd, and a bit disturbing. "Mr. Crier is expecting your call. Can you please hold while I check to see if he's available?"

"Sure," I said. I'd barely finished the word when there was a click, and pleasant classical music began to play in my ear.

There was a creak from the direction of the bed. I turned to find Dominic staring at me, a bemused expression on his face. He was shirtless. I smiled and took a moment to admire the view.

Dominic is short by most people's standards, which means he's reasonable by mine, since I'm only five foot two when I'm not wearing heels. He has the kind of lean, solid build that I look for in a dance partner, thick, dark hair perfect for running my fingers through, and dark eyes that go well with the puzzled expressions he seems to wear almost constantly these days. I'd thought he was good looking even when he was a member of the Covenant of St. George and things could never have been serious between us. Now he's a free agent, and he's mine, and he's gorgeous.

There was another click. I returned my attention to the phone as a jovial British voice came on the line, exclaiming, "Valerie! As I live and breathe, it's good to hear from you, sweetheart! You were always one of my favorites, you know that, don't you darling?"

"Hi, Adrian," I said, smiling broadly so he'd hear it in my voice. Adrian Crier was the sort of man who adored you while you were on his good side, and wouldn't hesitate to bury you once you got on his bad side. Naturally, I'd always done my best to stay on his good side. "I missed you, too. What's going on? Why am I getting emails all of a sudden?"

"Well, darling, it's because the number we had for you wasn't ringing through anymore, and we needed to get hold of you rather desperately. Is this number on my display good? Can we call you here if we need to?"

It was an unassigned burner phone; that's why I'd used it. I'd just have to keep reloading it with minutes until whatever Adrian was asking me to do was over.

No. I frowned at myself. Until I had *turned down* whatever Adrian was asking me to do. "This is a good number for me, yes," I said. "What's up?"

"Well, sweetheart, I don't know if you've been watching the ratings, but we're in a bit of a slump right now. People still care about dance—it's a vital part of the human emotional landscape—but they get down at heart when their favorites are eliminated, and they stop watching for a season while they get over it. Just like a breakup, wouldn't you say?"

No breakup had ever inspired me to the amount of self-destructive ice cream consumption *Dance or Die* had. I still injected a bit of awe into my voice as I replied, "I never thought of it like that, but you're so right. It's just like ending a relationship."

"We've been commissioned for another season, thank God, but the network is starting to look a little reluctant to commit. So we were passing the old idea hat around, and Brenna came up with the best suggestion any of us had ever heard! Got a guess on what it is?"

"Um . . . reduce the number of audition shows from eight to four so you don't have to deal with the ratings drop that always comes from people getting bored and changing channels during hour two?"

A faint sharpness came into Adrian's voice. "You know how important the audition shows are to our audience, Valerie."

"I know, I know, I love them, I watch them with my family, but I *understand* the level of technique we're seeing," I said, trying not to sound like I was covering a mistake. Even though I technically was. "Those shows establish why the lineup looks the way it does once the season starts. I'm just saying, sometimes people come up to me and complain about how long it takes to get to the competition. So I might give up some of those shows if it meant the ratings of the rest would go up."

"Ah," said Adrian, sounding mollified. "I suppose that's not bad thinking, even if it goes counter to what we try to do with this program. Brenna's idea does dovetail a bit with what you've been saying, darling, in that it would replace the audition shows for this season with a pair of clip shows—and given that we've already passed the window for auditions by a good measure, it's what we're doing. I just wanted to know if you were on board. You're one of our stars, you know, even if you didn't go on to set the competition world on fire."

"I've been busy," I said, too relieved by the return of "darling" to his vocabulary to think about the rest. Then my brain caught up with my ears. "Wait. On board with what, Adrian? You didn't say what her idea was."

"Oh, didn't I? Silly me. We're doing an all-star season, my dove. The top four from the past five seasons returning to duke it out and learn who America's Dancer of Choice *really* is."

"Whoa," I said.

"There's a quite decent prize package," he said, wheedling. "Two hundred and fifty thousand dollars, a feature in *Technique Magazine*, and a year's paid rent on a Manhattan flat. And the exposure, of course. It could kick your career to the next level."

My career was over. I had walked away from it willingly, and with no intention of going back. "That's tempting, Adrian, but—"

"The other three dancers from your season are already on board. We can punt and go to the girl eliminated in the number five position, but wouldn't it be better to bring back the dream team? Come on, sweetheart, be a peach and do it for me. Even if you don't need this, I do."

I hesitated. My career was over . . . but that didn't mean I couldn't have one last hurrah. "Can I call you back in an hour? I need to check my schedule and have a word with my boyfriend."

Dominic's expression darkened at the word "boyfriend." He held up his left hand, looking exaggeratedly from me to his wedding ring and back again. I mouthed the word "sorry" at him. He scowled.

"Just don't leave us hanging any longer than that, all right, darling? I need to get this locked down. Talk to you soon." Adrian hung up. I lowered the phone.

Dominic was still scowling. "Boyfriend? Was there a demotion in the night that I was unaware of? Because I didn't allow myself to be lectured by a woman in a skintight sequined jumpsuit just to be bumped back to 'boyfriend' as soon as—Verity?" His scowl faded, replaced by concern. "What's wrong?"

I must have looked pretty distraught if he was having that reaction. I put the phone down and thought about standing, but I wasn't sure my legs would work. Better not to risk it until I had a bit more confidence. "That was Adrian Crier, the producer of *Dance or Die*. It's his baby. He has a real thing for dance education, and he basically went into reality television so he could have a dance show one day."

"*Dance or Die*—that's the show you were on." Dominic and I had spent a comfortable night curled up in a motel room in Colorado watching all my dance routines and solos on YouTube, with me explaining how each number had gone right—or wrong. I'd been more brutal to myself than the judging panel had ever been, but when I was done, Dominic had been there to kiss me and ask for more videos. It had been therapeutic in the extreme, and at the time, it had felt like a fitting funeral for my dance career.

Apparently not. Or maybe not, anyway; I still had to talk to some people, starting with the man in front of me.

"Yeah, that's the show I was on," I said. "He wants to do an all-star season, with the top four dancers from the past five seasons. I was number two in my season." Me and Lyra, the only female top two in the show's history. We'd promised to keep in touch after the show was over. I hadn't heard from her since she'd won.

Dominic's scowl lifted. "He wants you to be on television again?"

"Yeah."

"Wouldn't that be dangerous, after . . . everything?"

"Maybe," I admitted. Dominic and I had left New York—and he'd left the Covenant of St. George—after a Covenant strike team had arrived with the intention of checking his work and starting their purge. They'd found out about me, and hence that my family line hadn't died out after all; they'd learned that Dominic was keeping secrets, including my existence, from the organization he was supposed to be loyal to.

In the end, the only way we'd been able to escape with our lives was by having my telepathic cousin Sarah rewrite their memories, turning me into a Price imposter and Dominic into a power-mad traitor. As far as the Covenant team was concerned, both Dominic and his self-made "Price" had died in the gunfight that ended their assignment in the States.

(It had been a neat solution, but it wasn't without its costs. Sarah had never used her telepathy that way before, and the backlash hurt her. Badly. She's been recovering with my grandparents in Ohio ever since. For a while, we'd been afraid she was never going to be fully herself again. That fear had proved unfounded—she's definitely still Sarah, if less cocky and confident in her own abilities than she used to be—but it was a terrifying experience, and not one that I'm in any hurry to repeat.)

"What would the benefits be?" asked Dominic. "If you danced again, and won, would it make you restart your dance career?"

I blew out a slow breath. "I don't know," I admitted. "I thought I was done with that part of my life, but I also feel like ... if I don't do this, I'll always be asking myself 'what if,' you know? What if I'd gone back? What if I'd danced so well that they gave me a second chance at the big stage?"

"Are you good enough?" He held up a hand before I could squawk indignantly. "You're the finest dancer I've ever known, but when we met, you were dancing for three hours a day. I haven't seen you practice your foot-work in weeks. Will you be able to meet your own standards on the floor?"

"Yes," I said. This, at least, I could say with certainty. "I haven't been doing my dance practice, but the rest of my physical conditioning is still good. I'd have to vary my daily exercise routines, and really focus on my feet and hips between now and the show. That's no big deal. I'm in better shape than most dancers can even dream of—and dancers are by and large a healthy lot that spends a lot of time in motion."

"And your Valerie identity, it's still sound?"

"No one's managed to blow it yet," I said. "I'd have to unpack my wigs, and see about getting a few new ones, since the old ones have been in storage since my last competition. But Verity Price has never danced profes-sionally, and we use so much makeup when I'm Valerie that she and I don't even have the same complexion. I'd basically have to pull my wig off and announce myself." It was all very Scooby-Doo. A wig and some makeup and nobody knew my name. But it worked, and that was what mattered.

Dominic nodded. "Valerie Pryor, of course, is not married to me."

"Yes," I said. "That's why I called you my boyfriend when I was talking to Adrian. I didn't want to have to explain to him why I didn't send him an invitation to the wedding. Not that he would have come, and not that there was actually a wedding, but you know what I mean."

"Miraculously enough, I do know what you mean," said Dominic. "Your approach to the English language is like a virus, and after long exposure, I've contracted a great deal of it. I may, by this point, be incurably afflicted."

I stuck my tongue out at him. Dominic laughed before sobering, sitting up a little straighter in the bed. He shouldn't have been capable of looking that grave while half-naked, but somehow, he managed it.

"Do you want this?" he asked.

I hesitated before saying, "Yes. Maybe it's selfish and maybe it's stupid, but . . . yes. I do."

"Then that means you must do the show, unless someone can raise a truly novel and valid argument against it," he said.

I blinked.

Dominic continued, "I know you. I love you, but that doesn't preclude understanding what a gloriously stubborn creature you are. If you don't do this, you'll forever be wondering whether you made the right choice when you became a fulltime monster negotiator rather than staying on the stage. The universe doesn't offer this manner of opportunity to just anyone, and I'd rather not watch you abuse yourself with 'what-ifs' when the chance to answer them all is right in front of you."

"If I win, I get a year's free rent on a studio apartment in New York," I said. "Is that safe?"

"There's been no Covenant movement in that direction. New York is a large city. You would be living as a redhead. I could bleach my hair and take a job at the Freakshow. I'm sure Ryan would enjoy the challenge of teaching me how to make a proper martini," said Dominic. "We would make it work."

The imagine of Ryan—the Freakshow's tanuki bartender, a tall, friendly, half-Japanese man with a waheela girlfriend and a perpetually sunny disposition—teaching Dominic to make cocktails was almost enough to make me start laughing. "You think so?"

"I've yet to encounter an obstacle we cannot surmount when working together, save for possibly the mice," said Dominic. "I really think so."

"Great." I unfolded my legs and slid off the desk. "Let's go see if Dad's back. I need to talk to my parents."

Dominic raised both eyebrows, giving me a meaningful look. I glanced down. I was wearing a sports bra and a pair of dance shorts, having simply stripped off my outerwear before collapsing into bed. Dominic, naturally, wasn't wearing anything.

"Oh," I said. "Let's get dressed first."

"What a wonderful idea," said Dominic, and slid out of bed.

Yup. Definitely naked.

"New plan," I said. "Let's have sex first."

Dominic grinned.

Three

"Anyplace can be a stage. All you have to do
is make yourself the spotlight, and shine."
——Frances Brown

*A small survivalist compound about an hour's drive east of
Portland, Oregon*

THE REST OF THE HOUSE WAS AWAKE by the time we
made it out of the room. There was no single thing
that made it apparent that sleep time was over—nobody
ran a flag up a pole or played the bugle—but there was
a soft, almost indefinable difference in the air between a
wakeful house and a sleeping one.

We descended the stairs to the living room, me in
front, Dominic a step behind. Antimony was curled up in
the corner of the couch, laptop balanced on her knees,
noise-blocking headphones covering her ears, and eyes
glued to a roller derby video. I stepped into her periph-
eral vision and waved. She glanced at me and jerked her
chin upward in the briefest of possible motions. I mimed
removing headphones. She frowned and shook her head
"no." I mimed removing headphones again, this time
more forcefully. Antimony heaved a sigh so heavy that it
seemed to come all the way from her toes and pressed
"pause" on her video before pulling the headphones
down to hang around her neck.

"What?" she demanded.

"Family meeting," I said.

"Is this about the Nessie you had Dad move last night? Because he sent me video. Pretty thing. Wish I'd been there. Meeting over, nice talking to you, have a wonderful day." She started to turn back to her laptop.

"No, it's not about the plesiosaur," I said, before she could put her headphones back on. "But it *is* about a project that might get me and Dominic out of the house for two months or so."

Antimony perked up. "Really? Aw, but I like Dominic." She put her laptop on the cushion next to her, unplugging the headphones and leaving them around her neck like an odd fashion statement. "Family meeting it is. Mom and Dad are in the kitchen making waffles for the mice."

"Are they also making waffles for the humans?" asked Dominic hopefully.

I gave him an amused look. "Didn't you just inhale an egg and toaster waffle sandwich like, four hours ago?"

"Yes, but if I'm not permitted sufficient sleep, I'll have to bolster myself with additional meals. It's the only way to keep me functional until you allow me a full night's rest." Dominic managed to make this sound reasonable, like he wasn't asking for anything more than he deserved.

Antimony rolled her eyes. "Um, *ew*, all right? Keep it in your bedroom." She turned and stalked off toward the kitchen.

Dominic blinked. "What did she think I meant? I was talking about how late we were out last night dealing with the plesiosaur. She shouldn't have expected to see us before noon."

"I know, honey," I said, giving him an affectionate pat on the arm. "Let's go get you some waffles."

This seems like a good time to take a second to explain the Price family.

See, up until five generations ago, we were good,

obedient members of the Covenant of St. George, an organization I've mentioned a few times, dedicated to wiping out all "unnatural" life on the planet. The Covenant defines "unnatural" as "not appearing on the Ark," which is both narrow and arbitrary, since no one's ever heard of an actual list of what may or may not have been on a boat that may or may not have existed. My great-great-grandparents, Enid and Alexander Healy, quit the Covenant and moved from England to Michigan when they realized how arbitrary it was. Since they had a lot of guns, the Covenant mostly left them alone after that.

Note the word "mostly." My grandfather, Thomas Price, was sent to Michigan to check on the Healys several decades later, where he promptly met and fell in love with Enid and Alexander's granddaughter, Alice. They got married and had two kids, he got sucked into a hole in the fabric of reality, and she dove in after him. Just your ordinary love story, right?

Alice and Thomas' daughter, Jane, married Theodore Harrington, a nice incubus with surprisingly pure intentions. They have two kids, Elsinore and Arthur—my cousins Elsie and Artie. We get along, mostly.

Alice and Thomas' son, Kevin, married Evelyn Baker, my mother, who's sweet, friendly, and was raised by her adoptive parents in Columbus, Ohio. Her mother, Angela, is a cuckoo, the same sort of telepathic cryptid as Sarah. Her father, Martin, is a Revenant, a sort of amalgam of resurrected people parts. Or, as I like to call them, Grandma and Grandpa. Since cuckoos and Revenants can't have children—something about cuckoos being giant telepathic wasps who just *look* like humans, and Revenants being, y'know, partially dead—they adopted all three of their kids. Mom came from a human orphanage; Uncle Drew had been orphaned by a gas leak in the bogeyman community where his parents lived. Cousin Sarah joined the family much later, when Grandma found her in a storm drain. Totally normal, right?

Anyway, Kevin and Evelyn—aka, "Mom and Dad"—had three kids. My big brother Alex, was currently finishing up an assignment in Ohio and would be home inside of the year; my little sister Antimony, who had yet to leave home, and had become weirdly territorial about her spot on the couch; and me. Our family tree was more of a bush, but it was a really stubborn bush, like a blackberry bramble. We stuck together, even when we didn't like each other much, and we refused to be uprooted.

Anyone who tried was going to learn all about our thorns.

Dad was extracting a waffle from the waffle maker when Dominic and I entered the kitchen. Mom was sitting at the table, a cup of coffee in one hand and a newspaper in the other. She likes to get her news the old-fashioned way, since it's hard to donate a website to the mice to shred as bedding. These are the adjustments necessitated by sharing your home with a colony of talking rodents.

They looked up and smiled at the sound of our footsteps, although Mom's expression was more guarded. She was raised by cryptids, and didn't consider herself human until well after her marriage and move to the West Coast. For me to come home with a former member of the Covenant of St. George was, well . . .

Again, there were multiple reasons we stopped in Vegas to get married before continuing on to Portland. Mom not burying Dominic in the backyard was one of them.

"I didn't expect to see you up and about for a few hours," said Dad, putting the waffle he'd just finished down on a plate on the counter. The mice waiting there hoisted the plate onto their shoulders and marched away with it, stopping in front of the microwave, where they began hacking it into more portable pieces.

"You're one to talk," I said, walking over to give Mom a kiss on the temple. "You weren't home yet when we went to bed."

"Your father decided pulling an all-nighter was better

than being groggy during his conference call with the university," said Mom.

"Ah," I said, understanding.

"Want waffles?" asked Dad.

"Please," I said, and sat.

Holding down a normal job while serving the cryptid community can be difficult bordering on impossible, since there's no way of predicting what kind of time will be required to, say, transport a plesiosaur from the city reservoir to a safer spot upriver. Some of us get around it by taking jobs within the cryptid community—Mom is basically a mobile first aid station, providing advice, medical care, and carefully researched remedies to anyone who needs her. Others find jobs that don't require rigid hours. Dad is known throughout the academic community for his skill with ancient languages and ability to translate virtually anything. The academic community doesn't know he accomplishes his linguistic feats by consulting with species who never allowed the languages in question to die out, and none of us see any reason to enlighten them. He gets paid, his presence on the books makes it easier to explain how the power stays on when people get nosy, and everything is fine.

(As a whole, our family doesn't want for funds. Grateful cryptids who don't place much value on human money have made substantial donations over the years. Dragons tend to pay in gold, which is always nice, and Aunt Lea is an Oceanid, which means sunken treasure. Between her and the finfolk, we could have been comfortable forever just thanks to things other people lost in the ocean. But there's "not wanting for funds" and then there's "being able to stay under the radar of the IRS." We're all more than willing to work occasionally, if it keeps the taxmen from our door. Nobody wants to negotiate an audit.)

Dad dished out waffles, bowls of strawberries, and— yes—more bacon, which Dominic promptly claimed in the name of the bottomless pit he called a stomach. Dad looked amused by this, and went to the fridge to get more. Feeding three growing, athletic teenagers had left both my parents with a very relaxed attitude about second helpings.

I waited until Dad had joined us at the table with another plate of bacon and a waffle of his own before I cleared my throat and said, "I had an interesting phone call this morning."

"Oh?" asked Mom.

"The producers of *Dance or Die* are doing an all-star season. They want the top four dancers from the last five cycles, which means they want me." I looked between my parents, trying to figure out what they thought of this idea. "They're going to start filming in Hollywood in six weeks."

"You can't be serious." I twisted in my seat. Antimony was behind me, headphones still around her neck, a disapproving expression on her face. "You said you were done. You said you weren't dancing anymore."

"Yeah, but that was before they asked if I wanted to compete again." I twisted further, trying to meet her eyes. "This is a huge opportunity for me, and it's going to look weird if I don't show up when everyone else does. Which is a bigger risk of exposure? Going on TV one more time, or triggering a bunch of 'whatever happened to . . .' junkies to come looking for me?"

"Yes, but, dear . . . what if you win?" Mom sounded genuinely concerned. I glanced back to her. "Artie managed to get into their computers last time, and he said you only lost by about a hundred votes. People love you when you dance for them. What if they decide that this time, they should give you the prize you deserve?"

"Then I spend another year in New York, in an apartment someone else is paying for, which would mean I wouldn't have to take back my job at the bar," I said. "I could follow up with the people I helped while I was there before, and this time I could do it without trying to juggle work, dancing, and the cryptid community. This could be really good for me, Mom, and for the cryptids of Manhattan."

"And you'd be back in the spotlight," said Antimony. "Can't forget about that." She sounded remarkably bitter. I didn't know how to respond.

I didn't have to. Mom did it for me. "Antimony, don't attack your sister. Verity has a point: she hasn't properly retired her Valerie Pryor identity. Is there any way you could turn them down without them making a big deal about it?"

"Not really," I said. "Adrian is the producer and the head judge, and I was one of his favorites. If I don't come back, he's going to say something about it on the air."

"Which makes people wonder why you'd refuse something like this," said Mom. "I think doing the show might be the best way to handle the situation. If you win, you can go back to New York for a year, and get the hidebehinds to help you arrange a murder."

"Mom," I protested, without any real heat. She was right, on both counts: I hadn't properly retired Valerie. I'd just abandoned her, like a shirt that didn't fit right. And if I wasn't going to *be* Valerie, I needed to get rid of Valerie. I needed to kill her off.

"I don't believe this," muttered Antimony, before asking more loudly, "Why can't she have her alter ego murdered now, instead of after the show? There's no need for her to risk exposure like this. Or did you forget what happened in New York? She broke cover! Sarah could have died!"

"That was an unforeseeable situation," said Dad. "Your sister did nothing wrong. She took the steps she had available to her, and she did her best to keep from exposing the family to danger. As for Sarah ... your cousin is an adult. She made her own choices, and we have to respect them."

"She only *made* those choices because Verity got caught," countered Antimony.

"I didn't get caught on the dance floor," I said. "I got caught because I was working. I was doing my job. I wasn't Valerie when the Covenant figured out who I was. There's never been any connection between my dance career and my identity."

Dominic, who once successfully tracked me to a tango competition, said nothing. I was grateful for that. I would have hated to make myself a widow.

"Your sister's appearance on *Dance or Die* didn't cause any rumors about the Price family being alive in North America, but it did make her acceptance into the Manhattan cryptid community easier," said Dad. "We're still rebuilding our family's reputation after all the time we spent in the Covenant. I think this is a good thing."

Antimony shook her head. "Unbelievable. Just unbelievable." She turned and stormed toward the stairs.

"Where are you going?" Mom called.

"To get my backpack," she called back. "I'm going to Artie's." Then she was gone, pounding up the stairs with such force that it was impossible to keep talking to her unless we wanted to start screaming.

I turned fully back to the table, pushed my waffle out of the way, and allowed myself to slump forward until my forehead hit the wood. "I remember being so *excited* to have a baby sister," I complained, voice only slightly muffled.

"She feels left out sometimes," said Mom. "It's like when you were all little, and you and Alex would play games she couldn't keep up with."

"Mom." I sat up. "She dug pit traps for us when we played hide and seek. *Pit traps*. Sometimes she put spikes in them, because she thought that made them look better. We could have been killed."

"But you weren't, and now you're better prepared for pit traps in the future," said Mom. "She's still figuring out who she wants to be when she grows up, that's all. Sometimes she gets jealous because you seem to know who you are."

That was an overly simplified version of a fight I'd been having with my sister for years. I decided to let it go. Bringing Antimony further into this was just going to complicate things, and I didn't want to complicate things. Technically, I was an adult, and didn't need my parents to approve of what I did with my life. At the same time, going on television *did* represent a risk of exposure, however small, and they deserved to have input, even if I was going to ignore any input that didn't come down to "you should go."

"You should go," said Dad. "I know you've mostly managed to get the dancing out of your system, and that's wonderful, but I also know you're never going to get it *completely* out. You need to do this, so you can be sure you made the right choice for you."

I stared at him. I'd been hoping for grudging approval, not full-out support. "What?"

"Your mother and I were delighted when you said you were done trying to be a dancer," said Dad. "But you made that choice while under duress. You'd been seriously wounded, and Sarah was very ill. Decisions we make when we're that stressed aren't always the best ones for us. We want to know that you made the right call. So go back on the show. Dance for a live audience one more time, and let the voters decide whether you belong in cryptozoology or dance."

"Thank you, Daddy," I said, blinking back tears.

Dad smiled. "Don't thank me. I remember how many bruises you came home with last time. I might as well be shipping you off to boot camp so you can think about what you've done. Now eat your waffle. You're going to need the calories."

He was right. I laughed, and ate, and tasted nothing, because my mind was already far away, in a mirrored room, listening to the choreographers bark instructions.

I was going back on the show.

First, though, I was going to have to get Valerie's life back in order. All my dance costumes and wigs had been packed up for the trip from New York to Oregon, and were still in their boxes in the storage shed out back. (We had a garage. We just didn't use it to store boxes, since we needed a place to park. We couldn't use the attic, either,

as the Aeslin mice had a tendency to co-opt whatever
was put into their space, and the barn was where we did
the taxidermy. After years of crap building up in closets,
spare rooms, and everyplace else that it was possible to
wedge a shoebox, Dad had finally thrown up his hands
and bought a prefab shed from the nearest hardware
store. After the hot tub, it was definitely the smartest
thing he'd ever invested in.)

Dominic watched me wade through boxes. He was
smart enough not to get too close, since he didn't know
exactly what I was looking for. "How many costumes do
you need to bring?"

"Most of the dances are choreographed, which means
I'll be dressed by the folks in wardrobe," I said, pulling a
strip of bedazzled fabric out of a box. It was barely wider
than a scarf, and ended with a foot of long white fringe.
"What do you think of this one?"

"I think it looks like a handkerchief with delusions of
grandeur," said Dominic.

"Great, put it in the 'take' pile." I tossed the dress to
Dominic. "I'll be expected to do solos as often as the
producers want to shove them in, and this is a new format: I could be dancing solo every night, if they feel like
being vicious. I need costumes for when I dance solo, and
having something eye-catching is a good way to drum up
a few extra votes. Besides, it's not like my costumes take
up much room." Competition Latin ballroom outfits
tended to be more rumor than reality, to steal a phrase
from my grandmother. There were big poofy feather
dresses, sure, but they were few and far between, and
mostly unnecessary in the styles I preferred.

"That's true enough," said Dominic. "When we
watched the videos of your last run on the show, I was
amazed some of those costumes had made it past the
censors."

"They cover the salient bits," I said, brightening as I
saw my wig box. I waded deeper into the pile. "We'll
need to fly to Los Angeles. Or at least, I'll need to fly,
since the producers will send me a ticket, and I don't

think you want to make that drive by yourself. If we go a little early, we can get you set up someplace near the cast housing. This will let us give your new photo ID a test run." A new identity had been part of my wedding gift to him, as well as a necessary component of bringing him home to meet the parents. If he hadn't been able to pass basic background checks, he would never have been allowed in the house. "Do you have a credit card for someone who *isn't* Dominic De Luca?"

Dominic shook his head. "No," he admitted. "There hasn't been a need since I've been here, and I didn't want to list this as my address."

I resisted the urge to groan. We should have been working on this weeks ago, as a matter of common sense, and it had taken reality television—which was literally the opposite of "common sense"—to make us get started. "Okay, we'll add that to the list of things to take to Artie. He should be able to whip together something good enough for emergencies, even if it's not good enough to be permanent. We'll get him to fake another ID for you in the process, something burnable. Decide what I'll be calling you. Make sure it's something you can answer to. I recommend something that starts with 'D,' since it'll be easier for you to recognize as your name."

"Is that why you go by 'Valerie'?"

"Yup," I said, hoisting the wig box and wading back toward him. "Similar enough to 'Verity' that it catches my attention across a crowded room; dissimilar enough that people aren't likely to connect the two. Same goes for my last name. 'Price' for me, 'Pryor' for her."

"You know, there are people in the Covenant convinced that if your family survived, they did so by being intensely cunning, unbelievably clever, and making bargains with one or more demons," said Dominic. "I'm reasonably sure no one's ever said 'why don't we look under a simple mnemonic?'"

"Simple means you have fewer moving pieces that can break; there's nothing wrong with simple." I dropped the wig box next to him and knelt to begin examining its contents. "And we've never made any deals with demons. A few deals with my Aunt Mary the crossroads ghost, but she always recommends against it, and for the most part, we listen. She knows what she's talking about."

"Once again, I have to ask: how many dead aunts do you have?" asked Dominic, a note of desperation creeping into his voice.

I glanced up from the wigs and grinned. "Just the two. Aunt Rose, who you met in New Orleans and may or may not see in the foreseeable future, and Aunt Mary, who we'll see again at Christmas. She always brings fruitcake from this old lady she knows in Denver who actually bakes fruitcake you can eat without breaking your teeth, it's amazing." This said, I looked back to the box. "Hmm."

"Hmm?" echoed Dominic.

"Yeah. Hmm." Valerie Pryor was a redhead. It was a decision based half on vanity—I always wanted red hair when I was a kid, and I was never allowed to dye it, since that would have made me stand out too much—and half on practicality, because again, red hair stood out. Between the costumes and the hair, few people remembered much about "Valerie's" face. They came away with an impression of color and semi-nudity, and didn't really look at things like the shape of my cheekbones.

Unfortunately, while my costumes had fared reasonably well during the move, my wigs were outdated and disheveled after their time in the box. It would look odd if I showed up on television with the exact same hairstyle I'd had three years ago, and if I tried to rehab the wigs, there was a chance I'd wind up damaging them.

"Is that real human hair?" asked Dominic, sounding somewhere between amazed and appalled.

"Yup. Expensive, but you're not going to find anything that looks more realistic, or does a better job of fooling tracking spells. I buy them from a wig shop in Salem. It's run by a very sweet harpy and her daughter. They have feathers in their hair, and pulling them out would hurt like hell, since living feathers have blood vessels in them. They make wigs instead. They do a good business among the gorgon community and with other cryptids who have reasons to hide their scalps." I was already running the numbers in my head on how many wigs I could afford. Dad would probably give me the money if I asked, since he'd approved this mission, and it would be nice to have something styled in a braid or updo, just to make the rumbas easier.

"I see," said Dominic. He paused, and then said, "When we met, I thought your dancing was frivolous. I suppose I still do, on some level. Your work is more important than the dance floor."

I glanced up, raising an eyebrow. He shook his head; he wasn't done.

"But your joy when you dance . . . it's radiant. The preparation, the work, the thought you put into every element of the presentation . . . this isn't frivolous. It may not be what I recognize as important, but that doesn't mean it's worthless. I'm glad you're going to do this reunion show. I think that, as your husband, I owe it to myself to take more time to watch you dance."

"That sort of thing gets you kissed, Mister," I said, before standing and doing just that. Dominic looped his arms around my waist and pulled me close. He'd always been an excellent kisser, from the time that I first put my lips on his in an alley in New York, but time and comfort had elevated him to an Olympic level. If there had been a gold medal for kissing, I would have given it to him hands-down.

When I finally pulled away, my cheeks were hot and felt like they were as red as my wigs. "Okay, handsome," I said. "Let's go call Artie about getting you that credit card and fake ID. We're going to Hollywood."

Four

"Chin up, shoulders back, trigger finger ready. Now go out there, my darling girl, and prove that you're the one."

—Enid Healy

The lobby of the Crier Theater in Hollywood, California, six weeks later

THE AIR INSIDE THE LOBBY was at least five degrees cooler than the air outside. It felt more like my native Portland than like Hollywood, land of sunscreen, tanning beds, and movie stars with thousand-dollar skin. I shoved my sunglasses into my oversized dance bag, blinking rapidly to adjust to the switch from outdoor bright to indoor dim. Everyone around me was doing the same thing, which gave me an excuse to hang back from the crowd and get a feel for the situation.

The building was familiar, of course: this was where we'd done my original season of *Dance or Die*. Holding our final rehearsals on the actual performance stage used for live shows made it easier for us to get comfortable with routines that we barely had time to learn, which cut down on injuries. Cutting down on injuries lowered the show's insurance rates, so everybody won. Besides, the theater was huge. There was plenty of practice space, and the plumbing almost never decided to back up and flood the bathrooms. Almost. Stepping into the Crier Theater was like coming home.

Dominic was a different but equally familiar presence behind me, although his blond-tipped hair and studiously "I am in a boy band, ask me about our new single" attire made him less familiar when I actually looked at him. Dominic De Luca wasn't the kind of guy Valerie Pryor would have looked at twice, much less gotten involved with. David Laflin, on the other hand, had all Dominic's natural hotness, combined with a much more modern sense of style. He was believable as part of her image. That was what mattered here. Image. Reality was boring if it didn't have a layer of sequins on top.

"Remember," I murmured. "If someone asks you a question you can't answer, just laugh and either look in a mirror or look at me."

"I am to be your boy toy," he said. He sounded amused. That was good. I couldn't have done this if he hadn't been willing to play along.

Six weeks seemed like a long time when I'd agreed to do the show. Six weeks hadn't been nearly long enough. Not when I needed to have my costumes altered, wigs made, and get a whole new identity set up for Dominic— a big task under any circumstances, and one that was made bigger by the fact that some of Valerie's paperwork was out-of-date. We'd managed to finish everything just under the wire, and now here I was, a week out from our first show, about to become reacquainted with the people I'd once thought of as my natural peers.

I wasn't ready. And that didn't matter, because I'd been spotted. A black-haired blur rocketed through the crowd toward me. I braced for impact, hoping Dominic would recognize this as the opposite of an attack. We didn't have an easy way for me to warn him without drawing attention to myself or looking unfriendly, and then it was too late, as a slim African-American woman in yoga pants and a beaded red halter top slammed into me, rocking me back several inches as she slung her arms around my neck.

"Val!" she squealed. "Oh my gosh Val you're *here* I heard from Anders who heard from Lo that you'd dropped out of your last two competitions and then the producers were having trouble finding you and I was so afraid you weren't going to come but here you are! You're actually here!"

"I'm actually here," I confirmed, giving Lyra a quick hug before attempting to extricate myself from her embrace. "I had a bad fall during training, and bruised my tailbone. Nothing permanent, it didn't need surgery or anything, but it was pretty messed up for a while, and I had to miss some competitions. I wasn't getting any traction, so I figured I'd come home to California and think about my options."

Lyra let go, stepping back enough to beam brilliantly in my direction. It was like staring into a searchlight. "This is some option, huh?"

"And how," I agreed. I half-turned, opening my posture as I gestured to Dominic. "Lyra, I'd like you to meet my boyfriend, David. David, I'd like you to meet Lyra, my season's dancer of choice."

"She says that like she didn't come in second," said Lyra, dialing her smile back and giving Dominic an appraising look. "So you're dating Val? You think you're good enough for her?"

"No, but as she doesn't seem to have realized that yet, I intend to take advantage of my time in her good graces," said Dominic, with the sort of solemnity he usually reserved for portents of doom and complaints about how long I took in the shower.

Lyra glanced back to me. "Ooo, I like him. Spanish?"

"Italian," said Dominic.

"I like him even more." She whirled and gave me another quick hug. "It's so good to see you again, Val. I know I was supposed to keep in touch better, and I'm sorry. Things got so *crazy* after I won our season."

"I understand," I said. I did, too. It was hard to remember to stay in touch when your life was blowing up around you. "I didn't make the effort, either. Can we agree to forgive each other?"

"Already forgiven," said Lyra, making a tossing

gesture. "Anders is here, by the way. In case you wanted to see if *he* was willing to forgive you."

I grimaced. "On a scale of one to never gonna happen, how much shit am I in?"

"I'd say a nine-point-five," said a voice from behind me. I turned and found myself looking at a perfectly fastened bow tie. I tilted my head back and shifted my gaze to the big blue eyes of one Anders Clarke.

He was easily six inches taller than me, built like a runner, something he attributed to a combination of genetics and never sitting still. Dance was a world of constant motion, and Anders made the rest of us look lazy. He was a human cartoon in impeccably polished tap shoes . . . at least, he always had been before. Now, he was standing frozen, a sad look on his classically handsome face. Very classically handsome: he could have stepped straight out of a Gene Kelly movie, even down to the cut of his suit. Anders was the only human man I knew who thought of suspenders as a valid fashion choice. Somehow, for him, they were.

"Anders," I said, starting to reach for him. That was when he finally moved.

He stepped away.

"I emailed you," he said. "After your phone number was disconnected. I emailed eight times, and you never responded."

"When did you start?" I asked.

He gaped at me. "When did I *start*? Because that totally makes up for you never answering me, or reaching out in the first place? We were partners, Val. You should've called."

"I was in Manhattan for a year, and I didn't get any email from you," I said. "I would've answered." I would have. I might not have been proactive about keeping in touch with the other dancers from my season—partially out of shame over my loss, and partially because there hadn't been enough hours in the day—but I answered the people who bothered to contact me. Guilt and curiosity had been enough to guarantee that.

"I started the day after the show ended," he said.

I blinked slowly. "Sweetie ... I didn't get any email from you. Not one single piece. What address were you using? Did you ever swing by Facebook and message me?"

"No, because you were already ignoring my email." Now Anders was starting to look angry. Never good. He took a long time to wind down, and we were going to be called in to meet with the producers soon.

Lyra, ever the peacemaker, pulled out her phone and shoved it in front of his face. "Is this the email address you were using?" she asked.

Anders blinked several times as he refocused on the screen. His anger was like a rolling stone: it gathered speed as it moved, and it was difficult as hell to pull it back. Then he blinked again. "No," he said, pulling out his own phone and scrolling through his address book before pushing it toward me. "This is."

We made a weird sort of triangle, standing there holding phones out toward one another, and it made me want to get my own phone out, just to complete the formation. I resisted the urge in favor of frowning at Anders' screen. "That's not my email address," I said. "That isn't anything even *like* my email address. Who gave you that address?"

"Jessica," said Anders. "You ducked out so fast after the finale that I didn't have a chance to get it from you, and I wanted to keep in touch."

Lyra and I both stared at him. Lyra lowered her phone to give herself a clearer view of Anders' face. We were a united front again, just like we'd been during our last weeks on the show, and I wasn't going to lie: it felt incredibly good. Lyra had never met Verity Price, would probably be appalled by Verity's world, but she had been Valerie's best friend. Even compartmentalized and held apart as my two worlds were, that mattered to me.

"You asked *Jessica* for contact information for *Valerie*, and you believed one, that she'd have it, and two, she'd give it to you accurately, without being an asshole about it?" Lyra planted her hands on her hips. "Did you fall and hit your head after you were eliminated, or did you just think the spirit of brotherhood would suddenly move her to *not* be a horrible human being?"

"She's not that bad," I said, with no real heat.

"Uh, excuse much? She called you a fake redhead on camera when they did alumni week. She tried to sue the show when they let Emily come back after she was eliminated, because they hadn't let *her* come back. She's awful. She's always been awful, she'll always *be* awful, and the fact that Anders listened to her for like, a second, makes *him* awful." Lyra directed a glare at Anders, who squirmed. "How dare you get mad at Valerie because of something Jessica did? That's like, awful squared."

"Valerie still changed her number without telling anyone," said Anders—a defensive rearguard action if I had ever heard one.

"My old phone got disconnected because someone blasted the number over Twitter," I said.

Anders and Lyra exchanged a look before saying, in unison, "Jessica." Then they were laughing, and I was laughing, and all was right with the world.

A chime rang through the lobby, shaking dancers out of their conversations and warmup stretches. I wrinkled my nose and turned to Dominic, who'd been looking increasingly confused during our conversation. He'd just been dropped into a world he didn't understand, complete with preexisting social connections and rivalries. He was doing the sensible thing and staying quiet. I loved him even more for that. Common sense is less common than you'd think.

"You can come in for this part; we're encouraged to bring friends and family to the producer meeting, since it makes the audience look fuller," I said. The instructions had been clearly spelled out on the last prep email from the producers. "You'll have to leave after the showboating, but at least this way you can get a look at the judges and our host."

"I understand," he said solemnly.

Lyra grabbed my arm, tugging me toward the theater

doors. "Come on, come *on*, Val. We want to get good spots on the stage!"

As if they weren't going to arrange us according to their own plan? This was all staged. Every bit of it. I was just surprised there weren't cameras here in the lobby — at least not cameras I could see. I glanced around, suddenly paranoid, and resisted the urge to check my wig.

Then Anders grabbed my other arm, signaling that all was forgiven, and the two of them lifted my feet off the ground and toted me into the future.

As I'd expected, the stage was marked with little pieces of tape, each with a name written on it. They were mixing the seasons, turning us from five sets of four into a mob of twenty dancers. We milled around the stage until we found our names. Then we stepped off again, waiting in the wings where the cameras wouldn't pick us up.

A statuesque blonde rose from the front row of seats and made her way onto the empty judges' podium. She walked with the easy sway of someone who'd been drinking since she got out of bed. I knew she wasn't drunk: she was just tall, wearing impractical shoes, and incredibly loosely jointed. I knew that, but I still held my breath as Brenna Kelly climbed the stairs, waiting for a fall that never came.

"Are we rolling?" she asked, glancing toward a production assistant. Whatever answer she got, she nodded, and said, "On my count, then. Five, four, three, two . . ." She stopped talking and smiled, an expression that took her from attractive to stunningly beautiful. It was directed at the camera, and hence, at America. "For five years, you've tuned in to watch as America's most talented and hardest working dancers took to our stage. You've seen their triumphs and their tragedies, their flights and their falls, and after every season, you've asked 'what happened to my favorites?'" Her smile softened, turning almost maternal. "I know I've often asked that question myself. Often enough, in fact, that someone listened, and said 'why don't we find out?'"

Brenna took a step back, gesturing to the stage with her free hand. "This season, we're doing something that's never happened before in *Dance or Die* history. We're bringing back your top four dancers, America—not just from last season, but from the last *five*. Our top twenty is made up of your very favorites, here to dance for you one more time, to prove that they deserve the title of America's Dancer of Choice."

She descended the stairs, never looking where she was putting her feet, hitting her marks impeccably. It was a form of dance in and of itself. She always insisted she had two left feet, but I couldn't have done that walk in those shoes without a choreographer. "But, of course, we can't do it without the people who started it all. Ladies and gentlemen, please welcome your judges."

Adrian was the first to appear—naturally. It was his show, and he wasn't going to let anyone steal that from him, even if the structure of the program forced him to give Brenna more camera time than he had. He strutted out of the wings, waving for the cameras, grinning. The dancers around me clapped. The families and friends seeded throughout the audience clapped. I clapped. There was no knowing whether we were being filmed right now, and a dancer who didn't applaud for Adrian might well find themselves falling, quite abruptly, from grace.

"Executive producer Adrian Crier," announced Brenna.

A woman with auburn hair teased into a glorious bouffant was the next to appear. She was smiling, but less broadly: she had Botoxed most of the movement out of her face years ago. It was sad. She was a beautiful woman, but as someone who worked in an industry where the most important thing a woman could be was young, she'd been forced to resort to increasingly desperate measures. Her hatred of Brenna—who was rumored to be the same age, and yet hadn't needed any such procedures—was legendary.

(Brenna was actually older. Brenna didn't need Botox because Brenna wasn't a mammal. This . . . wasn't something we could actually explain to anyone. Oh, well.)

"Our lady of the ballroom, the lovely Lindy O'Toole," said Brenna.

Lindy waved, smile never shifting, as she crossed the stage to take her place next to Adrian.

The third judge varied from season to season. I crossed my fingers, hoping for one of the faces I liked, and was rewarded when a skinny man in a bow tie, with the sort of smile that promised unexpected explosions, stepped out of the wings. He was waving with both hands, and looked happier to be there than any of us.

"Choreographer, producer, and all-around fabulous human being, Clint Goldfein!" said Brenna.

Clint sat down at the end of the judges' table. Lindy leaned over to touch his arm and say something inaudible, smiling like she hadn't seen him in months, even though she'd been backstage with him for who knew how long. That was show business for you.

My nerves were starting to tingle, and my stomach was a hot pit of terror. It was almost time to take the stage. I wasn't ready. I wanted to be up there right now. It felt like I was pulling myself in two different directions at the same time, and it couldn't help but be an awkward sensation.

Brenna stepped up onto the stage, standing on the edge as she smiled at the judges, and said, "It's so nice to have us all back together again. It's like a big family reunion for me. Adrian? How do you feel right now?"

"Well, Brenna, I've got to be honest with you, I'm as excited as you are," he said. "Every dancer we've ever had on the show has been magnificent in their own style—they wouldn't have made it through the audition process if they weren't—but there's always a bit of sadness at the end of the season, because we've seen these wonderful dancers leave us one after the other, and then we have to start all over again. The idea of being able to begin with the sort of technique and strength that we normally see at the end of the season . . . it's really exciting."

"Lindy?" Brenna turned her body slightly, so no one could accuse her of slighting the judging panel's only female member. She was a consummate professional in that regard.

"I'm so excited I could scream," said Lindy, her surgical smile not budging a bit. "I love all our dancers, you know I do, but some of the best ballroom people we've ever had are going to get a second shot at our stage, and I'm hoping there won't be any slippage in their footwork or their partnering. I'm expecting a whole new level out of this group of dancers. They know what we expect of them. We know what they're capable of. Put it together and it's going to be . . ." She sighed theatrically. She did everything theatrically. Since she'd frozen her face, her voice was all she had left to work with, and she made it do as much as she could. "Magical."

"I like a little magic," said Brenna, and turned to Clint. "All right, Mr. Goldfein. Sprinkle some of your magic dust on us, and let's get this show on the road, shall we?"

Next to me, Lyra snorted. I whapped her on the arm as a signal to be still. Out of the three judges currently seated at the podium, Clint was the least likely to go shoving foreign substances up his nose for fun. He wasn't an angel—he worked in Hollywood for a reason—but he'd always struck me as someone who genuinely enjoyed being alive, and didn't see any cause to complicate life with illegal pharmaceuticals. My kind of man, in other words, even if he was way too old for me and my particular code of ethics wouldn't have allowed me to sleep with a judge even if I *hadn't* been married.

"I don't have anything fancy to say about any of this," said Clint, grinning his wide, disarming grin. "I'm just thrilled to have everybody back with us."

"And so am I," said Brenna. "Let's bring them out now, shall we?" She turned to beckon us forward.

That was our cue. In a carefully rehearsed mob, we surged forward and took our places on the stage, settling with our butts on the pieces of tape staged for our benefit.

We were supposed to sit, so that we'd look like the eager, earnest students of dance we were meant to be. Some of us knelt; others settled cross-legged, or tucked their ankles like they were posing for a pinup calendar. I was in the front row between a dancer I didn't recognize and a dancer I vaguely thought had been on the season after mine. Lyra and Anders were somewhere behind me. They'd only been back in my life for a few minutes, and I already missed their presence desperately.

"Well, well, well, look at you all," said Adrian, beaming a toothy smile in our direction. "I can't believe we were able to get all twenty of you back again."

I tensed. I wasn't the only one. The show normally opened each season with auditions, milking them for every bit of artificial tension they possibly could. If you auditioned with a best friend or a sibling, for example, you'd both make it as far as the producers could justify, before one of you would be eliminated in the most vicious way possible. This season, by bringing back the twenty of us, they were missing out on all that drama . . . unless, of course, they were planning to eliminate one or more of us right now, when we were completely off guard.

Adrian's smile remained fixed and unmoving for a few seconds, giving us plenty of time to work ourselves into a low-grade panic. The dancers around me began to shift nervously, their chins dipping and their shoulders tensing. I forced myself to remain still, looking relaxed and content in my position. If someone was getting eliminated today, it wasn't going to be *me*. Why, they couldn't do the show without me! It was easier to look like I believed it than it would have been to actually start believing, but I hadn't been a dancer for most of my life without learning how to control my face.

Then he relaxed, moving into his patented sympathetic look, and said, "Come on, my darlings, you can't really believe we'd do that to America, can you?" The fact that he didn't need to say what "that" was should have been proof enough. Wisely, no one said anything. "None of you are getting eliminated today. We brought back our twenty top dancers because we wanted to show what you could do if you didn't have to go through the early stages of getting used to our format and learning how to work with our choreographers. We wanted to take all the stops off, and let you *run*. So no, there is not going to be a surprise elimination today: all twenty of you will be taking the stage in one week."

The mass visibly relaxed. Someone murmured, "Oh, thank God," and the dancers around them giggled, nervous and relieved.

"That doesn't mean we're not gonna put you to work," said Lindy, not to be left out. She fixed us with a stern look, only slightly diluted by the fact that she was still smiling. "You thought the choreography in your seasons was hard? Now we know what you're capable of, we're not going to be pulling any punches. You're going to work harder than you've ever worked before, and you're going to love every second of it."

The dancers broke into "spontaneous" applause. There was an element of honesty to what she was saying: we probably *would* love whatever we were told to do. We hadn't become dancers because we wanted to avoid challenges. I'd always been happiest when I was bruised, aching, and on the verge of collapse, and the same held true for most of the people around me.

Clint just beamed. "I'm so happy you're all back with us. I can't—you know eliminations are almost as hard on us as they are on you. You're the ones who have to leave, but we're the ones who have to watch you go. You're our best and brightest, and every time one of you walked away, you took a little bit of my heart with you. It's so nice to have my heart back." Coming from anyone else, it would have sounded utterly cheesy. Coming from Clint, it sounded sincere. He really did love each and every one of us, which was why he was everybody's favorite judge. No matter how badly you screwed up, Clint would be there to say you were wonderful.

"Now, Adrian, I know our format is a little different this season—what can our dancers expect?" Brenna moved back into the scene, stopping next to the outside line of dancers. A few people turned to smile up at her. Most of us kept our attention on the judges.

"Well, Brenna, for the most part, we're staying with the tried and true: we're going to be splitting our dancers into partnerships, and those partnerships will dance live on our stage, beginning with next week's performance show. America will vote, and each week the girl and the guy with the lowest votes will be eliminated, until the top four have been chosen. Then it's every dancer for themselves, and we determine who of our top twenty will be America's Dancer of Choice." Adrian sounded very invested in what he was saying. Forget world peace: what mattered was who America would vote for. "I know you're all aware of what's at stake, and I know you're all going to dance your best. Because we wanted to recapture the magic of your original seasons, we're going to be initially keeping the partnerships where they stood as of the end of your first appearance."

Some dancers murmured, looking dismayed: they'd lost their partners going into the top four, and would be dancing with people they didn't have much experience with. Others grinned or punched the air. I kept smiling serenely. My partner, Anders, had been with me from the beginning. I'd pulled his name out of the supposedly randomized hat. We knew each other incredibly well, and we'd be able to get back into the groove quickly.

"Initially," repeated Adrian. Both the cheers and the mutters stopped as we all went still, watching him with the wariness of mice sharing a tank with a snake. "In addition to voting on individual dancers, America will be voting on whether or not any given partnership should be broken up. If your partnership doesn't draw enough votes, you'll find yourself with someone new—and since we have dancers here from five seasons, that someone new may be someone you've never even spoken to before."

The feeling of unease on the stage was growing. We'd always been subject to the whims of the audience. Now we were going to be more at their mercy than ever.

"I want to stress again that you're with us because we expect truly great things from you. You are the best of the best, the dancers America couldn't forget, and by bringing you back to our stage, we're giving them what they want. Hopefully, we're giving you what you want as well: we're giving you a second chance to claim your title—or in the case of our five winners, to defend it. Only one of you will come away from this as America's Dancer of Choice."

"But they're all winners to me," said Brenna. She waded into our little sit-down, motioning with her free hand. "Up, up, my darlings, get to your feet, it's time to say hello properly."

When she came to me, she took my hand and pulled me into a standing position, smiling sweetly before she moved on to the next dancer, leaving a folded square of paper pressed into the center of my palm. I beamed at her, trying to look adoring and oblivious—two qualities Valerie Pryor had traditionally possessed in plenty—as I tucked my hands behind my back and slipped the square of paper into the waistband of my yoga pants.

Brenna continued on into the dead center of our merry band, gathering as many dancers in for a hug as she could. She towered over all but the tallest of the male dancers, like a swan moving through a flock of ducks, and the looks people gave her were genuinely happy. Brenna didn't judge us or blame us when things went wrong. She just liked us. That wasn't part of her job as host—she could have been businesslike and friendly and still kept her position—but it was a definite bonus. Brenna's rapport with the contestants was probably why the producers had never considered replacing her with a younger model, unlike all the other dance shows out there.

Once the hug was done, Brenna turned to the camera, raised her microphone, and said, "Here we go again! It's your top twenty, America, and each and every one of them is already a star. Who will shine brightest? Whose constellation will finally take its place among the heavens? Find out next week, when *Dance or Die* begins the greatest battle that has ever graced our stage. Don't miss it!" She winked. The show's theme music kicked in, and like the well-trained beasts we were, all twenty dancers began to boogie down. The contemporary dancers shimmied. The ballroom dancers shook. And the hip-hop dancers did things with their ankles that made my joints ache in sympathetic pain.

The music continued. So did the dancing. One of the cameramen was probably getting a pan shot, something wide and exciting that would play well under the credits. Someone grabbed my hand, spinning me into a wide curve. I caught a glimpse of a grinning man on the other end of my arm: Ivan, one of the ballroom dancers from season four. He had good technique and was well known on the jive competition circuit. Good. I went into a series of jive steps as I spun back toward him, and was rewarded with him matching me beat for beat before grabbing and dipping me. I stuck one leg straight up into the air, narrowly missing kicking Lyra in the nose, and froze there as the music stopped.

"Cut! Stop what you're doing!" shouted Adrian. All the dancers who hadn't stopped of their own accord stopped where they were. Brenna extricated herself from the mob, murmuring polite good-byes as she stepped back to let the judges have their way with us. I stayed where I was. If Ivan was willing to hold me up, I might as well see how long I could maintain a full extension. Like yoga with a partner.

Adrian looked less intimidating when he was upside down. As things settled back into a semblance of order, he also started looking amused. "Valerie darling, did you decide to become a fruit bat between seasons?"

"Nope," I said. "I just met this nice man, and I was trying to figure out whether I liked hanging out with him." I righted myself, planting my feet firmly back on the stage, and offered Ivan a smile as I pulled away. "He's okay."

"Glad you think so. All right, everyone, if you haven't checked in with the production assistants at the back of the room, you can go do that now. Fill out your paper-work and sign your waivers before we start putting you through your paces. We've got housing in the same complex as always, four to a two-bedroom flat. Roommates have been assigned, but if you want to negotiate a trade, feel free: just make sure everyone's comfortable." Adrian fixed us with a stern eye. "I'll expect to see you all back here at seven o'clock tomorrow morning to begin rehearsals for the first episode."

A hand went up. It belonged to a skinny redhead with hair several shades lighter than mine and cheeks brimming with freckles. Jessica. I wondered how many fits she'd had to throw to get her place on the show back. Technically, she'd been a part of her season's top four, but she'd never performed with them: she'd dislocated her knee so badly during rehearsals that she'd required surgery, and the number five dancer, Honey, had gone on in Jessica's place. If it had been up to me, Honey would have been the one tapped for this reunion, not Jessica.

(Jessica's involvement with the show had never ended, damn the luck. She'd become a choreographer's assistant after her elimination, and haunted the stage to this day.)

It looked like I wasn't the only one who felt that way. The people around Jessica gave her sidelong looks, some annoyed, some pitying. There was little of the easy camaraderie that seemed to pervade most of the dancers, even the ones who'd never met each other before.

"Yes, Jessica?" asked Adrian.

"Is everyone going to have a roommate?" she asked. "I'm a light sleeper."

"Every apartment will contain four people at the outset, with two bedrooms and four beds," said Adrian. "There is also a couch. You may attempt to convince whomever has been assigned to share a room with you that they'd rather sleep on the couch, but I'm not going to step in on your behalf."

"Shouldn't be a hard sell," murmured someone behind me. I bit my lip to keep myself from laughing.

"Are there any other questions?" asked Adrian. Without hesitating, he plunged on: "No? Good. We'll see you at seven tomorrow morning. Please fill out your paperwork before tripping over a cable and breaking an ankle or something, no one's getting sued today." He stood, adjusted his jacket, and strode away, with Lindy scurrying close behind him.

Clint paused long enough to throw us a smile just as bright as the one he'd been using for the cameras, if not quite as crisp. "I really am excited to see you all," he said, and trotted away.

"Guess we're doing this," said Anders, stepping up next to me.

"Guess we are," I said. "Can you and Lyra go find out whether we're all rooming together, and start making trades if we aren't? I need to go say good-bye to my boyfriend."

"Always knew you'd land a hottie," said Anders. "I should've moved faster to make sure it was me."

"Not getting my email address from Jessica would have been a start," I agreed, and kissed his cheek before heading for the stairs. I could have jumped off the stage—it was only a four-foot drop, and I have a tendency to leap off the sides of buildings at the slightest provocation—but I hadn't filled out my paperwork yet, and I didn't want to give the poor production aides panic attacks. They already had to work with Adrian and Lindy. They didn't need me to start torturing them, too.

Dominic was seated on the aisle about two-thirds of the way back, where he had a good view of both the stage and the aisles leading up to it. He'd been providing cover, in other words, making sure nothing was going to get the drop on me while I was playing good little dancer.

I rewarded him for his clever placement with a kiss. He kissed me back, so I felt compelled to kiss him again. This somehow turned into several minutes of us passing the kissing responsibility back and forth, my arms remaining locked around his neck the entire time. A few of my fellow dancers whistled or catcalled amiably as they walked past, but I ignored them. I had more important things to do.

Finally, Dominic let go and asked, "Well? Was it everything you hoped it would be?"

"It was pretty much exactly what I expected," I said. "I have to go see the official housing, but I should be able to sneak out after sunset. Meet you back at our usual spot?"

"Ah, yes; I'd missed this phase in our relationship. The intrigue. The subterfuge. The frequent need for tetanus shots." Dominic kissed me again. "I'll see you there."

I let him go, and watched, only a little regretfully, as he walked away. It was going to be weird, sleeping by myself. But who knew? Maybe this was going to get us back to New York.

"Nothing ventured, nothing gained," I said, and turned to head for the back of the room. It was time to fill out my paperwork and meet my roomies.

Five

"The only place you shouldn't sleep when you have the chance is a den full of bears and rattlesnakes, and if you're tired enough, even that turns negotiable."

—Frances Brown

The Crier Apartments, privately owned by Crier Productions, about an hour later

ADRIAN CRIER WAS A SMART MAN: everyone who'd ever had cause to work with him knew that. Being a smart man, he'd invested in Burbank real estate more than twenty years ago, which had helped to fund his production company. Among his assets were several apartment buildings, one of which was kept perpetually open in order to house the people who came to work on his various shows—people like us.

We'd all stayed in the Crier Apartments before, and there was something oddly comforting about climbing the exposed exterior stairs to the second floor. The building followed the kind of open design that only works in deserts and places that get minimal amounts of rain: all the apartments had doors that opened on the outside, and were built around a central courtyard that contained a fountain and a barbecue grill, as well as a great deal of aquamarine tile. It was like looking down into an empty swimming pool. It also echoed weirdly, something that was being clearly illustrated by the people who were shouting across it to their friends.

"I am so glad we're sharing a bedroom," I said to Lyra, as I unlocked the door to our temporary home. "I know you're not weird."

"And I know you *are* weird," she said amiably. "Do you still sneak out the window in the middle of the night?"

"Yup," I said. I opened the door and braced it with my suitcase before turning to take Lyra's duffel bag. As a jazz dancer, her costumes took up substantially more space than mine. Add that to the fact that I was using Dominic as off-site storage for half my stuff, and it was obvious why she needed help. "Do you still whistle in your sleep?"

"Sometimes." She eyed my single bag dubiously as she pushed past me. "Are you planning to get eliminated in the second week?"

"David's delivering the bag with my shoes in it later," I said.

Lyra smirked. "You know he can't come in, right? Show rules."

"Right." Show rules: no visitors were allowed in the apartments, and while our friends and family could visit if they wanted, no one was supposed to go and show them around. Everybody did, of course. We just had to make sure the producers never noticed.

The apartment was small enough to be compact and big enough to be cozy, skirting the line between "reasonable housing for four people" and "dormitory" with consummate skill. Lyra and I were the first to arrive. We claimed the back bedroom, farthest from the echoing courtyard, and I dumped my stuff on the bed next to the window. It would be easier to slip in and out if I didn't have to negotiate a sleeping body in addition to everything else.

Lyra looked at the bed I'd chosen and shook her head in amusement. "Oh, look, Val's next to the window.

Whoever would have guessed? Not me. Never me. I know nothing."

"Let's keep it that way," I said, taking a moment to nab the note from my waistband. As expected, it said "See me later." Brenna wanted to talk. "Do we know if the boys were able to trade for the other bedroom?" Anders and Pax—Lyra's original partner—had been deep in negotiations when we left the theater. We were allowed to set up coed rooming arrangements if we wanted, as long as it didn't distract from our work, and sometimes sharing space with your dance partner could be a real advantage. If you wanted to practice at three in the morning, you could do it in your living room, instead of in the courtyard. Big help.

"We are triumphant!" shouted Anders from the living room.

"Uh, yeah, they did it," deadpanned Lyra. We both broke down giggling.

We were still laughing when Anders and Pax appeared in the bedroom doorway, effectively filling it. Anders was tall: Pax was taller, a solid wall of Hawaiian muscle who moved with a grace that should have been illegal in the natural world. If he'd been human, I would have considered him a violation of several laws of physics. Since he couldn't have been much farther from the human genome without being made of silicon, I didn't have that problem.

Pax offered a shy, tight-lipped smile when he saw me looking at him. I smiled back. "It's good to see you," I said. "I'm sorry we didn't have a chance to talk at the theater."

"I wasn't talking much with anyone," he said. "My flight from Maui got in an hour before call. I was afraid I was going to be late and get myself eliminated early."

"How would they even have handled that?" asked Lyra. She sat down on her bed, looking coquettishly through her eyelashes at Pax. She'd been flirting with him since auditions. It had never gotten her anywhere, but she wasn't about to let that stop her.

Too bad for her that Pax wasn't likely to fall prey to her considerable charms: not when he had two wives and a husband waiting for him in the waters off Maui. He was Ukupani, one of the only known aquatic therian-thropes, named for the shark-god Ukupanipo, who'd supposedly created them. (Maybe He had. How would I know? I don't have much experience with gods, and I don't *want* much experience with gods, since people who meet gods tend to wind up pregnant with demigods. Not my idea of a good time.) This all meant that when he wasn't teaching dance classes on the island, he was splashing around in the Pacific Ocean, being a combination of man and shark, and birthing a million nightmares whenever someone happened to catch a glimpse of him.

Not that any of this was public knowledge. Pax was supposedly a single Hawaiian hottie, since female Uk-upani couldn't change shapes, and he was media savvy enough not to have mentioned his husband to the judges, or to anyone who might let it slip on the air. Adrian had a reputation for wanting his men to be manly, which carried with it an unfortunate whiff of homophobia. It sucked. Hopefully, this time we could do something about it.

"Probably have kicked off my partner, too, to keep things fair," said Pax.

Anders snorted. "As if they'd eliminate a winner? Lyra took our season. That means she's untouchable, at least until the second week."

"Cynic," accused Lyra.

"Realist," countered Anders.

I laughed. I was back among the people who understood this side of me, the side that wanted to cha-cha rather than negotiate peace between disparate cryptid communities. Pax caught my eye and nodded, agreeing with my delight. His situation wasn't quite like mine, but it was close enough that we both knew what it was like to hide half of ourselves from the world. We were still hiding, even here, but at least we could let our less-seen sides come out for a while.

"Hello?"

The voice was female, and coming from our living room. I stopped laughing, immediately tense. Pax and Anders turned, still blocking the doorway, ready to defend us from whatever might be coming. Then Anders groaned and stepped to the side.

"Ladies, it's for you," he said.

Lyra and I exchanged a glance before we stood and walked to the door, poking our heads out. There, standing in the middle of our living room like she belonged there, was Jessica. She had her arms crossed, and looked annoyed, probably because we'd made her wait.

"The door was open," she said, before either of us could say anything. "You probably shouldn't leave it open, it's like an invitation for people to come in and steal shit."

"Or to just come in," I said, stepping out of the bedroom. "How can we help you?"

"You're Valerie, right?" She looked me up and down, and then sniffed, like she'd just determined that I wasn't a threat. I bristled. "You were on the season after mine. I don't know if you watched the show before you tried to use it to get famous, but I came in fourth my year. I would've won if I hadn't been injured."

"How nice for you," I said. "We've met before, remember? You were Sasha's assistant during our season, where I came in second, if we're playing that game."

"I'm Lyra," said Lyra, slinging an arm around my shoulders. "Hi again, Jessica. Long time no irritate. I came in first. How can we help you?"

"I'm a really light sleeper, and Adrian said I should find someone who's willing to trade with my roommate and sleep on the couch." Her tone made it clear that her original roommate hadn't seen being kicked out of the bedroom as an acceptable solution. "It wouldn't be fair if I didn't get enough sleep and got eliminated, you know? I just need to find someone who wants to be a good sport."

"There are no good sports in this apartment," said

Anders. He managed to sound almost apologetic, like he was really sorry, deep down, about our lack of sportsmanship. "Sorry. I mean, if you wanted to crash on our couch, I'm sure we could work something out, but Lyra and Val are besties . . ."

Lyra and I linked our little fingers and held them solemnly up for inspection.

". . . and Pax has this whole thing about sleeping in the nude, which means we need to have a door to close between the world and his magnificence. Maybe try the next apartment down? They might be suckers. You never know."

Jessica looked, briefly, like she was going to stomp her foot in frustration. "This is the last apartment!"

"Well, then pray that whoever winds up with a room to themselves after next week is willing to trade with you." Anders dropped the sympathetic act. "Of course, you'll have to do this again once we're back down to an even number of girls. So I don't think you're going to have much luck."

"I won't forget this," said Jessica, and spun on her heel, stalking out of the apartment.

"Uh-huh, kiss noise, bye now," Anders called after her. He rolled his eyes as he looked around at the rest of us. "Can you say 'diva'? How does she survive in the real world?"

"I have no idea, but I don't have to care," I said. "Come on. Let's check out the kitchen."

Hours later—after a group barbecue in the courtyard, during which dancers I'd never met sucked down chicken breasts and tofu dogs like they were about to be made illegal, and everybody was introduced to everybody else, and just as promptly forgot everybody else's names—the apartment was settling peacefully into sleep. Lyra was still sitting up in her bed, writing the day's events out in her diary, but that was no big deal; she knew about my nocturnal habits. She looked over, a tolerant expression on her face, as she heard the window slide open.

"Going for a run?" she asked.

"Yeah," I said, trying to look sheepish. As far as Lyra knew, I was an insomniac with a fondness for night running. I'd promised her repeatedly during our original season that I wouldn't be in any danger, and after several nights when I'd returned home uninjured and capable of competing, she had grudgingly chosen to believe me.

"Bring back more eggs," she said, and went back to her diary.

"You got it," I said, and slid my legs out through the open window. My backpack was a mostly-empty weight against my lower back. After a quick, perfunctory glance to make sure I wasn't about to become a new YouTube sensation, I let go of the frame, and I fell.

There's something gloriously exhilarating about that moment where the body lets go and gravity takes over. It can be easy to forget how much effort goes into every movement the body makes. Even sitting still requires the muscles in your spine, thighs, and butt to work. But falling . . . falling can be a moment of perfect relaxation, at least until it's time to start thinking about not hitting the ground.

I dropped about six feet, far enough to build some momentum, and more importantly, to carry me to the first-floor windows. I grabbed the top of the sill and used it to twist myself around to where I could catch hold of the rain gutter. It was gritty under my hands. Honestly, if someone wanted to find out which apartment was mine, all they'd have to do was look for the window next to the rain gutter that had been inexplicably wiped clean.

Bracing my feet to either side of the gutter, I slid the rest of the way to the street. I preferred to travel rooftop to rooftop whenever possible, but the Crier Apartments were too far from the surrounding buildings to let me do that without risk of major injury. I let go of the metal pipe, wiped my filthy palms against the seat of my pants, and started down the driveway toward the street.

There was a car parked midway down the drive. It flashed its headlights at me, twice. I was still wearing my wig, still the perfect picture of a dancer sneaking out for a late-night snack run: I composed my expression into one of vague curiosity and trotted over to the car.

The passenger side window rolled down when I got there. Brenna looked across the leather seats, expression solemn. "Get in," she said. "I'll give you a ride."

I got in.

Brenna started the engine, rolling the window back up as she turned the car around. "Where are you heading?"

"You know the Be-Well Motel?" I unzipped my backpack and pulled out my wig bag. Then I reached up and peeled off my wig, tucking it into the bag before I started extricating bobby pins from my wig cap. My scalp itched like fire. I hadn't been Valerie for such a long stretch in months: I was going to have to acclimate all over again. Swell.

"Pretty familiar," she said. "Cheap as hell, you get what you pay for, rents by the hour, day, and week, and nobody asks any questions."

"Exactly," I said. The wig cap peeled away. I stuffed it into the backpack and began fluffing my sorely-abused hair. "I'm going there."

"You have a perfectly nice bed that the producers are paying for, you know," said Brenna. "Far be it from me to tell you how to spend your money, but . . ."

"But wasting money hurts your soul, even when the money isn't yours, I know," I said. "I'm not sleeping there. I'm meeting my husband there."

"Husband? Really?" Brenna glanced at me, startled. "You mean the short, broody man you were with back at the theater? You married him?"

"Yes, *I* married him, not Valerie. Which is why he's staying back and pretending to be Val's boyfriend if anyone asks. He won't be in the audience during the live show taping."

"Why not?"

"Ex-Covenant."

Brenna hit the brakes, slamming me forward. The seatbelt dug into my shoulder but kept me from going through the windshield, so I was willing to call it a win. I still yelped. I yelped again, this time in surprise rather than pain, when I turned and found Brenna staring at me, all wide eyes and impending rage.

"He's *what*?!"

"He's ex-Covenant," I said. "He quit when he realized he'd rather have a live girlfriend than a dead trophy, and when he started to figure out that cryptids were people. He knows about William, Brenna. He was there when I found him." When I'd been offered to him as a virgin sacrifice, technically, but I didn't see any need to tell people that. "He didn't tell the Covenant. He's a good guy. He just can't risk being caught on camera."

"Of all the irresponsible, unreasonable, *insane* things you could have done, you—"

"Went and did exactly what my grandmother did, only without the ten years of pining, flirting, pining some more, drinking the cooking sherry, and trying to date other dudes?" I shrugged. "This seemed more efficient. And better for my liver."

Brenna shook her head. "I take it back. I take it all back. You're not the best of a bad lot, you're as crazy as the rest of them."

"We're not crazy, we just have different priorities," I said. "You're one to talk, you know. You're the only dragon I've ever met who actually spends money on shoes."

The word "dragon" hung in the air between us for a moment, silent and accusing. Finally, Brenna blinked, and said, "You know, no human has ever called me a dragon before. Not even you."

"Times are changing," I said.

Brenna smiled. "I guess so."

I'd only been on the set of *Dance or Die* for a week before I'd realized Brenna Kelly was a dragon princess— the term we still used, out of long habit, for the female members of an extremely sexually dimorphic species. The males were giant, fire-breathing reptiles the size of a bus. The females were attractive, human-looking women with perfect skin, perfect hair, and a tropism toward amassing as much gold as possible. It was just that in Brenna's case, she preferred her gold to take the form of sequins and shiny shoes. She was the only materialistic dragon princess I'd ever met, and I had liked her instantly.

Getting her to like me back had been a bit more complicated, since once I'd known what she was, I'd felt obligated to tell her what *I* was: a Price, a cryptozoologist, and a liar, appearing on the show under a fake name. She'd responded with "You're a dancer first," and I'd known we were going to be friends.

Her smile faded as she drove on. "So, Verity, I'm sure you were wondering what I wanted to talk with you about."

"Not really," I said. "You're a dragon. I've never wanted to pry, but I assume you have a Nest?"

She nodded. "My sisters think I'm strange for enjoying spending money as much as I enjoy making it. As long as I give half my earnings to the Nest, they don't mind so much. I make valuable connections they can exploit for a profit. There's a lot of work for pretty girls who don't want to be big stars in this town. We can always find another photo shoot or music video that wants a few of us for set dressing. Private parties, too. Not the sex kind—we avoid that sort of intimacy with humans— but the sort where we just need to wander around being decorative."

"So I assume that when they heard there was going to be a reunion show, they pressed you to talk to me." I paused. "Wait. Adrian said the reunion show was your idea. Did you . . . ?"

"Please don't think badly of me. I just needed an excuse to talk to you without calling out of the blue, and I thought this might be a nice opportunity for you. Something I could do that wouldn't cost us a lot of money. We're hoping to need it very soon." Brenna cast a quick, hopeful look in my direction.

I nodded slowly. "I can put you in touch with Candy. She's William's primary wife, and she's handling all of the visitors who come to see him and discuss breeding."

Brenna looked appalled. "What? No. I don't want to borrow another woman's husband. None of us are looking to become the other woman. We're better raised than that. Our mothers saw to that."

"Then what are you looking for?"

"I understand how this is going to sound, because you're human, and your species has the luxury of doing things rather differently than ours." That apologetic note was back in her voice. "There's one male in the world. We didn't think there were any, and while we can keep having daughters by ourselves forever, we require a male if we're going to have any sons. William ... when you found him, you opened the doors for our species to continue, for us to have a future. But that means we don't have the option to be coy and demure."

"Uh-huh ..." I said, somewhat confused.

"You know the Manhattan Nest. Would you be willing to act as our go-between, to help us arrange the purchase of one of their sons?"

I said nothing.

Brenna, who was a dragon, no matter how human she sometimes seemed, said hurriedly, "We have money. We have *oodles* of money. There are over sixty of us in the Nest, and we've been in Los Angeles since the twenties. We own and rent property, we have investments, and we're willing to liquidate as much as necessary in order to offer a fair price. Every Nest has its own strengths and weaknesses, and we've learned that you have to spend money to make money—that's something a lot of dragons never grasp. So we have more funds on hand than most. We have sufficient space at the Nest to house a fully grown male, and we have all the deeds and property documentation to make sure he'd never have to be moved. We could be good wives, Verity. Not my generation, it's too late for us, but our daughters. They could grow up with their husband. They could learn to love each other. We could give them that."

I said nothing.

"Love is a human aspiration, and yours has been the dominant culture for so long that we want it, my sisters and I. We want it for our daughters. We don't want to pay for a conjugal visit with someone else's husband; we want to bring a husband home, and raise him in love, and see him grow to love his new family." Brenna slanted a glance at me, as if gauging my reaction. "We're *not* human. It's not in us to give something for nothing. I know if our positions were reversed, I would feel for the daughters of Manhattan, and I would still demand payment. It would show their seriousness, and their dedication to taking care of our boy. Please. They know you. They'll trust you. Please, help us."

Candy didn't necessarily trust me—she tended to view me as only temporarily outside the Covenant, which was an unfortunately common attitude in parts of the cryptid community—but William did, and money spoke loudly where dragons were concerned. I wanted to balk at the idea of selling a baby like it was a goldfish, but what other choice did the dragons have? Their species was on the verge of dying out. Male dragons were born the size of human infants. They could be moved while they were young. Once they became adults, like William, they were stuck.

"I'd need you, and at least one other representative from your Nest, to go to Manhattan with me," I said slowly. "William and Candy will want to meet you. You'd have to be willing to pay for transport. There's no way we'd be able to take the baby on a plane."

"You may never hear these words from another dragon as long as you live, but: we are willing to pay whatever it takes," said Brenna. "If you want to charge us a negotiation fee, we'll give it to you. Even if things fall through, we're willing to pay you for trying."

The Be-Well Motel was visible up ahead, neon sign

guttering like a bug zapper the size of a billboard. "I wouldn't charge you for this," I said. "Helping the cryptid community is my job."

"Does that mean you'll do it?"

My human sensibilities had their objections. I did my best to shunt them aside. Candy and I weren't the best of friends, but her fierce devotion to her Nest, her husband, and her children was unquestionably sincere. If she and William were willing to agree to this, I had no place objecting to it—and that meant I also had no place refusing to set up the conversation.

"Yes," I said. "I'll do it."

Brenna pulled up to the curb in front of the Be-Well and turned to look at me. Her eyes were bright with tears, catching and throwing back the neon glow until they glittered on her cheeks. "You don't know how much this means to me," she said. "We can never repay you."

"We'll figure something out," I said. "I'm honestly glad to help."

"Bring your boy by once the season's over, and I'll introduce you to my Nest," she said. "Meanwhile, anything you need, you just let me know."

I smiled. "Sure thing. It's good to see you again, Brenna."

"Likewise," she said.

I slid out of the car, taking a deep breath of the fragrant evening air. The smell of the neighborhood had changed as we drove from the relative sterility of the studio housing into a rougher, wilder neighborhood. Garbage, rotting leaves, and urine—not all of it canine— addressed my nose, undercut by the ever-present scent of the sea. This was the Los Angeles I felt most at home in, the one where danger and elegance existed side by side, beautiful and terrible and dangerous.

Brenna leaned across the seat as I closed the door. She pressed a button to roll down the window, and asked, "You sure you're all right to get yourself home again? You don't want me to swing around and pick you up?"

"Tempting, but I need a good run if I'm going to get

through tomorrow," I said. "I'll get myself home safe, I promise."

"Anyone else, I'd call you a liar," she said. "Be safe." The window rolled back up, and she pulled away, leaving me standing alone on the sidewalk.

Not totally alone: there were a few figures slumped against the base of a nearby wall, and someone farther up the block leaned against a post with the casual posture of the career lookout. I didn't know what he was looking out for, and I didn't care. I turned on my heel, slung my backpack over my shoulder and walked up the three shallow stone steps to the motel door.

The air inside smelled like Hot Pockets—hot dough and cheap cheese and indefinable meats, mixed into a hot, humid slurry that hung suspended in the lobby like an invisible curtain. The man behind the Plexiglas shield protecting the desk didn't look up from his magazine as I walked past. He always seemed to be there, night or day, and he only moved when someone was asking about a room or trying to hand him money. I suspected he was an Oread, given his immobility, but there was no polite way to ask, and it didn't really matter. This was supposed to be a place where no one asked any questions. It seemed only fair to extend that to the staff.

The stairwell was tucked into the far corner of the lobby, next to the gunmetal-gray elevator doors. I took the stairs. The Be-Well elevator was about as new as the carpet, which looked like it dated from the early seventies, and while I enjoyed falling, I wasn't a big fan of the uncontrolled plummet that I was sure was coming eventually.

Despite being wedged into a narrow space between two other buildings, the Be-Well had a decent number of rooms, largely due to it having a decent number of *floors*. We'd been there long enough to change rooms several times, finally winding up with the one we wanted: the rear corner of the fifth floor, looking out on the backside of a billboard, two convenience stores, and a gas station that had been closed for three years, but hadn't yet been sold.

The thin carpet on the stairs provided no padding. I only passed two people on the way up, a woman in a red dress who had her eyes glued to the screen of her smartphone, and a man who seemed more interested in talking to himself than he was in noticing me. We had found the perfect base of operations, seedy enough to be off most people's radar, but safe enough for me to not feel bad about leaving Dominic here while I spent my time on the show.

I had a key to the door of our supposedly shared room. I knocked anyway. The sound of a chain being undone followed, and Dominic opened the door. He smiled when he saw me.

"I know you selected red because it's an eye-catching color, but I've always preferred you blonde," he said, and leaned in, and kissed me.

I've always felt that the way a man kisses says a lot about him. Dominic kissed me like he hadn't seen me in a decade, instead of just an afternoon: hungry and hopeful and hard enough that I could feel it all the way down to my toes. He lifted his hands like he wanted to hold me, but didn't want to pin me in place, in case I wanted to pull away. So I kissed him even harder, looping my arms around his neck. He took it as the invitation that it was and put his hands on my waist, boosting me up until my feet left the floor and he could carry me into the motel room.

I kicked the door shut behind me as Dominic carried me inside. The slam was deeply satisfying, as was the way Dominic was still kissing me, eager and present in a manner that very few of the men I'd kissed had been able to manage. I was about to pull back and propose we continue in this vein for a while when another sound intruded: cheering.

I pulled away from Dominic and twisted to see a cluster of mice standing on the room's single low dresser, waving banners made from scrap paper and cheering their tiny hearts out.

"HAIL!" they cried. "HAIL THE RETURN OF THE ARBOREAL PRIESTESS!"

. . . and that, right there, was why his kisses were so passionate after being apart for only a few hours. We'd been sharing a tiny motel room with a splinter colony of Aeslin mice for weeks, and while it hadn't managed to completely eliminate our sex life, twenty-three talking rodents had definitely been enough to put some limits on what we did.

(I'd complained to my mother, during one of my weekly calls home. Her response had been laughter, and the most chilling thing she'd ever said to me: "Well, at least this way, you'll be ready when you have kids of your own.")

"Hi, guys," I said, unwinding my arms from Dominic's neck and allowing my feet to drop back down to the floor. "Did you pick who's going back to the studio with me?"

"We did, Priestess!" proclaimed a mouse, puffing out its tiny chest with pride. "Three Travelers in the Mysteries have been chosen, and will walk with you in Glory!"

"Cool," I said, glancing back at Dominic. He was looking tired but amused. Somewhere between Manhattan and home, he'd learned to live with the mice. "So how about you guys go down and raid the kitchen trash one last time before I have to get going? Give us, say, an hour?"

"Are you invoking the Sacred Law of Food for Privacy?" asked the mouse.

"If I say yes, will you leave?" I asked.

"It is most irregular to send us away, rather than giving the food to us directly," said the mouse. "But the Thoughtful Priestess did say, lo, Go Easy On Her, She Is Going To Be Under A Lot of Stress, and I believe that this is Going Easy."

"Thank you, Mom," I murmured, before saying more loudly, "Yes, it is. Thank you. Have fun in the kitchen."

"HAIL!" cried the mice, and dispersed, vanishing behind the dresser.

I turned back to Dominic. "Now, where were we?" I asked.

"You were telling me about the show," he said, taking a seat at the edge of the bed.

I blinked. "Actually, I was thinking make-outs, but okay. Um . . . I'm sharing an apartment with the other three dancers from my season. Anders, Pax, and Lyra. We started with same-sex rooming arrangements, but people were allowed to trade, so I figure most folks will have stayed with who they knew."

"This is good?" asked Dominic.

"Means my roommate is already used to the idea that sometimes I'll sneak out the window and go for a run in the middle of the night," I said. "She isn't going to get on my case about it, since I made it to the finale last time."

He smiled. "Ah," he said. "This is good. Are you enjoying the company of your peers?"

"Yes. No. Maybe. It's weird being Valerie again, and it's not like they're planning to ease us into things. We already have our choreography assignments for week one. We'll be heading to the theater tomorrow to get started."

Dominic raised an eyebrow. "What will they have you doing?"

"For week one, a group number—jazz with other elements—and then they've broken us down by style. I'm going to be part of a three-way Argentine tango."

His expression softened. "I remember dancing the tango with you. It was . . . bracing."

"Bracing? That's all you can say about dancing with me? That it was *bracing*? Oh, no." I held out my hand. "Get up."

Dominic raised an eyebrow. "Why? Where are we going?"

"The roof."

"You know, there was a point in my training where I should have learned not to go to rooftops with Price girls." He slid his hand into mine. I pulled him to his feet.

"I'm glad you were such a lousy student," I said,

grabbing my backpack from the floor before I tugged him over to the window. "I think it's time you learn just how bracing I can be."

Dominic came without resistance or complaint. His teachers would have been very disappointed in him. I, on the other hand, was thrilled.

Six

> "I've found that the difference between an opportunity and an obstacle often comes down to how many knives you have hidden in your clothing."
>
> —Alice Healy

The roof of the Be-Well Motel

WE HAD CHOSEN THIS MOTEL partially because it was cheap and partially because it had a large, flat roof that was accessible from the upper rooms, if you didn't mind climbing straight up the side of the building. (Technically, that meant the roof wasn't accessible, since most people don't view "climbing straight up the side of the building" as an option. Most people are silly.)

The roof was wide, flat, empty, and surprisingly free of broken glass and other debris, again because most people don't want to climb up the side of the building. I beat Dominic there by an easy eight feet, and was sitting down with my forehead pressed against my knees by the time I heard him climb over the edge.

There was a pause before Dominic asked, "Is there a reason you're demonstrating your flexibility right now?"

"Yup," I said, climbing to my feet and smiling at him. "If I'm going to brace you, I want you to know you've been braced."

"I *have* danced with you before," he protested.

"Oh, believe me, I remember." He'd followed me to

one of my last ballroom competitions, knocked my partner unconscious, stuffed him into a closet, and joined me on the floor, resulting in my faking an injury and getting myself disqualified. Good times.

But the past was past, and these *were* good times. I dug my iPod out of my bag, attached the speakers, and hit "play." Jesca Hoop began to play. Dominic looked at me. I raised a hand and beckoned him forward.

"C'mere, Batman," I said. "Let me show you how bracing I can be."

He laughed nervously as he walked over and put one hand on my hip, pulling me into an amateur's idea of a proper frame. "I assure you, I don't need a demonstration."

"Oh, but you do." I moved his hand until he was cupping the top of my ass, pulling myself so close to him that there wasn't room for air between us. "The Argentine tango is about connection. Intimacy. It's a seduction."

"You've already seduced me," he protested.

"Not like this," I said, and began to move.

Dominic's Covenant training had included basic ballroom dance for some reason: probably because they had weird ideas about fitting into European high society when necessary. He knew the steps of the tango. He could even execute them, in a boring, workmanlike way. I twisted my hips, our proximity forcing his to move in tandem with mine.

"Feel the music, feel your partner," I said. "I am the only thing that matters."

He looked at me, eyes dark and heavy-lidded, and I shivered. "I've known that for a long time."

The urge to stop dancing, shove him to the rooftop, and get naked was strong. Only the knowledge that even without broken glass, the roof would be *filthy*, stopped me. I kicked to one side, then the other, before raising my right leg and bracing it against his shoulder, essentially doing a split while still on my feet.

Startled, Dominic took a step backward, dragging me with him. I grinned.

"See? We're one creature with two bodies, and it's your job to make sure the connection doesn't break. Hold me up. Support me. Feel the tension in my muscles, and use it to follow."

We danced silently for a few minutes, Dominic trying to match me. The song changed, but I'd chosen Jesca because her beats were usually regular without being overwhelming. There was nothing on the album I couldn't tango to, and Dominic could at least hear the rhythm.

His cheeks were red when I spun out and back, pressing myself against his chest. "I feel oddly inappropriate doing this," he said.

"I'm your wife."

"Valerie Pryor isn't married," he said. "The way you hold yourself, the way you move . . . I know I'm dancing with you. I feel like I'm also dancing with her."

"Just hold on to that feeling," I said, running my foot up the length of his leg. "When you watch the show, remember that it's not your wife dancing like this with other men. It's Valerie."

"As long as you'll remember that when the show ends, you're coming home to me." He pulled me abruptly closer and kissed me.

The song changed. I barely noticed.

When we finally pulled back from each other, we didn't resume our dance. Instead, we stood there, cheeks red, and looked at each other. Dominic spoke first.

"Tell me something vital that requires there to be blood in my brain, or we risk the mice turning another sexual encounter into religious rite," he said, in a low voice that sent shivers down my spine.

I took a breath. "Um. Okay. You remember I told you Brenna Kelly was a dragon? Well, she wants us to go back to Manhattan with her." Dominic raised an eyebrow. I quickly outlined Brenna's proposal: the purchase-slash-adoption, the money, the idea of raising a husband with love.

"Ah," he said, when I finished. "The Covenant does something similar."

"Still not comfortable with that." I didn't like the fact that the Covenant ran what was essentially a monster-hunter breeding program. Knowing that my family had belonged to it until just a few generations ago didn't help.

Dominic took my hand and led me to the edge of the roof. He sat down. I sat beside him. Looking at me gravely, he said, "Do you remember when I asked if we were dating?"

"You mean when we were both naked, and you were like, 'hey, girl I've been sleeping with for months, are we a thing?'" I asked. "Yeah, I remember."

"I told you most of the knights of my generation would take lovers for the sake of the flesh, and then return home to suitable marriages," said Dominic. "I didn't want to do that, because I only wanted you."

"Yes, this rings a lot of 'wow that was an uncomfortable, horrible day' bells," I said. "What's your point?"

"My point is if you hadn't come crashing into my snare and my life, and if I'd remained the good Covenant soldier I was raised to be, I would have returned home to that marriage by now. I would have been lucky to meet the girl before I took her to the altar. Everything in our lives is curated. That includes our bloodlines. It's necessary, when the same families have been fighting together for so many years." Dominic looked at me solemnly. "I prefer how things happened with us—I'm delighted to have had the chance to fall in love—but arranged marriages haven't destroyed the Covenant. For the dragons, they may be the only way."

I blinked. "Okay, wow. This is the second conversation I didn't expect to have tonight. You think I should do it?"

"I think you've already decided to do it," he said. "I'm simply trying to make you feel better about the idea."

"I love you."

Dominic smiled. "I'm aware."

Between dancing and talking, it had been over an hour, and the mice hadn't appeared. That was a little odd: I assumed they had pilfered a lot of goodies from the motel kitchen and wanted to divvy them up before they went back to interacting with humans. The mice are loyal and dedicated to documenting as much of the family's history as they can, but they have their own lives, and those lives are not lived according to human rules.

"I won't be able to come tomorrow night," I said, leaning my head against his shoulder. "The first day of rehearsals is always a killer. I've done it before, though. I'll bounce back fast."

"I'll continue to do as I have done: hole up here, and watch the surrounding area for signs of danger or of Covenant presence. I've found plenty of danger so far, but nothing worth worrying about, and no traces of either Covenant monitoring or field teams. I suspect they're still hung up on the East Coast."

"Thank God for small favors," I said. The idea of meeting another Covenant field team was enough to turn my stomach. Dominic had been working alone when I met him: he'd been willing to listen to reason. When the field team had shown up, it had been a lot less pliable and a lot more dangerous. "You're sure you don't mind?"

Dominic smiled. It was one of the sweetest sights I'd ever seen. "If I minded being here for you, I would never have followed you to Oregon. I'll be fine. I'll watch you dance on the television, and be gloriously glad to have met you on that rooftop in Manhattan, since it means I can be here now to see you moving. It will be fine."

"You are the best." I glanced at the display on my iPod. "But I don't have time to show my gratitude right now. I gotta get back and go to bed if I'm going to survive the first day. Mice who are coming with me, front and center!"

"Are you sure they—"

"Have you *met* the mice?"

Sure enough, three Aeslin mice popped into view. One was carrying a Barbie-sized bag made from patches of cloth stitched together with dental floss. It bulged suspiciously at the seams, making me suspect the motel kitchen was missing more cheese than previously thought. Ah, well. It wasn't like it was the good stuff.

"All right: these are the rules," I said, sitting up straighter. "Rule one: no one sees you. Adrian will have the place tented and fumigated if someone says there are mice, and I refuse to explain that to my parents. Rule two: I know unquestioning obedience isn't your thing, but I need it. If I say hide, you hide. If I say run, you run. Understand?"

"We understand!" squeaked the mice in unison.

"Good." Now for the hard one. I took a breath. "There can be no cheering, no chanting, and no audible celebration of any kind."

The mice looked appalled. "But ... but Priestess," protested the mouse with the bag. "How are we to keep the catechism, if we cannot cheer for you?"

"Find a way," I said. "If you get caught, I won't be able to protect you. Especially not when we're at the theater."

Dominic gave me a curious look. "How did you manage the first time?"

"I took one mouse, because no one knew what sort of situation I was walking into, which meant I needed to have my 'black box,' but I wasn't trusted to take even a splinter colony," I said. "She's older now. She's one of the heads of my priesthood, and she was very sorry when she wasn't able to come with us." She was also one of the only mice I recognized on sight, thanks to the amount of time we'd spent together. Brave and foolish and funny. I missed her.

One of the tragedies of the Aeslin is that while their lives are much longer than the lives of ordinary mice, they're still so short. The mouse that was young and vital only three years ago was now solidly middle-aged, and no longer as eager to risk herself in the big, bad world outside the temple. Besides, she had a congregation to run, and dance classes to teach, since dancing was a large part of the rituals inspired by my time on *Dance or Die*. Watching Aeslin mice do the cha-cha was definitely an experience.

"We will try," said the spokesmouse, looking miserable. "Is it the only way?"

"It is the only way," I confirmed. "If you get caught, we're in trouble, and if you make noise where humans can hear you, you're going to get caught." Maybe I could convince Brenna to let the mice use her dressing room for any necessary rituals. She wouldn't be shocked by their existence, and I was in a unique position to ask for favors, given the situation. I wouldn't ask for anything that would give me an advantage in the competition—there was being smart about my resources, and then there was being a jerk—but helping the mice didn't fall under that category.

"We Shall Obey," said the mouse. All three had flat ears and drooping whiskers, and looked so miserable that I felt bad about silencing them. Sadly, I didn't really have a choice.

"You can raid the craft table if no one sees you," I said. That perked them up a bit: their ears lifted, and one of them gave a muted cheer. I pointed to my backpack. "Hop in, and don't get tangled in my wig. I'm going to need to put that back on pretty soon."

"Hail!" chorused the mice, and scurried into the backpack.

When I looked up, Dominic was watching me wistfully. "You're going, then?"

"I'm going." I picked up the backpack and stood, moving to kiss him briefly before I said, "But I'll be back before you know it."

"I know it whenever you're away," he said. "Be astonishing, Verity. Be the amazing, impossible, infuriating woman I married, and steal the show from all those other dancers."

"Remember to vote for me," I said, and stepped onto the edge of the roof, and off, and fell.

The Be-Well Motel was a rare thing for the area: a freestanding building with nothing directly connecting to the structure. Below me, the alley used for storage and employee parking beckoned like a dangerous asphalt river. If I fell that far, I'd never dance again, but I'd make an attractive smear on the pavement until the infrequent Southern California rains washed me away.

That wasn't going to happen. When I'd fallen far enough to gather the momentum I needed, I grabbed the ledge of the building and braced my feet against the brick, pushing off as hard as I could. The muscles in my thighs bunched and released, launching me across the alley toward my target: the billboard we'd so carefully positioned ourselves behind. For a moment, I hung weightless and suspended in space, my mind stretching out that fraction of a second until it felt like a year. Then gravity remembered our unfinished business and yanked me down, pulling me in a hard arc toward the back of the billboard.

I put out my hands, bracing for impact just before my palms struck the metal trellis. The jolt echoed all the way up to my shoulders, but there wasn't time to dwell on that: dwelling would lead to more plummeting, and plummeting was not in the plan. Instead, I gripped tight and swung myself up, hooking a foot on the higher part of the lattice. Then I pulled, and flipped myself up to grab the next row of pipes.

Hand over hand and foot over foot, I climbed to the top of the billboard and paused, looking back at the Be-Well. Dominic's silhouette at the roof's edge made me want to turn back, wrap my arms around him, and never let him go. I pushed the impulse down. We were here because we both knew what we had to do, and I'd learned my lessons well from watching my grandmother's endless quest to find my grandfather and bring him home: love is great, but it can be a poison. Sometimes you have to step away, or you'll never be able to break free.

I turned to the front of the billboard, looking out over the city. Then I jumped. It was a long trip back to the studio housing, and I was planning to enjoy every moment of it.

It took me a little over forty-five minutes to run along the rooftops, fire escapes, and other available supports and make my way back to the apartments. I checked my time before pulling my wig out of the bag and positioning it on my head. By the time the season was over or I got eliminated, whichever came first, I was going to be dealing with some stellar chafing. Anything for dance.

There was no one visible outside the building. I counted windows until I found ours, and then shinnied my way up the drainpipe to my bedroom. Lyra was long since asleep, her body a flawless curl beneath her blankets. Holding a finger to my mouth in a silent shush, I opened my backpack and let out the three Aeslin who would be secretly living with us.

They scampered to the pillow, waved their forepaws in the closest thing they were currently allowed to a "hail," and vanished behind the bed. I ducked into the bathroom and wiped away the grime from my journey before coming back out and crawling into my own bed. The pillow was a psalm to sleep. The mattress was a benediction. I closed my eyes, and sank instantly down into sleep—

—only to be jerked out what felt like seconds later by the sound of someone blasting an air horn in the central courtyard. I sat bolt upright, one hand going for the gun that wasn't under my pillow. Good thing, too: I might have had an unfortunate accident. My eyes were filled with grit. I wiped it away.

Lyra was also sitting up in her bed, looking groggy and displeased. "They're going to be filming when we emerge," she said. "Only reason they'd do the air horn. How's my hair?"

"Sheepdog-like," I said. "How's my face?"

"You were drooling in your sleep," she said. "Wonder Twin powers?"

"Activate," I agreed, and shoved my blanket off my legs as Lyra jumped out of her bed. Twenty seconds later, we were crammed into the bathroom, doing the best we could in what we knew was an artificially limited amount of time. Lyra handed me a brush, and I stood behind her, smoothing her hair, while she washed her face and applied a quick layer of "neutral" makeup. Then we switched positions, her brushing and braiding my wig while I slapped on lip gloss and foundation. The camera's eye was eternally unforgiving, and it would know if we came outside unprepared.

"Nice wig," said Lyra.

"Thanks." She was one of the few who knew that America had never seen my real hair. "It's new."

"I figured. You ready?"

"As I'll ever be," I said.

The boys were waiting in the living room. They didn't need as much time to get ready as we did, damn them, but they knew the rules of this game as well as we did, and they knew that we were already being judged.

"One," said Anders.

"Two," said Pax.

"Three," said the four of us in unison. We burst out onto the balcony connecting the second-floor apartments. Doors were opening on every side: we'd timed our appearance perfectly. We hadn't been paranoid about it, either—there were cameras in the courtyard, lenses positioned to get as many of the opening doors as possible. So we did what was expected of us. We came out screaming and waving our hands in the air, looking like there was nothing in the world that we appreciated more than being dragged out of our beds at some ungodly hour of the morning.

At least the sun was up, even if they'd probably only waited this long because they wanted better light levels. My legs were still pleasantly loose from my nocturnal running, which told me more than I wanted to know about how little sleep I'd gotten. But those were Verity problems, and this wasn't Verity's time. As Valerie, I put my hands in the air and screamed like this was the most exciting thing that had ever happened.

Adrian appeared out of the swarm of cameras, stepping up onto a low platform that hadn't been there the night before and wouldn't be there after he left. He was holding the air horn in one hand, and a megaphone in the other. "Good morning, all-stars!" he shouted, through the megaphone. We knew our cue: we roared approval and delight until our throats hurt. Adrian smirked, mugging for the cameras before raising the megaphone again. "Are you ready to get this party started?"

We were. We were *so* ready to get this party started.

"Well, then, come on!" Adrian beckoned, and we ran, barefoot and in our nightclothes—or what we were pretending were our nightclothes—for the stairs. I realized we'd all been put in second-floor apartments on purpose: with only twenty contestants, sleeping four to an apartment, we could have been in doubles, each of us with a private room. But then he wouldn't have been able to address us en masse like this, or get dramatic shots of shoeless dancers running down concrete stairs. Sometimes I really hated Hollywood.

When we reached the bottom of the stairs, we ran straight into a wall of cameras, followed by some producer shouting, "Cut! Did we get the shot?"

"They came out slower than I like, but we can edit that," said Adrian, pushing his way through the mob. "I think we had good energy, good sincerity, and besides, Lindy will kill me if I don't get back to the theater before it's time to assign choreography groups. Morning, all. Thanks for your quick response, car for the theater leaves in twenty. Please be presentable." Then he was gone, turning on his heel and pushing back through the swarm of cameras.

Some of which were almost certainly still running, knowing Adrian. I kept my smile in place, feeling my face relax into the easy routine of being Valerie, who was virtually unflappable. "Let's go get dressed!" I chirped, looping my arm through Lyra's. She matched my smile with her own, and side by side, we walked back upstairs, the boys trailing behind us.

Jessica, who'd clearly done the same math I had, was waiting on the balcony. "There are seven empty apartments in this complex," she said, without greeting or preamble. "What would it take for me to convince the two of you to move into one of them?"

I blinked. Lyra blinked. I recovered first.

"If there are seven empty apartments, why don't *you* move into one of them?" I asked. "You could have the whole place to yourself. Way better than just a single bedroom."

"Because then I'd look like I wasn't a team player," said Jessica. Her tone was disgusted, like she couldn't believe I'd be so stupid. "Everybody knows you two were BFFs during your season, so if you wanted to go off and have some girl time, they'd find a way to spin it that didn't make you look like total bitches."

"Do we get a vote here?" asked Anders. "Because Val's my BFF, too, and where she goes, I go."

"I'm not going to be the only dude rooming solo with a woman," said Pax. "I *know* where the camera takes that, and it takes me to a lecture from my mama as soon as I get home."

"So basically, we could all move into one of the empty apartments, and leave you with the problem you already have," I concluded. "Sorry, Jessica, no sale. Now if you'll excuse us, I want to be wearing something more substantial when I go to find out what sort of torture we're being put through this week." I stepped past her, my arm still looped through Lyra's, and Anders and Pax followed close behind.

I didn't look back to see whether Jessica was seething. I was a smart girl. I could make an educated guess.

"Showtime," giggled Lyra, hugging my arm.

I smiled at her, and opened our apartment door. Showtime, indeed.

So here's the thing about dance rehearsal: it's fascinating while you're doing it, because you're learning new choreography and forcing your body through its paces, even as your muscles protest and your lungs complain and your skeleton feels like it's about to turn into sludge and come dripping out the soles of your feet. And when you're done, you've learned something new, and you can make art with your body. That's the true power of dance. Painters and sculptors and designers, they take raw materials and turn them into art. Dancers turn *themselves* into art. We are poetry in motion when we do our jobs right, and we can stop your heart with the point of a toe or the angle of a limb. But describing rehearsal?

If there was an annotated dictionary with more elaborate definitions, "a detailed description of a dance rehearsal" would probably go under "boring." There's a lot of repetition, and a lot of "I tried, I failed, I fell, I tried again." Not the sort of gripping material that holds the attention, unless it's edited down to a series of sound bites and clever clips. There were cameras on us the whole time we were dancing, capturing every scrap of material that could possibly be worked into a montage.

As I'd predicted, we were learning multiple routines, and expected to master them in the course of a week. The big group number that would launch the season was a combination of fast, pseudo-jazz and our own styles, designed to give us each a "stand out moment," but really creating a confusing series of shifting angles, which we had to memorize without kicking each other in the heads. After that, we had two smaller group numbers, one for the girls and one for the guys. I didn't know yet what the guys were learning, although I was sure Pax and Anders would have plenty to say about it once we were all back home, icing our ankles and whining. We were learning the sort of loose-limbed, lyrical contemporary piece that was my bane. Dance should tell a story, but I shouldn't have to dislocate my shoulder to do it.

For the moment, however, I was learning my third routine for the week, and I was in my element. There were six ballroom dancers among the contestants, and four of us specialized in the Latin forms, so it had been decided that the big "ballroom style" number would be an Argentine tango. Sweaty, steamy, sticky, and best of all, familiar, using steps and postures I'd been doing in my sleep since I was thirteen years old. There were four women and two men, so we switched partners throughout the dance, forming duos and trios of swirling seduction. I was currently going through my steps with Lo, a beautiful Chinese-American dancer who'd taken the top prize in her season. We were almost the same height, and so we traded off who was leading constantly, spinning and caressing one another. Pretty intimate, considering we'd only met at the beginning of the rehearsal.

Our choreographer, Marisol Bustos, shouted instructions and we did our best to follow them. I'd worked with her before on my original season, and I knew she didn't expect perfection right off the bat: she just wanted to know that we were trying. Well, I was trying, and when she finally called, "Enough! Enough! You are hopeless and should take fifteen minutes to dwell upon your failures!", I was more than ready to collapse into a heap on the studio floor.

I wasn't the only one. Only two dancers remained standing—Lo, who looked more amused than anything else, and Ivan, the other ballroom dancer from her season.

"I think you were built in a secret government lab for creating tireless ballroom dancers," I accused without rancor, closing my eyes.

"Now that you know my secret, I'll have to incinerate you with my laser eyes," said Lo. Her toe daintily prodded my ribs. "Get up. There's water. You could use some."

"Everyone here is evil except for me," I grumbled, and rolled over, climbing back to my feet before I opened my eyes. The first thing I saw when I did was Lo's smiling face.

"Evil, perhaps, but in excellent shape," she said. "I heard you hadn't been working."

Of course she'd heard that. The ballroom dance community is smaller than anyone likes to believe, despite the number of talented amateurs and studios scattered across North America. Everyone talks, and while it's not like we all know each other personally, reputation is harder to run away from.

"There was some family stuff," I said, wiping my cheeks on the top of my shirt. "I thought I'd been getting enough practice in. Apparently, I'm going to need to work harder."

"Or risk elimination," said Lo. Her smile faded, replaced by solemnity. "I want to know that everyone here is giving it their all. I want to know that whoever beats me will deserve it."

"Maybe you'll win again," I said.

Lo snorted and started walking toward the table at the back of the room where the water service was set up. "America isn't going to vote for the same winner twice in a row. They loved us enough to reward us, and I'm grateful, but all you have to do is look at the Internet to know that there are always people who think the wrong person won. Those are the voters we're courting back this season. Everyone who feels like their favorite got robbed their first time around will be turning out, and the producers will reap the rewards."

"Why are you here if you feel like you can't win?" I asked, nabbing a small paper cup of water. The urge to dump it over my head was strong. I might have given in, if I hadn't known my wig would block most of it from reaching me.

"It's good exposure. I get to work with a wide variety of choreographers on someone else's time, while that same someone pays for my food and lodging. I'll be able to book more lessons after I show up on TV again. And it's *fun*. Are you really going to tell me you're only here because you might win this time?" Lo gave me an inquisitive look. Too inquisitive: for the first time since rehearsals started, I felt like my wig might be less convincing than it needed to be.

"No," I admitted. "I missed my friends from the show,

and I wasn't doing anything big. This seemed like a good way to see them again. Like summer camp in high heels."

Lo grinned. "I enjoyed you during your season. I voted for you, especially after your cha-cha in week two."

"Thanks," I said, returning her smile. I hadn't been watching the show regularly by the time Lo was on: something about being on assignment in New York had put a major crimp in my viewing schedule. Still, I'd seen enough to be sincere when I said, "I really like your footwork. Your quickstep is amazing."

"I think we're going to be friends," said Lo, just as Marisol banged her heel against the studio floor.

"Back to work! Back to work, and may some of you remember how to dance before the end of this day!"

Lo and I looked at each other, laughed, and dropped our paper cups in the trash before following the other dancers back toward rehearsal, and our future, which wasn't going to wait around for us to catch up with it.

We danced for the rest of the day, until our feet hurt and our thighs sang hosannas to the god of muscular torsion. And then we went back to our temporary homes and rubbed Tiger Balm on our legs and shoulders before collapsing into bed, a whole company of exhausted dolls being put away at the end of a long day's play. No one complained more than was absolutely necessary. We knew we were going to do it all again the next day.

And we did. We did it the next day, and the day after that, and the day after that, until we'd whittled away the week, and we were standing on the stage of Adrian Crier's specially-built theater, dressed in black and white rags, heads bowed, waiting for the music to begin. Brenna stood on the corner of the stage, her voice providing our only map through the darkness.

"You voted for them once, and you saw them rise to the top four, where one of them claimed the ultimate prize. Now they're back, ready to dance for you a second time—ready to prove that each and every one of them deserves the title of America's Dancer of Choice. Welcome, to *Dance or Die!*"

The music began to pound: "Disturbia" by Rihanna. The dancers began to move, sharp, staccato, and more synchronized than anyone who wasn't on that stage would ever know. I stopped thinking and just moved, following the beat, flinging myself into the air and trusting the people larger than I was to catch me before I could fall. We hit the verse and split into pairs, racing forward to take center stage for a few precious seconds while our names flashed on the screens to the sides. Anders hit a merciless tap sequence, heels echoing like gunfire, during his solo. I matched it with my footwork, hips shaking until my ragged skirt was a blur. Then I dropped backward, and he caught me, dragging my limp form back into the swell.

We danced. The song was only four minutes long, and we needed every precious second to get through twenty introductions married to a group number. At the end, we began to fall, one tier at a time: the dancers who had come in fourth collapsed, then the ones who had come in third, then second, and finally the five winners, all of us sprawling on the stage like the dead. The audience exploded into applause. Brenna Kelly appeared from the back of the stage, stepping over our prone and supine bodies, shouting about how amazing we were.

The show was going on, and we were going with it. It was really happening. I lay there, cheek pressed to the stage, catching my breath, and smiled.

I was dancing again.

Seven

"A mother is always proud of her children. Sometimes she doesn't understand what the hell it is they're doing, but that's also part of motherhood. If you always understand your kids, they're probably not telling you everything."

—Evelyn Baker

The Crier Theater, three weeks and two eliminations later

"LAST WEEK, they left their hearts on the stage, and America voted. Now it's time for me to tell you which three girls and which three guys are in danger. Are you ready?" Brenna's eyes skimmed down the line of dancers. The stage felt too small for the sixteen of us, standing with our partners in heart-dropping solidarity. Anders had one arm wrapped loosely around my shoulders, offering what comfort he could.

Intellectually, I knew we were unlikely to be in danger of elimination: we'd both danced incredibly well, and we still had a strong fan following. The fact that we'd reached the third performance week without dipping into the bottom proved that. Emotionally, I was holding my breath, bracing for the moment when Brenna called my name.

"Poppy. Emily. Jessica," said Brenna. "Reggie. Chaz. Ivan."

The six dancers she'd named stepped forward. Poppy

and Chaz were a partnership, and they clung to each other even harder once they were no longer in the back row of dancers.

"If I did not call your name, you are safe, and can leave the stage," said Brenna. We filed obediently away, heading for our dressing rooms. The first couple to perform would only have about ten minutes before they were expected back on stage. That was Lo and Will, a contemporary dancer. What they lost in time, they would gain in being the first to make an impression on the audience this week. Starting the show could bring big rewards, if you could be sure your eyeliner was straight.

Monitors lined the hall, allowing those of us backstage to keep up with what was going on at the front of the house. It was odd to see Brenna from the front, as the audience saw her, and not as a tall, occasionally terrifying figure moving among us. She looked sad, something I knew was more than half sincere.

"These are the dancers your votes have put in danger, America," said Brenna gravely. "This is the part I enjoy the least, because one guy and one girl will be leaving us tonight. But buck up! There's still a chance for each of these dancers to save themselves. All right? Off with you now. Go get ready." The six dancers rushed for the wings, and Brenna turned to begin giving the spiel that would lead us into the commercial break.

I continued on to my dressing room. I had my own routine to get ready for, and maybe more importantly, I didn't want to get caught by Jessica when she came looking for someone to wail at. She thought everything was unfair, from the choreography she was assigned to the fact that she was dancing with someone who wasn't originally her partner. Being in the bottom six would probably trigger the sort of fit that I didn't want to be anywhere near.

I was here to dance. I had danced my way through two weeks of eliminations after the performance-only week one, saying good-bye to Raisa and Graham in week two, and to Bobbi and Danny in week three. It was week four, and I was still standing, because I knew what was expected of me. The judges and the people at home, they just wanted me to dance.

And that was exactly what I was going to do.

With neither me nor Anders in danger, we'd been able to flirt, fight, and float our way through a contemporary routine set to a Yael Naim cover of "Toxic" by Britney Spears. There was no concern that this dance would be our last: we just did our best and left everything on the stage. We were the last routine of the night, and we were still streaked with acid-green chalk when we joined the other safe dancers in the pit in front of the judges' table, where we could watch the elimination.

"All right," said Brenna, standing in front of the line of six dancers in danger. "Adrian? I know you don't like this part, either, so I suppose we should get down to it. What have the judges decided?"

"Well, Brenna, we are unanimous tonight. But before I give our decision, I want to remind all our dancers that you're with us because we already know we love you, and that America loves you. It's just that we're a competition show, which means someone always has to go home, no matter how much we want to keep you all."

Anders squeezed my hand. I squeezed back. This was still nerve-racking, even when we knew we were safe, because next week, we might not be. Jessica had her eyes cast down at the stage, probably so the audience wouldn't realize she was glaring daggers at the people who'd dared to not vote for her.

"You're all magnificent dancers. We are so very proud to have seen your talent grow over your time with us, both in your original seasons, and over these past weeks. You are truly stars. Never forget that. Poppy, step forward. Chaz, step forward."

Poppy—a diminutive blonde from Utah who danced ballroom with the clinical precision of a surgeon—and

Chaz—a jazz dancer from Chicago who sometimes seemed to have no bones at all—stepped forward. Both were from season one. I turned to bury my face against Anders' shoulder. The judges weren't making any effort to whittle down the seasons symmetrically. They could take out an entire year with two eliminations, and they knew it.

"You will be leaving us tonight," said Adrian. Poppy and Chaz nodded as Brenna shooed the other dancers off the stage and began telling the eliminated contestants how much we were going to miss them. I doubt they heard a word she said. I certainly didn't. As with every elimination, the reality of the competition was slamming down on me, and I was suddenly, fiercely missing my normal, monster-filled life, where at least no one was going to vote me off.

Then the theme music was playing, and the remaining dancers were rushing the stage for good-bye hugs and mass goofing around, all while mugging for the cameras and reminding people at home that we were still here, we still wanted their votes, please don't send us home. It wasn't dignified, but as Pax swept me off my feet and held me up in a perfect *Dirty Dancing* lift, the weight of the competition eased off, and there wasn't anywhere else I would have wanted to be. I was a dancer. I was dancing again. That was all that really mattered.

We weren't allowed to roam around unescorted according to our contracts, but the producers understood that dancers were a weird and temperamental lot, so they didn't try too hard to force us all to leave the theater on time. Drivers had been assigned to each season, with the understanding that sometimes we would swap cars, and no one would be left behind.

I didn't feel like hurrying. The first people to get back to the apartments would be the ones starting the after party, and that wasn't the sort of responsibility I felt like having on my shoulders. Not tonight, not with my complicated feelings about the show warring for my full attention. So I sat at my dressing table and slowly wiped the chalk off my cheeks, listening to the theater emptying out around me.

Lyra lounged on the room's small couch, filing her already perfect nails. "Are you planning to sleep here tonight?" she asked.

"There was open space in the season one car," I said, wiping off another streak. Leanne, as the only remaining contestant from season five, had been consolidated into the season four car. It was like Tetris, only with highstrung, over-stimulated dancers instead of colored blocks.

"Oh, because riding with Jessica after *that* is the sort of thing I feel like doing," she said, and snorted. "Thanks, but no thanks. I'll wait until you're ready to go."

"Anders is doing the same cleanup job. You should go find Pax, see if he wants to practice your lifts."

"Nope. Pax is being standoffish and weird, so I'm giving him the cold shoulder."

I eyed her in the mirror. "Did you try to kiss him again?"

Lyra's coy smile was all the answer I needed. I sighed.

"You know that makes him uncomfortable," I said. My wig itched, but I couldn't take it off to adjust it in the theater. Lyra knew I wore a wig. So did Brenna. Everyone else would have been shocked and appalled, and it wasn't like we had actual privacy here. "Flirt with Anders instead. I promise I won't mind. I might even thank you. David's twitchy about me sharing an apartment with two men he doesn't know."

"Eh," said Lyra, and kept filing her nails.

Someone knocked on the doorframe. I glanced over my shoulder, and there was Pax, looking shaken and a little ill. "Val, do you have a second?" he asked.

It's hard to upset an Ukupani. Pax had always struck me as even more unflappable than most. I sat up straighter, putting down my washcloth.

Lyra, meanwhile, was pouting as prettily as she knew how—which was, admittedly, very pretty. She was a practiced pouter. "I have a second," she said.

"I just threw up in the stairwell and I need someone to help me find a mop," said Pax. "Do you really want to be here for me?"

Lyra's weak stomach had been legendary during our season, to the point of keeping a bucket backstage before competition, just in case. She wrinkled her nose and sank back into the couch cushions. "No," she said. "Take Valerie. She's good with gross."

"Thank you for your endorsement," I said, standing.

She waved a hand magnanimously. "But hurry up, okay? I want to get home before the party winds down. We might start switching partners next week, and I don't want people to think I'm no fun."

"Do my best," I said, and hurried out of the room.

Pax waited until we were halfway down the hall before he said, "I didn't throw up."

"I know." Ukupani were therianthrope sharks. They could eat basically anything, and I wasn't even sure they *had* a regurgitation reflex. Not the sort of thing I could ask about in mixed company. "What's going on?"

Now he looked even more uncomfortable, glancing around himself several times to confirm that we were alone before he leaned a little closer and asked, "Can you smell blood?"

"No," I said, the first hints of concern seeping into my consciousness. "Human noses aren't set up for blood detection. More's the pity. I'd ruin fewer cute skirts if they were. Do you smell blood?"

Pax nodded tightly. "I noticed it when I was walking Malena out to her car. You know she's a chupacabra, right?"

"I suspected." Chupacabra were oddly drawn to ballroom dance. Or maybe not that oddly—ballroom dance is *awesome*. "Did she smell the blood, too?"

"Yeah," he said. He ran a hand back through his hair.

"She's still here. It's cool if we cram in five people for the ride home, right? Because we told the season three driver she was going to be riding back with us."

It wouldn't be the worst thing we'd done to one of the studio drivers. Lyra could deal. "That should be fine. Where is she?"

Pax gave me an inscrutable look. "She's with the blood. It seemed . . . safer, than leaving me with it."

"Good call," I said, and gave his arm a reassuring squeeze, more grateful than ever for his vomit-based excuse. Lyra would have flipped her lid if she'd seen me touching her partner, and no amount of explaining would have calmed her down. She wanted him bad, and there was no way to explain that she was never going to get what she wanted. Not this time.

We walked down the hall to an unmarked door, one of the dozens dotting the theater walls. I'd never noticed it before, despite its proximity to the changing rooms. It was propped ajar with a chunk of concrete, keeping it from closing and possibly locking itself. It was also heavy as hell, which went with the fact that it was apparently made of solid metal. Pax took hold of the edge and wrenched it open.

"Thanks," I murmured.

"Don't mention it," he said.

The stairs on the other side of the door were metal. They creaked and groaned with every step as we made our descent. I would have been worried about falling, but the rail was bolted solidly to the wall, and Pax had long enough arms that even if the steps dropped out from under us, he'd be able to grab the rail while I grabbed him. We were going to be fine.

Then we reached the bottom, and I realized we were the only ones who were going to be fine.

Malena was crouched in one corner, her spine bent in a curve that would hurt most humans, but which looked utterly natural for her. She had her hair pulled up in a high, sloppy ponytail, revealing the spikes starting to break through her skin. The flesh around them looked inflamed. There was no blood. All the blood was reserved for the two people on the floor.

"Aw, damn," I said, stopping on the last stair.

Malena's head snapped up. She didn't say anything. Neither did Pax. All of us were silent, looking at the mess in front of us. The mess that had, until recently, been two of our fellow contestants.

Poppy and Chaz had been stripped naked and stretched out so that her feet were next to his head. Their arms were outstretched, creating a sort of box with their bodies. It was a very deliberate positioning. I pulled out my phone and took a picture of it. This was the sort of thing that needed to be studied at more length.

Malena flinched back from the flash, hissing under her breath.

"Sorry," I said distantly. It was difficult to fully commit to an emotion. I needed to stay a bit removed, because I needed to keep my wits, when all I really wanted to do was scream and run back up the stairs. Verity was trained for this sort of thing. Valerie wasn't, and I'd been living almost exclusively as Valerie for four long, relaxing weeks. My instincts were scrambled.

Speaking of instincts . . . "Pax, can you tell if they were both human? Are both human, I guess. You don't stop being human when you die." Not unless something reanimated you, which was less a change of species and more a change of status.

Pax inhaled. Then he nodded. "Both were human. Before you ask, no, I can't tell you whether it was a human that attacked them. I only smell blood from two sources."

"Same," said Malena curtly.

"Okay," I said, and went back to looking at the bodies.

They had been slit open, a long red line running from the hollow of their throats to slightly below their navels. If there was anything . . . missing, I couldn't tell; the flaps of skin were closed, just bloody. There didn't appear to have been any facial or genital mutilation. This had been a ritual killing, but the ritual was one I didn't recognize. The person or persons who had killed them had smeared blood in a wide circle around the pair, painting it directly onto the concrete floor. The edges were obscured by the blood that had continued to pour from the bodies, and any subtle markings that might have been there had already been lost forever.

The markings on the bodies, on the other hand, had not been washed away, because they weren't painted on. Someone had carved strange runes and symbols into their flesh, slicing all the way down to bone in some places. The carving appeared to have been done after the pair was dead: those wounds hadn't bled.

"I swear we found them like this," said Pax.

"I believe you," I said. "Malena, how did you get over there without stepping in the blood?" I couldn't see a clear path to where she was crouching.

"I can stick to walls," she said, her tone challenging. For the first time, I noticed her feet were bare.

Good. "Can you take pictures while you're sticking to the walls?"

Malena narrowed her eyes at me. "Yes."

I knew her tone. It was the voice of someone who expected me to regard them as both other and lesser because they weren't human. Normally, I would have taken the time to reassure her, to try to explain I wasn't going to judge. Under the circumstances, I needed my attention where it was. "Great. Come get my phone. I need you to get as close as you can—get directly above them, if your 'sticking to things' powers extend to the ceiling—and take pictures. As many pictures as you can. Zoom in, get all the details."

Now she stared at me. "I didn't figure you for a sicko."

"I'm not," I said. "Some of those symbols look familiar. I want to send the pictures to my dad, see whether he recognizes them." They looked a lot like the symbols William's captors had been using when they were sacrificing virgins in his name. Not identical, but similar enough that alarms were going off at the back of my brain.

William had been the living target of a snake cult that wanted to turn him into their devoted servant before they woke him up. No, they didn't realize what a bad idea that was, and if they had, they probably wouldn't have cared. People who think of virgins as a renewable resource are not usually the sort of people who listen to reason. Snake cults were bad news. I'd be happier if I didn't have to deal with one.

Malena shook her head and stuck her hands to the wall, boosting herself up Spider-Man style. She still looked mostly human. There was something unusual about her hands, and her feet were almost twice as long as they should have been, with an oddly flexible bend at the pad of the toes, but those were still morphologically possible. The orange-and-black scales unfurling along her shoulder blades and circling her wrists were harder to explain away.

She got her feet braced against the wall and scuttled along it, quick and nimble as a gecko, to thrust her hand out toward me. "Give me the phone," she snapped.

"Get as close as you can," I said, handing it over. Seeing her sticking to the wall like that was both disorienting and envy-inducing. If I had been able to wall-crawl, there would never have been a day when I couldn't be found lurking on the ceiling. Never.

Malena nodded before she scuttled up the wall toward the ceiling and began snapping pictures.

I turned back to Pax. "Did anyone see you come down here?"

"No." He shook his head. "I was talking with Malena, and everybody else went on ahead. She's a real nice girl, you know? And I figured we should stick together, since we're both therianthropes and all."

"Makes sense," I said. "Did you smell blood on any of the people who passed you? Specifically, did you smell *this* blood?"

He shook his head again. "No, and believe me, I would have noticed. Blood is the sort of thing that attracts my attention." He cast another uneasy glance at the bodies, and I realized I was reading his expression wrong. It wasn't discomfort born of squeamishness.

It was discomfort born of hunger.

"We have steaks in the fridge at home," I said quietly. "I can keep Lyra distracted while you bolt one of them raw."

"Can you make that two?" he asked, still looking at the bodies.

I elbowed him, pulling the motion at the last second so that he was barely grazed. "Hey, I thought humans didn't taste good."

"They don't," he said. "It's just ... there's so much blood."

"Pax, do you need to leave?" I watched him out of the corner of my eye, looking for any sign that he was about to lose control. I didn't feel like following the discovery of two bodies with a fight against one of my best friends in this competition. I'd do it if I had to. "Malena and I have things under control here."

"What are you going to do?"

This was the awful part. Well. The latest awful part in a long line of awful parts that had spanned most of my life. "The three of us are going to go cram ourselves into the car with Lyra and Anders, and we're not going to tell anyone what happened here. I hate to do it, but we have to leave the bodies for the janitorial staff to find."

"What? Why?"

I looked up. Malena was sticking to the ceiling directly over the bodies, my phone still clutched in one half-taloned hand. She was staring at me, expression aghast.

"Because you and Pax aren't human, and I'm here under an assumed name," I said. "I don't think any of us wants the kind of scrutiny that comes with this sort of discovery. Maybe more importantly, at least for me, I need to get those pictures to my dad. Spending hours explaining what happened to the police is going to delay that, and someone else could get hurt."

The janitorial staff would find and report the bodies

before we had to come back to this theater. Dumping the situation on their heads was a shitty thing to do, but that didn't change the necessity of it, or the sensibility of distancing the three of us from things as fast as we possibly could. Hopefully, Adrian had a good medical plan for his employees, and the people who found the bodies would be able to get some therapy after the fact.

Sometimes I felt like *I* needed some therapy after the fact. It was really too bad that was never going to happen.

"You're cold as hell, dancing girl," said Malena. She scuttled from the ceiling back to the wall and down to the floor, where she offered back my phone.

"I sort of have to be." I tucked the phone into my pocket. "You didn't panic when I walked in, so I'm assuming Pax told you I was a friend. Did he tell you why?"

"I was sort of busy hoping he wouldn't go all SyFy Saturday on me and bite my head off," said Malena.

"All those shark-themed monster movies are racial discrimination," grumbled Pax. He sounded a bit more like himself, and a bit less like he was going to start licking blood off the floor. I had to take that as a good thing.

"Yes, they are, and that was a sensible concern, Malena," I said. I held my hands where she could see them and be certain I wasn't reaching for a weapon, as I said, "My name isn't Valerie Pryor. It's Verity Price."

Slowly, Malena blinked. "Verity *Price*."

"Yes."

"As in, you're a Price."

"Yes."

"I don't suppose you're secretly the granddaughter of *Vincent* Price, and you're just hiding your celebrity pedigree?"

She sounded so hopeful that I sort of hated to let her down. Sadly . . . "No. I'm the daughter of Kevin Price. I'm a cryptozoologist. Sorry about that."

"Oh, great. 'I'm just going to go on reality television again, no big deal,' she said, right before she wound up in a room with two corpses, a hungry shark-man, and a *member of the Covenant of St. George.*" Malena shook her head. "I should've stayed in the desert."

"I don't belong to the Covenant," I protested. "My family quit generations before I was born. I'm on your side, and that's why I'm saying we need to get out of here. We can read about this on the Internet tomorrow." And I could wait a few days before bribing someone for the autopsy results. That would tell me how worried I needed to be.

I was pretty sure that I needed to be *extremely* worried.

Cramming five people into one of the town cars supplied for our use was easy once we put Pax in the front seat. He had the longest legs. More importantly, he was still light-headed from all the blood he'd been inhaling, and by putting him closer to the air conditioning, I hoped he could clear his head a little.

The party was raging in the courtyard when we got to the apartments—and I do mean raging. The celebration after the eliminations was always loud, enthusiastic, and guaranteed to leave more than a few dancers to face the next morning with hangovers. But we'd made it through another cruel cut, and the urge to rejoice was strong. Anders and Lyra tumbled out of the car already cheering and pumping their arms in the air. They took off running, leaving me, Pax, and Malena to watch them go.

"I don't think I can do this," said Malena, as the car drove away behind us.

"You have to, if you don't want to blow your cover," I said. "Pax and I will go up to the apartment so he can bolt a steak and I can contact my family. You're going to head for the party and watch to see whether anyone is behaving oddly."

Malena turned to stare at me. "What the hell makes you think I'm helping you with this? I was in the wrong place at the wrong time. That doesn't mean I've been recruited."

"Kinda does," I said apologetically. "Just see whether anyone's being weird." One of the jazz dancers had apparently been a cheerleader in a past life, and was organizing a human pyramid. "Weirder than usual," I amended.

"Do you really think one of us did this?" asked Malena.

"No," I said. "But we're going to need to know that for sure." Dancers wanted to dance more than they wanted to do anything else. Killing people would distract from the dancing. Whoever had done this, I didn't think we were going to find them here—and yet I needed to be sure, which meant we needed to start watching our surroundings.

"I thought I was supposed to be able to relax when I wasn't in the bottom three," muttered Malena, and stalked off toward the revels.

"Come on," I said to Pax.

No one came to ask us where we were going or why we weren't coming to the party as we made our way upstairs. We'd pay for that in the morning, when the main breakfast conversation was about whether or not we'd hooked up. That was fine: we could weather a few rumors more easily than we could weather Pax having an incident and eating half the dancers.

He made a beeline for the fridge once we reached the apartment. I kept going, making my way back to the bedroom I shared with Lyra. We both had laptops on our nightstands. Mine had a pink shell, and was covered in sparkly stickers. I ignored it as I dropped to my knees next to my bed, reached under the mattress, and pulled out a sleek, steel-colored notebook computer. It wasn't as big or as powerful as a full-sized laptop. I couldn't use it to manipulate graphics or play games. But it was small, it was fast, and best of all, it was equipped with its own wireless hotspot, thanks to the tireless efforts of my cousin Artie.

Pax was still rattling around in the kitchen when I returned. I sat on the living room floor, balancing the notebook on my crossed ankles, and activated the wireless. It would use the local cellular signals to boost itself, allowing me to get messages out without Adrian's network IT people seeing them. That was important. Somehow, I didn't think transmitting a bunch of bloody corpses over the Crier Inc. network connection would have been good for my career.

My lifestyle has equipped me with a variety of interesting skills and coping mechanisms. As it turns out, knowing how to word the "Hey, Dad, found some unexpected corpses in the basement of my dance show, can you check them" email was not one of those skills. I finally wrote a quick line warning him about gory contents and asking whether he could tell me anything about the runes cut into the bodies. Dad would be able to take it from there.

He took it faster than expected. My phone rang only a few seconds after I hit "send." The caller ID showed unknown number. I answered.

"Hello?"

"Where did you find those bodies?"

"Hi, Dad." Just hearing his voice was enough to relax me. He would know what to do next. He always did. "In the basement of the theater. Those are the two contestants who got eliminated tonight."

"You need to get out of there."

He always knew what to do, and I always refused to do it. "Why?"

"Because those runes are intended to summon a snake god, and if the snake cultists are carving them into dead people, I'd rather they not decide to carve them into you."

I leaned back until my shoulders rested against the arm of the couch. "See, and that's why I can't leave. I don't think we can convince Adrian to shut down the show—officially, the bodies haven't been found yet. Maybe when they are, he'll decide this is too dangerous, but I think he's just going to turn it into a bid for better ratings. Dancing for our fallen comrades and all that. Right now, I'm the only one here who could potentially make things better."

"I don't like the thought of you out there without backup. Your mother and I—"

"Are *so* not coming out here," I interrupted. "You have work to do, and there's nowhere for you to crash. Besides, I have backup. Dominic is here. The local cryptids include a chupacabra, an Ukupani, and a whole Nest of dragons that really wants to stay on my good side. I'll be fine."

"That isn't enough," he said. "These runes aren't amateur work, like the ones you found in the sewer. Someone has been working for a long time to bring their god to this plane of existence."

"Do you even know *which* god?" Pax stuck his head out of the kitchen, mouth bloody and eyes wide. I covered the receiver with one hand and mouthed "snake god" exaggeratedly at him. He looked blank, shrugged, and withdrew back into the kitchen. I uncovered the receiver. "Because there are a lot of snake gods out there. Maybe they're summoning Uncle Naga, and we can have a fun chat about how dance proves that bipeds have too much nervous energy. Again."

(Uncle Naga was a very nice, well, naga from a parallel dimension. His real name was unpronounceable by humans. He'd originally been summoned by a snake cult to eat my grandmother when she was a kid. Being a respectable professor of extra-dimensional studies who didn't believe in eating people he could have conversations with, he'd declined and has been a friend of the family ever since. And this is why we don't invite strangers over for Thanksgiving.)

"Naga cannot be summoned using these runes," said Dad. "Honestly, I'm not sure what *can* be summoned using these runes, only that I'd rather you not meet it face-to-face, and especially not without backup."

"Already told you, I have backup," I said. "I just need you to find out whatever you can about these runes, and pass it along, so my backup and I have a better chance of staying alive."

"I'll do my best," he said. "The two people who were eliminated tonight, they weren't the first, were they?"

"See, you say that, but I know you've been watching the show," I said. "I know because *your* mice have been sending Facebook messages to *my* mice. They really like the caps lock key. Someone should teach them about proper email etiquette."

"Thanks for volunteering," he said, before he sobered and asked, "The other people who have been eliminated ... are they all right? Has anyone talked to them?"

I didn't drop the phone. I may as well have. My mouth going slack, I stared off into the distance, considering the terrible implications of his words. Because we hadn't heard from them, had we? Danny—he'd been eliminated in week three. He was a ballroom boy. We should have swarmed him with hugs, covered him with kisses, and sent him infinite supportive messages on social media. That was part of how this *worked*. You made a fuss over the outgoing contestants to remind America that you were still there, still alive and kicking. And we hadn't done it.

Why not? Where the hell were they?

"Verity? Are you still there?" Dad's voice turned sharp. "If you're in distress, breathe in sharply twice. We'll find a way to get help to you."

"I'm fine, Daddy," I said. The last thing I wanted was for my father to start mobilizing the troops. He'd start with Dominic—that was fine—but there was no telling where he would go from there. "I was just thinking about what you said. I wasn't close to any of the people who've been eliminated. My season is intact. But it's still weird that I haven't spoken to any of them. I'll look into it."

"See to it that you do," said Dad, and sighed. "You know, Verity, when you told us that ballroom dance was your life's true passion, I thought it meant you would be *safer* than your brother. Basements full of bodies sort of go against that."

"I *am* safer than my brother," I protested. "I haven't been bitten by a werewolf or turned to stone. Compared to Alex, I'm little Susie Safety."

He chuckled ruefully. "I wish that weren't reassuring. All right: your mother and I will stay here. But I'm sending backup, and you're going to accept it, or I'm coming down there and carrying you home."

"What kind of back—" I began.

It was too late. He had already hung up.

I dropped my phone on the carpet and began hitting my head against the couch. It was soothing. I was still hitting my head against the couch when Pax emerged from the kitchen again. He walked across the room to loom over me, a concerned expression on his face.

"It didn't go well?" he asked.

I stopped hitting my head against the couch. "Dad says the runes are intended to summon a snake god, although he doesn't know which one, and that they're really old, which means they have a better chance of working. So he's sending me backup, because apparently what I already have here is not sufficient. He also says we should be checking up on everyone else who's been eliminated, because *that's* the sort of thought that helps me sleep at night."

"I see." Pax sat down on the couch, still looking down at me. "What's a snake god?"

I blinked. "Okay, that was something I hadn't considered. Um. So most major human and cryptid religions have snakes in them somewhere. There's the whole Garden of Eden shtick, the Rainbow Serpent, Medusa, all that fun stuff. And maybe that's because of monomyths and things like that—ask my mother if you ever want to have your ear talked off—and maybe it's because all religions are a little bit right, but it's at least partially because there are a really disturbing number of dimensions filled with nothing but snakes."

"Snakes," said Pax slowly.

"Yup, snakes. You know how dimensions work, right?"

He looked at me blankly.

"You . . . *don't* know how dimensions work?"

"You don't have to sound so surprised," he said, sitting up straighter. "I bet you don't know how the benthic zones of the sea function, but I understand them intimately."

"We all have our own strengths," I said, and shook my head, trying to switch into educational mode. "Have you ever seen a honeycomb?"

"Yes."

"So think of our dimension as one cell in a really, really big honeycomb. It's touching a bunch of other realities, all sort of parallel, all sort of not. What you get is determined by what direction you go—and don't ask how you know what direction you're going, I am *not* a dimensional traveler, and I don't want to be. That's my Grandma Alice's job. Anyway, if you're traveling on the horizontal," I swept my hand flat through the air in front of me, "you get humanoids, things that look like life in this dimension, but aren't necessarily the same. Cuckoos probably came from a horizontal dimension. If you're traveling on the vertical, you get things that aren't humanoid, but are statistically more likely to be like the people in this dimension—empathic, intelligent, friendly. And if you travel on the diagonal, you get weird shit. Frequently snakes. Like, three times out of four, snakes."

"But why?"

"Hell if I know. Hell if *anyone* knows. The universe seems to really enjoy making snakes." I pushed myself up off the floor, tucking my phone into my pocket. "Because there are so many snake dimensions, people have run into them at various points throughout history. And because humans are sometimes predictable in bad ways, there are always people who think summoning a giant snake from another dimension will help them get their heart's desire. I'm not sure what that says about people. Probably nothing good."

Pax stared at me. "That's it, I'm going back to the ocean."

"You're like the little mermaid in reverse." I flashed him a smile and offered him my hand. "Come on. Are you feeling less like eating people?"

"Yes, but we're going to need more steak," he said, taking my hand and letting me pull him to his feet.

"We can get more steak," I said. "For right now, we need to get out there and pretend everything is normal. You up for it?"

"No," he said dolefully.

"Good," I said, and dragged him out the door. Yes, there was an element of fiddling while Rome burned in heading for a party when two of our fellow contestants had just died, but sometimes, keeping up appearances was all you could do. We'd avenge them later. Maybe I was being a little paranoid: I'd own it if that were the case. Hell, I'd even be grateful. But I didn't think I was. When something like this begins, it doesn't end until a lot more people are dead.

Eight

"Walking into danger with your eyes open and your mind clear is a sign of bravery, not foolishness. Well, sometimes foolishness. But as long as you walk back out again, you can pretend that part doesn't matter."
— Enid Healy

The Crier Apartments, privately owned by Crier Productions, sometime after midnight

THE PARTY WAS AS AWFUL as I expected. People kept asking if I'd seen Poppy or Chaz, then laughing and making snarky comments about sore losers when I said I hadn't. It was triggering a weird sort of déjà vu; I was pretty sure I'd seen this scene play out over the course of the last few weeks, as people slipped away from us. I might even have been one of the ones asking where they'd gone.

Thinking about it made me want to grab and shake every single person I saw, and when I realized my hands had started balling into fists without my having consciously decided to hit somebody, I pleaded a headache and left. Lyra was still laughing, dancing on top of a picnic table with one of the contestants from season four. I decided to let her have her fun. She'd pay for it in the morning, and maybe the hangover would make the bad news feel a little less personal.

The front of the apartment was empty when I stepped

inside and started toward my bedroom. It was time to take off my wig, shower, massage my scalp, and get ready for bed. Nothing was going to stop me from getting a few hours of much-needed sleep.

Nothing except for maybe Dominic, perched on the windowsill above my bed like some bizarre bird of prey. He was even wearing his leather duster, which he usually only broke out for monster hunting these days. I stopped in the doorway.

"Close the door," he said.

I closed the door. Then, without being told, I grabbed a chair from the closer of the room's two desks, and wedged it up under the doorknob. If Lyra came back, she could knock.

"Come over here," he said.

Those were the words I needed to snap me out of my surprise. "What are you *doing* here?" I hissed, voice low. "You know you're not supposed to be this close to the studio housing. They have a lot of security around this place. You could have been arrested. You could *still* be arrested. You're supposed to text me and let me come to you!"

"Yes, there are a great many things we're supposed to do, aren't there?" Dominic stayed on the windowsill, eyes narrowed and jaw set in a hard line. "For example, when my *wife* discovers dead bodies in the place where she spends most of her time, I expect her to notify me. I certainly expect her to call me before she goes to a party, rather than leaving me to find out from an email CC."

I paled. "Oh. Dad already got results?"

"You are the most insufferable, infuriating, *insane* woman I have ever—yes, he found some documentation of those runes you photographed. You remember, the ones *carved into the corpses of your fellows*." He finally slid off the windowsill, striding toward me. "Verity, how could you?"

"Look, I know you're mad, but I was never directly in danger," I protested. "They were dead by the time I got down to the basement. I didn't see the killer."

"You think that's why I'm angry? Please. Danger is a natural part of what you've chosen to do with your life. I hope you don't get yourself killed while I'm not with you, but I accepted the possibility long before I asked you to marry me." Dominic shook his head. "I'm angry because you didn't call. Because I had to find out from someone else, as an afterthought, and I've rarely been so worried, or felt so helpless."

"I'm sorry," I whispered. "I didn't think." I'd followed procedure. I'd encountered a problem and notified the family. But I had more than my blood relatives now. I had Dominic, and he was *here*, and he'd needed me, and I hadn't called him. I was a terrible wife. He was probably going to divorce me. It would be just what I deserved. It would be—

Dominic put his hands on the sides of my face, pulled me closer, and kissed me. I could feel the relief radiating off him, so clear and vibrant that for a moment I thought this must be what it was like to be an empath. Artie had tried to explain what it was like to feel other people's emotions to me more than once: in that moment, in that kiss, I finally understood what I'd been missing.

Finally, Dominic pulled back, and said, "If you ever do that to me again, *ever*, I will lock you in the trunk of the nearest available vehicle and leave you there until I feel you've thought sufficiently about what you've done."

"I'm sorry, did you just threaten to put me in time out?" I put a hand at the center of his chest and pushed lightly. "Nope. Not going to happen. But I'll try to be better."

"That's all I've ever asked."

"So if Dad found some info on these runes, does that mean you're up to speed?"

"Yes, although not with whatever unreasonable plan you've concocted to deal with the situation."

"I'm going to go back to the theater tomorrow, and wait to see whether Adrian shuts down the show," I said. "If he does, we get the hell out of Dodge. If he doesn't, I keep my eyes open and you start lurking around the theater more, in case you're needed in a hurry. Dad thinks these may not have been the first bodies—just the first ones we've found. Someone may have gotten to the janitorial staff. I'm not sure yet. I need to wait and see."

Dominic blinked. "That actually sounds reasonable. Who are you, and what have you done with my wife?"

"Ha, ha," I said, before kissing him again. "Get out of here. The last thing we need right now is for you to get caught. I'll come see you tomorrow night, and you need to clear your calendar for this weekend."

"Why?"

I grinned. "Because we're going to the flea market."

After Dominic left and I'd taken my shower, I was able to manage almost five hours of uninterrupted sleep before the alarms went off and it was time to get moving again. Despite my corpse-and-intrigue–filled evening, I was still perkier than most of the other dancers as we lined up to wait for the town cars. Apparently, dead bodies aren't as bad for you as wine coolers. Not a surprise, but still good to have it proven.

Malena wandered over to our waiting area, nodding genially to Anders and Lyra before asking me, "All good?"

"All good," I said. "I'll let you know if that changes."

"Or you could not let me know," she said. "That's always an option. Catch you on the backbeat." Then she was gone, heading for her own waiting zone, while Anders and Lyra turned to stare at me.

"Are you making *friends*?" gasped Lyra. "With people who aren't *us*? Be still my heart, I never thought I'd see the day."

"Quiet, you," I said, before punching her on the arm. "I'm a friendly person. I know how to make friends."

"Knowing how to do a thing and actually doing the thing are not the same thing," said Anders. "You've never socialized with our competition."

"I socialize with you," I protested.

"I was your partner for the whole season. If you hadn't been willing to socialize with me, you would have spent all your free time sitting in a corner looking sad," said Anders. "It still took me two weeks to get more than five words out of you when the cameras weren't on us."

"You only started socializing with me and Pax after I got dropped on you during a group rehearsal," said Lyra. "Ours is a friendship born of unstable footing and guilt."

"Okay, so I'm mostly focused on my dancing," I allowed. Lyra was wrong about why I'd started being friendly with her: the drop had been an excuse. I'd been trying to get closer to Pax, who was the first Ukupani I'd ever met. Scientific curiosity has always been a powerful motivator where I'm concerned. "That doesn't mean I'm unfriendly. I can make friends."

"Malena's a nice girl," said Pax. "If Val wants to make friends, I say we let her."

"It's just so beautiful," said Lyra, miming wiping a tear from the corner of her eye. "Our little Valerie's learning how to play nicely with the other children."

"I will kill you all in your sleep," I said.

Lyra was still laughing when the town car arrived.

The ride to the theater was harder than usual. I had to keep pretending nothing was wrong, even as the feeling of impending doom grew stronger. Soon, we'd find out how Adrian was planning to react to the bodies in his basement. In the meantime, I had to keep people from realizing I'd already known.

Worse yet was the possibility that Adrian wouldn't say anything; that the bodies wouldn't have been found, and I would have to decide how to play things from there. Not fun.

The cars let us out behind the theater, at what we all thought of as the stage door. We filed dutifully inside to learn what we'd be doing for the next week—or to find that the whole show had been canceled on account of the vicious murder of two of our own. I saw Malena through the crowd, casting worried glances at me and Pax. For once, I was the person with the least to lose. I was the only one of the three of us who was human, and while intense media scrutiny might result in my having to spend a few years hiding from the Covenant of St. George, I didn't need to worry that I'd lose control, change forms, and eat a judge.

I found Pax's hand and squeezed. He didn't say anything, but he squeezed back.

We arrived on the stage in a mob. Adrian and Lindy were already at the judges' table. Cameras were set up around the edge of the stage, filming everything.

"Morning, all," said Adrian. "We have a few announcements before you pull your choreography assignments."

This was it. They'd found the bodies, and the show was going to continue as a memorial. The other four eliminated contestants were fine. Everyone would know to be much more careful, and we'd dance to honor the dead. Maybe it said something bad about my priorities, but I was relieved to know that we wouldn't be going home just yet.

"Remember that as of this week, America will be voting on whether or not to mix up your partnerships. If you want to keep your partners, you'll all need to work on your connection to one another, and on seeming like you actually enjoy what you're doing. If you feel like a new partner would be a good thing, then by all means keep smiling at the audience when you're supposed to be having a romantic moment."

Lindy chose that moment to speak up. "We still have a *lot* of excellent ballroom dancers here, but we're already down two. I'd rather not lose one of you every week. So get your shoulders down and ground your feet like you actually remember what your choreographers taught you. Got it?"

"Yes, Lindy," chorused the remaining ballroom dancers dutifully, me among them. It was no secret that Lindy favored the ballroom dancers—or that she'd come down on us like a ton of bricks if she felt we'd given her a reason.

(I never really had to give her a reason. My friendship with Brenna was enough to label me as a bad girl in her eyes. Lindy was professional enough that she'd never used it as an excuse to throw me under the bus, but during my season I'd been praised less than the other ballroom girls, a trend which was continuing into the present day. Oh, well. It wasn't like I needed her validation when I had all of America picking up their phones to vote for me.)

"Brenna will be here in a moment, and then you'll draw your routine for the week. We'll do it twice, to make sure you have a style that works for you; once that's done, you'll go and meet with your choreographers." Adrian looked around the group. "Any questions?"

I had one. *Why aren't you saying anything about the murders?* But I couldn't ask that without betraying that I knew more than I should have, and so I kept my mouth shut and stared at him, willing him to say something.

He didn't say anything.

Brenna appeared with the hat from which we'd draw our "random" dance assignments. Someone hit the theater lights, recreating the diffuse theatrical lighting that accompanied the shows, and it was time to get back to work, no matter how much I didn't want to. If I was going to find out what was going on, I was going to have to play by their rules.

Anders and I drew the quickstep, which meant a lot of hopping and running and incredibly rapid footwork, all performed while trying to recall Gene Kelly and Cyd Charisse in their heyday. We were going to be dancing to "Candyman" by Christina Aguilera, doing a Tarzan-and-Jane concept routine, and since it was a dance built on energy and precision rather than complicated tricks or lift sequences, our choreographer didn't need to modify it much to accommodate our skill levels. We spent the first two hours of the day warming up, learning the basic steps, and getting a feel for the piece. It was pleasantly non-hectic—something I knew wouldn't last when we hit lunch and got our group routine assignments.

"Anyone mind if I duck out to powder my nose?" I asked.

Anders, who was currently flat on his back on the studio floor, breathing heavily, waved me off. Our choreographer flashed me a grin.

"Just hurry back, we're about to start learning the fast part," he said.

"Can't wait," I said, and slipped out of the room.

As soon as the door was shut behind me, my posture changed. Valerie was a dancer. She was graceful and loose and always ready to turn a simple motion into something profound. Verity—the real me—was all those things, but first and foremost, Verity was a hunter. Where Valerie walked like the whole room was hers to claim and conquer, Verity slunk, compact and poised to strike. Valerie posed. Verity attacked.

Sliding from one identity into the other was more difficult than usual, because I was on Valerie's territory. The back halls of the Crier Theater belonged to her, especially in the middle of the day. Anyone could come out of a room and catch me outside my rehearsal and walking oddly. I couldn't think about that right now. All my attention was on stripping myself back down to my training, and finding out what the hell was going on.

There was no smell of decay wafting up from the basement. I hesitated for a moment before I flicked on the light and started down the stairs. Halfway down, I froze.

The bodies were gone.

The floor was clean, all traces of blood washed away. The place would probably have lit up like Christmas morning under a black light, but the naked eye found nothing wrong. There was a scuff from behind me, like someone coming to a stop. I whipped around, falling into a combat stance, and relaxed as I saw who it was.

"Pax," I said. "You scared me."

"I scared you?" he demanded. "You just looked at me like you were going to rip my larynx out with your bare hands. I need my larynx. Those things take forever to grow back." He looked past me to the floor, expression going from surprised to grim. "I figured you'd come here eventually. I've been checking every ten minutes or so."

"That must be making Lyra super happy," I said.

"Between the so-called vomiting last night and now this, she thinks I have food poisoning. I'm a 'trooper.'" He grimaced. "The door was cracked when I passed it to start rehearsal, and I realized I couldn't smell any blood. I checked the room as soon as I could get away, and found it like this."

"*No* blood?" I turned back to the empty basement. "They can't have cleaned it that completely."

"I'm telling you; my nose doesn't lie. There's no blood in this room. Before you ask, no, I didn't smell any blood on anyone last night, or on Adrian and Lindy this morning. Either they've got the best cleaning crew in the business, or they weren't involved."

Slowly, I sank into a sitting position on the stairs, holding onto the rail with one hand for balance as I looked down at the spotless concrete floor. There was no blood. There were no bodies. If not for Pax being as confused as I was and the pictures in my phone, I might have taken it for a very vivid, very terrible dream.

"What the hell is going on here?" I asked.

Pax didn't answer.

We had to get back to our partners before they noticed anything amiss. After a few more moments of staring at the empty basement, we'd returned to our respective rehearsal rooms and done our best to make it seem like nothing was wrong. That was where my Valerie persona gave me a thin advantage. I'd been treating her like someone completely distinct from myself for so long that all I had to do was shove my own concerns to the background and let her have the wheel. Valerie didn't care about dead people. Valerie just wanted to dance.

Our group number for the week was a lyrical jazz number, where Lyra floated like a leaf and the rest of us struggled to get our legs to bend in places that didn't usually come with joints. I left Valerie in charge, allowing her to follow the steps while I tried to puzzle through the situation. Two dead dancers, and no outcry, not even from their former roommates. I could see Jessica not caring that Poppy had never come to collect her things, but Reggie? He and Chaz had been pretty close. And what about the other eliminated dancers? Someone needed to check their social media accounts. If they'd gone completely silent, we'd know they were gone.

But first I had to survive rehearsal. Our choreographer was a punk rock Tinker Bell that I suspected of being a succubus, although I didn't have any proof. Artie would have known in a second—Lilu always recognize their own kind—but as that would have required getting him out of his basement and bringing him to a rehearsal space full of sweaty females, it was never going to happen.

(None of my cousins are exactly what I'd call "normal." Cousin Artie was the winner of our private weirdness armada, being a reclusive half-incubus comic book nerd with a supposedly secret crush on our telepathic cousin Sarah. I say "supposedly" because everybody in the family knew he was in love with her—everyone except Sarah, who somehow managed to be as oblivious as he was. For a couple of really smart people, they could be remarkably dense sometimes.)

The thing about working with anyone who can be described using the phrase "punk rock Tinker Bell" is that they'll work you to death while exhorting you to "dig a little deeper" and "reach your true potential." Sasha was the sort of natural disaster every dancer dreams of working with, right up until they get the opportunity. After an afternoon in her studio, I was exhausted, and my dreams were a lot more focused on the idea of smothering her

with a pillow. Not to death. Just into a peaceful uncon-
sciousness from which she'd wake in a year or two.

Rehearsal finished at seven o'clock, and we dragged
ourselves out to the town cars, where we collapsed like
so many boneless puppies. I wound up with Lyra half in
my lap. She had more experience with the steps Sasha
was drilling into our heads, but that just meant she'd
been expected to master more, faster, while the rest of us
were forgiven for our occasional bouts of clumsiness.

I needed to go see Dominic. My legs felt like they'd
been hollowed out and filled with cicadas in place of the
bones. The thought of running across the rooftops of Los
Angeles made my stomach flip.

"Is she a robot?" asked Anders. He'd allowed his head
to flop backward, apparently lacking the strength to hold
it up any longer. "You can tell me. She's an alien robot,
here to soften us up for the invasion. Let's destroy her."

"I don't think she's a robot," said Pax.

"But she doesn't sweat. Have you noticed that? She
throws us around like we're toys, and she never sweats. I
think she's a robot."

"You're a robot," said Lyra.

We all fell quiet, considering her words with the seriousness that only comes naturally to the truly exhausted.

"Nah," said Anders finally. "But Jessica's probably a
robot."

The argument about whether Sasha or Jessica—or
both—were robots occupied us all the way back to the
apartments, where we rolled out of the town car and
slouched dolefully toward the stairs. Halfway there, Lyra
perked up.

"Dibs on the shower," she said, and broke into a run.

Lyra was the first to reach the apartment, with the rest
of us close on her heels, clamoring about our need to use
the shower before she did. She unlocked the door, and
the four of us virtually fell inside, where we stopped, all
of us, and stared at the woman sitting on our living room
couch. She was writing in a leather-bound journal, looking utterly relaxed.

She wouldn't have looked out of place in the new edition of *Tomb Raider*: early twenties, with short, ragged blonde hair, cut-offs, and a tank top. Tattoos covered the exposed skin on the left side of her body, wrapping around her collarbone and running partway up her neck. The family resemblance between her and me was unmistakable, even with my wig.

She raised her head. We picked ourselves up off the floor. I started to open my mouth and froze, unsure what I was supposed to call her. "Grandma" wasn't going to go over very well with my companions, or be something that I could readily explain.

Fortunately, she solved the problem for me. "I was wondering when you'd get home," she said, and stood. "Sorry to break in like this, but the security guys were starting to give me the stink-eye for sitting on the curb. I had to come over the wall or risk being arrested."

"Who the hell are you?" demanded Anders, pushing himself forward, putting himself between her and the rest of us. I don't think protecting Pax was the goal, not from the way he positioned himself directly in front of Lyra, but he was gallant enough to stick an arm across my chest, barring me from the potentially dangerous intruder.

Well, not "potentially dangerous." She was my grandmother. She was *definitely* dangerous.

Alice grinned. It was a wry, lopsided thing. My grin would look like that if it ever got dragged down a hundred miles of bad road, and through more than fifty years of fruitlessly searching for my one true love. I'd pass, if I had the choice. No one should have to smile like that.

"I'm her sister," she said. "My name's Elle."

"You have a sister?" said Lyra, head whipping around as I suddenly became a lot more interesting than an intruder in our living room.

"You have a punk rock sister who picks locks?" demanded Anders.

Pax didn't say anything. He was the only one from my season who knew about my family, and when I glanced back at him, I could see him running through the possible candidates for the role of "Elle." He reached his conclusion while I watched, turning white.

"Oh," he said.

"Okay, break it up." I ducked under Anders' arm. "Nice to see you, 'Elle,' but what are you doing here? You know my contract doesn't allow unmonitored contact with my family while I'm on the show." Thank God there weren't cameras in our apartments. Adrian would have filmed us twenty-four/seven if he'd been able to get away with it, but he didn't want to pay the insurance fees for putting cameras in our kitchens. That, and we were dancers: many of us had a tendency to wander around completely nude. None of that footage could be used, or even kept, for fear of a pornography charge.

"Sorry, Val, but I got thrown out of my latest apartment," said Alice, calm as anything. She raised an eyebrow, daring me to challenge her. "There were noise complaints from the neighbors."

"Loud music?" guessed Lyra.

"Gunfire," said Alice.

Lyra didn't say anything.

"So I figured you've got room, right? There's a whole bunch of empty apartments downstairs. No one's even going to notice that I'm here." She turned and flashed her most winsome smile at my roommates.

It's weird. Grandma Alice is a heavily tattooed dimension-hopping marauder who regularly carries grenades clipped to the belt of her cut-off jeans, but for some reason, people *want* to like her. Lyra and Anders smiled back immediately. Pax, who was still pale and wide-eyed, did not. He also didn't run out of the room, which would have been a perfectly reasonable reaction under the circumstances.

"Look, if security catches me, I'll say I was squatting when the dancers arrived, and stuck around for the anonymity and free grub," said Alice, turning back to me, like I was the one she had to convince. "I won't get you in trouble, I promise."

"All you *do* is get people in trouble," I said. "It's like a holy calling with you."

Alice's eyes widened. Too late, I realized my mistake, and managed not to compound it by slapping my hand over my mouth—although it was a near thing.

Every priestess is important to the Aeslin, but they have their hierarchy. The longer a priestess has been alive, the more rituals she'll have, and the more excited the colony will be when they see her. Normally, this is balanced out by the fact that people die and their catechism ends, becoming a fixed loop in the Aeslin year. Unfortunately, Grandma Alice was too busy to settle down and get old like a normal person, and the Aeslin have been maintaining her worship for almost eighty years without a break, making her the senior priestess of our family. So far as I knew, she was the only priestess to have two separate liturgical lines. She was the Noisy Priestess when she was home and the Pilgrim Priestess when she was off looking for Grandpa Thomas, which meant she had double the usual number of rituals and catechisms focused on her. And now she was in my apartment, and I had mentioned holy callings.

We stayed frozen for several seconds, staring at each other and waiting for the cheering to begin. When it didn't—when merciful silence, broken only by the shouting from the people who were starting to gather in the courtyard, reigned—we relaxed, in the sort of familial unison that was just going to make her claim to be my sister more believable.

"Fine," I said, more harshly than I meant to. "As long as no one's going to rat you out, you can stay." I turned to my roommates. Maybe one of them would save me. Maybe one of them would object, and Alice would have to go stay somewhere else. I could call Brenna. Maybe there was room at the Nest for my occasionally murderous grandmother and her collection of grenades.

Instead, Lyra broke from the pack and slung her arms around my neck, pulling me into a tight, exuberant hug. "Oh, *Val*!" she squealed. "I'm so happy for you!" She turned to Alice and said, "It's always been really upsetting to me how Valerie's family doesn't support her dancing. Your sister's a genius, you know. She's amazing, and your whole family should be coming out to watch her dance."

"That's what I've always said." Alice was clearly amused, eyes glinting with barely-contained mischief. "So I'm here for the rest of the season."

"Thanks," I said, through clenched teeth.

"Any time," said Alice. "I'm going to take the apartment right downstairs. Give me a few minutes, and then come down to talk to me? We should catch up, *sis*."

"Wouldn't miss it," I said, and watched my grandmother—regularly named the most dangerous human woman in four dimensions—pick up her backpack and walk out of the living room.

Lyra hugged me again. "I changed my mind, you can have first shower. This is amazing!"

Was it my imagination, or did I hear muffled cheers from behind the couch?

It probably wasn't my imagination.

Lyra let me go. "You and your sister must have so much to catch up on!"

"Oh, yeah," I said. "Definitely."

So very much . . . like murder.

Nine

"I didn't start out with a lot of family. One thing I've learned is that people who love and accept you are worth their weight in silver bullets. You hold them fast, and you never let them go."

— Frances Brown

The Crier Apartments, privately owned by Crier Productions, about fifteen minutes later

LYRA WAS RIGHT: I felt better after a shower and a wig change, although my scalp still itched. I changed into a pair of yoga pants and a jogging top, rubbed a layer of Tiger Balm into my calves, and went bounding outside. There were no cameramen in evidence, giving us a rare moment of peace.

An impromptu rehearsal circle had formed at the center of the courtyard, which explained the yelling. About half the season was bending, swaying, and stretching their way through Sasha's lyrical jazz routine. Under normal circumstances, I would've felt obligated to join them. The thought made my thighs ache. Fortunately for me, I had something more pressing to attend to.

I slipped down the stairs and headed for the apartment under ours, glancing nervously around. No one looked my way. I opened the apartment door and stepped inside. Alice—who was sitting on this couch just like she'd been sitting on ours—looked up from the rifle she was field-stripping and smiled.

"There's my girl," she said. "Shut the door and come talk to me. It's been too long since we've had a nice talk."

"Grandma, what are you doing here?" I shut the door. "I'm not supposed to have guests. I'm *definitely* not supposed to have guests with grenades."

"Your father called me. Fortunately, I was in a place with phone service, or he'd have summoned your Uncle Mike." Alice raised an eyebrow. "Far be it from me to criticize Mikey—he's a good kid—but do you think he would have fit in with your new friends better than I will?"

"You don't fit in with my new friends at all," I protested. "They're in their twenties, and they dance for a living. You're . . . not in your twenties, and you kill things for a living." And for food, and sometimes, I suspected, for fun. It was hard to tell with Grandma Alice. She was the only human I knew who lived primarily off-dimension, and that sort of thing had to be bad for her sense of social norms.

"No, but I look like I'm in my twenties, and I'm believable as your semi-estranged sister who wants to mend some bridges." Alice began reassembling her rifle, still looking at me. "I know this isn't ideal, Very. I'm not here to blow your cover or get you into trouble. I'm just here to make sure that you're safe. Snake cults aren't something to mess around with."

"I already handled a snake cult in New York," I said.

Alice's expression turned hard. "No, you handled a bunch of amateurs who'd been lucky enough to stumble across a sleeping dragon. They were working out of the pop culture version of the snake cult bible, and they had no idea what they were doing. What kind of forces they were playing with. Do you honestly think I crossed three dimensions because I thought you couldn't handle yourself? Please. Your father sent me the pictures you took. The people you're dealing with here, the people who killed those poor children, they have a *much* better idea of the rituals they're trying to enact."

My knees felt suddenly weak. I allowed myself to fold to the floor, settling cross-legged as I stared at her. "You think it's going to be that bad?"

"I think some of those runes were things I'd never seen before," said Alice. "Some of them I'd only ever seen in Thomas' notes. Even *he* didn't know what they all meant. There have been snake cults as long as there have been people, Very, and some of them had the chance to get extremely good at what they did before their neighbors sensibly rose up and slaughtered them."

"I don't think the words 'sensible' and 'slaughter' belong in the same sentence," I said.

"They do when it's that or watch your children get swallowed by a snake the size of a freight train," said Alice. She snapped the last piece of her rifle back into place. "What did you find at the theater today?"

I shook my head, chasing off the image of snakes big enough to have their own SyFy Channel franchises. "Nothing," I said.

She blinked.

"I mean it literally: there was nothing." I explained the situation, from the empty basement to the lack of blood trace evidence.

By the time I finished, Alice was frowning. "You're saying an Ukupani couldn't find *any* signs that someone had been killed there?" I nodded. Her frown deepened. "Ukupani are some of the best long-range hunters in the world. They can scent a drop of blood in the water from up to a mile away. If he couldn't detect any signs of blood . . ."

"They bought a lot of bleach," I concluded.

"No," said Alice. "You would have been able to smell that much bleach. But there are spells and charms that absorb blood, use it to power things. Whoever drew those runes on the bodies was an actual magic-user, not just someone screwing around."

I stared at her. "Oh," I said, after a moment. "Crap."
Alice nodded. "Yes," she said. "Crap."

Magic is real, in the sense that sometimes the world does things that can't be explained using science as we currently understand it. Magic isn't real, because once something becomes explainable, we start thinking of it as "science," and we no longer pretend it doesn't exist. It's sort of like cryptids. Creatures that were once considered impossible and mythological become completely plausible as soon as someone figures out how to explain them. The wheel turns, and the world changes.

Here is what we know about magic:

There are people who, for whatever reason, can affect the world on a molecular level. They can convince things to appear out of thin air, open portals between places, or—yes—tear holes between dimensions. Most of the time, it's the symbols that matter. You don't have to be a mathematician to copy an equation, and the answer will be the same whether you did the work in real time or wrote it down from memory. Most so-called "wizards" and their ilk are working from copies of copies of copies of the original crib sheets, sketching out spells and charms that they don't really understand. They're not harmless, but they're not as dangerous as they could be, either.

The problem with working from someone else's notes is that mistakes will start creeping in, which was why Dad could tell the age of the runes we'd found carved into Poppy and Chaz. Degradation of information was inevitable . . . unless they had someone on their side who understood what they were doing. Someone who could check their math, and could, say, draw a charm to completely purge the blood from a room. A magic-user, someone for whom the use of this particular language came as naturally as Sarah's use of math or my use of the tango.

Magic-users are pretty rare. It's partially training and partially genetic, and both factors have suffered greatly at the hands of the Covenant. The last magic-user in our family was Grandpa Thomas, who had a small talent for elemental magic and a large talent for moving things with his mind, at least according to Grandma Alice, who—as has already been established—was not the world's most reliable source. Still, if we assumed she was telling the truth about that, then we had a baseline for how rare the talent was, since no one in the two generations following their marriage had shown any tendency to set the curtains on fire with their minds. Two children and five grandkids, and still nothing had manifested.

For the snake cultists to have a magic-user . . . well. That wasn't good. And that may have been the understatement of the year.

When I got back up to my own room, I curled up on my bed and sent Dominic a text, asking him to answer if he was up. My phone buzzed a few seconds later.

JUST GOT BACK FROM PATROL. THE AREA'S QUIET. NO SIGNS OF SNAKE CULT ACTIVITY. WHAT'S GOING ON?

There were so many ways to answer that question, and half of them required a flowchart. I decided to go with something from the other half, and replied, DAD SENT BACKUP. MY GRANDMOTHER'S HERE. JUST WANTED TO WARN YOU.

This time, there was a longer pause before his return message. DID SHE BRING SARAH?

He was thinking of my maternal grandmother, Angela Baker. Grandma Angela is a cuckoo, like Sarah. But she's not a fighter, and she's not a receptive telepath—she can project her thoughts, but she can't pick up the thoughts of the people around her. Not so useful when what I needed was to find the people who were responsible for the murders of my cast mates.

WRONG GRANDMA, I replied. THIS IS GRANDMA ALICE.

No pause at all this time, but his next text was in all caps: ALICE HEALY?!?

PRICE-HEALY, TECHNICALLY. SHE TOOK HER HUSBAND'S LAST NAME WHEN THEY GOT MARRIED. Grandma was the traditional sort, in some ways. Mostly the ways that gave her a higher chance of getting blood in her hair.

I'M COMING OVER.

NO! I CAN'T HAVE PEOPLE COMING IN AND OUT AT ALL HOURS. WE'LL COME TO YOU. I hadn't been planning to go *anywhere* tonight—I was exhausted, and we didn't have any new information to go on—but if I needed to introduce my grandmother to my husband in order to prevent some sort of incident, I'd find a way.

I WILL EXPECT YOU INSIDE THE HOUR, was Dominic's last text. He stopped responding after that. I should probably have been worried, but I was honestly relieved. His silence gave me time to figure out how I was going to sneak out when I wasn't going alone.

Grandma Alice isn't a free-runner; like most of my family, she views my tendency to throw myself off tall buildings as just short of suicidal, although—being her—she also found it sort of adorable. When your grandmother with no sense of self-preservation thinks you're being cute, maybe it's time to reconsider your life choices.

On the plus side, she *did* like to drive, although the legality of her license was questionable. She definitely knew how to hot-wire a car, since she'd tried to teach me when I was six (just one of a long series of decisions that eventually led to my father saying she wasn't allowed to be alone with us until we turned sixteen). Between the two of us, we could probably manage to scrounge up a vehicle. I slipped my phone into my pocket, pulled a few knives from under my mattress and tucked them into my shirt, and stood. Time to get moving again.

Pax and Lyra were in the living room. He was giving her a foot rub; she had a cold cloth on her forehead. Anders was nowhere to be seen. Pax looked up at the sound of footsteps, raising his eyebrows.

"Going somewhere?" he asked.

"Just downstairs to talk to Elle," I said. I managed a smile that didn't look entirely ghoulish. "Don't wait up, okay?"

"Val, wait." Lyra sat up enough to meet my eyes. "I know I'm the one who said this was okay, but I'm worried. It's cool that your sister's here and all—it sucks that your family doesn't support you—and I don't have any problem with her squatting until the show's over, but you already sneak out the window most nights, and now you're going downstairs to hang out with her. Is this going to affect your work?"

It was such a reasonable question, about such an unreasonable situation, that it was all I could do not to start laughing. Instead, I forced my smile to get a little wider, and said, "With my sister here, maybe I won't feel the need to sneak out as much. I'll be fine, Lyra. I've never gotten so little sleep that I couldn't dance the next day."

"I know. But I want it to come down to the four of us again, you know? Let's prove we were the best season, and take home the grand prize for ourselves."

"Easy for you to say," grumbled Pax good-naturedly. "You already won once."

"Lo says the audience probably won't vote for one of the previous winners to take it all again," I said. "Something about the perception that their favorites got robbed. So if it came down to the four of us, I think your chances would be really good, Pax."

"Let's get there and see," said Lyra. She closed her eyes and lay back down, wiggling her toes as a signal for Pax to continue the massage. "Just be careful."

"I will," I said, and let myself out of the apartment.

As was customary on a night following a Sasha rehearsal, the party in the courtyard had devolved into quiet conversation and people working the kinks out of each other's shoulders, calves, and feet. There was nothing sexual about it. Massage might be an erotic thing for some people, but for dancers, it was a necessity of life, keeping our muscles from rebelling in the middle of the night and reducing us to wobbling knots of pain. No one looked my way as I padded down the stairs and let myself into the apartment that Alice had claimed as her own.

She was gone. The living room was spotless, giving no sign that my grandmother, or her gear, had ever been there. I stopped in the doorway, blinking.

Then I realized I could smell cookies.

"Gra—Elle?" For all I knew, she had company, and I didn't want to need to explain why I was calling my sister—my apparently *younger* sister, and don't think *that* didn't make my head hurt—"Grandma."

"In here, sweetie," she called, from the direction of the kitchen.

I stuck my head in, and sure enough, she had produced a practical white apron and a pair of oven mitts from her cavernous backpack and was baking chocolate chip cookies. This seemed somehow natural and completely bizarre at the same time. So I asked the most pressing question I could think of:

"Where did you get the eggs?"

"The nice thing about this dimension—apart from the gravity; you should never take gravity for granted, dear, you never know when it's going to be taken away from you—is the availability of things called 'grocery stores.'" Alice opened the oven and pulled out a cookie sheet covered in perfect, golden brown cookies. She'd been baking cookies for decades, and had somehow mastered the arcane art of getting the exact right ratio of chocolate chips to dough.

My mouth watered. I swallowed, frowned, and said, "You're supposed to be keeping a low profile. How is baking cookies keeping a low profile?"

"I'm going to make noise by being in here: it's inevitable," she said, beginning to transfer the cookies to a cooling rack with a spatula. I was starting to wonder whether her backpack was so large because she carried a full pastry kitchen with her at all times. "This way, if someone hears the noises coming from the apartment that always smells like cookies, they'll be more likely to assume that

I'm harmless, and not kick the door in. Plus, cookies make excellent bribes. Especially fresh-baked cookies."

"Some of the dancers are gluten-free and vegan," I said.

Alice looked at me blankly.

"It's a whole new world, Grandma," I said. "Dominic wants to meet you."

"Dominic—that's your boyfriend, yes? Your father told me about him. He seemed to think I'd be angry because you'd started dating someone from the Covenant." Alice shook her head, a small smile painting her lips. "As if I'm in any position to judge? Your grandfather was still officially a member when I fell in love with him."

"I hope that non-judgment extends a little past 'boyfriend,'" I said. "I married him."

Alice blinked. "You did what?"

"I married him. We went to Las Vegas, and got married." I braced myself for the shouting that was sure to follow.

Instead, she picked up a plate of cookies from the counter and thrust it in my direction. "Oh, darling, that's wonderful! Congratulations to you both. Have a cookie."

It was my turn to blink. I picked up a cookie automatically, asking, "You're not mad?"

"That you eloped? Sweetheart, at your father's wedding, I punched the mother of the bride in the face so hard that she took out half a row of chairs when she fell over. I wasn't invited to your aunt's wedding, but I understand the groom's side of the family caused more than enough commotion. The last peaceful ceremony in our family was mine, and it was only peaceful because the priest performed it in Thomas' living room, for an audience of Aeslin mice and spiders." Alice shook her head. "Marriage is a sacred bond. I think where it gets screwed up is when we try to include everybody else. Did you take his name?"

"He's taking mine. His family is dead, and the Covenant sort of disowned him."

"That's nice." Alice produced a Ziploc baggie from

her baking supplies and began filling it with cookies. "So he's in town, and he wants to meet me? That's good. We should probably come up with some sort of plan of attack before the killers show up again."

"Yes," I agreed, and took a bite of my cookie, to give me a second before I had to say anything more. It was a great cookie. I love my grandmother's cookies. But she was right. We needed a plan, and we needed one five minutes ago. I swallowed and said, "I don't think it was a coincidence that the two eliminated dancers were killed right after the end of the show. They're sort of the definition of 'won't be missed for a few days.' Everyone assumes they were embarrassed and left immediately, or got swept away by the producers. Whoever they have waiting for them back at home will assume they're sad and going radio silent for a day or two."

Alice looked momentarily wistful. "It must be nice to have the sort of life where a few days of radio silence doesn't mean that something has gone horrifically wrong."

"Yeah," I agreed. I knew that sort of life existed. I've never had the chance to have one, and neither had she. "I checked the Twitter feeds for the dancers who've been eliminated. There's been some activity, but it all feels ..." I stopped, struggling for the words that would explain the impression I'd gotten from their pages.

"Like camouflage?" offered Alice.

"Yeah," I said, relieved. "It's all generic. 'Sad to be eliminated, glad to be home,' and 'good luck to the remaining dancers.' No personal messages. Nothing like 'oh, I love you' or 'vote for my friends this week.' It feels static and wrong."

"So maybe they didn't make it home at all," said Alice. "Can people tell lies on these 'feeds'?"

"Grandma, if I try to teach you about Facebook and social media, we're going to be here all night," I said. "Just believe me when I say you can't trust *anything* you read on the Internet until you confirm it."

"Fair enough," said Alice. "Now what?"

"Now we get moving before Dominic freaks out and

decides we've gone off to fight something without him."
I'd feel better once I'd seen him, and verified with my
own eyes that he was all right—and that my grandmother
wasn't going to kill him for being Covenant. Alice's sense
of family responsibility was sometimes second only to
her protective streak, and she did *not* like the Covenant.
Given the way they'd treated Grandpa Thomas, I couldn't
exactly blame her for that. I just didn't want her taking it
out on my husband.

"I'll get my keys," said Alice, tossing me the baggie of
cookies as she walked out of the kitchen.

I trailed after her. "Keys?"

"To the motorcycle I bought," she explained. She
grinned at my expression. "Sweetie, I know you want to
grow up to be Batgirl, and I think that's a very respectable life choice, but I'm an old lady. I might break a hip
if I tried traveling the way that you do."

"Yeah, right," I said, with a snort. I considered reminding her that Batgirl had traveled via motorcycle for
most of her career, and that calling me "Catwoman"
might be more accurate—or better yet, Spider-woman—
but decided I had more important things to focus on.
"You bought a *motorcycle*? From whom?"

"Someone who was selling a motorcycle," she said. "I
had money. She wanted it. She had a motorcycle. I
wanted it. Some things are universal. I don't know what
I'm going to do when people stop believing in newspaper ads. I can't keep up with the Internet and all those
gadgets you kids use to keep in touch." She stepped into
the back bedroom. The curtains were open, providing a
clear view of the empty parking lot behind the apartment complex.

"I can never tell if you're joking when you say things
like that," I said.

"That's the intention," she replied, and opened the
window.

We slithered through the narrow opening and out
into the warm night air, which smelled of hydrangeas
and exhaust fumes. Alice led me across the lot to a hole

in the fence. She squeezed through, and I followed, onto a narrow, weedy cul-de-sac where the houses were more rundown than anything that had been visible from the fence's other side. A little girl with grayish skin was sitting in the yard of the nearest house, playing tea party with her dolls. She went still when she saw us.

Alice said something in what sounded mostly like French. The little girl brightened, nodded, and flashed a sharp-toothed smile before she went back to her party. I gave my grandmother a questioning look.

Alice smiled. "I rented a part of their garage for the bike. I just told her I was the weird day-walker who paid her grandfather enough for her new doll, and everything was fine."

"I thought ghouls liked to live in secluded places when they couldn't live underground," I said. "You know, abandoned houses near cemeteries and slaughterhouses."

"Would you want to raise a child near a cemetery or a slaughterhouse?" asked Alice.

She gripped the bottom of the garage door and hauled upward. I moved to help, and she shot me a grateful look as the door slid up, revealing a garage packed stem to stern with boxes, piles of yard equipment, and old, tangled Christmas lights. A space had been cleared off to one side, the scrapes in the dirt on the floor showing how quickly the job had been done. There was a motorcycle parked there, old and battered but still sturdy-looking, like it had been driven a long way to get here, and was more than ready to drive back.

"There she is," said Alice. "California has helmet laws, right?"

"Right," I said uneasily. I've never been a big fan of motorcycles. They seem like an even faster route to a horrible death than the usual cars. "I like helmets. They're like exoskeletons for your skull. Please tell me you have helmets."

"I have helmets," said Alice. She reached into the pile of boxes, withdrawing two brown lumps that looked like they came from roughly the same era as the bike itself.

Privately, I resolved to walk home. "Don't make that face. They're not cute, but they're street-legal, and they'll protect your head. Not that I'm planning to have an accident. Road rash isn't my idea of a good time."

"Grandma, your idea of a good time involves gutting things."

"True enough," said Alice, apparently unoffended. "Blood is good for your hair, and internal organs are good for your skin. Put your helmet on, and don't talk back."

I rolled my eyes, pulled off my wig, and put the helmet on.

The little ghoul girl was still playing tea party when the motorcycle came zooming down the driveway, my grandmother leaning forward to reduce our wind drag, me clinging to her for dear life. The little ghoul raised a hand in a wave. To my dismay, Alice returned it. I hugged her tighter, and she laughed, and drove on into the night.

Crossing the city was easier on a motorcycle than on foot, even for me. Alice seemed to have at least a basic understanding of traffic laws—she understood they existed, and she understood she didn't like them, but if everyone else was playing by the rules, she should pretend to care. She only broke a few speed limits and drove on the sidewalk for about six blocks during a particularly nasty patch of traffic. Apart from that, she was a model citizen.

I still kept one eye on her rearview mirrors, waiting for the red-and-blue lights to start behind us. We were wearing helmets, but that was where our dalliance with being responsible drivers ended, and I had no faith that whatever license she was using would stand up to any sort of scrutiny . . . or hadn't expired thirty years ago.

Luck was with us for a change. No police appeared by the time the neon sign of the Be-Well loomed ahead of us, and Alice was able to snag a parking space out front, using the weird alchemy of good fortune and random happenstance that had kept her alive for all these years.

"I'm walking home," I said, sliding off the bike and pulling off my helmet. My hair, offended by going from under-a-wig to under-a-helmet, stood up in untidy hedgehog spikes.

"No, you're not," said Alice, removing her own helmet more carefully. *Her* hair was perfect. *Her* hair was always perfect. I'd seen her so drenched in blood that she looked like Carrie after the prom, and her hair had still managed to look amazing. As useless superpowers went, it was probably one of the more pointless, and I envied it fiercely. "You left your wig in the garage, remember? Unless you're planning to explain to your dance buddies that I scared you so bad it turned your hair blonde, you're going back with me."

I groaned and stomped into the motel. Laughing, Alice followed me.

Hearing two women in the lobby was apparently novel enough to catch the clerk's attention. He looked up from his magazine for the first time when there wasn't money being shoved in his direction, and looked us both up and down before making an appreciative sucking noise. Alice's eyes narrowed.

"Please don't knock his teeth out, we've already paid our rent for the rest of the month," I said, grabbing her arm before she could do anything.

"Men used to be more respectful," she said, shooting one last glare at the clerk before allowing me to lead her to the stairs.

"You and I both know that's not true," I said.

Alice smiled, glare fading. "And thank God it's not, or your father would never have been conceived."

"Ew! Grandma, ew! Don't say things like that! How can you say things like that with your face? Your actual grandma face? You're supposed to be all innocent and baking cookies and forgetting that sex was ever a part of your life."

Alice snorted. "Sweetie, if that's what you think, old age is going to be a series of small miracles for you."

"Like you'd know what old age was like? The oldest I've ever seen you look was thirty."

Alice's expression turned wistful. "That was a good run," she said.

We'd been climbing as we talked, and were almost to the room where Dominic was waiting to meet us. I saw the chance to solve one of the great family mysteries within my grasp—how *did* Grandma Alice keep slipping backward in physical age?—but decided, regretfully, that this wasn't the right time. We had more important things to take care of.

"Yeah, well, Dominic and I are hoping for a good run, so please don't punch my husband, okay? He's a good guy."

"I wouldn't," said Alice, sounding offended. "I trust your taste in men."

"You, and absolutely nobody else." I knocked twice, paused, and knocked twice more.

There was a clatter from inside as Dominic undid the chain. The door swung open and there he was, expression blank as he studied us.

Alice, for her part, studied him right back. She didn't even pretend to be subtle about it: she just stared, looking him up and down with bald frankness. Finally she grinned and said, "It's nice to meet you. You're my first grandson-in-law. I'll be honest, none of us expected Verity to win *that* particular race."

"Hey!" I squawked.

Dominic nodded gravely. "I am Dominic Price, born Dominic De Luca. You are Alice Price-Healy, daughter and wife to traitors."

"In the flesh," said Alice.

"It's an honor to meet you, ma'am." Then, to my surprise, Dominic bowed.

Alice grinned. "Oh, I *like* him. I like you, Dominic. Did the Covenant send you to infiltrate our family so you could kill us off once and for all?"

"No, although I'm sure they would have if it had occurred to them," said Dominic, straightening up. "You are the last of our great deceivers, after all, and your death would mean much to those who keep the historical records. Alas, the people in charge are nowhere near that creative. I'm afraid I married your granddaughter because I was in love with her, and because she said yes when I asked her if she would. Between the two, it seemed rude to refuse."

"Fair enough," said Alice. Her levity faded. "It seems like we have a lot to talk about. Can we come in?"

"Please," said Dominic, and stepped aside.

We went in.

Dominic closed the door behind us.

Ten

"My mama left me when I was too young to be without her, and I always swore I would do better than she did. Turns out the only thing I was better at was leaving."

—Alice Healy

The Crier Theater, the next morning, after a lot of coffee

B Y THE TIME THE CLOCK STRUCK TWO and I asked Alice to take me back to the apartments, we had what seemed like a halfway viable plan. Dominic would stop patrolling and lurk around the theater during rehearsal instead, watching for signs of suspicious activity, while Alice took over canvasing the city. She knew more about snake cults than he did, and would have a better chance of seeing something. The rest of the mice would come back to the apartments with us, where they could keep an eye on both available priestesses. And I would dance.

It seemed like a small contribution in the face of things. Dominic was risking arrest if someone decided he was trespassing or loitering. Alice was risking all sorts of things involving knives and shouting, since snake cults don't take kindly to being spied on. Whereas I was just risking a sprained ankle and a few pulled muscles.

Dominic walked us to the door, Alice chatting merrily away to the rapt mice that filled her pockets and covered her shoulders. He snagged my arm before I could step into the hall, turning me to face him.

"Be careful," he said, in a low voice.

"Not my style," I said, and kissed him, long and slow and languid, like we didn't have an audience, like I wasn't about to walk away.

When we broke it off, his cheeks were flushed and his eyes were bright. "Incorrigible," he said, and shut the door between us. That was probably a good thing. It was the only way to keep me from telling Alice I was going to make my own way home before I jumped his bones, and I *needed* to get some sleep.

New experiences I didn't know I was missing: riding a motorcycle while accompanied by more than a dozen cheering Aeslin mice.

Lyra was sound asleep when I came in through the window. I smiled at her, wistfully. It must have been nice to be that oblivious to how dangerous the world could really be. Then I tied a scarf around my head to hide my hair and crawled into bed.

I was out before my head hit the pillow.

Sasha clapped her hands. "All right, again, from the top, and this time I want to believe it! Five six seven eight!"

I revised my earlier thought about the risks of dancing. I was looking at a sprained ankle, a few pulled muscles, and maybe a homicide charge if Sasha didn't relax before the end of the rehearsal.

The fourteen remaining dancers spun and leaped and flung ourselves into one another's arms, moving with one unified goal: to remind the audience how much they loved us, and how much they wanted us to stay. Sasha was a hard taskmistress, but she was also an inspired choreographer, and every one of us knew how lucky we were to be working with her. All we wanted was to please her. Nothing was going to break our concentration —

Nothing but the sound of a body impacting the studio floor, followed by a wail of pain. Dancers stumbled to a

halt around me. I caught myself on Anders' arm, craning
my neck to see who'd stumbled.

"Medic!" shouted Sasha.

The crowd parted and there was Jessica, splay-limbed
on the floor, a line of blood running from her nose to her
upper lip. She was glaring daggers at Reggie, the only
other remaining dancer from her season. He looked
alarmed and faintly mortified, like this was the last thing
he'd been expecting when he came to this rehearsal.

"You dropped me on *purpose*!" she accused, loudly
enough for everyone to hear.

Now Reggie looked even more alarmed. "I didn't, I
swear I didn't! I just—you jumped before the beat, and I
wasn't braced yet! I'm so sorry, Jessica, I didn't mean to
do it."

"That's a pretty major accusation," said Sasha. "Are
you going to be able to back it up?" The sympathy was
gone from her voice. I remembered watching Jessica's
season while I prepared for my own. Nothing had ever
been her fault. Somehow, every mistake she'd made had
been something she could blame on someone else, even
when she'd been alone on her side of the stage. Sasha
apparently remembered that, too.

Jessica hesitated. "I was *on* the beat," she said finally.
"I'm sure of it."

"Good thing we record everything, isn't it?" Malena's
question was sweet enough that it could have been mistaken for genuine concern if she hadn't been smirking.
Jessica shot her a venomous look. Malena smiled back,
and her expression was, if anything, sweeter than her
question. "If there's any question, for insurance pur-
poses, I'm sure we'll be able to see who was at fault."

Jessica was saved from needing to answer by the appearance of the medical team, who swept through the
group and surrounded her, already asking questions
about what hurt, how badly, and whether she thought
she could stand. Sasha rolled her eyes, turning away from
the scene.

"Everyone, take fifteen," she said. "We'll either continue or start figuring out how to perform with one less girl."

"What?" squawked Jessica.

"Miss, please be still," said the medic who was taking her blood pressure.

Sasha ignored them. "Fifteen minutes, and then it's back to work," she said. "Now scatter."

We scattered.

I found myself on the stage with Lyra, Anders, Pax, and Malena, who was becoming an unofficial fifth member of our group. I was fine with that, for obvious reasons. Lyra wasn't quite as pleased.

"Doesn't your season miss you?" she asked, putting her hand on Pax's arm, as if to claim territory. "I mean, everyone else is mostly sticking with their own year."

"Mac is more interested in keeping up with his ballet company than he is in being social, Emily and I never liked each other, and Troy is banging Lo. Turns out neither of them is into threesomes, which is cool by me, since I'm not into dudes who practice their remedial Spanish on me. He calls me 'senorita' one more time, he's going to be short a couple of fingers." Malena looked mildly at Lyra. "Do we have a problem?"

"I just want to be sure you're hanging out with us for the right reasons," said Lyra.

"I'm a dancer, you're dancers, me and Valerie are pretty tight thanks to that thing where the tango is more intimate than sex and we've tangoed together, and like I said, I don't get along that well with the rest of the folks from my season." Malena shrugged. "If you want me to split, I'll split, but I'd prefer it if you could be chill. I'm just looking for people to hang with."

To her credit, Lyra looked abashed. "Sorry," she said. "I didn't mean to . . . sorry. Pax, can you help me with my leg extensions?"

"Sure," he said, and walked with her to the other side of the stage. Anders was already sitting on the edge, flexing and unflexing his feet; their departure left me and Malena alone at the back. If we kept our voices low, we wouldn't be overheard.

"More intimate than sex?" I asked.

She shrugged. "It worked. Real answer is I figure if shit gets bad, you and shark-boy stand a better chance of keeping me in one piece and breathing than anybody else I'm going to find around here. You are thus elected as my new best friends."

"Swell," I said. "Have you noticed anything unusual?"

"You mean apart from the tattooed squatter in the apartment under yours? Nah. I've been watching, but there hasn't been anything. No smell of blood, either. If somebody's carving up the janitorial staff, they're doing a good job disposing of the evidence." Malena studied her nails. "I figure I'll keep staying in well-lit areas with lots of other people around, and not get caught in whatever weirdness is going on."

I glanced over my shoulder, making sure Lyra and Anders were still too far away to hear me. Then I looked back to Malena, and said quietly, "The tattooed weirdo is my Grandma Alice. She's here to help make sure we don't all die."

"What?" Malena yelped. Everyone turned to look at us. She smiled weakly. "Get out of town, Val, you don't dye your hair? Wow. You've got some great genes in your family tree."

"We all hate her for it," called Lyra, before she winked at me and went back to extending her left leg over her head.

"Way to draw attention," I hissed. In a weird way, I was pleased. Any jealousy Lyra might have been harboring over my new friendship with Malena had just taken a blow. After all, *Malena* didn't know I wore a wig.

"Sorry," whispered Malena. "I just didn't expect . . . your *grandmother*? Like, Franny Brown's kid?"

"Yeah." My great-grandmother, Frances Brown, was originally from the Southwest. It made sense that a chupacabra would have heard of her, although I hadn't been expecting her to be remembered that clearly. "She's here to help. Don't worry about her."

"Worry about her? I should kiss her. On the mouth, with tongue." Malena shook her head. "Franny Brown was a great friend to our community."

I blinked. "Okay, that's cool. I didn't know that."

"Yeah. She needs anything you can't help her with, you tell her to come talk to me. I'd be happy to be of service. I'd be *honored*." Malena shook her head. "Wow."

I needed to get the conversation away from my family before someone wandered into it that shouldn't have. "So nothing else has seemed strange?"

"No." Malena looked at me. "Maybe it's over, huh?"

"Maybe." I hesitated before saying, "Look, this Sunday, we're going to head for the flea market downtown. You want to come with us?"

"What for?" asked Malena.

"You speak Spanish, we're going to be buying a lot of knives, it could be a handy combination."

Malena blinked at me. Then, slowly, she grinned. "It's a date."

"There you losers are." Malena and I turned. Jessica was standing in the wings. There was a soft thump behind me as Lyra got her foot back on the floor. Jessica folded her arms, lip pushed out in a pout like the world's biggest toddler. "Sasha said I had to find everyone to pay for being the one who stopped rehearsal, because now it's *my* fault I got hurt. This is so unfair."

"Thanks, Jessica," I said. "We'll be right there."

"Whatever." She turned on her heel and stomped away, hips swaying so hard that I worried briefly that she was going to dislocate something.

"What a bitch," said Anders, stepping up next to me.

"That's an insult to dogs everywhere," said Malena. "She's a—"

"Let's get back to rehearsal!" I chirped, linking my arms with theirs and starting to march, Wizard of Oz-style, toward the others. The sooner we got back to work,

the sooner we'd be finished, and the sooner we could find
out what was really going on.

We didn't find out what was really going on. Malena and
Pax excused themselves enough times to get on Sasha's
nerves, but they failed to find any suspicious traces of
blood anywhere in the building.

(Oh, they found blood: they found *plenty* of blood. As
Jessica had demonstrated, it was impossible to have this
many dancers in one theater without getting blood on
every surface it was possible to get blood on. Bloody
noses, scraped knees, broken toes, torn-off toenails . . .
we were a slow-motion horror movie in unforgiving
shoes, and we had trained our whole lives for the opportunity to demonstrate that yes, it was possible to acciden-
tally bleed on the ceiling.)

I danced. It was what I knew how to do, and what I
could contribute to the quest. As I danced, I watched the
people around me, trying to decide whether any of my fellow contestants could be a killer. Lo moved with the grace
and elegance of a striking viper. Did that make her capable
of murder? Mac was strong, stable, and stoic, three things
that made him a great ballet dancer, but could also make
him a stone-cold killer, under the right circumstances. Jessica was a selfish, delusional brat who might do anything to
get ahead. Even Sasha could potentially pick up a razor
blade, if she thought that it would benefit her somehow.

By the end of rehearsal, I was a bundle of nerves, and
we were no closer to knowing who our enemies were.

Once again, Malena rode back to the apartments with
my season, compacting herself into the back between me
and Lyra and smiling like butter wouldn't melt in her
mouth. The party was already going when we arrived.
Someone had put chicken on the grill. We sniffed the air
appreciatively, drifting in a group toward the smell of
food . . . and stopped when we saw the woman at the
grill, once again wearing her sensible apron.

"Chicken's up," said Alice, meeting my eyes and smiling. She thrust a paper plate at me. When I didn't take it, Malena did. The chupacabra looked suddenly shy, like she couldn't believe she was getting actual food from Frances Brown's actual daughter. "Did you want a breast or a thigh, Val?"

"Breast," I said automatically, before rattling off, through gritted teeth, "Elle, can I talk to you?" The words were sharp and staccato, with no pauses between them for breath.

"Of course!" she replied, and handed her tongs to Ivan, who had been hovering around keeping an eye on the grill, before grabbing two more plates of chicken. "Lead the way, O dearest sister of mine."

I didn't say anything, but my glare promised murder. Alice laughed, following me across the courtyard to her pilfered apartment. The door wasn't locked. I held it open for her, and she followed me inside.

"I know what you're going to say, and I promise, I *did* think this through," she said, as soon as the door was closed. She turned to face me, smiled blithely, and handed me a plate of chicken. "I got caught."

I blinked. "Come again?"

"I was sneaking back into my apartment, and I guess I timed things wrong, because the first town car pulled in before I could close the door. They asked what I was doing here, I said I was your sister and begged them not to report me, they asked if I had any useful skills, I said I was an excellent cook." Alice shrugged. "Apparently, as long as I'm willing to run the grill, I'm not actually an intruder. Tomorrow's taco night."

"I can't . . . you can't just . . . oh, my God." I sat heavily down on the couch, looking at the plate of chicken balanced on my knees. It looked tasty. My stomach rumbled. Dance is a sport, and it burns a lot of calories. "You're *sure* no one looked like they were going to rat you out?"

"That Jessica girl didn't look happy," said Alice. "I promised to make fruit smoothies in the morning. That seemed to help. She doesn't seem like the sort who enjoys waiting on herself."

"No, I'm pretty sure she'd hire people to dance for her if she could get away with it, and thought she could get the credit." I took a tentative bite of chicken. It was better than it looked. Stupid Grandma and her years of experience at cooking things over an open flame. I swallowed before asking, "Did you find anything useful, besides the location of the grilling tools?"

"They were in the same shed where these people keep the grill," said Alice. "It wasn't a big mystery."

I raised an eyebrow and waited.

Alice laughed, apparently feeling like she'd been annoying long enough. "I went to all the cryptid bars I knew of, and then I went to three more that have opened since the last time I was here. Some pretty nice places, if you don't mind martinis made with spinal fluid. Anyway, I asked around, and nobody knew anything about a new snake cult in town. I had people in two separate places ask me if I meant the gorgons over in Newport Beach. So far as magical asshole activity, this town seems to be going through a quiet patch."

"That's surprising," I said.

"Not really. There are lots of nonhumans in Southern California. They settled here because they thought it would stay small, if you can believe it. Beautiful weather, but no big natural resources—no gold or oil or flourishing fur trade. When the humans started coming and ruining the neighborhood, they stood their ground. Most snake cults are made up of frustrated humans who feel like they should be higher on the supernatural pecking order. As if being the dominant species on this planet wasn't enough of an accomplishment." Alice shook her head as she sank down onto the couch next to me. "I'll hit the supply shops tomorrow, see whether anyone's been buying the materials for a big summoning. Given what you said about the blood, though, that seems likely to be a dead end. Someone who can scrub the blood from a room that way isn't going to need saltpeter and silver to accomplish whatever it is they're trying to do."

"No, probably not," I admitted. "Malena's going to come with us to the flea market on Sunday. She speaks Spanish, so she can help us with some of the vendors."

"Malena—that's the pretty chupacabra girl, isn't it?"

I nodded. "She's really psyched about you being Frances Brown's daughter. I wouldn't be surprised if she asked for an autograph."

Alice laughed ruefully. "Of all the things I have and haven't earned in my lifetime, that's among the most perplexing. But I'm glad she's coming with us. Maybe that will stop her from putting me on too high of a pedestal."

"I think it may be a little late for that," I said. I would have said more, but a knock from the back of the apartment pulled my attention away. I frowned and stood, leaving my chicken behind.

Alice had already drawn a wicked-looking knife from somewhere inside her clothes. I wasn't sure where: she was wearing cut-offs and a tank top, and the knife looked too large to have been hidden under either. I shook my head and motioned for her to put it down. Then I turned and walked toward the source of the knocking.

Dominic was standing outside the window of the back bedroom. I groaned theatrically as I opened it.

"What part of you people are supposed to stay far, far away from here was too difficult for you to grasp?" I asked.

"The part where your grandmother gets to be here with you and I don't," said Dominic. He boosted himself through the window, casting me a brief smile before he said, "And besides, this requires less running across the city on your part. I'd like you to continue to do well in this competition for as long as you choose to do so—or for at least as long as it takes us to catch our killers. A good night's sleep will help."

"You know what doesn't help me stay on the show and catch the killer?" I asked. "Being kicked out because I was caught hosting a family reunion in our apartment complex. Seriously, you can't be here. Neither one of you should be here."

"HAIL!" shouted a tiny, ecstatic chorus. "HAIL THE CONFLICT OF PLACE!"

I went stiff. Then, slowly, I turned to see the Aeslin mice clustered on the floor next to a suspiciously cartoonish mouse hole. The edges were perfectly smooth; I wouldn't have been surprised to see a tiny welcome mat on the floor outside.

Keeping my voice carefully neutral, I asked, "Have you been cutting holes in the walls?"

"And lo, did the Precise Priestess speak unto us, and say, Have You Considered Hiding In Plain Sight? And we did take our knives of cutting, and our saws of sawing, and begin Making Improvements." The spokesman— spokesmouse—of the group sounded so proud of itself that I couldn't really get angry, just exasperated.

"That doesn't mean cutting holes in walls we don't *own*," I said. "Antimony doesn't have any authority here."

The mice looked confused. Confusion on a mouse was adorable, which made it even harder to stay mad at them.

Then Alice swept into the room. "Who wants chicken?" she asked.

The mice cheered.

Several minutes and two plates of barbecued chicken later, we were settled in the living room (with the curtains firmly closed, as I didn't feel like tempting fate). Dominic sat on the couch. I sat in front of him on the floor, where he could rest a hand on my shoulder while I stretched the kinks out of my legs. And Alice, who was never very good at holding still, paced.

"So no one in town knows anything about a snake cult, and no one at the theater is acting weird," I said. "Well. Any weirder than usual. Dancers are inherently weird. It's part of the job description. What do we think the chances are that the murders were a matter of convenience? Maybe we have a snake cult working its way through the reality shows of Burbank, and we just had our turn on the rotation."

Alice stopped pacing and looked at me, expression unreadable. "Would that make a difference to you?"

Damn. "No," I admitted. "We'd still need to find them and stop them before anybody else got hurt. We'd just need to widen our search area by kind of a lot."

"I'm glad to hear that," said Alice. She resumed her pacing. "If it weren't for the cleanup job, I'd think you were onto something. Cleaning something *that* completely isn't easy, especially when it's something liquid. It takes a lot of energy out of the witch who spins the spell. Thomas didn't just magic away the dust on his books, because it would have left him defenseless, and blood's a much harder set of commands."

"I thought you didn't have any magic of your own," said Dominic.

"I don't, but I came home bloody a lot, and sometimes I dripped on things that weren't supposed to be stained," said Alice. "Once I dripped blood on a book that could have summoned something nasty from beyond the walls of the world. Thomas cleaned that up *real* fast."

"So the fact that our killer or killers cleaned up the mess the way they did proves they were intending to be in the theater again," I said.

Alice nodded. "Exactly. Bleach would have been good enough to do the job, if they hadn't been worried about coming back there. Cleaning it so well that even an Ukupani's nose can't find traces of blood tells me they're intending to use that space again."

"But when?" asked Dominic. "They've made no moves that I can see."

"There hasn't been anyone else eliminated," I said. "If I were them, I'd wait until after the next show. That way, it's less likely to be noticed."

"All right, then: when's the next show?" asked Alice.

"Thursday night," I said. "We have five days."

She nodded gravely. "Okay. Let's hope the flea market has a *lot* of knives."

For once, I didn't argue.

Eleven

"Being a smart shopper doesn't just mean clipping coupons and watching for sales. Sometimes it means understanding when you need that Kevlar vest a lot more than you need to wait for it to go on clearance."
—Evelyn Baker

The South Riverside Flea Market, Sunday morning, way too early for this crap

THE LINE TO GET INTO THE FLEA MARKET snaked from the admissions booth, where a bored-looking attendant exchanged hand stamps for crumpled dollar bills, all the way to the gravel parking lot. We stood patiently, waiting for our turn to step inside and experience the wonders of things sold off blankets and folding card tables. We were far enough from the comfortable unreality of Burbank that I wasn't wearing a wig, and I could almost hear my scalp singing hosannas in the crisp morning air.

Getting away from the complex had been easier than expected. Lyra was a heavy sleeper when she didn't have to get to rehearsals, and while she was probably going to be pissed when she woke to find me gone, there was no way she could have come with us. Alice had snuck out the back window of her pilfered apartment, while Malena and I had simply walked out the front gate with shopping lists in our hands, chattering about specials at Safeway. The guard on duty changed at nine AM. Even if the man who watched us go had been awake enough to make a note about our departure, no one was going to raise an alarm if we didn't check back in. Two dancers heading to the grocery store was not cause for major concern.

Dominic had been waiting on the corner with the engine running and Alice already in the back seat. Malena and I just had to climb in and we were off, heading for the one-stop super-shop for the makeshift monster hunter.

(Alice was her own walking arsenal. Dominic and I weren't too shabby ourselves, especially since we'd driven from Portland, which meant we'd been able to bring a certain amount of gear. But there was "a certain amount of gear" and then there was "prepared to take on a snake cult." Whatever happened, I wanted us to be ready.)

"Why are we here?" asked Malena, wrinkling her nose as someone walked by carrying a mounted stag's head. "Half this stuff looks unhygienic in the extreme. The other half's just gross."

"All sales final, all sales made with cash, and nobody asks your name or looks for ID," I said. The line moved forward. "Not the place to go for guns or heavy ammo, but we'd have to buy a live elephant for anyone to remember us in a week."

"Besides, some information brokers who have ties in both the human and not-so-human communities show up at these things," said Alice. "We might be able to get a lead on what's going on around here."

Malena glanced nervously at the people around us, eyes landing on Dominic. She knew he was my husband, not my boyfriend. She *didn't* know he was a former member of the Covenant of St. George, or that he'd still belonged to the Covenant when we'd started dating. There were some things that wouldn't be fair to drop on her while we were all still getting to know each other.

"She made a whole speech about monsters and men in a coffee shop the first time we met," he said solemnly. "No one paid her any attention, but still. I feel your pain."

"No one's listening to us," I said, flapping a hand dismissively. "Eavesdropping is fun, but when people start talking about monsters and nonhuman intelligences and income tax law, everyone around you assumes you've been watching *Game of Thrones* again."

"You watch *Game of Thrones*?" asked Malena, with even more suspicion, like I'd just proven myself to be completely untrustworthy.

"I don't have time to watch anything, but I don't live under a rock. I pick things up." I stepped up to the ticket booth and forked over four dollars. All four members of my group received hand stamps, and we were in.

Most of the week, the flea market was a vacant lot that was formerly a drive-in theater. The marks were still there, if you knew how to look for them: the grid painted on the blacktop, the distant "flea market office" building that looked suspiciously like a repurposed concession stand. The rise of Netflix and cheap cable might have spelled the end of the drive-ins, but their bones lived on, and had been used to construct new hybrid creatures, half yard sale, half mega-mart, all a little shady. Things that fell off the back of trucks had a tendency to wind up here, as did bootlegs of the movies that would once have been shown on the drive-in screen. People were everywhere, minding their own business and mining other people's junk for treasures.

"Everybody got their shopping lists?" I asked.

Nods all around.

"Great. Then let's scatter, and get this over with." I started down the nearest aisle. Dominic stuck with me. Malena trailed after my grandmother, looking both terrified and elated by the opportunity to spend time getting to know her better.

You're welcome, Malena, I thought. A little alone time with my grandmother would either cure her hero worship or elevate it to terrifying new heights. Either way, it would be interesting.

"Do we really need this much rubber hosing?" asked Dominic, pulling my attention back to my own assignment.

"Potentially," I said, looping my arm through his. "It has a lot of uses, including draining flooded areas. If we find another blood bath like the last one, I need to be prepared to take samples without disturbing the scene. Lower a hose, suck a little—but not enough to start breathing anything nasty—and voilà."

Dominic gave me a sidelong look. "Samples."

"Yes."

"Of the blood."

"Yes." We'd reached a stall selling old gardening equipment, including an assortment of machetes. I stopped to check the quality of their steel. "We need to know if these people are being drugged, and if so, with what. That's going to tell us more about the snake cult that's pulling this crap. We have so little data at this point that everything is important."

"So the rubber hosing is predicated on someone else being killed."

I looked up from the machetes and nodded. "It is. I'd like to say we could stop it from happening again, but without more resources than we have, and without any real leads, I don't know that we're going to be that lucky."

"A pity, then, that we cannot set up cameras in the theater."

Cameras. I gaped at him. "You're a genius. If we weren't already married, I'd ask you to marry me, just for that."

"While I am always glad to have you reaffirm your decision to marry me, what did I say that was so genius? We can't set up cameras. We have neither the technology nor the training."

I handed the stall's owner a ten dollar bill and tucked my new machete into my shoulder bag. "No, but we don't need to. Cameras have already been set up for us. Reality television, remember? And my cousin Artie is amazing with computers. If there's any sort of cloud storage setup for the theater, I bet he can get in and see what's what."

Dominic smiled. "I appreciate this plan. Please tell him that it was born of my genius."

"Will do," I said. "Come on, genius. Let's go find some lye."

We found some lye. And some bleach, and some saltpeter, and an assortment of rare spices being sold as attractive ground cover. We also found a lot of knives, many of which found their way into my bag. Only some of them would be suitable for the kind of combat I prefer—the kind where I throw knives at people, and they stay as far away from me as possible—but there's no such thing as too many knives. There's only more knives than you have room to hide under your mattress, and I was planning to solve that by sending the bulk of the new armory back to the Be-Well with Dominic.

A stall at the end of one of the last rows crammed into the lot boasted a sign reading "TAROT AND TAXIDERMY." I exchanged a look with Dominic, who seemed nonplussed.

"Well, there's definitely taxidermy," I said, indicating a mounted bison head that looked like the cousin of the deer we'd seen on our way in. It was next to one of those faux jackalopes that used to be popular in certain kinds of novelty shop.

(Faux jackalopes were popular even when jackalopes were more common, back when there were so many of them that people *had* to admit they existed. It's just that real jackalopes look sort of like jackrabbits on steroids, with sharp claws and muzzles too long to fit most people's ideas of what a rabbit looks like. It was much more profitable to slap horns on some innocent bunny and claim *it* was the real deal, especially when you were selling to people who'd never seen a prairie in their lives. People are weird, and there's nothing new about that.)

Or wait . . . I narrowed my eyes, taking a closer look. The jackalope had a long muzzle and what looked like tiny daggers set into its digging paws. It wasn't a fake. It had just been a baby when it died, which was why it was so much smaller than I expected a jackalope to be. And based on the condition of the fur and the quality of the glass eyes set into its fur-covered skull, it had been preserved within the last twenty years.

"Come on," I said, and stepped into the stall.

California is flea market heaven. It rains rarely enough that it's safe to have a remarkable variety of open air goods, and the vendors tend to become comfortable enough in their positions that they really nestle into a space, decorating and customizing it to their heart's content. The front of the tarot and taxidermy stall looked like any other, with long, uncovered folding tables heavily laden with wares. But the back half was taken up by a gauzy tent that looked like something out of a Renaissance Faire, complete with rainbow streamers and multiple layers of netting. Someone was inside, their shadow moving against the net.

I stopped without reaching for the curtain. If the stall's owner was in the middle of a tarot reading, they wouldn't take kindly to being interrupted. Instead, I cleared my throat to let them know I was there before turning to study a stuffed and mounted furred trout. Like the jackalope, it appeared to be the real deal.

Dominic stepped up next to me, apparently reaching the same conclusion, as he said, in a low voice, "I thought these were extinct."

"Not extinct, just mostly being preserved in private fisheries until science is ready for them," I said. "The last time there was a wild spawning, some assholes poisoned the river to stop whatever weird disease they thought was making the fish all moldy."

"There will always be things people aren't prepared for, which must be covered in mirrors and greasepaint, until they seem believable enough to be borne," said an Irish-accented voice behind us. It was light, female, and amused, like the speaker was the only one who knew the punchline to the world's best joke.

I turned.

She was taller than me—who *isn't* taller than me? In

a world of giants, I've learned to treasure my high-heeled shoes—and about my mother's age, with a smile that matched her voice for warmth and amusement. Her hair was black, with streaks of lilac gray. It looked dyed, rather than natural; everything about her looked carefully designed. I couldn't be sure without a blood sample and an X-ray, but I was willing to bet she was human.

"So you recognize a furred trout," she said, sliding her hands into the pockets of her jeans. The silver foil printing on her T-shirt was so faded that I couldn't make out the name of the band it had been intended to promote; the graphic was nothing but the ghosts of gothic type and heavy metal guitars. "Short, blonde, and holding yourself like you think you might have to kill me—are you Alice Healy's girl?"

"Is there *no one* who does not know your family?" asked Dominic. I glanced at him. His jaw was clenched so tightly that a muscle in his cheek was twitching.

Poor boy really didn't understand what he was getting into when he married me. "We sort of tend to attract attention," I said, and focused back on the stall owner. "I'm her granddaughter. How do you know my grandma?"

"She gave her children to Laura Campbell to raise, remember? The routewitch community took notice."

I felt a small knot of tension uncoil between my shoulders. My Great-Aunt Laura had been missing since before I was born—the history of the Price family in America is a patchwork of unexplained disappearances and unanswered questions—but she raised Dad and Aunt Jane when Grandma Alice couldn't. And Great-Aunt Laura had been an ambulomancer, which made her part of the routewitch community. Routewitches were magic-users of a sort, pulling their strength and spells from the long sweep of the road. They gathered power through travel, and through artifacts that had been carried around the world, amassing power with every step. Flea markets were their cathedrals, truck stops their holy ground, and while they were as capable of being deceitful and untrustworthy as anyone else, we had enough of a history with them that this encounter had just become a lot less dangerous.

"Verity Price," I said, sticking my hand out toward the woman. "I'm Kevin's daughter."

"The older one, if I'm not mistaken: I know one of Laura's last predictions related to the younger." The woman took my hand. Her palm was callused enough to feel almost scaled. "Bon. Siobhan, actually, but 'Bon' serves me well enough." She looked to Dominic as she let go of my hand. "And you, young man. You've traveled a very long way, from the other side of the Atlantic, if I know my road-ways. British?"

"Italian by birth," said Dominic. "British by much of my upbringing. My name is Dominic."

"He follows your lead, doesn't he?" Bon looked back to me. "I've never met a Covenant boy who'd give his name to a routewitch without a fight."

"Ex-Covenant," said Dominic. "They'd kill me as soon as look at me at this point."

"Oh, you *are* your grandmother's bloodline," said Bon, looking amused. "What can I do for the latest generation of the Price family? I'm sure you didn't wander into my flea market because you were in desperate need of a mounted boar's head—although if you are, I'd be happy to work something out with you."

"Do you do your own taxidermy?" I asked. My head was reeling. Meeting Bon wasn't as big of a coincidence as it seemed. Our kind of people have always frequented flea markets and rubbish sales, since they're a great place to trade the things we're likely to need. I just hadn't been braced for someone with quite this much of a connection to my family history.

"No, I buy it from a family of Sasquatch up near Vancouver," said Bon. "It keeps me running the West Coast twice a year, and helps them clean out their garage. Everybody wins."

"Nice," I said. I looked around one more time, assessing the people around us, before I focused on Bon. "I'm in town because I'm appearing on a reality show—*Dance or Die*. There's a situation at the studio. Could I ask you a few questions?"

"Now we get down to it," said Bon. "My cards told me not to skip the flea market this week. Come in." She walked back to her tent, sweeping the curtain aside with a grandiose motion of her hands. The gauzy ribbons danced and fluttered in the breeze from her passing.

I followed her.

Dominic followed me.

The air was at least four degrees cooler inside Bon's tent, which was lit by a pair of camp lanterns hanging from the roof. A carved wooden table occupied the center of the space, presumably for tarot readings. There were two chairs on one side of the table, and a single chair on the other side. All of the furnishings were plain, not buried in lace or doilies: this was a practical place in a very impractical location. The noise-dampening qualities of the tent were more surprising than anything else about it: once the gauzy curtain fell back into place behind us, I couldn't hear a thing from outside.

My surprise must have shown, because Bon smiled and said, "I keep track of my space in other ways. If I need to deal with a customer, I'll duck out."

"What about shoplifters?" I asked.

Her smile turned feral. "I've been coming here for a long, long time. People know better than to steal from me. Now what is it you needed to know?"

"Have there been any rumors of a snake cult starting up in Hollywood?"

Her smile died. "A snake cult?"

"Yeah." I pulled my phone out of my pocket, flipping through the gallery until I found the pictures of the bodies in the basement. It was getting harder to make myself remember their names. I didn't want them to have been people I knew and liked, even if we weren't friends; I wanted them to have been strangers, a delivery mechanism for the unspeakable, and not people I would have to mourn for when this was all over. "I took pictures of the runes we found. They're sort of carved into naked dead people. Sorry about that."

"What will you do if someone steals your phone?" Bon asked, reaching over and plucking it out of my hand.

"Abandon this identity before I track down the thief and make them regret their life of crime," I said.

"Sometimes she makes jokes which imply she thinks of me as Batman," said Dominic. "I don't think she looks in many mirrors."

"Prices never do. They know they wouldn't care for what they'd see," said Bon. Her attention was fixed on the phone. She swiped her thumb across the screen, images of gore and tragedy reflecting on her eyes. Finally, she closed them and offered the phone back to me, saying, "That's definitely a snake cult. No one else would be that careful in their cruelty."

"Yeah, we get a good class of assholes in the snake cults." I tucked the phone into my pocket, watching her carefully. "Dad says he thinks they have at least one magic-user working with them. The quality of the runes is too high for it to be a copy."

"Well, they could be a bunch of disgruntled art students working from a really crisp source document, but that seems less likely." Bon opened her eyes. "I think your father's right. They've got at least one magic-user, maybe two, with them. How long would they have had to work on the bodies?"

It was always chaotic backstage after a show. There was removing and returning costumes to be worried about, and wiping off the worst of the makeup. Some of the girls would try to remove the top layer of hairspray from their hair with warm towels before they went home, on the theory that it was better to have a wet head than to be standing in the shower when the hot water cut out. (Since my real hair was never subjected to the stylists, I didn't have to join in on that particular struggle.)

"About twenty minutes, tops," I said finally. "That

assumes they were able to get their victims into the basement where we found them without losing any time."

"Were you able to study the bodies? They may have been knocked out."

"The last snake cult I encountered used tooth fairy dust to subdue their sacrifices," I said. I still had nightmares about that sometimes. "Unfortunately, the bodies disappeared after we took the pictures, and there wasn't time for a full examination. There haven't been any more deaths that we know of." Yet.

"Yet," said Bon.

I grimaced. I hate it when people put voice to my depressing mental asides. "Yeah," I said. "These two were killed right after they were eliminated from the show. There may have been four previous deaths that we didn't catch in time. We're going to watch whoever gets eliminated this week like hawks."

"What if you get eliminated?"

This time, I smiled. "Then whoever's doing this is going to find out why you never follow a Price girl into a dark alley."

"I feel we're getting off topic," said Dominic. "Can you tell us anything about the movement of snake cults in this state?"

"The state's a little big, but I can tell you about the snake cults in this area," said Bon. "Make-it-big schemes have always been huge in Hollywood. We've had more snake cults, demon summonings, and crossroads bargains per capita than anywhere else in North America. Last year I think we even surpassed Mexico City for people trying to barter with the dead, and that's not easy. People want to be stars, and they don't mind cutting corners to get there. This is a place that thrives on luck, you know? I always wondered why your family didn't settle here. Healy luck and all."

"Sometimes Healy luck is incredibly bad," I said. "I think we didn't want to risk it." But more, Hollywood was where you went when you wanted people to pay attention to you, and that was something most of my family had never wanted. When I'd decided to want it, I had changed my name and my hair color and my past, and even that hadn't been enough to get me away from the gravitational pull of the work I'd been raised for.

"That shows sense. Most of the people who come here don't have much of it." Bon dropped herself into the chair reserved, based on position, for her use. Dominic and I sat on the other side of the table. It seemed like the appropriate thing to do. "We've had snake cults here since the 1920s. A lot of people think—even if we can't prove it—the snake cults are why Maleficent turned herself into a dragon in Disney's *Sleeping Beauty*. He'd been around Hollywood long enough to know the score."

I stared at her, appalled. "Are you telling me Walt Disney was a snake cultist?"

"Nah. He summoned a demon once and bound it into one of his roller coasters, but that's not the same as being a snake cultist." Bon shook her head. "Still, he was here, he had to have heard. Snake cults are the pyramid scheme of instant fame and fortune. If you want one, you need to collect a bunch of loyal cultists you can feed to your snake god when you get it."

"Pardon me if I sound ignorant, but . . . these people are attempting to summon *snakes*," said Dominic. "Not djinn or creator gods. *Snakes*. How can a snake give you anything apart from venom and a quick death?"

"Snake gods don't come from this dimension, at least not anymore; there's some argument on whether the Titanoboa was big enough to have qualified for snake god status, and whether, if it was, there are still examples of the genus out there somewhere, slithering around and swallowing the people foolish enough to summon them. But that's neither here nor there." Bon leaned forward, resting her elbows on the table. "The point of the snake god is not the snake god itself, although the cults that worship them would probably disagree. It's the stuff they bring with them when they tunnel through the dimensional walls."

"It's the shape of them," said Alice. We all turned. She was standing in the entrance with a duffel bag slung over her shoulder that hadn't been there when we had arrived at the flea market, and from the way it bulged at the bottom, it was packed to capacity with things she thought would be useful. "They're long and smooth—not many limbs to siow them down. So the snake gods pierce through dimensions and get covered in the membrane that keeps them apart, and magic-users can use that membrane to fuel things. It's raw possibility. Luck and lies and all the tricks you could wish for, wrapped around a giant snake like a second skin."

"Alice." Bon stood, a smile lighting up her face. "I wondered if I'd be seeing you."

"Bon, you old troublemaker." Alice dropped her duffel bag—it clinked when it hit the floor—and moved to wrap her arms around the other woman. Bon towered over her, but looking at the two of them, there was no question that, in a physical fight, Alice would mop the floor with Bon. "No one told me you were in Southern California these days."

"I had a little falling out with the current Queen of the Routewitches and thought it might be a good idea to head for the other side of the country," said Bon easily. She let go of Alice, dropping back into her chair. "You here about the snake cult thing?"

"My granddaughter needed me," said Alice, gesturing toward me.

"Your granddaughter needs to do whatever it takes to keep more people from winding up dead," I said. "So these snake cultists, they don't really want to summon giant snakes from beyond the walls of the world? They just want a quick way to get their hands on pieces of reality, and the snakes make a good delivery mechanism?"

"Something like that," said Bon. "A lot of snake cults *do* want the giant snakes, because they've lost track of what makes this particular bad idea work. That's also why you don't hear many stories of snake cults who got what they were looking for. The ones who actually manage to summon giant snakes wind up being slowly digested as often as they accomplish their goals. Maybe more often these days, since most people don't remember the binding spells."

"Do you?" asked Dominic. There was something low and dangerous in his voice. I put a hand on his knee, hoping it would be enough to hold him in place. If it wasn't, I was going to witness the remarkable sight of my grandmother punching my husband in the throat. Family reunions were tense enough without adding that extra layer of awkwardness.

"I'm a routewitch, son, not a magician," said Bon. She didn't sound offended. If anything, she sounded amused. "I pull magic from roads and travel, and it's mostly tied to foresight and prophesy and the dead. You want someone to talk to ghosts or tell you where there's going to be a bad accident, I'm your lady. You want to know what the road knows or find a missing person, I'm happy to help. But if you want to summon a giant fucking snake from the other side of the universe, I'll be leaving."

"Bon was with the Campbell Family Carnival for a while, as their fortune-teller," said Alice. "Laura vouched for her. She's not involved with the snake cult that's killing your friends. I'd stake my left eye on it."

"That is . . . very specific and somewhat disturbing," said Dominic, relenting and leaning back into his seat.

I took my hand off of his knee. "So you don't know of any snake cults currently operating in the Burbank area?" The background information was nice, but it wasn't going to do us any good if it didn't lead us to whoever was killing people on the set.

"Not right now," said Bon. "There's one in Anaheim, but there's *always* a snake cult in Anaheim. Blame Disney again. So many of his villains thought 'well, I'm in trouble, better turn into a giant snake' that it's seeped into the public consciousness as the solution to all problems."

"Turning into a giant snake is *never* the solution to your problems," I said. "It actually ranks somewhere between 'cut off own hand, replace with chainsaw' and 'summon indestructible dream demon.' Bad plans one and all."

"Forgive me if I'm committing some terrible faux pas that I'd be able to avoid if I were more aware of the role of the routewitches in the extranatural ecosystem, but what, then, can you do to assist us?" Dominic's voice was calm, measured, and wary. He was waiting for the other shoe to drop. I couldn't blame him. Every time he thought he'd reached the bottom of the weirdness well, I pulled up another bucket of unexplained phenomena and impossible realities.

"I can tell you that anyone who uses those runes," Bon gestured toward me, and hence toward my phone, "knows what they're doing, and will probably be able to get their defensive wards in place before anything breaks through to our level of reality. That's the good part. No one is going to get eaten by mistake."

"What's the bad part?" I asked.

"A lot of people will probably get eaten on purpose. Snake gods are hungry when they rise, and if you want to keep a snake happy, you feed it." Bon pressed her lips into a thin, hard line. "Worse yet, those runes . . . they're not trying for one of the *smaller* unspeakably large snakes. This is going to summon them something enormous, and two deaths won't be enough to fuel it. Neither will six deaths."

"How many will be?" I asked.

"Honestly, I can't say. But I'd guess at least ten, probably more like twelve or fourteen." Bon's expression turned grim as she looked around the tent. "You've got a lot of bodies ahead of you if you don't figure out who's doing this."

Well, damn.

Twelve

"The world is going to get in the way sometimes. That's what the world does. What you have to do, what you have to be prepared to do, is plant your feet and tell the world that you're not going to be the one who gives ground."

— Enid Healy

The Crier Theater, four days later

WE HAD LEFT THE FLEA MARKET—collecting Malena from a stall that sold live birds, where she'd purchased a box of pigeons which she had proceeded to suck dry in the car—and returned to the apartments with our newly-acquired weapons and our newly-heightened sense of urgency. Explaining what we'd learned about the situation to Malena while she picked feathers out of her teeth had been odd, but not odd enough to make me stop.

In the end, we were better armed and better informed, but no more aware of who was behind the situation. Dominic had dropped us off with a dire warning to be careful, and we'd slipped back into our rooms without attracting too much attention. It helped that Sunday was everybody's free day; no one was looking for anything out of the ordinary. No one but us—and even we couldn't find it. Even Artie hadn't been able to work his particular brand of incredibly nerdy magic. Oh, the theater had cloud storage, but it was used solely for rehearsal footage and show recordings, not for the security in the halls.

(One good, if largely irrelevant, thing had come of his trawling through the systems: we knew for sure now that it had been Jessica, and not Reggie, who'd been in the wrong when she got dropped. It was basically useless information, but Pax had passed it on to Reggie without letting on how he knew. Reggie had been a lot more careful around Jessica since then, which was all to the good. She wasn't *quite* sabotaging the other contestants. She was still enough of a snake that she should have been attracting a cult of her own.)

The days had fallen back into the same pattern of rehearsals, costume fittings, and frantic searches of the theater. Having Malena on our side meant she and Pax could constantly sniff around for signs of blood or ritual herbs. Sadly, that didn't mean they'd been able to find anything, and by the time the night of the show arrived, we were all consumed by nerves.

Anders picked up on my anxiety—it would have been hard for him not to. He stepped up behind me while I was checking my makeup before the opening jazz number. Sasha had bent us into the shapes she wanted, and all that remained was getting through the next five minutes without breaking an ankle. Or a neck. To be honest, I was more worried about the latter.

"You okay?" he asked, looming in my mirror. He focused on my reflection with an intensity that made me borderline uncomfortable.

I didn't let it show. He'd always been attracted to me, and he'd always taken "no" for an answer. I just had to act oblivious and things would be okay.

"Nope," I said, using eyelash glue to secure one more rhinestone to my cheekbone. We were dancing the seasons tonight, and I was supposed to be a winter wind. A little weird, sure, but that was lyrical jazz for you: the only thing that kept it from being even weirder than contemporary was the need to keep us all contorting into shapes that the human body was never meant to achieve.

"Nerves?" he asked.

"Nerves, and family trouble." We'd find out which dancers were in danger after the group routine. Anders might be a little too focused on me sometimes, but he was still my partner, and I still loved him as a friend. I always would.

I dropped the eyelash glue and spun around in my chair, grabbing for his hands. Anders blinked at me, surprised but not displeased.

"Poppy and Chaz rushed out of here so fast last week that I didn't get to say good-bye," I said. His face fell as he realized I wasn't about to confess my undying love. I pressed on. "I don't think either of us is going to be in danger, but I want you to promise that if we *are*, if either one of us gets eliminated, that you'll stick around so we can say good-bye. Please. Promise me."

Anders blinked again. "Dude, Val, what's gotten into you? I expected nervous. I didn't expect psycho." He tried to pull his hands away, eyes widening at the strength of my grip. "Yes, okay? Yes, I promise, if either one of us gets eliminated—which isn't going to happen—I'll find you backstage. No matter what."

"I'm so glad to hear that. I don't think I could bear it if I didn't get to say good-bye to you." I'm not sure which of us was more surprised when I hugged him: me, or Anders.

He relaxed into my embrace after the initial stiffness, and he was smiling when he pulled away. "Here I thought you weren't a hugger."

"I'm not," I said, turning back to my mirror before he could realize how uncomfortable I was. This was another of the places where my real life and my fantasy life diverged. *Verity* was a hugger, but *Verity* only hugged people who wouldn't be surprised when they felt a gun pressing against their hip or a sheathed knife digging into their stomach. Anders had no idea how many weapons I was carrying. That had been foolish, and worse, it had been weak. I needed to be strong, now more than ever.

If I wasn't, someone else was going to die tonight.

"Special circumstances, huh?" Anders patted me on the shoulder. "It's going to be fine, Val. We danced like gods last week. Nobody's going to eliminate us."

"Hope you're right," I said, picking up my eyelash glue and carefully tacking one last rhinestone into place. I glittered whenever I moved. Exactly like I was supposed to.

"I'm always right and you know it," said Anders. He opened his mouth to say more, and stopped as a long, low bong resounded through the room. A wry smile twisted his lips upward. "Ask not for whom the bell tolls . . . you ready?"

"Ready," I said. I stood and took his arm, and he led me from the safety of my mirror to the dangerous familiarity of the stage.

Sasha might be a punk rock Tinker Bell who thought the human body came equipped with easily replaceable joints, but there was no question that she was a damn fine choreographer. The fourteen dancers still in the competition—the fourteen dancers who were still *alive*—flung ourselves through the routine like our lives depended on it. And they did. Even if only Malena, Pax, and I knew the danger was literal, and not just a risk of elimination, there was a very good chance that anyone who failed to dance well enough would die.

This wasn't what I'd signed up for. I leaped into the air with the rest of the winter wind girls, and Pax snatched me before I could hit the floor, wrapping his spring-draped arms around me and lowering me to tangle around his ankles. The summer girls fell into the boys of fall, and the stage was an unending maze of motion. We were *dancers*. We risked our lives every day. Everyone I knew had a story about someone who'd never dance again thanks to a bad fall or a blown knee, and half of us had a story we wouldn't tell unless it was late and we

were drunk, about someone who'd misjudged their partner during a trust fall and ended up with a broken neck.
Nothing was forever, nothing was *real* except for this
moment on the stage, all of us spinning and falling and
leaping and *alive*.

Why was it on me to keep us that way? Why did I
have to be the one who'd been born into a family with so
many ancestral debts to pay that we might never stop
fighting? It wasn't fair. Even though I'd already chosen
the world I belonged to—more than once—part of me
just wanted to dance, and always would. And that was
the part of me I'd never be able to satisfy.

The music ended. The seasons froze, fourteen dancers
holding ourselves rigid in improbable positions, backs
bent, hips twisted, and limbs akimbo.

Then the show's theme music began, and Brenna
Kelly strutted onto the stage, walking through the mass
of dancers. We straightened and bowed to her as she
passed us. She rewarded us with smiles and blown kisses,
chirping, "Hello, my darlings! Wasn't that amazing?
Hurry now, go and get yourselves ready."

That was our cue. We scattered, running back to the
dressing rooms, where the wardrobe assistants were
waiting to scrape the makeup off of our faces and brush
enough of the hairspray out of our hair to render it mal-
leable. We had eight minutes—only four of which would
actually be broadcast—to get into our costumes for the
intro. The unlucky couple that would be dancing first tonight would also have to get into their hair and makeup
before they could go back out, and so the assistants
swarmed over them first, giving me time to slip into the
bathroom and trade my teased-up wig for one that had
already been styled in victory rolls and delicate waves.

(None of my fellow dancers seemed to realize I wore
a wig, except for Lyra, who'd caught me, and Pax and
Malena, who'd been told. I was reasonably sure *everyone*
from the wardrobe department knew, and just didn't
care. It made me easier to style than the other dancers,
since they had one less dancer yelping every time they

hit a snarl, and so they were happy to keep my secret, if only out of enlightened self-interest.)

I got out of the bathroom and plopped down in a seat, where a makeup assistant appeared and used a cloth soaked in a chemical-smelling fluid to remove the rhinestones and makeup from my face. It burned, and I wondered if I was also losing half of my epidermis. Oh, well. Sometimes you have to suffer for your art. They were finished in record time. I yanked my simple black practice dress on and strapped my shoes to my feet just as the bell rang again and the whole group of dancers stampeded for the door. The show was going on.

Since we were still in the couples phase of the show, introductions consisted of one male dancer and one female dancer running onstage and performing roughly eight seconds of steps between them. Anders and I were the first to be introduced this week, courtesy of his name's place in the alphabet. He tapped. I grabbed his hand and used it to steady myself as I performed an impressive-looking flip that would have gotten me disqualified from any formal competition. Then we fell back, swaying rhythmically as we watched the other dancers go through their paces.

None of them looked calmer or more anxious than I expected. If any of my fellow competitors had been involved in the deaths of Poppy and Chaz, they were good at not showing it. I switched my attention to the judges as much as I could without losing my place in the rhythm. Adrian had his usual expression of faint disapproval. Lindy was smiling—although with as much Botox as she'd had, I wasn't sure she could do anything else. The third spot at the judges' table was occupied by a grinning Clint, clapping his hands in time to the intro music. He saw me looking and winked. I winked back, still grooving, and felt better about the show, if nothing else.

Clint genuinely *liked* the dancers on *Dance or Die*. Adrian viewed us as a path to better ratings, and Lindy seemed to hate everyone equally, but Clint was second only to Brenna in showing affection and fondness for the dancers. If he was here, the judging would be even-handed and constructive, even if everything else went horribly wrong.

"It's your fourteen remaining dancers, America!" crowed Brenna, and we walked forward, the boys strutting, the girls sashaying, to strike our pose at the middle of the stage. The crowd cheered like so many supersized Aeslin mice. The lights beat down, hot as a summer sun, and I was home.

It was really a pity I wasn't going to be allowed to stay there. But then, I never was.

"—hate this part, so let's go on and get it over with," said Brenna. She looked down the row of girls, a line of worry etched between her eyebrows. I realized with a pang that we hadn't told her about the snake cult. Between rehearsals, Alice showing up, and our own attempts at an investigation, there hadn't been *time*. How could a week not have been enough *time*?

Brenna was worried because she might be sending me home, and she needed to stay on my good side if she wanted an introduction to William. I was worried because whoever was eliminated tonight might be in deadly danger . . . and I hadn't told her. She was *right there*, and should have been among the first to know.

What else had I missed?

"The girls in danger of elimination tonight are . . ." Brenna opened the envelope, sighed, and read, "Leanne, Malena, and Raisa. Thank you, girls. The rest of you may leave the stage."

We filed off as she was reading off the names of the boys in danger. I lingered in the wings. Anders and I were up fourth: I had time, and I wanted to know which of the male dancers were on the bottom.

"Pax, Mac, and Will," said Brenna, and the bottom dropped out of the world. The rest of the boys walked off.

Anders was one of the first to make it clear of the cameras. He stopped in front of me, a bleak, anxious look on his face. "Pax was never on the bottom during the first half of our season. What the hell went wrong?"

"Better dancers, tougher competition," said Jessica, stepping from behind one of the dangling curtains. She was smirking. "Maybe you're going to have extra room in your apartment sooner than you thought."

The urge to slap that stupid smirk right off of her face was almost strong enough to override my common sense—but only almost. Assaulting a fellow contestant would see me eliminated on the spot, and then my friends would be defenseless.

"Not funny, Jessica," snarled Anders.

"*Hysterical*," she said, looking him dead in the eye.

"Break it up," I said, stepping between them. "Pax isn't going anywhere. He's too good a dancer to have pulled the lowest number of overall votes. Now if you'll excuse me, *some* of us are interested in staying in this competition." I slid my arm through the crook of Anders's elbow, so I was holding him close without clinging, and pulled him with me toward the dressing rooms. We separated at the last minute, him going into the men's, me going into the women's. We were all dancers here—none of us actually *cared*—but the show's producers needed to at least pretend they were holding to Middle American standards of decency.

Someone grabbed me as soon as I was inside the room, yanking me behind a rack of costumes. I pulled the knife from my thigh holster—worn high enough that it hadn't been visible during my flip earlier, and low enough that I wasn't goosing myself in uncomfortable places, and don't think *that* hadn't been a learning experience—and whipped around, ready to stab my assailant in the throat.

Only the fact that Malena was even faster than I was saved us both from a very bad experience. She hissed and let go. "Stand *down*, Jesus! All I did was grab you!"

"Keep your voice down!" I countered, making the

knife vanish back into my dress. "Didn't anyone ever tell you not to grab people?"

"I didn't expect you to respond by pulling a goddamn *harpoon* out of your crotch," she snapped. "How is your boy still among the living? You should have stabbed him the first time he rolled over in bed."

"He's a sound sleeper." I cast a glance over my shoulder to the costumes she'd pulled me through. They weren't currently moving. Maybe we were going to get lucky, and no one had noticed my impromptu disappearance. I looked back to Malena. "You need to stick close to me or Pax tonight. If you can't find us, look for Alice. I know she's lurking around the back of the theater."

"She'd better be. Shit, V—" Malena caught herself before she could use my real name, and continued with a, "I didn't expect to be in the bottom this week. I thought Troy and I danced better than this."

"You did," I said. "The voters make weird decisions. Now we just need to make sure that if you're eliminated, you never go anywhere alone. *Anywhere.*"

"What if Pax and I both get eliminated?" Malena asked.

I grimaced. "Then we hope whoever killed Chaz and Poppy will go after the two of you, because I'm honestly not sure I can stop this if I'm the only one in the theater who knows what's going on."

Malena's glare could have melted metal. "I didn't sign up to play the bait in your little crusade."

"No one signed on for this 'little crusade,' Malena. People are dying, and we're trying to stop it." A bong sounded, signaling the first couple to take the stage. "If you and Pax are eliminated, they're not going to know what hit them. I still hope that doesn't happen. I'd much rather have the two of you helping us track down our killers. Either way, I'm hoping no one dies tonight."

"You know, when I came here, I was just hoping for a shot at the big money," grumbled Malena. "I'm coming up on my twenty-sixth birthday. It's time to start thinking about having kids. That'll be a lot easier if I can actually afford them."

"I think we all came here for that," I said. "I know Poppy and Chaz didn't sign up because they were hoping to get their throats slit."

Malena looked at me gravely. "Do you think we're going to be able to stop this?"

"Honestly, Malena, I don't know. But we're going to do the best we can." That's all we could ever do, and all my family had ever done: the best that we could. It was a real pity that even our best had never been enough to keep everyone we cared about alive.

The rest of the show passed with the kind of speed found only in tense situations and anxiety dreams. Anders and I danced our quickstep with as much enthusiasm as we could muster, but I knew I was letting him down; I was too worried about what might happen after elimination to focus on my energy and my connection with my partner. The judges knew it, too. Getting criticized and warned about potentially being in the bottom next week was painful. Having Clint look at me like I had personally disappointed him was worse.

At least I had stayed on the beat and kept my feet moving. Maybe I'd put myself in danger, but Anders should be safe. And maybe if I kept telling myself that, the universe would take pity on me and somehow make it true.

Brenna called the six dancers in danger back to the center of the stage after the last couple finished. The rest of us moved to stand in the space between the judging platform and the audience, still in our costumes. The nervous energy rolling off the group was palpable. I was struck once again by how *simple* this had all seemed once, how blissfully removed from the world I'd grown up in. The last time I'd been standing here, I'd been thinking only about winning, proving I was America's Dancer of Choice, and that I could have a life beyond the one my blood had fated for me.

Now I was worried about whether two of the people

up on that stage were going to survive the night. I was worried about the fact that of the three contestants who knew about the deaths, two of them had their heads on the chopping block. If Malena and Pax were both eliminated, and we didn't catch the killers before the theater closed for the night, I was going to be the only person left who knew what was going on and had free, unfettered access to the building.

Brenna and the judges had been speaking while I fretted over the future. Now she turned to them, and said, "Well, Adrian? Please don't leave us in suspense any longer, my heart can't take it." Neither could the dancers who stood beside her, their hands locked together and their faces set in near-matching expressions of grim stoicism. There could be no crying or visible distress: the two who survived tonight's elimination would need votes to stay on the show, and the public didn't respond well to the idea that someone was a sore loser, no matter how untrue it was.

Please, Adrian, I thought. *Just get it over with.*

Adrian leaned forward. "Well, Brenna, we've discussed it, and our decision tonight is unanimous. The girl who'll be leaving us tonight is . . . Leanne."

Leanne pulled her hands away from the other two, covering her face. Now that she'd lost, she was allowed to show how crushed she was.

I didn't really know her. I didn't know how much of her heartbreak was real, and how much was a careful affectation, designed to appeal to the audience, in case there was a miracle that might get her back on the show. It had happened before. Right now, it didn't matter, because she'd just been cut, and I grieved for her, even as I was grateful Malena would be staying.

"All right, Malena and Raisa, you can leave the stage." Brenna put her arms around Leanne, giving the girl a hug that lasted just long enough for the other two dancers to make it down into the pit. Then Brenna let her go, waving her toward the wings, and walked over to where the three boys in danger waited.

The same drama played out in slow motion for the second time: the brief critique by the judges, Brenna's plea that they get it over with, and finally, Adrian's verdict.

"Once again, we are unanimous. The boy who will be leaving us tonight is Mac. Thank you so much for your time; your journey ends here."

Mac bowed his head, shedding a single manly tear. Brenna embraced him. The closing music began, inviting us all to mob the stage, hug our departing comrades good-bye, and dance for the cameras.

Pax grabbed me as soon as I came into range, spinning me in until he could murmur in my ear: "What do we do now?"

"We stay on them," I replied, and spun out again, this time flinging myself at Malena in what I hoped would look like a friendly hug. The fact that we'd never shown any real affection for each other before didn't matter: we were originally from different seasons, and could be expected to form new bonds during this one. Anders was glaring at me. I did my best to avoid him as I brought my lips to Malena's ear.

"Follow Leanne," I whispered.

Malena nodded, and pulled away to dance with Ivan, matching him step for step. The cameras spun around us, capturing every moment, right up until the lights flashed to signal the end of the credits. That was everyone's cue to get offstage.

It was my cue to get ready for an ambush.

The Crier Theater was built to accommodate all sorts of productions, from the recording of *Dance or Die* to concerts and theater companies. Consequently, the ceilings were unusually high everywhere backstage, to allow for the movement of stage flats and complicated equipment. Moving through that space was like moving through a dream of the theater, unconfined and smelling always, faintly, of sawdust.

Being a free-runner means I spend my life assessing my surroundings in terms of "how hard would it be to climb that?" Most of all, being a free-runner means I've had a long time to figure out the big blind spot that almost all humans share:

Humans virtually never look *up*.

I was among the first off the stage, and the absolute first to hit the women's changing room. My Jane of the Jungle costume was simple to shuck off and hang on the rack, and it was a matter of seconds to pull on my street clothes. I swapped my stage wig for my usual loose red ponytail, and filled my pockets with knives. By the time the first of my fellow dancers was coming through the door, I was pushing my way out into the hall, murmuring vague phrases about not feeling well. Some of them looked at me sympathetically, but no one tried to stop me. They all knew I hadn't danced my best tonight.

As soon as I was alone in the hall, I grabbed the nearest curtain and shinnied up it to the rafters. Once there, I ran along the beams meant to hold our hanging lights to a position above the basement door. I crouched, holding a beam for support, and waited.

Malena arrived a few minutes later, sauntering casually until she saw she was alone. Then she skittered straight up the wall, stopping when she was roughly on the level with me. She blinked. I raised my free hand in a small wave.

"All present and accounted for?" I asked.

"The other seven girls were still getting changed when I left the room, and I don't smell blood," she said. "Where's your grandmother?"

"I have no idea." Probably in the basement, if I knew Alice. She was good at staying out of sight when she wanted to, and while we hadn't planned for this moment in excessive detail—having too many variables meant it was better to wing it and play to our strengths than to get tripped up by a plan that wouldn't work—she'd want to be where she could break some faces, if it came to that.

Dominic was outside, and would stay there until

someone signaled him to come in. We'd need to find a better way of getting him into the theater if this continued for another week. *Please,* I thought, *don't let this continue for another week. Please, let us find the people who killed Poppy and Chaz, and stop them, and move on into a world where I could just dance, and not worry about anybody getting murdered. Please.*

There was motion below. Malena and I both went very still, and watched as Pax walked down the hall, looking quickly from side to side. Like the humans, he didn't look up. That made a certain amount of sense. Ukupani were aquatic in nature. Just being out of the water was disconcerting enough to keep him from looking for an ambush.

He opened the basement door and stepped inside, disappearing.

"He didn't do it, did he?" whispered Malena.

"No," I said, with absolute certainty. "If he had, he would never have been stupid enough to involve me." Ukupani didn't have a history of worshipping snake cults. I'd needed to explain the concept to him, and Hawaii was too small to have ever sustained anything the size of Titanoboa. Hawaiian terrors tended to come out of the sea. I fully expected that if anyone ever managed to summon Cthulhu or something like that, it would be anybody's guess whether the squamous terror rose from the waters off Massachusetts or Maui.

"I still don't smell blood," said Malena. She was starting to sound unsure.

I paused. "Wait. If all three of us are here—I thought you were keeping an eye on Leanne."

Malena's eyes widened. "She wasn't in the dressing room. I thought you were keeping an eye on her."

"*Shit*," I hissed, and swung around to dangling from the beam I'd been sitting on. From there, it was easy work to grab one of the guide ropes and lower myself, one hand over the other, to the floor. It wasn't the fastest means of descent, but it prevented rope burns, and that was important to me. I was going to need my hands.

My feet had barely hit the floor when someone sighed

behind me. "Val, Val, Val, do we have to have a talk about the insurance rates and keeping out of the rafters again? I thought we went over this."

"Um." I turned, forcing a sickly smile as Clint walked toward me. He was shaking his head in disapproval. Every encounter I'd ever had with the show's judges told me to bow my head and look regretful. Every lesson I'd ever had about getting caught climbing somewhere I wasn't supposed to be told me to turn and run.

I settled for a compromise, leaning back on my heels and smiling sheepishly. Clint was still dressed for the judging table, and tonight's bow tie was covered in purple grapes hanging heavy on bright green vines. He looked concerned.

"I'm serious, Val. You're a great dancer—usually. What happened tonight? I expected better from you. There was no fire in your performance, and that song *demanded* fire." Clint tilted his head. "Is everything okay back at the housing? Are you getting along with the other dancers? You know you've always been one of my favorites. I want things to be as comfortable for you as possible."

"Everyone's been great, honest," I said. "I just climb when I'm stressed, that's all. I know I didn't do so good tonight. I didn't even need you to tell me."

Clint nodded. "I could see the knowledge in your eyes when you came over to talk to us. See, that's part of why you're one of my favorites. You have a degree of self-awareness that's unusual in a dancer of your age. You didn't answer my first question."

I paused, reviewing the conversation in my head before deciding to go with the excuse that would best match the rumors he might have already heard. "My sister's in town, and we don't talk much." Referring to my grandmother as my sister was never not going to be weird. "I just let her throw me off my game, that's all. I'll work harder next week."

"You'd better, or next week could be your last," said Clint gravely.

His back was to the basement door. He didn't see it

open, or see Pax's startled expression when he was confronted with Clint's unmistakable silhouette.

Be smart, I thought, while nodding and trying to keep a downtrodden expression firmly in place. "I know. I just have to hope America will show me mercy. If we get something in the ballroom category for next week's show, I think I can carry Anders through it, and remind people why they let me make it to the finale last time."

"Remind them of more than that." I wasn't expecting Clint to move when he did. He stepped forward, grabbing my hands before I could shift out of the way, and said seriously, "Remind them how they blew up the message boards when Lyra edged you out for the title. Remind them that they *love* you, and that they want *you* to be America's Dancer of Choice."

Years of living with Aeslin mice had given me the odd ability to hear it when someone stressed a word hard enough to capitalize it. I smiled and tugged my hands away from him. "I'm flattered, Clint, but I don't think we should be having this conversation. If the other dancers start thinking you're favoring me, it's going to make rehearsals awfully uncomfortable."

"Adrian has his favorites every season. You know he does. Bits of fluff who know how to waggle their asses for his approval. He's never slept with any of them—Lindy would have his balls if he tried—but that doesn't change the way he looks at them. He's undressed them with his eyes a thousand times." Clint's expression hardened, mouth thinning into a disapproving line. "He cuts deserving dancers because he wants to keep his favorites as long as he can. Why shouldn't I come down on the side of the dancers who actually deserve to be here? You're *good,* Valerie. I expected you to turn us down because you were setting the competition stage on fire, or starring in some new Broadway extravaganza. What happened after you left us?"

I remembered who I was, I thought. Aloud, I said, "It's hard out there for a dancer. I guess I just got overwhelmed." Which was technically true. I'd been overwhelmed by the discovery of a giant sleeping dragon under New York City, and by the presence of a Covenant field team. I'd been overwhelmed by the effort of doing my job and starting my career at the same time, and when I'd been forced to choose one over the other, I'd chosen the one I couldn't imagine living without.

And now I had to do that again. Insulting a judge was a quick way to wind up on the bottom, but I didn't see where I had a choice if I wanted to find the others.

"I'm really sorry I was climbing; I just needed to clear my head," I said, taking another step backward. "I was hoping to catch Leanne before she left to get her things. I'm sorry. Can we talk later, maybe?"

"I thought I saw her on the stage," said Clint. He closed the distance between us, taking my arm firmly in his. "I'll walk you."

Shit. There was no way to get out of this: not without blowing my cover, and potentially getting myself tossed out of the theater. "All right," I said, glancing over my shoulder toward the basement door and hoping that Malena would take the hint.

This was all on her and Pax now.

Clint chatted vaguely during the walk back to the empty stage. I don't think I heard more than one word in three. I was too busy watching the corners of the hall, waiting for something to lunge out at us. If there were any dancers remaining in the building apart from the ones I knew about, our route avoided them; it was just Clint and me, right up until we stepped out onto the echoing vault of the stage.

It always seemed larger when it was empty, without the bodies of my friends and colleagues to fill it. The big floodlights were off, but the smaller stage lights were still on, preventing accidents among the stagehands and cleanup crews who were doubtless sweeping through the building.

"Don't you always feel more alive when you're on stage?" He finally let me go, taking a few quick steps away before twirling on his heel and offering his hand with a flourish. He was grinning, looking absolutely delighted with himself. "Miss Pryor, may I have this dance?"

I didn't have a good way to refuse. I *wanted* to tell him "no," to turn and run and find my people—but they were good people. They could do this without me if they had to, and keeping Clint from pursuing me through the theater was as important as getting back to them in a timely fashion. Still, I tried. "I'm not wearing good dancing shoes," I demurred.

"So? I've seen you dance barefoot and in six-inch spike heels. I think you can manage a basic waltz in sneakers, don't you?" His hand remained outstretched. "I'm not hitting on you, if that's what you're worried about. I'm just concerned. You're not the brilliant dancer I used to know. Something's eating you. I want it to stop."

"Life moves on," I said, and slid my hand into his. He promptly spun me in, and then back out again, moving slowly enough that I could follow him, yet fast enough to make it clear he trusted my capabilities. It would have been flattering, if I hadn't been so worried. "I had to stop dancing for a while before the show called. I'm not in the best shape."

"Liar," he said fondly, beginning to waltz me around the stage. Our steps matched like we'd been practicing together for years. I forced my shoulders down, trying not to let my tension show. Ballroom dance is serious business for those who perform on a competitive level, and we've all learned how to hide our fear. "You're in impeccable shape. If fitness were the only thing we judged, you'd be in the top three easily. You might just walk away with the whole show. What's eating you, Valerie?"

"Life," I said, with a very small shrug. "It's been hard. I thought I'd leave here and find this glorious career waiting for me, and instead, I found a lot of failed auditions, some competitions where I didn't even place, and a revolving door of partners. I never expected it to be easy. I definitely didn't think it was going to be impossible."

"It's not," he said. "Why didn't you call me? I would have arranged some private auditions for you. I can open doors, you know. If you want it, I can make it happen."

"What would it cost me?" There was no music, but the waltz was so familiar that neither of us needed it. We didn't dance around the stage; we glided, and his hand was a hot weight on my waist, not crossing any lines of propriety apart from the ones that had already been left far behind us. There was nothing sexual about it. Clint had never pressured me for anything in that direction. So far as I knew, he'd never pressured *any* of the dancers. It was just *there*, reminding me that escape was impossible, that I was the dancer and he was the judge, and if I ran, he would pursue.

I couldn't even blame him for that. He thought he was helping. He thought he was keeping me from losing faith and losing focus, when what he was really keeping me from was the chance to save a life.

Dominic, Alice, get in here, I thought, and wished Sarah were with me. I hadn't realized how much I'd come to depend on the presence of our resident telepath until she was gone. We wouldn't even have had to worry about how to get her into the theater. Sarah was a cuckoo. Cuckoos went where they wanted to go, and nobody stopped them. Most of the time, no one even realized they were there. That was what made them so damn dangerous.

"You'd have to promise me you were going to be serious," Clint said, and his voice was solemn, and his eyes were grave. "I know how good you are, Valerie. Sometimes I think you don't. Sometimes I think this is all just a game to you."

"I promise, I don't think of this as a game." He twirled me gently out. I automatically scribed a wide arch in the air with my hand before spinning back in again, returning to our frame. My body knew the way, even if my mind wanted nothing more than to get away from here and back to my mission. "Everything I do, I do as seriously as I possibly can."

Clint nodded. "That was what I was hoping to hear. You could be one of the great ones, Valerie. We could be talking about the things you did for dance for the next fifty years. Don't throw that away."

He stopped dancing. So did I. Then, without another word, he took his hand from my waist, raised our joined hands to his lips, and kissed my knuckles. Then he turned and walked away, leaving me alone on the stage.

Thirteen

"There's no crime in missing the shot. The only crime is being too damn slow to take it."
—Frances Brown

The Crier Theater, four seconds later

I STAYED PUT FOR A COUNT OF TEN, watching to see if Clint would come back. He didn't. I turned and bolted for the wings, heading for where I'd left Malena and the others.

The show had been over for long enough that the halls were deserted: even the technicians, janitors, and countless production assistants who could usually be counted on to lurk in unexpected places were gone, leaving me free to run. I sped up, grabbing a corner with my left hand in order to slingshot myself around it, only to stop dead as my momentum carried me straight into Dominic's chest. He was close enough to my height that my head hit him in the throat, and he staggered backward, closing his arms around me in an effort to stabilize himself.

I didn't pull away, even though every instinct I had said not to let myself be trapped. Instead, I leaned to the side, and we hit the wall with a thud that resounded all the way through my spine.

"What the hell, Ve—" Dominic caught himself before he blurted out my real name. He frowned instead, and demanded, "Where were you? We've been looking everywhere!"

"Didn't look on the stage," I said, and ducked out of his arms, stepping backward. "Where is everyone else?"

"Trying to find our eliminated contestants," he said. "Pax thought they were with Malena. Malena thought they were with you. Alice thought they were with anyone but her."

"So we've lost them." Which meant that they were probably dead. I swallowed the urge to stomp my foot, and simply asked, "How the hell did we *lose* them?"

"Leanne left the girls' changing room to use the restroom, and didn't come back; Mac never made it to the changing room at all," said Dominic. "Perhaps more interesting is the question of why no one finds this strange."

That stopped me. "What?"

"Pax asked Troy—the other male dancer from Mac's season, who you would think might feel some camaraderie or responsibility for the man—where Mac was. Troy looked confused and reminded Pax that Mac had been eliminated." Dominic's expression was grim. "I know the dance world can be cutthroat and cruel, but you've always led me to believe there was slightly more compassion in it."

"There usually is," I said. Sarah's brand of telepathy wasn't the only way of changing people's minds. There were compulsions, illusions, all manner of charms that could be cooked up by your local witch or Letiche—and in a city like Burbank, where everything was available for the right price, finding someone who'd cook you a charm without asking questions wasn't hard. Assuming their pet magic-users hadn't done it themselves. "We need to find the others."

"We split up to look for the missing contestants."

"I get that, and it was a smart move given the information available at the time, but I'm telling you we need to find the others." I shook my head, feeling the bobby pins holding my wig in place dig into my scalp. "Something's making people not care about the disappearances. Do we want to risk Pax or Malena going missing, knowing that nobody's going to give a shit?"

Dominic's eyes widened. Then he nodded. "This way," he said, and turned to run.

He was only a few inches taller than me, but that was enough to give him a longer stride. That was a good thing, since otherwise there was no way he'd have ever been able to keep up with me. Dominic was in good shape. He trained hard and worked harder. I was a dancer and a fighter whose only chance of survival was rooted in speed, and I'd been training nonstop for the past three weeks. Really, the only surprise was that I was less than ten feet ahead of him by the time I hit the last corner between us and the hallway leading to the basement.

Alice and Pax were there, standing in front of the open door. Alice had a pistol in her hand, holding it low against her hip, as if that would keep her from getting in trouble if theater security came around the corner and saw her with the gun. I slid to a stop and looked up at the same time. Malena was anchored to the wall some twelve feet up, her feet bent at an inhuman angle.

"Where have you been?" demanded Alice. "We've been looking for you everywhere."

"Dominic said the same thing, and I don't think you have," I said. "I was on the stage with Clint. Half the hallways in this place would have led you straight there. I think someone's messing with us. Malena!"

"What?" The voice drifted down from above, not accompanied by the chupacabra. She was in hunting mode. It would take her a while to shake that off.

That was good. I needed her in hunting mode. "Go to the top of the wall and start looking for anything that seems like it doesn't belong there. Dried flowers or herbs or stones."

"*What*?" Now she just sounded confused.

Alice, on the other hand, looked horrified. "Memory charms."

"Or confusion charms," I said. I looked up again.

Malena hadn't moved. "Come on. We need this if we're going to find them."

"You need my foot up your butt," she muttered, and skittered away, moving with a fluid, insectile grace completely at odds with her still mostly human appearance.

Content that she was trying, I turned to Alice and Pax. "Do either of you *remember* going to look for me, or did you just assume it had happened?"

"Pax and Malena told me they'd gone looking," said Alice.

"I looked," said Pax.

"As did I," said Dominic.

"Okay, where?" I asked.

Silence followed.

"That's what I thought. Look: my family's spent so much time around cuckoos and Lilu and other things that scramble your head that we're a little resistant. Not immune, but . . . we do okay." I shook my head. "If I don't remember looking for people I couldn't find, and Alice doesn't remember looking for people she couldn't find, but we're all mysteriously losing track of the folks we're supposed to be keeping our eyes on? Someone is messing with us."

"Does this fit the bill for something that doesn't belong?" asked Malena, just before a bundle of dried flowers wrapped with a string of stone beads hit the floor. Pax jumped. Alice slanted a narrow-eyed glare up at the rafters.

"Yes, it does," I said, as I moved to pick up the bundle. The flowers were thin and fragile, but they'd been red before they were dried; hints of color still showed on the petals. I sniffed, and was rewarded with a dusty, venomous sweetness. "I think these are resurrection lilies."

"The stone is howlite," said Dominic. I glanced at him. He continued, "We used to carry disks of the stuff when it was thought we might be going into an area containing a cuckoo. There was no proof it helped us to remember ourselves, but the thought was that any protection, however scant, was better than none."

"Howlite is supposed to be calming," said Alice. "It reduces stress, anger—all the things I live by."

"And resurrection lilies are used in a lot of memory charms," I said. "Someone's looping memory in the halls. Keeps us from noticing when we lose track of people, keeps us from realizing that we're wasting time doing things we don't have to. This is bad."

"We can get counter-charms from Bon," said Alice.

"That's not going to save Mac and Leanne," I said.

She didn't have an answer for that. Sadly, neither did anybody else.

Malena searched the rafters and found six more howlite and resurrection lily charm bundles. Once they were all collected, she slipped out through one of the high windows, on the theory that if we got the charms out of the building, we'd have a better chance of finding our missing people. (They weren't powerful enough to make her forget what they were while she was actually touching them. As for the wisdom of having her move them, rather than destroying them . . . if we didn't find Mac and Leanne, we could put the charms back and hopefully keep the people who'd created them from realizing how much we knew, at least for a while longer. Especially since we didn't know anything *useful*. We had enough bits and pieces to be a danger to ourselves, but not enough to be a danger to anyone else.)

Dominic made a small, startled sound. I turned to see him blinking, looking suddenly confused. Pax looked much the same.

"What's up?" I asked.

"I never went looking for you; I found you by mistake," he said, expression turning horrified. "I was angry with Malena for refusing to come off the wall, and stalked away. I all but ran into you after that—before, I would have gone to my grave swearing I'd sought you, and failed to find you anywhere."

"Welcome to the wonderful, terrible world of memory charms," I said. "It's all right. I wasn't hurt, and you didn't do anything wrong."

"No," he said. "It most certainly is *not* all right, and we'll be discussing this later, at length. Right now, we need to find your missing dancers." He turned and stalked away, heading down the hall toward the stage.

A hand touched my shoulder as I watched him go. I looked behind me. There was Pax, frowning deeply.

"You know, if you don't want to discuss this with him later, he can't make you."

I blinked before I realized what he was implying, and burst out laughing. It was a relief, almost, to feel like laughing again, even though I knew the situation was dire. "No, no, nothing like that, Pax, I swear. He's just worried, and he didn't get a lot of coping mechanisms when he was a kid. I promise, he only wants to talk to me. And maybe make out with me. A lot."

"If you're sure . . ."

"I'm sure. Now come on, you're the Ukupani. Do you smell blood?"

Pax closed his eyes and breathed deeply. As he did, he went perfectly still, becoming a statue of a man. Nothing moved except his chest, and once his lungs were full, even that stopped. He was motionless as only a predator could be, carved from stone and ready to return to life the moment his prey was within range.

Then he opened his eyes and pointed down one of the side halls. "Blood," he said, voice suddenly thick with hunger and longing. "So much blood."

We ran. Malena would just have to catch up with us once she was back in the theater. I had faith that she could; Pax was great for following the smell of blood, but Malena was a distance hunter, and she could follow the smell of *us*.

The hall ended at a closed door. I was the first to reach it, followed by Alice and Dominic, with Pax bringing up the rear. We all stopped, hesitating as we looked at it.

"Anyone know where this leads?" I asked.

Silence told me no one did.

"Great," I said. Producing three throwing knives from the waist of my pants, I signaled for the others to be quiet before leaning forward and turning the knob with my free hand. The door swung inward, revealing a flight of stairs leading down into the dark. My nose was nowhere near as sensitive as Pax's, but it didn't need to be.

The smell of blood was strong enough that I could pick it up on my own.

"Come on," I said, and reached through the door, feeling around for a light switch. There wasn't one. Bracing myself against the potential for things to go terribly, incredibly wrong, I started down the stairs. The others followed.

It was impossible for us to descend silently into the dark. We had to hunt for our footing, and the stairs were metal; our footsteps clanked, not every time, but often enough to alert whatever might be lurking below to our presence. Something scraped on the wall above my head.

I decided to risk it. "Malena, find the light," I hissed.

The scraping intensified, moving away. I realized my mistake and covered my eyes a split second before the lights came on, bathing the room in burning light. Behind me, Dominic made a small, disapproving sound. Alice said a bad word in what sounded like Latin, identifiable as profanity only in its inflection. Pax didn't say anything.

The brightness was a momentary distraction. I uncovered my eyes and turned to the floor, already knowing what I was going to see. The blood had been notification enough, like a marquee sign leading toward horror and the grave.

Mac and Leanne were stretched out side by side, his head by her feet, her head by his. Their hands were joined in the space between them, pinned to the floor by a spike of what looked like ivory, or polished bone. Like the others, they were naked, their bodies laid bare to the unforgiving world. Runes were carved into their skin, so deep in some places that bone glistened through the gore, blindingly white in contrast to the red around it. The runes were larger this time, more elaborate.

The others saw it, too, but it was Alice who put it into words: "They're not afraid of getting caught. Those pictures you showed me before, those were a mess, but this ... they took their time and made sure every little detail was Just. So." She shook her head. "This is sick."

"What are the differences between this scene and the last?" asked Dominic. He had a high, tight note in his voice, like he was stepping back from the situation and putting it behind a glass wall, something clear enough to let him see, but solid enough to distance him. It was his Covenant training coming to the fore, and I almost envied him the ability to become divorced from the terrible things that were going on.

I had no such training. My training was less about killing and more about saving: it never let me step back. Instead, I took a step down, moving closer to the mess, and said, "Some of the runes are the same, but there are more of them, and some I've never seen before. The spike is new. That's physical evidence of what they're doing. The last two victims weren't holding hands."

"They're not sliced down the middle," said Malena. I glanced up at her. She was still sticking to the wall, and her transformation toward her more canine form was continuing; spikes had broken through the skin of her neck and shoulders, and her complexion was shifting toward a dusky gray. It was a slow process. She'd be able to talk for a while yet, even if she chose to keep transforming. "There's no way the killers could've gotten to their guts."

"So we either have two ritualists, or the ritual is evolving." I pulled out my phone and began snapping pictures. "Malena, I'm going to need you to take the overhead shots again."

"We need that spike," said Alice.

"We can't take it," said Dominic. His voice was sharp.

We all turned to look at him. He shook his head, and said, "Whoever is doing this, they use the confusion charms to keep people from realizing the eliminated dancers have vanished without a trace—everyone thinks they've seen the missing people with someone else. Our killers aren't aware that they have an active opposition in the building."

"Yet," said Pax.

"Yet," agreed Dominic. "Nothing stays secret forever. But if we steal that piece of ghoulish equipment, they'll realize someone knows what they've been doing. They'll change their ways. I don't think they'll stop. People like this, *monsters* like this, don't stop simply because they've been discovered. If anything, they kill faster, destroy faster, because they no longer have secrecy to protect them."

"He's right," said Alice. "Every snake cult I've ever seen has gotten a lot nastier once people knew for sure that they were there. It's like rattlesnakes. They're pretty good neighbors until you flip their rocks over."

"Don't compare these people to rattlesnakes," said Malena, and her voice was filled with the sound of bones rearranging themselves, teeth sharpening to new points. I remembered with a jolt that she and Mac were from the same season. They had danced together. He hadn't been her regular partner, but he'd been the Pax to her Anders, and now he was dead, bled out on a cold stone floor in the basement of the theater, and there was nothing she could do to bring him back.

"Rattlesnakes only bite when they have to," Malena continued. I could hear the sorrow under the sounds of shifting now. I had just needed to figure out how to listen for it. "These people, they're biting for the fun of it. They're biting because they want to *get* something. They're not rattlesnakes. They're *monsters*."

"You're right, and I'm sorry," said Alice, glancing in my direction. I nodded slightly, thanking her without words. The last thing we needed was for Malena to launch herself at my grandmother because she'd been insensitive. "We need to stop this."

"That won't bring them back." Malena scuttled lower on the wall, holding out her hand toward me. "Give me the phone. I'll get those pictures you want."

"See if you can get close-ups of the spike," I said. "If there are any carvings or anything, we need to know about it."

Malena nodded once, closing her sharp-nailed fingers around the phone. Then she scurried off, starting her photo project.

I turned. Pax was black-eyed and shaking, staring at the pool of blood that covered the floor. "Dominic, take Pax up to the hall. The two of you need to keep an eye out, in case the people who did this come back." And in case the smell of blood overwhelmed the Ukupani's ability to keep himself under control. I had faith in Dominic's ability to restrain Pax without hurting either of them too badly. There was one big advantage to Pax losing control, rather than Malena: if his transformation became too advanced, he'd lose the ability to breathe oxygen, and would pass out before automatically reverting to an air-breathing form. Malena would just keep going until she had more ripped-off faces for her collection.

"Thank you," said Pax, and virtually fled back up the stairs, with Dominic following close behind him. Alice watched them go.

"Do you think the cultists will come back?" she asked, turning back to me.

"Not for a while," I said. Malena was clinging to the ceiling now, taking overhead shots. "I think they'll leave the bodies here for a few hours, and then magic as much of the mess away as they can. There won't be any sign of what happened here by morning."

"I see." Alice shook her head. "I should have realized there was a confusion charm on the building. It only makes sense, given the way you described everyone else's behavior. Verity, I'm sorry."

"Don't be. You had no *reason* to suspect." I took another step down and crouched, trying to get a better look at the spike that held our latest victims' hands together. "I'll call home when we get back to the apartments. Daddy can FedEx us some anti-telepathy charms."

"I have a better idea," said Alice. "I meant it when I said we could get counter-charms from Bon. She's a routewitch, and she knows me well enough that my word is good when I tell her she'll be paid."

"Do routewitches usually take money?" My Aunt Laura was a routewitch, but she disappeared before I was born, and I've never had that much direct dealing with them. They were mostly active on the highways and in truck stops, and those weren't places where you found many ballroom dance studios.

"They take distance," said Alice. Her expression went briefly unreadable. "I've traveled a very long way."

Malena dropped from the ceiling onto the stairs behind me. It was abrupt enough that I jumped as I whirled to face her, and behind me I heard the click of Alice removing the safety on her gun. There was another click as she put it back. Malena thrust the phone at me, stone-faced and slowly reverting toward her usual human form.

"Here," she said. "Enough gore to keep a teenage boy happy. I need to shower forever. We done here, or are we gonna hang out and see if we can't murder the shit out of the people who did this?"

I hesitated. There were five of us, and I might be up for elimination next week; even apart from the need to save the lives of my fellow contestants, my own life was potentially in imminent danger. At the same time, we had no idea how many snake cultists there were, or whether they were human or something else. If we stayed, if we waited, we could be wasting five lives for a chance at saving two.

The thought was followed by a wave of guilt. Since when was my life worth more than anyone else's? Since when did I get to value my friends above the people I was supposed to be protecting and taking care of? No. I couldn't think that way.

"Yes," I said. "We wait."

Hopefully, we wouldn't be waiting for nothing.

There were no other entrances to this particular basement: just the one door, leading down to the abattoir the previously innocent space had become. Malena crawled up the wall while I took to the rafters. Alice elected to wait just inside the basement door, sitting on the steps and waiting for someone to come and make her night more interesting.

Pax and Dominic were a problem. Neither of them were climbers, and we couldn't put Pax on the other side of the door with Alice unless we wanted him driven wild by the smell of blood. In the end, we'd sent Pax down the hall to hide in the curtains and watch for people who might be coming to check on their handiwork, while Dominic went outside to watch the parking lot. It wasn't a perfect solution, but this wasn't a perfect place to put together an ambush. The basement was a killing jar . . . if we could get our killers inside. Until then, they had all the hallways and hidey-holes of a very large theater at their disposal, and we needed to be careful.

I crouched in the rafters, balancing on the balls of my feet, and waited for the signal to move. Malena clung to the wall nearby. She looked calmer, and more human, than she had in the basement. She wasn't as upset by the smell of blood as Pax was. That didn't mean it hadn't been getting to her. It could be easy to forget, sometimes, how weak the human nose was when compared to most therianthropes. As a chupacabra, Malena was attuned to the smell of rot and offal. It was probably perfume to her heightened senses. Leaving her to marinate in it would still have been cruel.

"You okay?" I murmured. The theater had been

designed to muffle backstage noise as much as possible, with sound baffles in the walls and foam padding on the bottoms of the rafters. Our killers would have to be bats to hear me.

(Bats weren't off the table—the Batboy story has some real cryptid roots—but they weren't likely. None of the batlike cryptids we've found so far have been therianthropes, and I was pretty sure I would have noticed people with giant leather wings trooping around the halls.)

"Mac didn't like me," she replied, her voice pitched as low as mine. "He said Latin ballroom was primitive and dirty when compared to ballet. I said he was a racist fuck-hole. We weren't friends, you know?"

I couldn't think of anything to say. I just nodded, hoping she could see how sorry I was from my expression. Hoping she would understand my silence.

Malena grimaced. "But, man, he could dance, and when a couple of the guys got on my case for having a funny diet—that whole 'all-liquid, all the time' thing looked sort of like an eating disorder to them, I guess—he told them to go stuff themselves. Said I was a brilliant technician who was wasting herself on an inferior form of dance, and that I was worth twenty of them. He wasn't a *nice* guy, but he was a *good* guy, you know?"

"I do," I said quietly. I've known my share of good guys who wouldn't know nice if it bit them in the ass. Sometimes I liked them a lot better than the alternative.

"He was a good guy," said Malena again, almost meditatively. She went silent after that, and I let her. She was the one who'd just suffered a loss, not me. She knew what she needed better than I did.

The hallway beneath us was motionless. The stage techs were gone, and all the other dancers would be home by now. I wondered whether the charms that kept anyone from noticing when the eliminated dancers disappeared would also prevent them from noticing that Malena, Pax, and I hadn't come back. If we died here tonight, would our friends make up stories to explain why it was perfectly reasonable that we had left our things in our apartments before quitting the show?

The thought of Anders and Lyra trying to explain the number of knives under my mattress was briefly entertaining, but only briefly. The Aeslin mice would have to find their way from Burbank to Portland if I disappeared, and while that might sound like the premise of a children's book—colony of talking, intelligent rodents travels hundreds of miles to reunite with their human protectors—the reality would be cruel, and bloody, and probably end with the deaths of all the mice who'd volunteered to accompany me. The Aeslin counted on us to protect them. I couldn't protect them if I was dead.

Seconds slithered by, piling up until they transformed into minutes. The minutes began doing the same, until I had no real sense of time; I just knew my calves ached from holding my position for so long, and that it was getting difficult to keep my eyes open. Carefully, I shifted around to plop my butt down on the rafter and dig my phone out of my pocket. It was almost midnight. We'd been waiting here for more than two hours, and nothing had happened.

"This doesn't make any sense," I muttered. "Something's wrong."

"What do you mean?" asked Malena. She twisted her head at an angle that a human spine would have been hard-pressed to achieve, narrowing her eyes. "I didn't hear anything."

"That's what's wrong. Grandma's not an ambush predator. She should have gotten bored by now." And she hadn't. The basement door was still closed; Alice had yet to make her reappearance. "Something's wrong."

I pressed my knees together, lifting my weight up onto the heels of my hands. Then, without a pause to think about what I was doing, I pushed myself forward, off the rafter and into free-fall.

The descent was exactly what I needed to clear my head, and as I fell, I felt the sleepiness slip away, leaving me awake, alert, and plummeting. The first two were good things: the third, I'd been counting on. Spreading my arms so that I was swan-diving toward the rapidly approaching floor, I snagged one of the guide ropes used to hoist things up into the rafters, pulling myself in and looping my arms around it so as to maximize my drag without ripping all the skin off of my hands. My speed of descent dropped by more than half. I hooked a foot around the rope, and suddenly I was sliding as gracefully as a fireman down a pole.

I tightened my grip on the rope when I was a foot or so above the ground, bringing myself to an abrupt and relatively painless halt. Unwinding my foot from the rope took a second longer—long enough for Malena to race down the wall and step onto the floor, shaking away her lingering reptilian attributes with a rattle of spines that were there when the noise began and gone when it finished.

"What the fuck?" she demanded.

"Gravity and I have an agreement," I said. "I treat it with respect, and it doesn't smear me across the nearest flat surface." The basement door seemed larger now that I was on a level with it—larger, and more dangerous. I took a deep breath, stepped forward, and turned the knob.

The stairs on the other side were empty.

The place where Alice should have been was unoccupied. I stared at it for a moment, trying to process what I wasn't seeing. Then I bent and touched the concrete. It was cool. She'd been gone for a while.

There was a rustling sound behind me as Malena stepped closer. I didn't turn. "Go find Dominic and Pax," I said tightly. My hand found the butt of my gun almost without my consciously deciding to draw it. If Alice was missing . . .

My paternal grandmother was one of the deadliest people I knew. The rest of us were good, but she was the result of Covenant training and techniques combined with decades of doggedly pursuing traces of her lost husband across a hundred hostile dimensions. For our attackers to have taken her without making a ruckus was almost as unbelievable as it was terrifying.

"What are you going to do?" asked Malena.

I looked at the stairs, stretching down into the dark, and swallowed. There was really only one thing I *could* say, much as I disliked it.

"I'm going to find my grandma."

Fourteen

"I don't figure I'll have a headstone. I don't honestly figure I'll have a grave. Just a dark spot on the ground somewhere, and the knowledge that when it mattered, I wasn't good enough. I guess I never really was."
— Alice Healy

The Crier Theater, descending a flight of stairs down into the dark, like that isn't the worst idea ever

I WALKED DOWN THE STAIRS, taking my time, sure with every step that this would be the one where my foot found my grandmother's body. The door was open behind me, providing enough light that I wasn't worried about missing a step and falling, but not enough light for me to see what was ahead.

"Grandma?" I didn't dare shout. I could still hiss, calling down into the dark in the hopes that if she was wounded, she would hear me and respond.

There was no answer.

My foot hit level ground. I squinted my eyes shut as I felt along the wall for the light switch, finally clicking it on to reveal ... absolutely nothing.

The bodies were gone. The blood was gone. *Alice* was gone. There was no sign that anything bad had ever happened in this room; it was just a gray box with a few folding chairs against the walls, too out of the way and inconvenient to be used even for storage. I stayed where

I was for several seconds, staring in disbelief at the emptiness.

"Grandma?" I whispered.

The room, in the way of empty places with high ceilings, bounced my voice back at me. Not enough to form a true echo, but enough to make sure I knew I was absolutely, unquestionably alone.

That was the final straw. I launched myself at the nearest wall, shoving the folding chairs aside as I scrabbled at the concrete, looking for a crack, a seam—anything to betray the presence of a hidden door or secret passageway. I was willing to accept that we were up against people who could use magic to clean a room without leaving a trace. I was a lot less willing to accept that they could somehow get into and out of that room without using the *door*.

If they were capable of teleportation, we were fucked, and I was going to find a safer line of work. Like naked alligator training at the Gatorland amusement park over in Florida.

I'd just knocked over the last row of folding chairs when someone grabbed my elbow. I whirled, free hand already cocked back and ready to swing. My eyes registered Dominic's presence in the nick of time, and I halted with my fist barely an inch from his nose.

He raised an eyebrow. I stared at him, panting and panicked. He let go of my elbow. I lowered my hand.

"What happened?" he asked, and his voice was soft enough to make me feel even worse about nearly punching him. He was clearly trying not to startle me more than he already had.

There's a special sort of awful feeling that comes with making your husband look at you like you're some sort of dangerous animal. Up until that moment, I had never fully experienced it. After that moment, I could have gone a long, long time without feeling it again.

"Blood's gone," I said. I straightened, hearing footsteps on the stairs, and looked over in time to see Pax making an appearance. That was good. The less I had to explain later, the better off we were going to be. "Bodies are gone. *Alice* is gone. There has to be a hidden door. They can't be teleporting. That takes a ridiculous amount of power. Someone would have noticed."

"No, but perhaps they can be manipulating the stone, or using a dimensional rift," said Dominic. "There are more ways to be secretive than I care to consider. The first bodies were found in a different underground room, were they not? How many such rooms does this establishment have?"

I paused. "I don't know," I admitted, after a moment's thought. "One basement-level room is weird enough in California. Two . . . this place could be half belowground for all I know." Belowground . . . I smiled.

Dominic nodded approvingly. Pax took a step back. Apparently, my smile wasn't as reassuring as I'd always thought it was.

"You've put a piece in its place, and now you're calm enough to tell me about it," said Dominic. "Pray, do, and do not make me worry about you *and* your missing family."

"She's your family, too, remember; marriage has a lot to answer for," I said. "We're *underground*. This is earthquake country, and we're *underground*. That's not the sort of construction decision you make on a whim. Adrian built this place. Either he did a lot of excavation that would have looked weird to his network sponsors, or he built on top of something that already existed. Malena!"

Malena's head appeared at the top of the basement door. From the angle, she was clinging to the wall again, hanging upside down. I didn't know enough about chupacabra to know whether that was normal for her species, or whether it was something uniquely Malena.

"What?" she asked, shouting down the stairs rather than descending.

"We need to look for more underground rooms. There's a chance Alice is in one of them." I didn't think she would be, but now that I was starting to put together the etchings and outline of a plan, I was going to see it through.

"Got it," she said, and vanished again.

I turned back to the boys. "We're going to check all the rooms that could share a wall, or even a corner, with this one. And then we're going to go talk to some friends of my grandmother's about colonialism."

Pax looked baffled. Dominic, who was more accustomed to the way my brain worked, smiled, utterly content with this turn of events. I was in motion now. As anyone who's ever worked with dancers could tell you, that was when I was at my most dangerous.

We didn't find any traces of Alice—or any blood—nearby. We did find four more underground rooms, one of which was only accessible by going through a door hidden in the back of a janitor's closet. Dominic and I had been forced to go into that one alone: both Malena and Pax had wrinkled their noses at the smell of the cleaning chemicals on the shelves, and refused to go any farther until we confirmed that something was actually down there.

Nothing was down there. Nothing but spiders and concrete and the faint scent of mold. Most of the underground rooms had been like that: perfectly squared corners, perfectly smooth walls, and wasted storage space. The ones that did have things stored in them seemed almost haphazard—folding chairs in the room where we'd found the bodies, a few pieces of old stage equipment in another, and some sad-looking costumes in a third. The stairs were an obstacle, sure, but given how over-packed all of the aboveground storage rooms were, I would have expected the crew to have been bleeding off more of the excess. So why weren't they?

Dominic and I returned to ground level, where a quick glance at my phone confirmed that it was coming on one in the morning. "All right, here's what we're going to do," I said. "Dominic, no one knows your face. Go hail us a cab. That way, if Adrian has anyone watching the theater, he won't see one of us doing it. We're all going to ride back to the apartments, and then Dominic and I are going to go see some friends of my grandmother's."

"Nope," said Malena.

I raised an eyebrow. "Excuse me?"

"I said, nope. Nuh-uh. Not going to happen. Because from where I'm standing, it sounds like you just said 'hey, other half of the party, we're officially in a horror movie now, so how about you two go off on your own, don't worry, nothing bad will happen.'" She smiled tightly, and her teeth were sharp as rocks protruding from the desert floor. "My mama didn't raise no fools. We ate them. I'm sticking with you."

"Malena is right about safety in numbers, but I'll go back to the apartment anyway," said Pax. "Anders and Lyra need someone to keep an eye on them, and if you're not there when Lyra wakes up, she'll assume you went for a run or something. If I'm not there, she'll decide we're having an affair. I don't want to have that fight with her. Do you?"

"Not in this lifetime or any other," I said, suppressing a shudder. Lyra was a good friend, and always had been. But between her crush on Pax and the need to keep certain aspects of my life secret from her, sometimes she seemed like just one more obstacle—an obstacle that had to be placated from time to time, to keep her from feeling like she was being replaced.

Valerie didn't have those problems. Valerie was just another dancer, and anything she needed to hide would be mundane and understandable. Sometimes I envied Valerie, even though I knew that her life was simple only because she didn't actually exist. Maybe that was always the secret to a simple life. Reality was the complicating factor.

"Meet me at the back of the theater," said Dominic, disappearing through the nearest exit. We waited a count of thirty before following him.

The night outside was as dark as Burbank ever got.

The sky was painted with soft orange light from the streets below it, and illuminated billboards rose above the buildings at irregular intervals, disrupting any decent stretch of shadows. Batman would have taken one look at the cover available here and vanished right back to Gotham, never to venture forth again.

I loved it so. If only it hadn't been connected to so many things that weren't worth the effort it took to keep on loving them.

"All this cloak and dagger security is cute, but I'm not sure it's necessary," said Malena as we walked toward the back corner of the theater to wait for Dominic and the cab. "Those confusion charms you found are going to have people convinced that they saw us half a dozen times over the course of the night."

"Yes and no," I said. "They can make people suggestible, and they can falsify general memories, but they're all here, at the theater. If Lyra decided I was sneaking around with Pax, a bunch of memory charms wouldn't be able to convince her otherwise. She'd use that to explain why she wasn't concerned when she couldn't find me. Really powerful memory charms could rewrite a lot more, but none of us would be going to rehearsal. We'd decide we'd already been, and go hang out in the lobby." Dancers loved to dance. Dancers loved to move. Dancers loved the moment where a new routine came together and the whole world made sense. But no dancer, ever, had loved being shouted at by a choreographer who couldn't believe the arrogant stupidity of the dancers they had to work with. Each and every one of us would skip it if we could.

Malena nodded thoughtfully. "So they have to split the middle. Powerful enough that we don't notice when things are out of place, but weak enough that they don't disrupt the show. Do you think it could be one of the choreographers? They like it when we come to rehearsal."

"I know it's not one of us; I know it's not Brenna," I said. "That's about where my knowledge runs out."

"How do you know it's not Brenna?" asked Pax. "She's close enough to the dancers that any of us would follow her into a dark corner without thinking twice. She's tall, too. Strong. She could probably subdue most of the dancers on this show without a problem." He didn't add that he was one of the few dancers too strong for her to take down. He didn't need to.

I was too busy gaping at him to point that out. He'd just identified one major flaw in our intelligence gathering: namely, the fact that protecting the status of the various cryptids I knew had been so drummed into me for so long that I'd never thought to ask whether they knew each other. "I know because Brenna asked me for help the first night of the show," I said. "She and her sisters need me to broker an introduction to the dragons of New York for them."

There was a moment of stunned silence as Pax and Malena worked through the implications of this statement. Then they exploded, both of them speaking at once.

"—can't be serious, there's no way in hell that Brenna Kelly is—"

"—she's too *nice* to be a dragon princess, it doesn't make any—"

"—thought they were only interested in gold, not in reality television—"

I put up my hands, motioning for them to quiet down. "I didn't tell you before because it wasn't mine to tell; I'm telling you now because you need to know that she's a friend. Dragons can be greedy and self-interested. In this case, that works in our favor. If she and her sisters want access to the male of their species, they won't do anything that might get me hurt." I didn't bother reminding them that "dragon princess" was an outdated, inaccurate term. It was going to take a while for the phrase to work its way out of the language—assuming it ever did. A female cat was a queen, and a male harpy was a harrier. Why shouldn't a female dragon be a princess? There were definitely more insulting words in the world.

"So it's not Brenna because the profit is in a successful show, not a bunch of dead dancers," said Malena. "Shit. Brenna Kelly's a dragon? Shit. I gotta tell my mother she was wrong when she said no one had ever been able to hide forever."

"She didn't hide forever," said Pax, with a faint note of black amusement. "Verity blew her cover. Good going, Verity."

"I do what I can," I said. A yellow cab came gliding around the corner with Dominic in the front passenger seat. He pointed at us, clearly signaling the driver. The vehicle pulled to a stop and we all piled in.

I looked back as the cab pulled away. I couldn't help myself. The Crier Theater loomed behind us like some vast, hulking beast, squat and hungry and obscene. My grandmother was in there somewhere, or had been, when she was lost. We had to get her back.

We had to.

The drive home was silent, save for the crackle of the radio and the occasional muttered directions from Dominic, who seemed content to be the most memorable one in the car. Our cabbie hadn't been within range of the confusion charms, and might remember us later if anyone asked. A short redhead, a tall Latina, and a massive Pacific Islander didn't get into cabs in this area every day. I spent the time bent over my phone, sending the new assortment of gruesome snapshots to my father. Hopefully, this would tell him more about what we were up against. If it didn't, I didn't know what we were going to do.

We asked to be dropped two blocks from the apartment. Better safe than sorry, especially when talking about people who were treating my colleagues like their own private hunting ground. Dominic paid the driver, and the four of us stood on the sidewalk, watching as the cab slid off into the night.

"Pax?" I said, once I was sure we were alone.

"I'll do my best to get inside quietly. If Anders wakes up, I'll tell him we were hung up at the theater trying to console Malena. He knows we've been getting close to her recently. He'll believe it."

"All right. If you see Lyra—"

"If you see Lyra, tell her I took Verity home with me after we left the theater; too upset to deal with the fact that we'd lost someone from my season," interjected Malena. "Feel free to make like Mac and I were super close, instead of just people who'd danced together a time or two. Sell it as hard as you can, and we'll be besties if that's what it takes to make it look legit."

"You do make the most remarkable friends," said Dominic dryly.

Malena looked at him and snorted.

I touched Pax on the arm. "Be safe," I said. "If anything seems out of place, come find us. Don't be a hero."

"I have a family at home to worry about," said Pax. "I have no interest in being a hero."

"See, I have family, too," I said. "Having a family seems to be the trigger that keeps forcing people to heroism."

"You're a good person, Verity, but I swear, I'll never understand humans," said Pax. With that, he turned and walked away, heading for the apartments and leaving me alone with Dominic and Malena.

Both of them turned to look at me, Malena expectantly, Dominic with the sort of quiet patience that had seen us both through so many potentially life-ending encounters. They were good backup. Maybe not as good as my entire heavily armed family, but still ... with these two standing beside me, there was a chance that I would come through this alive. That was more than I'd had a few weeks before.

I'd take it.

"My grandmother bought a motorcycle when she got to Southern California," I said. "Since there's no parking at the apartments, she's been keeping it with a local family of ghouls who live nearby. They have a garage."

"So?" asked Malena.

"So ghouls are like bogeymen: they prefer to live underground. They don't here in Southern California, which is odd until you account for the earthquakes—but even then, they usually have tricks and techniques that let them build in seismically unstable areas. So why are they living in houses? Why not burrow and reinforce the walls?"

"Maybe they did, and something came and took their burrows away from them," said Malena slowly. "Like how chupacabra used to mostly live in cactus patch burrows, until humans decided it was time to clear the land. No cactus, no convenient cover for your scrape. No convenient cover for your scrape, you may as well get a condo."

"That is the most practical approach to industrialization I have ever heard," said Dominic.

Malena shrugged. "You do what you gotta do. Besides, it's hard to run plumbing into a burrow, and this girl likes her showers."

"I think someone *did* come and take their burrows away," I said. We were almost to the hole in the fence, following the path Alice had shown me earlier. Dominic and Malena looked at me. I shook my head. "That sort of subterranean construction would have needed to be done before this area was so overbuilt—if not, it would have attracted a *lot* of attention. We know the ghouls moved to California before it became part of the United States. They were in this area when it was still a part of Mexico. So I ask again, why would they be living in houses?"

"They wouldn't," said Malena. "Not unless they had to."

"Exactly," I said, and ducked through the hole in the fence.

The cul-de-sac on the other side hadn't changed: it was still run-down, still smaller and shabbier than the Burbank I was accustomed to. Dominic looked around without comment. Malena walked a little straighter, clearly more comfortable now that we were in a place where the shadows were not only allowed, but encouraged to gather.

The little girl was on the lawn again, her tea party set up in front of her with all the care and precision of a royal wedding. She looked up as we approached, tensing. I realized I was still wearing my wig. I was about to reach up and snatch it off when Malena smiled, showing a mouthful of inhumanly sharp teeth.

The little girl visibly relaxed before asking Malena a question in that same almost-French language she'd used when speaking to Alice.

"Sorry, pudding," said Malena. She had a slight lisp now, no doubt brought on by the size of her teeth. "Spanish, I can do. English, I can do. French, I can't do. Do we have any languages in common?"

"I speak French," said Dominic. "That was not French."

"It was Acadian," said a male voice. I turned and found myself looking at a group of three male ghouls. There was no mistaking their species: not with their grayish skin and jagged teeth. All were fully grown, and taller than me. None of them looked pleased by our presence. "No one here speaks it, so it serves us well within the community. Keeps eavesdroppers at bay. There a reason you're talking to our Aurelie? Last time I checked, it was considered socially inappropriate to talk to someone else's children without their permission."

My grandmother trusted these people enough to rent garage space from them. I took a breath, took a step forward, and said, "My name's Verity. Alice Price is my grandmother. She's renting space in your garage."

Their spokesman frowned. "That didn't so much answer my question as it danced around it in a big circle."

I relaxed. "You know me."

"The dancer? Yeah, we know you. She's right proud of you, you know. Why are you here, and who are your friends?"

"Malena," said Malena. "I'm a chupacabra."

"Dominic," said Dominic. "I'm ..." He hesitated, clearly looking for a definition that wouldn't send us plunging into deeper water. He finally settled for, "I'm married to the dancer."

"I can vouch for him, and you know my grandmother can vouch for me," I said. "Please, I need to talk to whoever's in charge here. It could be a matter of life or death."

"You got that right," said another voice, again from behind us. This time, it was female. I risked a glance back. Three ghoul women had appeared on the lawn. One of them was holding Aurelie, who looked more annoyed about the disruption of her tea party than anything else.

It must have been nice to be young and unaware of the dangers of the world around you. I didn't have that luxury anymore, if I ever really had. I looked back to the men, and said, "She's missing. Alice is missing. She disappeared in the basement of the Crier Theater, where we were trying to catch the snake cult that's been sacrificing my fellow dancers. I know we're not welcome here, and I know we're not friends of yours, but please. If you know anything about that place and what's underneath it, we need to know. I need to get my grandmother back."

The ghoul who had been speaking for the others blinked slowly, looking at me in confusion and disbelief. "Alice Price-Healy, missing? Are you sure?"

"She went into the basement to wait for the killers. She never came back out, and she wasn't there when we went down to look for her." I nodded. "Missing."

The three ghouls looked at each other, confusion and concern struggling for control of their expressions. Whatever they were thinking, they weren't making an effort to hide it, and I wished once again that Sarah were with us.

Finally, the spokesghoul turned to us and said, "Come inside. We need to talk about the theater."

Fifteen

"The only bad neighbors are the neighbors who try to kill you, discredit you, or steal your lawn equipment. All the rest can be good, in their own ways."

—Enid Healy

The sitting room of a family of urban ghouls, trying not to worry about being eaten alive

THE HOUSE WAS SURPRISINGLY NORMAL INSIDE, although my impressions may have been influenced by my own weapon- and taxidermy-draped childhood. The furniture was the mix of Ikea and Goodwill that I expect in any home that doesn't have its own interior design team. The wallpaper was old enough to have faded into a dusty purple, and the windows were covered by blackout curtains. That made sense: ghouls are primarily nocturnal. Keeping the windows covered during the day would let them keep their own hours.

We walked through the living room to the converted bedroom that served as their sitting room. I noted the toys scattered on the floor. Aurelie might be the only child living here, but she certainly didn't lack for the trappings of childhood.

"You know, there's a witch in Ohio who makes fashion dolls for cryptid kids," I said, as our guide motioned for us to take our seats. All six adults had followed us inside, after putting Aurelie back down on the lawn.

Apparently, she wasn't in any danger if we weren't there. Humans ruined everything. "I could give you her info, if you wanted."

One of the ghoul women perked up. "Really? Because we've just been buying her the gray-skinned Monster High dolls and telling her to ignore the stuff about them being zombies."

"Really," I said. The spokesghoul was starting to look impatient. I offered her an apologetic smile, and said, "I'll bring it by later."

"For a woman who has managed to mislay a member of her family, you certainly spend a great deal of time discussing fripperies," said the ghoul.

"I'm so worried about her that I feel sick," I said. He gestured toward our seats again. This time I sat, sinking into the slightly musty-smelling embrace of a couch that must have been almost as old as I was. Dominic and Malena settled wordlessly on either side of me. "Alice is the oldest, most dangerous member of my family, and she's *gone*. How am I supposed to defeat something that can take her out? How am I supposed to tell my father I lost his mom? But I can't stop paying attention to the world just because I'm scared. I'm too well trained for that."

The ghoul nodded. "Your grandmother was a good woman, and she spoke highly of you. That doesn't make you our friend. We have allowed you to enter our home because it was better than having this conversation on the street. Please don't mistake pragmatism for welcome."

"What my father is trying and failing to say is that we'd appreciate it if you didn't show up here all the time; our neighbors can be a little nosy," said the woman I assumed was Aurelie's mother. "They like the idea of getting us in trouble with our landlord."

"Never going to happen," said one of the other women. She slanted a glance in my direction and said conspiratorially, "The house is owned by a dragon princess. As long as we pay our rent on time and don't burn it down, she doesn't give a fuck how pleasant we are to live near. May the Great Rot bless and keep the greedy ones."

The dragon princess was probably part of Brenna's Nest; it's rare to have two groups of dragons in the same metropolitan area, even when it's as big as Los Angeles. I managed a wan smile, turning my attention back to the group spokesman. "You said we needed to talk about the theater. Please. What can you tell me?"

He took a deep breath. He looked older and wearier when he let it out again, like he'd used all his energy in getting us this far. "The Crier Theater was built over a warehouse complex that used to belong to us."

"Not just us," interjected Aurelie's mother. "Us, and the bogeymen, and the hidebehinds. A whole bunch of the subterranean species. We all clubbed together to build the place."

"Note how my daughter says 'we' when she didn't exist at the time. Then again, neither did I. But my grandparents were a part of the group that put up the money, back when this land was more open, and it was easier to bury such things in the bowels of the permits department." The old ghoul heaved a sigh. "I was born there. I grew up there. I saw my first communion there, and met my wife beneath the warehouse roof. It was glorious. We'd built a world right under the noses of the humans, and we never once saw the sun when we didn't want to."

There were a lot of questions I wanted to ask, some of which would probably lead us down very dark roads—like "What did you eat?" Ghouls are the only obligate carnivores we know of among the hominid species, and their meat of choice is usually human. They'd been content feasting on corpses until embalming and cremation became the norm. These days, they mostly go for live prey. A lot of disappearances can be traced back to the ghoul community. Since I didn't want to get into a fight with these people while I was asking them for help, I held my tongue.

"We owned that land fair and square. Bought it in

parcels and kept it in the family for as long as we could.
We even paid our taxes reliably and on the regular,
which is more than most of the humans around here
could be bothered to do. But they got us anyway. Said we
were an 'eyesore,' and started chasing loopholes." The
elder ghoul's voice turned bitter. I still didn't know his
name. That was probably intentional. Humanize the
child, because she was vulnerable, and they didn't want
her getting hurt. Hold themselves apart, hold themselves
back, because they were adults and could damn well defend themselves.

I hated that we lived in a world where that sort of
calculation was necessary, where we could search the sky
for aliens and ignore the sapient species living in our
neighborhoods and shopping in our stores. Even more, I
hated the fact that I was helpless to change it.

"Let me guess," I said, as gingerly as I could. "Estate
taxes?"

The ghoul nodded. "They came at us with lawyers. Said
we hadn't filed the correct paperwork for inheritance, and
we'd have to come up with money if we wanted to keep
our place—a *lot* of money, because the land had become
valuable while we were squatting on it and keeping to
ourselves. Taxes got them through the door, and then they
found a hundred code violations that needed to be fixed,
a thousand upkeep flaws that needed to be resolved. We
were smart enough to know they'd just keep coming, all
those clever humans and their wicked lawyers, until they
had what they wanted. So we sold while we could still
make a little money. Enough to resettle ourselves, even if
we'd never be as comfortable, or as much at home."

"Couldn't you move somewhere else and start over?"
asked Malena. The ghoul turned to look at her. So did
Dominic and I. She flushed, but shrugged and pressed
on: "There's lots of open land in New Mexico. You could
build another warehouse, or buy an old airplane hangar,
and try again. Hell, there are whole cities for sale, if you
know where to look. Some of them even have liquor
licenses."

"I was born in Southern California," said the ghoul. "My daughters went to school here, met their husbands here. My wife was consigned to the Great Rot here. I don't want to go anywhere else."

"Neither do I," said Aurelie's mother. She cast what could only be described as a fond look at her father, and said, "I'm a Valley girl. This is where I'm supposed to be. Aurie may feel differently when she gets older, when she gets tired of having humans in every direction. She'll be the one who moves to a warehouse in the desert, not me. Although I guess I'll follow her once there are grandkids."

"Grandchildren change everything," said the spokesghoul.

Right. "That's why I'm here," I said, trying not to sound impatient, even as I stressed the words as hard as I dared. "My grandmother is missing. If you were missing, sir, don't you think Aurelie would want to be able to go after you? I need to know about the Crier Theater. Please."

"I'm getting there," he said—but he didn't sound annoyed. If anything, he sounded approving, like he'd been hoping I'd push a little harder. "They tore down our whole complex. People rejoiced. Said it was a beautification project. The people who'd bought the land built a shopping complex there. It failed—something about sabotage and rats in the walls that kept chewing the wiring—"

"You say 'rats,' I say 'vindictive hidebehinds who didn't appreciate being rendered homeless,'" interjected his daughter.

"—and the place sat empty for a good ten years," finished her father. "We were starting to put together a plan for buying it back and making our new home in the mall when that Crier fellow swooped in with his big network bank account and bought the whole thing lock, stock, and barrel. He tore it down, and built his new theater over the bones."

"Which explains why there are six basements," I said. "The shopping mall wouldn't have seen the need to fill them in, and Adrian might not even have known they were there." Or maybe he had, and that was why there were unmarked doors in the halls. He'd left the unused spaces accessible but ignored. That was better than hiding them. Hidden things got found, after all.

The elder ghoul stared at me for a moment. Then, slowly, he said, "No."

"No?" I asked.

"No," he repeated. "No, there are not *six* basements. That was our *home*. Haven't you been listening? For fifty years, we lived and died in the warehouses he tore down to build his theater."

The warehouses had been torn down before Adrian got there, but somehow I didn't think pointing that out was going to make me any friends just now. "What are you saying?"

"He's saying six basements wouldn't be enough for a community the size of ours," said his daughter. "That place is a honeycomb. There are *dozens* of underground rooms. Some of them probably still have hidebehind illusions covering the doors, too. We may have all lived in the same place, but that didn't mean they ever trusted anyone who wasn't part of their clade."

"Well, Verity, I'm impressed," said Dominic. "You seem to have found the only reality show filmed atop a labyrinth. Good for you. That's some remarkable bad decision making."

I slanted a look in his direction. "Are you making fun of me?"

"Me? Make fun of you? Never. I'm simply doing my best to mock your way of looking at the world, to conceal my own sudden, bone-deep terror."

"Right." I took a deep breath before putting on my most winsome smile, looking back to the ghoul, and asking, "I don't suppose you have some sort of a map?"

The ghoul blinked.

They had a map. It was incomplete, missing most of the areas constructed by the hidebehinds, but it was a *map*, and all it cost us was the promise of eight hundred dollars and a favor to be determined later. (I would have been happier with more money and less favor. "Favors to be determined later" are the way people wind up breaking into tombs looking for the lost idols of spider gods who really just want to be left alone. To select a purposefully nonspecific example.)

"So now what?" asked Malena. She was walking on my left, keeping close. I couldn't blame her. The ghouls had followed us out of the house and were on the lawn with Aurelie, watching us go. They weren't the only ones. I wouldn't have wanted to wager a guess as to how much of the neighborhood was nonhuman, expats from their private, lost community—but I was assuming it was more than just the one household. Shadows moved on front porches as we passed them, and bushes rustled in ways that implied watchers larger than the average raccoon.

"Now we head back to the theater and start searching the basements for signs of our missing people." I couldn't say "bodies." Not yet. Alice was one of the most dangerous women in the world. She couldn't be dead. It wasn't believable.

"I'm sorry, but no," said Dominic.

I actually stopped walking to stare at him. Malena did the same. If anything, she looked more surprised than I did.

"What did you just say?" I asked.

"I said no," he said. "You can't return to the theater right now."

"Dominic, my grandmother—"

"Is a terrifying force who can take care of herself. That, or she's no longer in a position to suffer. Either way, we need to retain access to the theater. I can get inside, but that won't help us in the daylight." His expression, as much as I could see it through the gloom, was grim. "You must return to the apartment. Get enough sleep to let you dance tomorrow. Both of you. I'll go to the theater and search until the morning shift arrives. I'll meet you out back with the map and with anything I've managed to learn before I go to get some rest."

It was a good plan. It was better than "we all run around half-cocked and hope things work out for the best." It still felt like a betrayal. "I should be there. She's my grandmother. And we shouldn't be splitting the party."

"She's my family, too, and I don't have other commitments," said Dominic. "Let me do this. Let me help. As for splitting the party . . . that was inevitable. I can't exactly have a sleepover. At least this way, I'm doing something useful."

"You heard the man," said Malena. "I *really* don't want to get eliminated. I don't know if you've noticed, but we're eight for eight in losing the people whose names come up. My plans depend on me not being dead."

"Fine, fine," I said. "But you're coming back to the apartment with me before you go."

Dominic frowned. "Why?"

"Because you're taking some of the mice with you."

Now it was his turn to look unhappy. "Must I?"

"Yes. You must. If anything happens to you, I need to be able to find out what." I started walking again, forcing him to follow me if he wanted to remain in the discussion.

Malena grabbed my arm. I turned to look in her direction, and she scowled at me.

"Mice? What the hell are you talking about? I'm sleepy, too, but the sleep-dep hasn't kicked in yet. Have you been staying up all week?"

"Oh, right, you don't know. Malena, I have a colony of Aeslin mice living with me." I ducked through the hole in the fence. "They remember everything they see. We should have moved them to the theater a week ago. They'll help Dominic search the place, once we explain what we need."

Malena's mouth fell open, her eyebrows shooting toward her hairline like they'd just decided to secede from her face. "You've got to be kidding. Aeslin mice are a myth."

"No, they're an endangered species, and there's nothing mythical about them."

She turned to Dominic, apparently expecting him to side with her. Instead, he shook his head and said, "The mice are real. The mice comment on my hygiene, diet, and sleeping habits. The mice are not a myth, much as I might sometimes wish otherwise."

"Okay, I need to get some sleep, but before that happens, I have *got* to see this."

I almost laughed. "Come on. Let's get this over with."

Breaking into the apartments was easy, thanks to Alice's lax approach to simple human things like "locking the goddamn window." We slithered into the apartment below mine, me first, followed by Dominic, and finally Malena, who had the good sense to remain outside until she was sure the coast was clear. I motioned for her to close the window. Once it was shut—and locked, for a change, although that wasn't going to last—I moved to the center of the room, cleared my throat, and announced, as loudly as I dared, "I seek audience."

There was a long pause. Longer than normal: normally, the word "audience" would have them popping out of nowhere like a bunch of tiny rodent jack-in-the-boxes, all cheering wildly. But even talking pantheistic mice need their beauty sleep, and it was well past the hour when most of the faithful would have taken themselves off to bed.

After several minutes had ticked by, Malena flung up her hands in disgust. "This is the weirdest prank a pair of humans has ever tried to pull on me, you get that? There's something wrong with your entire species."

"And lo did the Violent Priestess speak unto the congregation, and she did say, 'Ain't Nothing Wrong with Most People which couldn't be Fixed with a Good Smack Upside the Head,'" squeaked a small, rapturous voice from the direction of the floor. Malena jumped nearly a foot straight up. The mouse continued, unperturbed,

"Then she did deliver a Good Smack Upside the Head to her husband, the God of Unexpected Situations, and All Was Well."

Malena turned to stare at the wainscoting. The mouse, which was sitting politely with its tail tucked around its feet and its cloak slung back over its shoulders, fluffed its whiskers forward as it stared back.

"Greetings, therianthrope," it said deferentially. Aeslin mice were remarkably canny about some things. Being polite to predators was one of them.

"Uh, mouse," said Malena. "Mouse, talking. Talking mouse. In the apartment. There is a talking mouse."

"Okay, it's fun to listen to you chaining your way up to a complete sentence, but we don't have time for this right now," I said and knelt, holding out my hand for the mouse to scamper onto. Once it was settled on my palm I straightened, turning to present the mouse to Malena. "Malena, Aeslin mouse. Aeslin mouse, Malena. Malena is a friend, and will not eat you. Right, Malena?"

"Uh, sure," said Malena, sounding unsettled. That was a common—and sensible—reaction to meeting an Aeslin mouse for the first time. She wasn't screaming and running away, which put her ahead of a lot of people. "Hello, mouse."

"Greetings, friend who will not eat me," said the mouse. It turned to me, forcing its whiskers forward in an expression of polite curiosity. "Why do you beg audience, Arboreal Priestess? Have we displeased you in some way? For the hour is Late, and you have said, many times, that we must Let You Sleep."

"You can hear the capital letters," said Malena, sounding even *more* unsettled. "Did you notice that? It talks, and you can hear the capital letters."

"You get used to it," said Dominic.

"What he's not saying is that before you get used to it, the mice make lots and lots of comments about your sex life," I said. I focused on the mouse. "I asked for audience because I need your help. Can you wake the colony?"

The mouse looked conflicted. Normally, that would

have been amusing enough to distract me from the business at hand. Normally, it wasn't almost two o'clock in the morning, with the clock counting steadily down toward the start of rehearsals. "Why?"

"The Noisy Priestess is missing. We need to find her, but if we want to retain our access to the place where she disappeared, I need to get some sleep. Dominic is going back to the theater, and I want you and the rest of the colony to go with him." Aeslin mice could fit in places where no human could ever go. They could escape through cracks and squeeze through holes in the foundation. And they never, ever forgot anything they saw or heard.

There was no guarantee the Aeslin eidetic memory would be enough to override the compulsion charms on the theater, but there was a chance. Given the situation, I'd take whatever chances I could find.

The mouse looked horrified. "The Noisy Priestess, missing? Vanished from our sight? I shall Ring the Bells. I shall Sound the Alarms. I shall—"

"You shall wake the colony and get them down here, to accompany the God of Hard Choices in Dark Places back to the theater," I said firmly, before the mouse could work itself into a full-blown panic. "I'll be there in the morning. You can sleep in shifts, and report whatever you find to either one of us, Malena, or Pax. You remember Pax, right?"

It was a foolish question, designed to snap the mouse out of upset into indignation. It worked exactly as intended. The mouse sat up straighter, pushing its whiskers back in pure outrage, and squeaked, "The man who is not a Man, but is also a Fish," it said. "I know him well. We all know him well."

"Good, then you know you can trust him," I said, bending to set the mouse back on the floor. "Go gather the rest of the colony. Tell them it's an emergency."

"I go," said the mouse, and put action to word, vanishing through a hole at the base of the wall almost faster than my eyes could follow.

I stayed where I was, crouched and looking at the empty space where the mouse had been. I was so tired. My grandmother was missing, and all I could think about was how nice it was going to be to crawl into my bed, pull the covers up over my eyes, and forget about all this for a little while.

It was a very Valerie reaction. Maybe I'd been trying to become her a little too hard, and was starting to lose track of the difference between my pretend self and my real one. Even more worryingly, maybe I was starting to forget which one was which.

A hand touched my shoulder. I looked up. Dominic was standing beside me, looking concerned.

"Get up," he said, offering me his free hand. I took it. He pulled me to my feet. "You'll be no good to anyone, not even yourself, without a few hours of rest and some food in you. You're not letting your family down. If anything, by seeing to yourself, you're proving you're worthy of the trust they put in you. Now let me prove myself worthy of the trust you put in me."

"I don't like the idea of leaving you alone," I said.

"I won't be alone. I'll have the mice, and they are a formidable force for good, when not attempting to convince me to portray the entire Covenant in their recreation of your Grandfather's final meeting with the elders." Dominic raised our joined hands to his mouth, pressing a kiss against the back of my knuckles. "Go. Rest. I'll see you in the morning."

"You're both *way* too calm about the talking mice," said Malena.

I had to laugh at that. It was a small, anxious sound, but it was a laugh, and I felt better afterward. "You have no idea," I said. Leaning forward, I kissed Dominic quickly and properly, savoring the feeling of his lips on mine. Then I stepped away, pulling my hand from his. "Come on. Let's get some sleep. It's going to be a big day tomorrow."

Sixteen

"Your real friends will love you for who you are, no matter how many heads or limbs or ovipositors you have."

—Evelyn Baker

The Crier Apartments, nowhere near enough hours later

"WHERE THE HELL WERE YOU LAST NIGHT?"
Lyra's voice cut through the fog of sleep like a knife through a swamp bromeliad. My eyes snapped open a split second before I sat bolt upright in bed, turning to stare at her.

She was standing next to my bed, arms crossed, and a deeply irritated look on her face. "Oh, good, you're awake. Because *I* was awake until almost midnight waiting for you to come the hell home so I could yell at you. What the hell, Valerie?"

That was enough to bring me the rest of the way from disoriented grogginess into full wakefulness. "Lyra, please, stop shouting. What time is it?"

"It's good that we're both talking about time, since you don't seem to have any for me these days," she snapped. "I knew things would be different with your boyfriend and sister hanging around—and don't think I haven't been tempted to report them *both* to Adrian, with the way you've been letting yourself get distracted—but I didn't expect you to go and replace me with a newer model. What's Malena got that I don't have, huh?"

Scales and the ability to walk on walls. I blinked. "Are you *jealous*?"

"Uh, yeah, I am, bitch," she said, without unfolding her arms. "You're supposed to be my best friend. Do you know how few really good friends I have? I'm always dancing, or rehearsing, or auditioning. I don't have *time* to make friends. I came back to this show partially because it would mean seeing you again, and here you are constantly running off with other people." Her face fell. "Did I do something wrong?"

"No! Lyra, honey, no!" I jumped out of the bed and hurried to put my arms around her. "I've just been . . . it's all hard on me. I'd stopped dancing."

Her eyes went wide. "What?"

There it was: the words were out. I took a deep breath, and repeated, "I'd stopped dancing. When I couldn't get work after the show, I decided to do something else with my life. I hadn't danced in months when Adrian contacted me."

"But . . ."

"I came back because I still love it, but I'll be honest, I feel like an alcoholic who took a job at a bar. This isn't my world anymore. Unless I win, I can't *let* it be my world anymore. I'm trying not to fall so much in love that I can't walk away when it's all over." Every word I said was true, and I hadn't been expecting to say any of them.

"Oh, Val," she said again. "I didn't know."

I shrugged. "I didn't tell you."

"How about this Sunday, we have a girls' day, just you and me? We can get pedicures and talk about how much our legs ache."

"I'd like that," I said. "Thanks. What time is it?"

"Oh!" Lyra winced. "I was so surprised, I just forgot! You slept through the alarm, the cars are leaving for the theater in ten minutes. I came to wake you up."

"*What*?!" I let her go, grabbing my makeup kit as I launched myself for the bedroom door. There was no one between me and the bathroom, and I was able to lock myself inside, beginning the quick and dirty process of putting my Valerie-face on.

Ten minutes later, I was standing on the sidewalk with the rest of my season, a fresh wig pinned to my head and just enough makeup on that I wouldn't look dead when the cameras came into the rehearsal room. Pax glanced at me, eyebrows raising as he took in my black yoga pants and loose gray tank top. They were audition clothes, "don't stand out too much" clothes, not "go to the rehearsal and keep the camera locked on you the whole time" clothes.

"You okay?" he asked. The real question—"How much sleep did you get?"—went unasked, but it hung between us, fat and ripe and poisonous.

"I'm good," I said, mustering a smile. "I was just more stressed out about last night's competition than I expected, and I guess I slept doubly hard because of it. I'm totally fine."

"You never oversleep," said Anders, pushing himself into the conversation without a trace of shame. "Remember how you used to wake me up by crouching at the foot of my bed like some sort of freaky gargoyle? You never missed a morning."

"Everybody has a bad day," I said.

Anders slipped his arm through mine, pulling me close. It was a fraternal gesture; there was nothing romantic or inappropriate about it. It still felt unearned. "Like last night?" he asked, voice going sharp and low.

"Like last night," I agreed. I was having trouble finding my inner Valerie today, and without her, I was an interloper in this place. All around me were dancers laughing, gossiping, totally ready for the cars to come and sweep them off to the waiting theater. Even Jessica was smiling as she chatted with Lo. It was like everyone else had fallen into some weird parallel dimension where people weren't dying and everything wasn't awful.

No, wait. I was the one in the weird parallel dimension. I was the one in the dimension where I had no choice but to know how terrible things really were.

Malena sidled up to me as the cars pulled up to the curb. She was wearing more makeup than I was, and her lips were painted a bright, bloody red that lent her the air of a ticked-off warrior goddess, ready to bite the heads off anyone who annoyed her. She pushed herself between me and Anders, forcing him to let me go. I decided she was my favorite.

"I hate everyone," she announced, sans preamble. "Can I ride with you? If I have to listen to Emily and Troy handicapping the remaining dancers for one more minute, I'm going to get myself disqualified."

"There are only three people in your car now," said Lyra, with all the tact and delicacy of a charging rhino. It made sense, after this morning. It was still a complication I didn't need. "Why do you need to cram yourself into ours?"

"Because I asked nicely, and because I'd rather ride with my friends than with a bunch of jerks who insist on plotting out how, exactly, they can win their way to the finals," Malena said. "It doesn't help that Troy's my partner, but cares more about exploring the magical promised land of Emily's pants than about noticing when he's making me uncomfortable. I'm riding with you guys."

Lyra looked like she was going to protest again. All that was going to do was slow us down, and so I made an executive decision, stepping forward, pulling open the car door, and gesturing for Malena to get inside.

"I'll ride in the middle," I said, with more perkiness than I actually felt. "I needed a nap anyway, and I always fall asleep when I'm squished between two people in the backseat."

"Middle child syndrome," said Malena, and winked as she scooted into the car.

Lyra frowned. I grimaced apologetically and got in. Maybe this wasn't the safest thing I could have done when she was already jealous of how much time I was spending with Malena, but I didn't have time to screw around. I needed to get to the theater.

The theater. The more I woke up, the more I

understood that Dominic and the mice had been there alone, all night long. There were no texts on my phone, and there had been no calls; they were probably fine. They were probably fine.

Maybe if I told myself that a sufficiently large number of times, I'd start believing it.

Lyra sulked for the whole drive, while Anders chattered at Pax about the surfing in Hawaii and whether or not Pax was hoping to be home in time for the big waves. Pax gave mild, noncommittal answers. I wondered whether either of them realized the other had effectively no interest in surfing. I didn't feel like pointing it out. I was too busy resting my head on Malena's shoulder—something she endured with stoic amusement—closing my eyes, and trying not to dwell on the worst-case scenarios at hand. There were so many ways things could have gone wrong once Dominic and the mice were alone. Maybe he hadn't texted because he wasn't there anymore. Maybe he and my grandmother had found the same shallow grave. Maybe—

"Val, I'm sorry to interrupt you while you're drooling on my shoulder, but we're here." Malena's words were accompanied by a hard poke in the arm before she brought her lips close to my ear and hissed, "Open your eyes, there's something you need to see."

I opened my eyes.

We'd pulled up to the back door of the theater, which was open and clogged with bodies as the remaining dancers forced their way inside. Pax was already out of the car, with Anders and Lyra close behind him. Apparently, remaining crammed in the car was not on their agenda for the day. I barely registered their absence. All my attention was on the dark-haired, exhausted-looking man standing off to one side and trying to look unobtrusive.

Dominic had acquired a clipboard and badge somewhere, which made my heart leap with something between pride and delight. He'd been paying attention when I talked about the way to integrate yourself into a setting. He looked like a stagehand, and unless he was giving orders or handing out coffee, none of the dancers were going to look at him twice.

"Don't dawdle," said Malena, holding the door for me as I got out of the car. "I can't stop the assignments for you, and you *know* Adrian will notice if you're late."

"I got it," I said, and launched myself at Dominic, wrapping my arms around him and hugging him as hard as I could. I didn't care who saw us. Dancers loved to gossip, and if they wanted to add "is sleeping with a stagehand" to their collection of rumors about me, I had dealt with worse. Sometimes the worse had even been true.

Dominic waited until I let him go and pushed myself back before he said, in a soft voice, "We found many things, but nothing which will lead us immediately to our goal. The map is behind the wardrobe rack in the women's dressing room. I've annotated it as best I could. The mice can tell you what was found in each area. They're still searching, and may need you to help them update the map. There is one mouse in your makeup drawer. It has promised not to jump out and frighten anyone who doesn't really, really deserve it."

I did a quick review of the dancers remaining on the show. "Please tell me you didn't show it a picture of Jessica."

"I didn't, but I was tempted." He deposited a quick kiss on my temple, leaving his lips there for a moment after the pressure of the gesture had faded. "Did you sleep?"

"Not enough."

"Will you be able to get through this day?"

"When you met me I was working as a cocktail waitress, acting as a social worker to half of New York, and still managing to keep fit for competitions and classes," I said, taking a step backward and giving him my best coquettish smile. It lacked a certain sincerity and sparkle, but it was close enough to what I needed it to be. "I'll be fine. You go rest up, and then get back over here. We may be able to finish searching the place after rehearsal is finished."

Dominic's expression was solemn. "Just because we didn't find her, that doesn't mean it's time to assume the worst. She is a brilliantly dangerous woman."

"All the more reason to kill her quickly," I said. "I have to go. I love you."

"I love you as well," he said. "Stay safe." He turned and walked away. He didn't look back before he went around a corner, and was gone.

I was the last one to the stage. Adrian looked up when I entered, and scowled.

"So, the fabulous Valerie Pryor is finally deigning to grace us with her presence," he said. "This is no time to get a swelled head, sweetheart. I don't know if you were paying attention last night, but if you're not in the bottom three this coming week, I'll be a monkey's uncle."

Some of the dancers tittered, Jessica among them. I ducked my head, trying to look humble and chastened.

"I know, I'm sorry," I said. "I haven't been feeling well. I had to stop by the bathroom for some cold water."

As I'd hoped, Adrian's expression shifted, becoming concerned. It was nothing to do with me: even if I hadn't been one of his specific favorites, the show's insurance insisted all medical issues be taken with the utmost seriousness. "Are you well enough to dance today, darling? We can provide a fill-in for your partner, if you're not."

The responsible thing to do would have been to say that no, I wasn't well: I needed to go back to the apartments and sleep off whatever virus I'd managed to pick up. Sadly, it wouldn't have been that simple. The show's medics would have been required to get involved, and by the time they finished filling me with fluids and lecturing me on nutrition—two things that seemed to happen for everything from food poisoning to broken toes and concussions—I would have lost even more time than I was going to waste dealing with the choreographers. I shook my head.

"I think I'm all right. I promise to say something the second I feel otherwise, but after last night, I don't think I can afford to miss the first day of choreography." I didn't have to fake the crack in my voice. Let them assume I was worried about my place on the show, and not about the life of my grandmother and my friends. The best lies were always built on a foundation of truth.

"All right, dear, all right," said Adrian. He waved me to my place on the stage, and didn't say another word about my tardiness.

The drawing of our dance styles from the hat went quickly after that. Anders and I got the Argentine tango, to my immense relief. I—or rather, Valerie—had been nationally ranked in that style more than once, and I could handle the rehearsal in my sleep, no matter how difficult our choreographer tried to make it. Pax and Lyra got hip-hop, while Malena and Troy pulled contemporary. Malena looked unhappy about that, but there wasn't time to reassure her before we were all being hustled off to our individual rooms to get to work.

It was more than an hour before I could duck away, making a vague excuse about needing to go to the bathroom. We were with Marisol Bustos again, the show's go-to for the Argentine tango, and she seemed relieved to have me stepping out of the room for a few minutes. It would give her time to focus her attentions on Anders, who frankly needed them much more than I did.

(Which wasn't to say that she was going to go easy on me in the days ahead. I knew Marisol, and worse, Marisol knew what I was capable of. I could underperform today, since I had the whole "I don't feel well" excuse going for me, but come tomorrow, I'd either need to step up my game or see the show's medics. That meant I needed to take care of this *today*.)

I hurried down the hall, bypassing the restrooms on my way to the dressing room. Luck was with me, maybe for the first time since I'd decided to come back on the show: there was no one else there. Quickly, I made my way to the main wardrobe rack, crouched down, and whispered, "I seek audience."

"HAIL!" The cry was muted—the mice were making an effort—but loud enough that I glanced over my shoulder, waiting for a PA or stagehand to stick their head in and ask what I was shouting about. When no one appeared I relaxed, marginally, and turned back to the wardrobe rack.

The mice were starting to appear, lining themselves up neatly as they bristled their whiskers and waved their paws in the air, jubilant over my appearance. Only about half the colony was present; the rest must have been running around in the basements, looking for signs of Alice. They'd been making the most of their time in the theater: fully half of them had strings of beads or sequins wrapped around their necks, and one was clutching a bag made from an ankle sock, stuffed to its absolute limit with feathers.

"Have you been chewing on costumes?" I asked.

"No, Priestess," said the mouse at the front of the group. "All we have Taken, we have Found, for did not the Well-Groomed Priestess say unto us, What Has Been Discarded, You May Have, But Don't You Little Monsters Nip My Embroidery?"

"I'll believe it," I said. "I'll try to find you a shoebox to put everything in. I can sneak it back to the apartment, no problem."

The mice cheered again. Then they sobered, and the lead mouse said, "We have not found the Noisy Priestess. We have failed you."

"Woe," moaned the mice, in unnerving unison.

The last thing I needed to deal with was a crisis of faith on the part of my Aeslin mice. "You haven't failed me," I said hurriedly. "Anything worth doing is worth working for, right? We're being challenged right now.

That means we have to stick with it, and we'll find her."

Whether or not we'd find her alive . . .

No. I couldn't dwell on that, or on the fact that maintaining my cover meant I was dancing while my grandmother was missing and potentially dead somewhere underneath the theater. For the sake of the mice, I had to remain positive.

That was a lie, too. For the sake of my heart, I had to remain positive. If I let my positivity fade, I would lose my grip on Valerie: she would collapse like the house of cards she was, and I would have to face the fact that I didn't belong here, I never really had, and everything was going wrong around me.

"You are Wise," said the lead mouse solemnly. "We have searched three more of the chambers below the ground. Dark they are, and vile, and filled with scuttling creatures."

"They were delicious," piped another mouse.

"Assuming you mean the scuttling creatures, there; go on," I said. "What did you find?"

"No sign that anyone had walked in those dark places for many days and nights, Priestess," said the lead mouse, shooting a glare at the mouse that had dared to interject. The Aeslin enforced a fairly strict hierarchy among themselves. It was possible for a mouse who wasn't part of the priesthood to go years without speaking directly to a family member. It had always seemed a little unfair to me, but since I wasn't a part of the colony, I figured it wasn't my place to say anything. "There was neither trace nor track of the Noisy Priestess."

"Okay," I said, despite the fact that this was anything *but* okay. "How many rooms do you have left to go?"

The mouse slicked back its whiskers, looking despondent. "Truly, we Do Not Know," it said. "Each time we think we have reached the end, we find another door, another chamber. Two of the rooms we have searched so far were not present on the Helpful Map."

"Which means you're starting to find the hidebehind

areas, which were never on the map to begin with," I said. "Great. Do you need me to do any annotating?"

"Please," said the mouse, with all the solemnity of someone who had just had a great and unexpected favor bestowed upon them.

I fished the map out from behind the wardrobe rack and spent five minutes making notes to match the things the mice told me. Here was a door, here was a staircase with two treads missing, here was a good place to hunt centipedes. Dominic's handwriting was large and spidery and reassuring. Mine was tight and compact, filling in the space between his notes.

When I was done, I handed the pencil back to the lead mouse, said, "Come find me if you find any trace of her," and left to the sound of muted rodent cheering, fleeing back to the rehearsal room, where Marisol was just starting to get impatient waiting for me.

Thank God for the Argentine tango. Any other dance form and I would have been falling on my ass. As it was, Marisol kept snapping corrections to my form and ordering me to get my face under control. After the third time I'd mechanically performed the same piece of footwork, she clapped her hands and shouted, "Stop!"

We stopped.

Marisol turned off the music before turning on me and demanding, "You! What is *wrong* with you? A broken heart? A broken ankle? Tell me you have broken *something*, and that you're not making a mockery of my rehearsal without an excellent reason!"

"I'm not feeling well," I said, without hesitation. The trick to a good lie: keep it simple, keep it consistent, and for the love of God, keep it unprovable if you possibly can. The second people start demanding proof, you're done.

"Valerie, I have seen you dance with walking pneumonia. You slid yourself across that stage like you were the rightful queen, and everyone else your subjects. Do not stand there pleading a little stomach flu and pretending it justifies the performance I'm seeing out of you today." Marisol's expression changed, turning calculating. "Unless you've got a secret . . . ?"

For a single panicked moment, I thought my wig had slipped. Then I realized she was looking speculatively at my midsection. "No!" I yelped. "No, I'm not pregnant, I'm just . . ." Anders was in the room. Anything I said would be relayed by him to Lyra and Pax, which meant—given Lyra's fondness for swapping stories with the other dancers—that it would be relayed to the rest of the show by the end of the day. Dammit. I took a breath, and said, "I'm not feeling well, and I didn't really sleep last night. My grandmother isn't doing so good. I guess when you combine the two, I'm not up to my usual standards. I'm sorry."

Marisol blinked. "Your grandmother? I thought—" She stopped herself. It was too late: I already knew what she thought, because I was the one who'd told the original lies. Little Valerie Pryor, whose family didn't want her. Too obsessed with dance to be a good girl, too obsessed with winning to be a bad girl. To have me saying I was upset because my grandmother wasn't well probably made about as much sense to her as a gorgon going vegan would make to me.

I didn't have to work to bring the tears to my eyes. The real challenge was keeping them contained. Once summoned, they threatened to overspill and overwhelm me. "She's always been happy for me to be whoever I want to be. She's just one of those people, you know? But we don't get to see each other much, because she lives really far away. I got the call last night."

Even Anders looked sympathetic. I was all too aware of the cameras rolling. Adrian would get this footage before the show next week, and he'd play it, even if America's vote put me solidly in the bottom three. This was the last time the judges could save someone. A story about a sick grandmother might be enough to make them save me.

The thought made me feel ill. I didn't want to use my

grandmother as a rope to pull myself to safety; I wanted to save *her*. More, I wanted to cling to the idea that she was still alive, somewhere in the dark beneath this building. I wanted her to be fine and furious with the world, kicking and biting and gnawing through her own chains if that was what it took. Grandma Alice was a constant. She was going to outlive the rest of us, because that was the way the world *worked*, and now here I was, proving to the world that I was the weakest of her grandchildren. This was going to be on television. My parents would see me using her as an excuse.

And I didn't have a choice in the matter. I stopped holding back my tears and let them run down my cheeks as I gazed miserably at Marisol, waiting for her to say something.

She looked flustered. "My poor dear, I had no idea—I didn't know you were in contact with any of your family. Why don't you take some time to compose yourself? I can work with Anders while you're indisposed, and I know you'll be able to catch up anything you miss."

"Yeah, Val," said Anders, looking equally concerned. "We don't start learning the group choreo until after lunch. That should give you a couple of hours to put your head together and get back on your feet."

"Thank you both," I said, still crying. Now that I'd started, I couldn't seem to stop. Before either of them could say anything else I turned, grabbed my dance bag off the bench near the door, and left the room.

This was an unexpected reprieve. I was going to do as much with it as I possibly could.

For most people, going from well-lit dance studio to underground labyrinth full of weird smells and damp patches would seem like some sort of punishment. For me, it was a normal day's work.

I descended the stairs as carefully as I could, wishing I had more for light than the bare bulbs overhead. They

were bright enough when I was directly underneath
them, but they were spaced out such that there were
bands of darkness between them. I'd never appreciated
the practical applications of interior decorating so much
in my life. A couple of Tiffany lampshades and this whole
hallway would have been lit up like Central Park at
Christmas.

"Are we almost there?" I asked.

"Very nearly, Priestess," said the Aeslin mouse on my
shoulder. It was clinging to my earring with one paw,
keeping itself stable as I descended. "The second search
party did say, lo, we are going this way, and the rest of us
did say, yea, though you walk through the hallway that
was not on the map, you should fear no evil."

"Gonna pretend you haven't started parodying the
Bible and just keep walking, if that's all the same to
you."

"As you say, Priestess."

It was sometimes difficult to tell when Aeslin mice
were joking. They *did* have the capacity for humor, and
could be amused by the damnedest things. I resisted the
urge to turn and eye the mouse. If it was still holding my
earring when I moved my head, I could wind up knocking it off my shoulder, and that would make the remainder of my descent a lot more interesting than it needed
to be.

The stairs were in reasonably good shape, considering
that I was now at least two levels below the street and
still going down. The air was damp and tasted of mildew.
"How did you find the hallway if it wasn't on the map?"

"The wall appeared intact, Priestess, solid as stone and
capable of withstanding any attempts to breach it. But
the air flowed through it all the same, as from a crack the
size of a valley." The mouse's whiskers tickled my ear.
"We sent the juniormost priest to see what was on the
other side, and she stepped through the stone, and was
gone. When she returned, she reported a great, wide hall,
lit with these same bulbs, filled with these same shadows."

"Was the false wall still there for her after she came

back through? I mean, could she still see it when she looked?"

"The false wall never rippled or changed, Priestess. It was like smoke—visible to the eye, but invisible to the nose or paw."

The mouse was describing hidebehind work. It had to be. They were experts at hanging an illusion on the smallest available hook, spinning scenes like spiders spun their webs. It was part of what kept them so well hidden. In a world where even the most secretive cryptids were being dragged, one by one, out into the light, most cryptozoologists had never actually *seen* a hidebehind. So far as I was aware, there were no pictures of them, only paintings and sketches done from rare eyewitness accounts. I'd spoken to the hidebehinds of Portland at great length—had even served as an impromptu marriage counselor for a couple who used to live under the supermarket downtown—and I couldn't say for sure whether I'd ever seen one. They were that good at what they did, and what they did was disappear.

That left me with one big concern. "Will you be able to find your way back to the false wall when we get there?"

The mouse's whiskers tickled my ear again, this time in quick, staccato bursts: it was laughing. "It can be easy to forget, Priestess, that you are in some ways less attuned to the world around you than we are, for you do not need to be: in your divinity, you may face all challenges without flinching, without need to be prepared to scurry and hide. The air passes through the wall, and will ruffle my fur and carry the scent of such dangers as might await us beyond the veil that is no veil. I will lead you true, Priestess. You will be Proud of Me."

"You're riding my shoulder into the dark below a theater, where no one can hear us scream. Trust me, mouse, I'm already proud of you."

I couldn't see the mouse on my shoulder, but I could feel it puffing out its fur with satisfaction and delight. Sometimes it was easy to keep the Aeslin happy.

Sometimes it was incredibly hard.

My foot hit the bottom of the stairs as I passed outside the sphere of the last of the overhead lights. Darkness fell, surprisingly profound, especially considering how close I was to the stairway. Glancing upward, I could see the naked bulbs glittering like beckoning stars, offering an escape from the certain death that waited up ahead. That, too, was hidebehind work. They were good at all sorts of illusion, from visual to emotional, and they never missed a trick.

"Now where?"

"Walk forward, Priestess, and do not be afraid; the wall will not harm you."

Being afraid of a wall was only common sense, considering I was walking blindly into the dark. The mice were good about not steering us wrong. I took a deep breath and kept going, taking three long steps into the black—

—and into the light. One second I was in the dark underground hall, and the next I was in another, much brighter hall. The overhead lights were equipped with small button shades that distributed their illumination smoothly over the entire area, putting the mold-speckled walls and linoleum floor on full display. It was clear no one had done any cleaning down here in quite some time.

It was equally clear that people had lived here, once. The linoleum was the sort usually installed in low-rent apartment buildings and public kitchens, places where mud might be tracked in from the outside, where children played and messes were made. It didn't look industrial or cold. It looked like the front hall of a community center, one that had been inexplicably abandoned by its residents.

Or maybe not so inexplicably. The entry was hidebehind construction, and the hidebehinds had been a part of the original community. They must have left with the rest, either because they no longer felt safe, or because they couldn't bring in the supplies they needed without passing through the human-controlled parts of the building. I looked up, following the exposed wiring between the lampshades. It vanished into the corner of the hall. I was willing to bet that this hallway, and any others like it, had been illicitly wired into the city power grid, providing a low drain so constant that no one had ever noticed it.

"This is where you left the other group, right?" I asked.

"Yes, Priestess," squeaked the mouse. "They were to continue searching the rooms until their shift passed, or one came seeking them."

"Okay, that's good. That means we're not totally alone down here." I started walking forward. Either the hide-behinds hadn't made any effort to conceal the doors on the other side of their clever gate, or there were more rooms down here than made sense, strictly speaking. It seemed like I passed a room every five or six feet. Most of the doors were closed, but the space between them and the floor was enough for a determined Aeslin mouse to squeeze through.

"Shall I call them for you, Priestess?"

"Yes, why don't you d—" I stopped mid-word. "Wait."

There were footsteps coming down the hall, sharp and quick and unmistakably bipedal. They were coming toward us from around a corner up ahead.

The hall was effectively featureless, leaving me no-where to hide except the obvious. I whirled and tried the knob of the nearest door. Locked. I tiptoed as quickly as I could back down the hall, my heart hammering against my ribs. I wasn't unarmed—I hadn't voluntarily gone anywhere without a weapon since my eleventh birthday party—but if this came down to a fight, I couldn't be sure that I was going to win. I didn't know what was coming down that hall, and my parents didn't raise me to charge in blind when there was any other option.

The second knob turned under my hand. I pushed the door open, not letting go of the knob, since I didn't want it to bang against the wall, and ducked inside. The room was dark, but that didn't matter as much as getting out of the hall.

Easing the door most of the way closed, I braced myself against it, ear to the wood, and listened.

The footsteps got louder. A female voice, muffled by the semi-closed door and distorted by the hallway, said, "I thought we'd be done by now."

I couldn't recognize the speaker, not with the way the environment was working against me, but I could pick up on her tone. She was *pissed*.

"I told you, this isn't an exact science." The second voice belonged to a man. Apart from that, I couldn't say. "Sometimes it takes four, sometimes it takes fourteen. There's a reason we brought back the last five seasons."

"Yeah, ratings, and that arrogant bitch insisting we had to stick to the Top Twenty format even when we weren't having auditions. Why does she have so much pull with the network?"

"She's the face of the show. They need to keep her happy." The man's voice was calm, even reasonable: he was clearly the one in charge, and doing his part to manage his companion's mood.

I was glad I was hidden, and no one could see the relief in my expression. The only person who could be described as "the face of the show" was Brenna—even Adrian wasn't as recognized as she was, and wouldn't be identified as quickly on the street. Brenna had been instrumental in putting together the All-Star season, but she hadn't been part of the plan to sacrifice us to the snake god. I'd already been pretty sure of that. Having it confirmed was still reassuring. For one thing, it meant there wasn't an entire nest of dragons arrayed against me.

"This is all pointless. We could use anybody."

"This particular snake god prefers talented sacrifices. Young people at the height of their powers. We give it what it wants, and it will give us what we want. Feeding it the staff would just anger it. You just need to have patience."

"I don't want to have patience. I want to have results."

"Soon," said the man.

Their footsteps faded off down the hall, leaving me and the mouse alone in the dark. I started to ease the door open, to look after them, and froze as I realized that it wasn't that dark anymore.

The wall behind me was glowing. Nothing that glows—apart from stars on a ceiling, or glow sticks at a rave—has ever been a good thing.

Well, crap.

Seventeen

"The difference between a last stand and a Tuesday afternoon is all in how many bullets you had at the start."

— Frances Brown

Somewhere below the Crier Theater, woefully underprepared for whatever's about to burst through that glowing wall

THERE WAS TIME TO RUN: I was at the door, and a step would see me in the hall, putting more distance and some barriers between me and whatever was coming through the wall. But there'd be nothing to stop it from following me out, and more, something that could pass through solid stone might be the answer to the question that had been gnawing at us all. Where were the bodies going?

I was about to find out.

"Get down," I hissed, pulling the pistol from the small of my back. The mouse obeyed without hesitation, tiny claws digging into me as it ran down my front. The light from the wall got brighter. I tensed, readying myself for whatever happened next.

The light began consolidating into straight lines, one about seven feet up from the floor, the others descending from its ends. I realized what it was a bare second before the middle went black and someone stumbled into the room.

The semi-spectral door continued to glow, but it

wasn't enough for me to see what I was aiming at. I took aim anyway, clicking off the safety with a swipe of my thumb. The newcomer straightened, head snapping toward the sound. Then it spoke, calm and clear and far more collected than I was feeling at the moment.

"Verity Alice Price, if you shoot me, your father is going to tan your hide."

"Grandma?!" I started lowering my gun. Then I stopped, eyes narrowing, and took more careful aim. "Prove it."

"For your sixth birthday I got you a ballerina Barbie and a bear trap. A real bear trap. No bear, though. Your mother thanked me for the thought, but said a real bear would have been a bit much, given you were no bigger than a whisper, and she didn't want you getting eaten."

"Grandma!" This time I clicked the safety back into place before lowering my pistol and shoving it into the waistband of my yoga pants. "Are you hurt? What are you doing down here? *How* are you down here?"

"Can I ask one?" For the first time, I heard the weariness in her tone. "*Where* is down here? I've been trying every door and egress charm I had on me, and most of them opened on dimensions you don't want to visit. I was down to my last three options. If this hadn't worked, I would have needed to go back to Naga for another set, and that could have taken months."

No one in the family really understood how Grandma managed her particular brand of dimensional transit, not even Mom, who sometimes joined her on her journeys. (Mom used a more traditional blend of door-opening herbs, supplied by a Letiche she'd known since college.) Uncle Naga was involved. The rest was more than she'd ever been willing to tell us.

"We're in the subbasement of the theater, behind a set of hidebehind illusions," I said. "I got a map from those ghouls you're renting the garage from."

"How did they—"

"The theater was built on the top of their old home, and Adrian didn't bother to fill in the underground levels. I don't think he realized most of them were *here*. Not all the rooms are on the map, and some of the ones that are have illusions blocking the door."

There was a prickling on the front of my shirt as the Aeslin mouse accompanying me ran back up to my shoulder, clung, and jubilantly cried, "Hail and welcome! Hail to the return of the Noisy Priestess, who was missing, but not on Pilgrimage!"

"Hello, mouse." Alice managed to inject a note of warmth under the exhaustion in her tone. "Thank you for helping my granddaughter look for me."

"It was an Honor," said the mouse, virtually vibrating with joy.

The light from the wall guttered and went out, leaving us in darkness. There was a pause before Alice asked, "Do you have a flashlight?"

"No, but I have a door." It had been long enough since the footsteps in the hall had passed that I wasn't worried about running into their owners—and if I did, well. I wasn't outnumbered anymore. Even exhausted, Alice was worth her weight in pissed-off badgers.

Opening the door flooded the room with light from the hallway. I squinted. Alice walked forward until she was standing beside me, her own eyes narrowed against the glare.

"This isn't hidebehind work," she said. "The construction is pure bogeyman."

"It was a composite community," I said. I was trying not to stare.

The tattoos on her left shoulder were gone. Not covered in dirt, or scarred—cutting a charmed tattoo could sometimes release whatever effect it had been designed to contain—*gone*. The skin was smooth and clean, like it was never tattooed in the first place. There were clear places on her arm as well, cutouts shaped like birds or eels or strange, twisty things from the bottom of the sea.

Alice saw me looking and smiled wryly. "I told you, I've been burning charms as fast as I could. It leaves a mark."

"I always wondered how you got your tattoos to change." It was an inane comment. It was the best I could do in the moment.

"They're one-use only, and they don't do subtle; whoever grabbed me didn't come with a damn glowing door," said Alice. She looked around the hall, expression calculating. "How far underground are we? And what time is it? There were some temporal distortions in there."

I didn't want to ask what that meant for her—how long she'd been trying to get back to us, or how long it had been since she'd slept. Those were questions for later. "It's Friday morning. Around eleven, I think? You only went missing last night."

"Thank heaven for little favors," she said.

The mouse on my shoulder, not to be outdone, proclaimed gleefully, "HAIL!"

"That, too," said Alice.

"As for how far underground we are, I went down two flights of stairs, each about twenty feet long. So we're deep enough to be a problem if an earthquake hits. And there's more." I took a quick breath, gathering my thoughts, before I launched into a summary of what I'd overheard while I was hiding in the room where Alice had emerged.

When I was done, she was frowning, and so was I. Another thought had occurred while I was speaking, and this one was unsettling, to say the least. "Grandma, if you were trying all night to get back to us, how is it you came through in the room I was actually *in*? That seems like a pretty big coincidence."

"Coincidence is just another word for an accident that doesn't kill you," said Alice. "My transit charms are set to drop me as close as possible to a family member, if there's one in the area I'm traveling to. It wouldn't do me any good to finally find the dimension where your grandfather is and wind up on a different continent, now would it?"

Reminding her that Grandpa Thomas wasn't likely to

be anything more than bones and memory by this point didn't seem like a good idea. I just nodded.

"As to why I came out down here . . ." Alice's frown deepened, turning pensive. "Which direction did you say they came from?"

We walked down the hallway side by side, pausing only so I could set the Aeslin mouse on the floor near a convenient break in the wall. It scampered off to locate the rest of the colony and pass on the news that Alice had been found. They would keep searching the theater for confusion charms and signs of what the snake cult was up to, but they'd do a better job if they weren't consumed by worry for the family's senior priestess.

The difference in our stride was almost startling. We were roughly the same height, but where I stalked, she prowled, like she was daring something to jump out and have a go at her. It was the difference between a brawler and a technician, and while I wouldn't have wanted to meet her in a dark alley, I was reasonably confident that in a real fight, I would have been able to get out of the way before she could lay a finger on me. Give her a gun or a blunt instrument, and the tides would turn in her favor. Everyone had their own strengths and weaknesses.

That thought brought me back to our snake cultists. What about *their* strengths and weaknesses? Their magic-user must have been the one urging patience, and saying the spells they were using weren't an exact science. Magic was never an exact science; only science got to use that particular label. Magic was more like cheese making than chemistry, depending frequently on "when it feels right." When the spell felt right, they'd be able to rip a hole in the wall of the world, and their target giant killer snake would come tumbling right through.

If the male had been the group's magic user, the female voice belonged to . . . who? A female cultist, an administrator, a lure? It wasn't Brenna, which was still a relief, but apart from that, I had no real idea who it was or what purpose she would be serving. Lindy, maybe. Lindy never did like the dancers as much as she pretended to, and there were certainly ways that a snake cult could have appealed to her. But it was hard to imagine her willingly sacrificing her ballroom dancers to a giant snake, no matter *what* she'd been promised.

Alice's thoughts had apparently kept pace with mine, because she asked, voice low, "Have any of the other dancers seemed off to you?"

"Jessica always seems off," I said. "Doesn't mean I think she's murdering people. I mean, I guess she could be, but it's . . . messy. She doesn't like messy. Anders has been a little touchy-feely lately. He had a crush on me the first time we danced together. He could be testing the waters to see how serious I am about 'Daniel.'"

"What about Lyra?"

I blinked. "From my season? The one who beat me? That Lyra?"

"Yes." Alice glanced in my direction, gauging my response. "I don't know much about the competition, but I know enough to check a roster, and your season is the only one that hasn't lost anyone. Season five has been totally eliminated. Pax is in the clear because he's a giant shark. You dance with Anders, which would make it hard for him to sneak around behind your back. It might not be a bad idea to take a good look at Lyra, and see what there is to see."

"Lyra couldn't kill anybody," I said doggedly. "Lyra's my friend."

"Sweetie, if being a friend of the family made you immune to murderous impulses, no one would like us anymore."

"No one likes us now."

"That's beside the point."

The hallway ended at a steel door. It was bigger than the doors around it, with a frame that appeared to have been hammered straight into the wall. "Probably the sewer exit," I said, and opened it.

We both stopped. We both stared. Neither of us said a word.

The room on the other side was roughly the size of

the theater above—we were probably *under* the stage, considering the direction and distance we had traveled to get here. It was a great cavern of a room, stretching upward into the unbroken dark, lit by bulbs strung like outside Christmas lights along the walls. There was no furniture. There were no decorations.

There were only the bodies of my eight fellow dancers, arrayed at the center of the room like the spokes of a wheel. Smears on the concrete floor showed where they had been rearranged as their number grew, going from a simple cross shape to something more elaborate. Their heads were at the middle, and their hands were joined, one to another, until they formed an unbroken circle. Whatever magic had been used on them was preserving their bodies; Raisa and Graham, who were eliminated in week one, looked as freshly killed as Mac and Leanne, who'd been dead for less than a day.

Something pressed hard against my mouth. I realized it was my hand. I was crying, too, but that seemed to be of little consequence. They weren't going to sweep *this* room looking for bodily fluids. The blood would obscure anything else.

Alice squeezed my shoulder. She didn't say anything. I appreciated that. It was dangerous to stand here in the open like this, but I needed a moment to center myself. Until now, I'd been holding out the hope that the bodies we hadn't found hadn't existed—that maybe a few people really *had* been eliminated and secluded themselves, maybe triggering the idea that "hey, we can kill them without anyone noticing" in our snake cultists. But no. All eight of them were there, silent and unmoving on the floor.

"Okay." I lowered my hand. My voice was thick with tears. I swallowed them away, squaring my shoulders, and said, "Now we can study the bodies."

"That's my girl," said Alice.

We didn't want to rush, but we didn't want to dawdle either: with no way of knowing when our snake cultists might come back, or how many of them there were, we needed to do this in as quick and efficient a manner as possible. Much as I hated to treat my former competitors as a chore to be completed, it was the best way to take care of things. Step back, distance, separate. Do not let them be the people that I knew they once had been.

The hands weren't sealed together; they were just joined, fingers folded over each other until they were reasonably sure of holding. Bobbi and Danny had holes in their palms that matched the ones in Mac and Leanne's, making me suspect the ivory spike was an "every other time" thing, even if I still had no idea why. The runes on each body were subtly different, but echoed the same forms. I took pictures, lighting up the chamber further with small flashes from my phone.

"This is a food preservation spell," said Alice, crouching next to Poppy's body and looking critically at the edges of her wounds. "I've heard of it being used to preserve murder victims, usually when there was a question of whether or not the killer would be brought to justice. It keeps the meat from rotting. There's a price, of course."

"There's always a price," I muttered, and took another series of pictures.

"These bodies are probably covered in a *shell* of frustrated bacteria by now. Don't touch them, and we're washing our hands as soon as we get out of here."

That was enough to make me glance away from my phone. "What? Why?"

"Because I don't want to explain to your father why I let you melt, that's why." Alice stood, moving away from the bodies. "Take your pictures, and then let's get out of here. I feel the strong need to bathe myself in bleach."

". . . oh." Magic didn't supersede the natural world: it just modified it for a while, making some things more possible and other things less likely. Preserving flesh beyond the usual rot-by date would mean keeping the bacteria that would normally be breaking it down at bay.

Not destroying it—not unless you wanted the flesh to be preserved forever. Which brought me to my next question: "How do people eat things they've preserved with these spells if they're always covered in flesh-eating bacteria?"

"There's another set of spells you can use to break the seal when you're ready. Sort of a low-grade local sterilization. It's still not what I'd call *safe*, but it's better than what you'd get if you decided to lick the contents of your pantry."

I wrinkled my nose. "Grandma, that's gross."

"Maybe so, but it's true." Alice stepped daintily over Poppy's legs, walking back over to me. "Do you have all the pictures you need?"

"Yes." I looked around one last time. The bodies of the dead seemed to look at me accusingly. I should have saved them. Maybe not all of them—I couldn't have known anything was wrong when Raisa and Graham had died—but the more recent deaths were absolutely on my head. I just needed to make sure there weren't going to be any more. "Dad should be able to narrow down the school of magic from what we've got so far."

"Good; let's get out of here." Alice started for the door. I followed her.

We were halfway there when it slammed shut and two shadows peeled away from the walls, resolving into rangy male bogeymen in dark jeans and button-down shirts. One of them was holding a pair of knives. The other had a sawed-off shotgun. Both grinned, showing their teeth in what was probably meant to be a threatening display. We were petite human women in a room full of corpses, after all. By all rights, we should have been terrified.

Too bad we'd never been very good at doing what by all rights we should have done.

"You're not going anywhere," said one bogeyman. The other didn't say anything: he just kept grinning, which was either intended to freak us out, or . . . no, he didn't look like a naturally jubilant person. He was trying to freak us out.

"Oh?" asked Alice. Her voice was suddenly an octave higher, filled with the sort of confusion I was used to hearing from first-year dance students. She sounded like she only had two brain cells left, and they were engaged in a fight to the death over who got to pick today's shade of eyeliner. "Are you sure? Because I thought we were going over there."

She pointed to the door. Her hand was empty. Anyone who'd ever met her would have recognized that as a final opportunity for escape. If they backed down now, Grandma might not feel obligated to kill them.

The bogeyman with the shotgun racked a shell into position. "We were hired to keep this room secure. We'll get paid extra for the pair of you. You're pretty. Our boss might like your corpses for his little art project."

"Oh, wow, how much do you know about the sculpture?" I made my eyes big and round, trying to project innocence in his direction as hard as I could. I was better at coquettish banter than I was at seeming like butter wouldn't melt in my mouth, but it was worth a try. I couldn't let Alice have all the fun. "It's really avant-garde. Like, is that real meat?"

"Those are human bodies, bitch, and you're going to join them," replied the bogeyman.

Alice and I exchanged a look.

"Sexist," I said.

"Speciesist," she said.

"Asshole," I said.

"Agreed," she said.

"Eyes front while I'm killing you," snapped the bogeyman, who'd been looking increasingly confused throughout this exchange. Apparently, his targets weren't supposed to banter.

Here's the thing about chatting when you're expected to shut up and let yourself be attacked: if you do it carelessly, it can get you gutted. But if you do it well, before things get bad, it can put your enemies so far off-balance that they don't know what to do next. It's confusing and difficult and problematic. Spider-Man is a master of the art of the battlefield quip. Since he's fictional, the rest of us have to make do with a blank expression and a perky comment about the size of the enemy's knives.

"Gosh, mister, did you know that your knives look really sharp?" I asked, turning my attention to the silently grinning bogeyman. He was starting to look a little white around the eyes, like we'd deviated so far from the script that he no longer knew where to begin. "I mean, *really* sharp. You could probably cut yourself if you're not careful."

"He's going to cut you," said the other bogeyman, lip curling upward. "Enough talk. Killing now."

"Works for me," said Alice, and her eyes were suddenly bright, and her hands were suddenly holding a pair of pistols. My own hands were full of knives.

The bogeymen had time for one wide-eyed "oh, shit" moment before we were in motion, and the fight was joined.

There are jokes about bringing a knife to a gunfight—or the other way around—but the truth is that sometimes it's the right thing to do. I charged the one with the shotgun while Alice advanced on the one with the knives. She was straight-backed and calm, firing three shots before my target had the time to pull the trigger even once. Her target howled.

I was preoccupied with *my* target, who was taking aim at the center of my chest. It would have been a good shot if he'd been dealing with someone who hadn't been training for speed and flexibility since grade school. I saw the tendons in his hands twitch as he pulled the trigger, and dropped into a split as the thunder of his shot split the air where I'd been standing. I flung two knives while he was racking his second shell. They struck him in the knees, and he joined his partner in screaming.

"You know, there was a joke I thought you'd make that you skipped," I said, rolling off the floor and running at him. He was standing, but barely; his knees had buckled when the knives hit. He must have had some training.

There was no other way he could be on his feet after that.

Just before I hit him I pulled back, smiled brightly, and said, "I expected you to say that no one was going to hear us scream." Then I punched him in the throat. He made a strangled choking noise and fell backward, landing on the concrete like a sack of wet laundry.

There were no more gunshots coming from my grandmother's side of the fight. I turned to find her standing over the body of the knife-fighter, a petulant look on her face.

"I broke mine," she said, only half apologetically. She raised her head. "Is yours in any shape to be questioned? Because mine isn't."

"I think so," I said, nudging the fallen bogeyman with my toe. He groaned slightly. "He's alive."

"Great." Alice made a gesture with her hands. The guns vanished back into her clothing, returning to whatever complicated holster she had hidden under her red tank top. All the women in my family were experts at making our weapons disappear, and most of the techniques I knew had been invented by her. She was a pioneer in the field of concealed violence. "Let's get these boys out of here before their bosses come back."

In the end, the most logical thing had been to carry both bogeymen—the living and the dead—down the hall to the room where Alice had made her appearance. As far as we could tell, it wasn't in use by our snake cultists, and while it was dark, the day Alice didn't have a candle somewhere on her person was the day I lost all faith in humanity.

Her bogeyman had leaked as we carted it down the hall, her holding the torso—where the bullet holes were—and me taking the legs. Alice and I used the body to prop my bogeyman up in a sitting position while she went back to mop up the spillage. I lit her candle and sat cross-legged on the floor, waiting for the survivor to wake up.

Seconds ticked by. The door opened behind me. "Is he awake?" asked Alice.

"Not yet," I said.

"Sorry I killed mine," she said—and she did sound apologetic. "I get a little enthusiastic sometimes."

"I know, Grandma. At least you didn't use a grenade." Scraping bogeyman off the walls and ceiling would have been a lot of work, and would have been necessary if we'd wanted to keep our presence in the underground complex a secret. Not fun.

"No," she said. "I didn't think it was appropriate."

The bogeyman groaned. I leaned forward, pressing my palms into the floor and beaming at him. When he opened his eyes, the first thing he saw was my smiling face. He groaned again.

"Hi," I said cheerfully. "Who are you working for?"

He scrabbled backward, stopping when his hand hit the body of his companion. His eyes went wide, and he froze, like a scared rabbit in front of an oncoming car. I kept smiling.

"See, here's the thing," I said. "Right now, you've got some nasty damage to your knees—that probably hurts, huh? I mean, knives are meant to hurt people, that's what they're *for*—but that's all the damage we've done. To you. Your friend, he's pretty dead. I hope he wasn't too important to you. My grandmother gets upset when people come at me with knives."

The bogeyman cast an alarmed glance at Alice. His already grayish complexion, which looked sallow and strange by the candlelight, got even paler as he put two and two together. There weren't many people my age who could go around claiming someone who looked younger than them was their grandmother. If I could . . .

"We didn't have a chance to introduce ourselves before," I said. "Hi. I'm Verity Price. That's my grandmother,

Alice Price-Healy, standing over there. You know, the one who killed your friend."

"Oh, God," moaned the bogeyman.

"What? Didn't your bosses tell you there were monsters in the dark when they left you alone down there?" I leaned closer still, shifting more of my weight onto my hands. "Tell us what you know, and we'll let you live. Don't tell us, and we'll find a way to make you tell us. You probably wouldn't enjoy that very much."

"He could be into pain, dear," said Alice. "It's not nice to judge."

"Sorry, Grandma," I said. I smiled at the bogeyman again. "Sorry. Sometimes I get carried away, too."

"I'm not telling you anything," spat the bogeyman. "You think my life is worth more than my severance package? Bullshit. You Price girls think you're so smart, like you can fix everything just because you've got some big human savior complex, but you can't. You're not everywhere, and where you're not, we have to find ways to handle things for ourselves."

"Severance package?" I asked blankly.

"Verity, grab him," said Alice. She sounded alarmed enough that I moved, lifting my hands off the floor and lunging for his wrists.

I was close. I wasn't close enough. I'd been so focused on intimidating that I hadn't thought about restraint—and why would I have needed to? We'd taken his shotgun away. He was injured and outnumbered. There was no chance that he was going to hurt either one of us.

He wasn't trying to hurt one of us.

A knife, ribbon-thin and sharp enough to gleam in the light from Alice's candle, slid out of his sleeve as he raised his arm to his throat. With a single decisive motion, he sliced lengthwise, and his flesh parted in a river of red. I shouted, a wordless exclamation of dismay, still moving toward him.

Then Alice's arms were around my waist, yanking me away from the arterial spray. She was faster than I had been, maybe because she'd caught on more quickly than I had: she got me clear without a drop of blood hitting my clothing.

"You have to go back upstairs," she said, pulling me back even further. "You can't be covered in blood, or people are going to ask questions."

"*You're* covered in blood," I said, pulling away. She let me go, and I turned to face her. "Won't that raise questions?"

There wasn't that much blood on her when I actually looked, and what there was matched her tank top almost perfectly. She could easily write it off as grease stains or mud. I'd never really stopped to think about my grandmother's wardrobe choices. Suddenly, they were starting to make a terrible kind of sense.

"I'm planning to sneak out the back door as soon as I collect the mice, since I can't be here during the day," she said, tone calm and level. "I need a shower and some sleep. I'll drop the mice back at the apartment, do what needs to be done, and then get my bike and go to check in with Dominic. We need to find Bon."

"For the counter-charms, right." The reality of what just happened was starting to sink in. My heart was hammering against my ribs, and my stomach was filled with sour churning. I wasn't going to throw up—I was too much of a professional for that—but oh, I wanted to. "Grandma, that man just killed himself rather than let us question him. What the hell are we in the middle of?"

"He mentioned his severance package. Bogeymen are all about commerce and contracts. The snake cult probably offered him enough money for keeping their secrets that it was worth his life to get that payout." Alice looked over my shoulder, back to the bogeyman. Her expression softened. "Poor man didn't have a choice. If the contract terms were strict enough, he could have found himself in the position of needing to die or provide an additional sacrifice from his own family. No bogeyman patriarch would be willing to do that if there was any other way."

"Fuck."

Alice nodded. "Yes."

This snake cult wasn't playing softball. Whatever they wanted, whatever they were hoping to achieve, there was no body count too big to make it happen. We were the only ones who were standing in their way . . . and I still had to get back to rehearsal.

Sometimes life just isn't fair.

Eighteen

"Heroes save everyone. Heroes sacrifice themselves for the sake of people they've never met. We're not heroes. We're never going to be. But if that means we make it home alive, I'm all right with that."

—Alice Healy

The Be-Well Motel, about seven hours later

DOMINIC ANSWERED THE DOOR when I knocked, taking in my bedraggled appearance and spiky hat-hair (well, technically, "wig-hair," but that had a confusing connotation) without comment. He opened the door wider, letting me inside. The smell of Chinese takeout assaulted my nostrils a beat before the mice started cheering.

"I thought you were dropping the mice at the apartment," I said.

Alice, who was sitting cross-legged on the room's single bed with a carton of shrimp fried rice in her hand, smiled brightly. "They decided they'd rather come with me for Chinese food and debriefing."

"They're *Aeslin mice*," I said. "They would rather do *anything* that involves food."

"HAIL! HAIL THE WISDOM OF THE ARBOREAL PRIESTESS!" exulted the mice.

"See?" I said. Dominic was waiting patiently nearby. I turned and leaned up to give him a quick kiss on the cheek. "Hi."

"Hi," he replied. "Did the remainder of rehearsal go well?"

"This week's group number is a hip-hop piece set to 'Dragula,' so yes if you like being screamed at to be a better vampire, and no if you're not comfortable doing a dance routine where six of the people have wooden stakes in their hands. Somebody's going to get impaled." I walked over to investigate the Chinese food. "Lyra isn't speaking to me because of the whole 'ditching her for Malena' thing, Anders is telling everybody they have to be nice to me because my grandmother is dying, and Brenna should be here in about twenty minutes, so I can fill her in on what we found under the theater."

"You mean Malena," said Alice.

"No, I mean Brenna," I said. "She's the show's host, and she's part of the local Nest. She needs to know what's going on. Also, the people I heard talking in the subbasement confirmed that she wasn't part of the snake cult, which makes her one of the safest potential allies we have left." The salt-and-pepper prawns were gone, except for a single piece of chitin and a few slices of pepper. I made a sad face.

Dominic tapped me on the shoulder. I turned, and he presented me with a fresh carton of prawns. "I know how much you enjoy the cockroaches of the sea," he said. "Alice was just explaining her plan to find Bon."

"She won't be at the flea market, but she won't have gone far, either," said Alice. "We need to figure out where the routewitches camp in this area, and Bon will be there."

"Which gets us the counter-charms, got it," I said, sitting down on the floor and opening my Chinese food. "It's Friday. The show—and elimination—is next Thursday. We need to find these snake cultists and stop them before that happens."

"On the plus side, we know they're not going to kill anybody before then," said Alice. "The only bodies we found in that room were people you knew."

"Oh, yay: only my friends are in danger." I didn't want to be hungry. My stomach grumbled, and I picked up a pair of chopsticks. "I have rehearsal tomorrow. If that's when you're visiting Bon, I won't be able to come with you. Or we could wait until Sunday and just go see her at the flea market."

"I was hoping to be able to pick up the charms on Sunday, if she doesn't have something already prepared," said Alice. "There's a chance she'll need a little time, and I want us to have them before we go back to the theater Monday morning."

"We'll need them for Pax and Brenna, as well as the three of us and Malena," I said. Putting it that way, I actually felt pretty good about the team we were assembling. I couldn't ask Brenna to fight for us—dragon princesses weren't exactly set up for dealing a lot of damage, and she couldn't beat anybody to death with her spike-heeled shoes—but I wanted her to understand what was going on around her. Having a good source of inside information couldn't hurt anything. It might help.

"That's going to cost," cautioned Alice.

"That's why we have credit cards."

"Routewitches don't take money for things like this. They take . . . distance. Distance traveled, distance seen." Alice sighed and plucked at her shirt. It was another tank top, this one dusky gray. "The shirt I was wearing earlier might work. I went through a lot of dimensions trying to get back to here, and I was wearing it the whole time. That's got to have a little oomph behind it."

"I am glad, I think, that no one in my immediate family was ever a witch," said Dominic, in the slow, careful way he used when he was trying not to offend someone, but knew it might be unavoidable. "It seems very complicated, and like there are a great many rules to be learned and then avoided."

"You're not wrong," I said.

Alice opened her mouth to speak, and froze as there was a knocking at the window. It was light, more a rapping than anything else. We all turned.

"Okay, first person who whispers 'nevermore' is getting kicked," I said.

The rapping came again.

"I'll answer that, shall I?" said Dominic. He walked over to the window, pushing his duster back to expose the hilt of the knife I'd given him for our six-month anniversary. And people say romance is dead.

He unlatched the window and eased it upward, shoulders tense as he prepared for the worst. What he got was Malena's head appearing in the opening, upside-down.

"It is windy as shit and it smells like diapers out here," she said. "I'm coming in."

"By all means," said Dominic, letting go of his duster as he stepped to the side. "I assume coming uninvited through motel windows is a point of chupacabra etiquette, and I should applaud your manners while shaming myself for my ignorance."

"Nah, I'm just rude," said Malena, swinging herself in through the window. Her hands and feet—both bare— were twisted into claws, covered with tiny black-and-orange scales. Spikes had broken through the skin of her shoulders, and pushed up the fabric at the back of her tube top in a disconcerting way. She saw me looking and shrugged, looking almost sheepish. "This is as far as I can go before my face starts getting weird and my tail starts popping out. It's actually a little uncomfortable to stop here, but it's better than getting shot for a monster when I start knocking on windows."

"Right," I said.

"Is that Chinese food?" asked Malena, changing subjects. Her hands and feet shifted back to the human norm, scales replaced by smooth brown skin, as the spikes on her back retracted. In a matter of seconds, no one could have ever guessed that she'd been the monster at our window. That was the trick with chupacabra: they hid in plain sight, except when they didn't want to.

"Malena, why are you here?" I asked. It was a little past seven o'clock in the evening: while she could probably have made a large portion of her trip in the sewers, clinging to the walls to keep her pants clean, she would still have needed to walk aboveground at least partway.

The risk of being seen didn't seem to balance the reward of free Chinese food.

(Although for a dancer, it might come close. When we're working, we're like teenage boys: constantly hungry, and willing to go to great lengths for a free meal. Forget saying "hey kid, go into this cave and bring back the magic lantern for me." You'd have much better luck with "hey kid, go into this cave, there's an unguarded buffet.")

"Because I figured you were going to try cutting me out of things about now, and while I should probably be down with that—I mean, hello, opportunity *not* to rush headlong into certain danger? Sign me up—I'm really not." Malena bared her teeth. "Mac was one of mine. Now he's dead. Whoever's doing this needs to pay. Plus Brenna was on her way over, and she was willing to give me a ride once I showed her my claws."

Which meant Brenna now knew that Malena was a chupacabra. That was a relief: it meant I didn't need to worry about blowing Malena's cover. As a human, it wasn't my place to run around outing cryptids who didn't want to be revealed.

Malena wasn't done. She turned to Alice, frowning, and asked, "Where the fuck did you go? You scared the shit out of all of us." She sounded affronted, like scaring her was some great and profound crime against the laws of nature. Maybe it was. I didn't know much about chupacabra culture, but I wouldn't have been surprised to learn that it was based on firm principles of "don't freak out your neighbor, save that for the humans."

"Somebody who could open masked portals grabbed me from behind, and the next thing I knew, I was in another dimension," said Alice. She made it sound perfectly reasonable, like this was the sort of thing that happened every day, and was no more problematic than breaking a nail.

Dominic didn't take it quite so calmly. He stood up straighter and asked, "How could you tell?"

"The air." We all looked at her blankly. Alice shrugged.

"Most Earth-type dimensions have a breathable atmosphere. Getting access to the ones that don't is surprisingly hard. The spells have all these countermeasures and protections built in and anyway, you can't do it without more prep than my attackers had. They just shunted me to the nearest place they had access to, which hadn't had an industrial revolution on the continent corresponding to North America yet. Everything smelled and tasted different. You develop a palate for that sort of thing once you've been dealing with it for long enough."

Malena was the first to speak: "Lady, you need better hobbies."

"I knit," said Alice.

There was a knock at the door. I put my carton of shrimp down and moved to open it, letting a flustered-looking Brenna into the increasingly cramped motel room.

"Sorry I'm late to the party," she said. "I had to circle a few times before I found a parking space."

"There's a garage across the street," said Malena.

Brenna shrugged out of her coat, expression unrepentant. "It charged five dollars an hour. That's highway robbery, and I'd never be able to explain the expense to my sisters. They're only all right with the size of my car because the studio pays for half my gas, and we can use it on our Costco runs."

Dragons bought in bulk. Of course they did. If there was something that could be done to pinch a penny, they would do it, and so well that it made human coupon clippers weep and beg to learn their secrets. I closed the door.

"How much did Malena tell you?" I asked.

"Just that she wanted a ride," said Brenna.

I looked to Malena. She shrugged. "I figured you were going to do the debrief and I didn't want to take the bus. I'm intrinsically lazy."

"Right." I took a deep breath. Brenna *loved* her dancers. This was going to suck. But the best way to deal with it was quickly. Turning to Brenna, I said, "All the dancers who've been eliminated are dead. There's a snake cult operating inside the building, and they've been using the eliminated couples as sacrifices to try and manifest their god."

Brenna blinked. She didn't say anything.

"I have pictures of the bodies, if you don't believe me. Please, try to believe me. You don't want to see these." I didn't want to have seen them, and I had a lot more experience with death than Brenna did. She was a sheltered dragon princess from an established Nest. There was a good chance she'd never seen a dead body in her life.

Finally, she spoke. "You can't be serious," she said, voice quavering. "We would have noticed. *I* would have noticed. They're my babies. You're all my babies."

"The snake cult has confusion charms tucked all over the theater," said Alice. "Once someone was added to the forgetting portion of the spell, you would have just stopped caring. It's not your fault."

"Who the hell are you, anyway?" Brenna rounded on Alice, appearing to notice her for the first time.

"It's cool, Brenna, she's my grandmother—that never stops sounding weird." I shook my head. "Brenna Kelly, meet Alice Price-Healy. Grandma, meet Brenna. No one is stabbing, shooting, or immolating anyone in this hotel room."

"Please," added Dominic. "I have to sleep here."

"HAIL!" rejoiced the mice. "HAIL THE LACK OF STABBING, SHOOTING, AND FLAME!"

I wasn't sure whether they couldn't pronounce "immolation," or whether it just hadn't fit into their chant. It wasn't worth arguing about. Besides, I had something else to worry about: Brenna, who was staring, open-mouthed, at the colony. This was the usual response to the mice, especially from people who hadn't been warned about them in advance.

We just didn't have time for it. "Yes, they're Aeslin mice, yes, they're supposed to be extinct, and yes, they're with me," I said, before she could say anything. "They're good at keeping other people's secrets, although most family secrets do sort of tend to get worked into the colony's religious rites. Please don't shout."

"Aeslin mice," said Brenna, and for a moment, she smiled. "I never thought I'd see the day. We live in a glorious time, Verity. A glorious, glorious time."

"A glorious time filled with corpses," said Malena, bringing the mood in the room crashing back to the ground. Brenna's smile faltered before fading altogether.

She turned back to me. "Are you telling me the truth?"

"I am," I said, with a quick nod. "I'm so sorry. The confusion charms must have been there from the start of the season. We might not know what was happening to the eliminated dancers even now, if it hadn't been for Pax catching the scent of blood on his way to the car."

"They're cleaning up after themselves so completely that even I can't smell anything after they vacate a room," said Malena.

"I think I may know how," said Alice. We all turned to look at her. "If their magic-user has the equations for dimensional shifts, they could easily be moving the bodies to a nearby level of reality, then leaving the blood behind when they take the rest of the body to a permanent resting place."

"The fuck you say?" said Malena.

Alice leaned over and picked up my abandoned carton of prawns. "This is one thing. If I dumped it out on the bed—which I won't do, Dominic, so there's no need to give me that look—would it still be one thing, or would it become many things?"

"That's semantics," said Brenna.

"That's magic," said Alice. "I could use a spell to shift 'Verity's order of salt-and-pepper prawns' into another dimension, and then use another spell to shift just the carton, or the carton and its contents, back. It's all in how you word it. The whole topic honestly makes my head hurt, but that's why I'm the blunt instrument. Thomas was always the scalpel."

Bringing my family history into an already tense

situation wasn't going to do any of us any good. Quickly, before someone could ask who Thomas was, I said, "So we have eight dead dancers, we have confusion charms all over the theater, and we have a magic-user or users good enough at what they do that they can move people and corpses into other dimensions without a lot of prep work." That last statement earned me some blank looks. I explained: "Even if they came prepared to move the bodies, they wouldn't have been expecting Alice. Since she didn't come back covered in blood, I'm assuming she was placed in a different dimension than all that blood they've been moving around. That means a magic-user who can access multiple dimensions, without having put in a lot of prep work toward doing it."

"That doesn't necessarily imply a lot of strength," said Alice. "They could be very good at doing one specific thing. It's our bad luck that the thing in question is basically a fight-ender when used correctly. It's hard to punch something that's in a different dimension altogether."

"This gets better and better," I said. "Next up, they actually summon the snake god, and we have to deal with it."

"That might be true," said Brenna hesitantly. "They can't let the show make it to the finale. They just can't."

Malena and I stared at her, matching expressions of dawning horror on our faces. Alice and Dominic looked confused.

"I'm missing something," said Alice. "What am I missing?"

"The finale is where they crown America's Favorite Dancer," I said. "The judges and the top four always get to pick their favorite routines from the rest of the season, and then those dancers come back and perform them one more time."

"If *all* the eliminated dancers are dead, they won't be able to have a reunion show," said Brenna. "It would make people notice the disappearances. Either these people expect to have their snake god by then . . ."

"Or they're going to disappear if they haven't

succeeded by the time the call is going out for people to return," I said. "So we're looking at what, we hit the top four and a bunch of people just disappear? That's still a lot of deaths between here and there. It has to stop."

"They're killing based on the elimination cycle, which gives us until Thursday," said Malena. "You have any big monster-hunter genius ideas?"

"We get the confusion counter-charms from Bon, and make sure we're all watching carefully when we're in the theater," I said. "We have a map to the subbasement. We know where they're keeping the bodies. We can find them."

"They have to be someone close to the show, or they wouldn't be able to come and go freely—and they definitely wouldn't be able to get the eliminated dancers to go anywhere with them," said Brenna. "I don't care how many confusion charms you put in the theater. A dancer who's just been eliminated isn't going anywhere with a stranger."

"So we're looking for one of our own, and we need to look fast," I said. "We're running out of time."

No one said anything for a moment, not even the mice. Finally, Dominic broke the silence.

"Would anyone like an eggroll?" he asked.

It was as good a way to move forward as any.

Brenna's big car came in handy for more than just Costco runs: it was big enough, and empty enough, that she was able to give me, Malena, and Alice a ride back to the apartments. Dominic remained behind, with half of the mice. It would make sleeping complicated—since they were assigned to me, not him, they weren't in the habit of obeying him when they didn't feel like it—but it would also mean he could get to the theater early, before first call, and make his way down into the basement levels while the rest of us were still getting out of bed.

(Was I thrilled by the idea of my husband venturing

into the basement of the building with only the mice for company, when there were confusion charms on the place to keep us from noticing right away when somebody disappeared? Hell, no. It was still the best plan we had, and stood a halfway decent chance of getting him inside without trouble from security. We knew we had time before anyone else was killed. That didn't mean we could afford to sit around twiddling our thumbs until the deadline arrived. We needed to *move*.)

As for moving . . . Brenna stopped at a light, casting a glance in my direction before she said, with forced joviality, "It's early yet. Mind making a stop before I drop you lot off?"

"Depends," said Malena. "Will there be an ambush?"

Brenna looked at the rearview mirror, eyebrow cocked inquisitively. "If there was going to be an ambush, would I tell you?"

"You might. I mean, if I were planning an ambush, there's a chance I'd be so surprised by someone coming right out and asking that I'd just tell them."

"But then it wouldn't be an ambush anymore, dear," said Alice. "You'd need to call it something else."

"No ambushes," said Brenna, an air of desperation creeping into her voice. I guess we could be a bit much to deal with, when you weren't expecting us. "I just want to swing by the Nest and warn my sisters about what's been going on. I figure it'll be more believable if I show up with the lot of you."

"They'll be okay with you bringing humans around?" I asked.

Brenna shot me a quick, amused glance. "It's *you*. They'd be all right if I invited you to come shopping in their closets, at least right now. Until we have our meeting with the dragons of New York, you can do no wrong that doesn't end in bloodshed."

"Well, okay, then." I twisted in my seat to look back at Malena and Alice. "You two all right with a stop? Keeping the dragons up to date can't hurt anything."

"More importantly, I can invite them all to this week's

show, once they know what they're getting into, and we can use them as extra eyes," said Brenna. "Adrian will never object to a sudden influx of pretty women in the audience. They don't directly impact ratings, but you'd never know that to hear him rave after we've had a good night."

"I thought people had to pay for tickets to the live show," I said.

Brenna looked amused. "They do, up until there are seats going wanting. If we hit day of show without selling out, then there are people who get paid to come and cheer. My sisters have made a pretty decent sum off of showing up and pretending to be excited on camera."

Another illusion shattered. And here I'd been thinking all this time that I was performing for packed houses because people wanted to see us dance. "Oh," I said.

"Buck up: they usually don't get to come," said Brenna, turning down a side street. "There's still a loyal audience for the show, and people honestly do enjoy the live performances. There's an electricity in the air that just doesn't come across on the screen."

"My whole family watches," said Malena. "My grandfather insists. Once a week, everyone gets together in his living room, and then they all vote for me, even when I'm awful."

"Isn't family great?" asked Alice.

I snorted.

The drive to the Nest took about twenty minutes, passing through dark residential neighborhoods and only slightly better-lit commercial ones, until we came to a small, ratty looking motel with a "No Vacancy" sign flashing in the parking lot like a blind eye. It was a prime example of 1950s Southern California design, with neon and exposed balconies accented by dead grass and battered cacti. Brenna pulled into one of the few open spaces, a beatific expression on her face.

"Be it ever so humble," she said blithely.

"Humble?" asked Malena, craning her neck to see the second floor. Nothing moved behind the curtains, but there were lights on; either someone was home, or the dragons had decided that wasting a little electricity to maintain their cover was okay. "This place isn't *humble*. This is where people go to get themselves *murdered*. To death. By white dudes wearing hockey masks."

"Why specifically white dudes?" asked Alice. Brenna was getting out of the car and so we all followed suit, closing our doors behind us. The car beeped once as Brenna pressed the button to lock it. She might live here, but even she didn't trust the neighborhood.

"You ever see anybody else slap on a fucking hockey mask and run around filleting coeds for no good reason? It's always some bored white guy. It's like Scooby-Doo. People think it's teaching you all these big lessons about how monsters aren't real, when really it's just showing kids over and over again that when something seems out of whack, there's probably some old white dude behind it."

Alice looked thoughtful. "You know, you may have something there."

"I do not have the spare brain to have this conversation right now," I said, and hurried after Brenna, accompanied by the faint cheers of the Aeslin mice riding in the hood of my sweatshirt.

We were taking Aeslin mice to visit a Nest. May the heavens have mercy on our souls.

The lobby of the motel was as small and shabby as the exterior. A lovely woman in her late twenties sat behind the desk, poking listlessly at a smartphone with tape on one corner to hold the screen in place. She didn't look up as we entered, just said, "You're late," without any heat or rancor. I would've known she was a dragon even if Brenna hadn't been the one to lead me here. There was something about her combination of perfect hair, perfect skin, and secondhand sweatshirt that screamed "secretly a princess, not here for you to save."

"I had to help Verity with some things," said Brenna sweetly.

The woman's head snapped up, eyes suddenly wide. She scanned us all in a quick, economical gesture before settling on me. "Verity?" she asked. "Verity Price? Is she—I mean, are you Verity Price?"

"Yeah, I am," I said. There was no point in stretching out the suspense of the moment. It would have been cruel, given the circumstances and the power imbalance between us. "It's a pleasure to meet you."

She put down her phone. "I—I mean, I—I mean—" She stopped. "I don't know how to have this conversation."

"That's because we're not having it yet, Chantelle. I'm sorry," said Brenna, before her Nest-sister could embarrass herself—or me—any further. "Verity isn't here because the dragons of New York have agreed to see us. She's here because of problems on the show, and we need to talk to Osana."

"Sorry," I said, when Chantelle looked to me for confirmation. "I'm working on it, but I've been sort of busy appearing on national television for the last few weeks. I'll let you know as soon as I have some sort of answer."

"Please make them answer 'yes,'" said Chantelle. The raw need in her voice was startling. It's rare to hear a dragon beg for anything—not even mercy. Chantelle was begging. "Please. I want my daughters to have sons. I want to die knowing my species isn't going extinct within my children's lifetimes. Please make them understand why they should sell us a baby boy. We'll be the best aunts any dragon ever grew up with. We'll teach him everything he needs to know, and he'll be loved. No one will ever be more loved than he will, because he'll be our future. Everyone deserves a future."

There was a moment of uncomfortable silence when she finished speaking, like none of us knew how to react. Even Brenna was quiet, maybe because she understood what Chantelle was saying a little *too* well. I was essentially in control of the future of their species, or at least the future of this Nest; without me to make their case and help them move the baby across the country, they'd have no more chance of getting a mate for their daughters than anyone else, and less chance than many. They needed me, and they didn't know what to offer in exchange for a favor that could quite literally change their lives forever.

So I forced myself to smile, and I said, "I'll do whatever I can to make the dragons of New York understand how good you'd be for their son, and why they should listen to your request. William's a friend of mine. I'm sure he'll pay attention when I speak."

Chantelle clapped a hand over her mouth. "Thank you," she squeaked, voice muffled by her fingers.

"Verity's nice that way," said Brenna. She put her hand on my shoulder, steering me toward the office door. "We'll be back in a bit, all right? Keep watch on the register."

"Yay, guard duty," said Chantelle, dropping her hand—but she was smiling, and her eyes were bright with tears.

Alice waited until we were through the door to the manager's office before she asked, "What was that all about?"

"We've asked Verity to help us purchase a husband from the dragons of New York," said Brenna blithely, as she pulled a set of keys out of her pocket and walked to the door on the other side of the room. "They should be having sons about now, and we have only daughters, naturally enough. We'd like to get some new blood in."

Alice said nothing.

Brenna must have interpreted her silence as a criticism, because she turned back and said, with great good cheer, "I know it's not the human way, but it's the way we have, and we need a husband for our little girls."

"I wasn't judging," said Alice. "I was just thinking about the logistics, that's all."

"Baby dragons are small," said Brenna. "They have to be. Females have human-esque hips, and we're the ones who lay the eggs." She unlocked the door and pushed it open, revealing a tunnel on the other side. "Come on, then. Osana will have seen the light go off on the security board, and she hates it when people dawdle in the tunnel." With that, she started into the dark, leaving the rest of us with little choice but to follow her.

The tunnel ran the length of a football field, passing under the motel before beginning to slant up again. The walls were shored up with concrete and wood pilings, and looked similar in construction to the sub-layers of the Crier Theater. "How long has this been here?" I asked.

"The original tunnel was built in 1922, when we acquired the property that would become our main Nest," said Brenna. "We hired local contractors for the bulk of the work. The expense stung, of course, but better to pay for something that would last than to be patching and renovating every ten years, right?"

"Local contractors," I said. "Not human ones, right?"

Brenna looked appalled. "And have humans know where we lived? No offense, Verity, you and your family ... you're a special case. But most of the species is dangerous, callow, and not to be trusted."

"Preaching to the choir," said Malena. "There's a reason most humans didn't even think chupacabras were an urban myth until fifty years ago. We've always been there. We just didn't feel like getting skinned and sold to tourists in six-inch squares."

Alice didn't say anything. But I could see her profile, and the downturned corners of her mouth made it clear that she was far from happy. Whether she was upset by the defamation of humans or thinking about all the humans she hadn't killed in the last fifty years was harder to say. My grandmother wasn't much on species loyalty. None of the members of my family are, when you get right down to it. It's just sometimes difficult to know where her loyalties actually lay. She isn't a danger to people she's related to. Everyone else is a different story.

I had another question, and this one felt considerably more pressing. "If the same people built the tunnels here and the ones under the Crier Theater, why were you able to hold on to your property while they lost theirs? Why didn't you help them?" I was wagering she would know what I was talking about.

I was right. Brenna shot me a startled look. "We kept our property because we invested in the local area, and made sure the place was run-down and unappealing to human residents. We own half the buildings in a three-block radius. We *do* have humans living here—we couldn't manage absolute control—but with us fighting gentrification and them happy to have rents they can afford and a relatively low crime rate for an area in this apparent state of disrepair, they mostly keep to themselves. They even afford a reasonable smokescreen if someone from the Covenant comes sniffing around."

Dragons frequently became black holes for an area's wealth. I had never heard of them investing in infrastructure before, but it made a certain amount of sense: they could always recoup their money by selling some of their property, since anything in the Valley would go for way more today than they had paid for it fifty years ago.

"As to why we didn't help them . . . they didn't ask," Brenna continued. We'd reached a sturdy door, set into a metal frame. She produced a set of keys from her purse and began undoing the locks. "Honestly, we didn't even know anyone was looking to buy the land the theater's on now until it was already done. We have little contact with the wholly subterranean communities. They're mammals. Mammals are messy and unpleasant to deal with on a day-to-day basis. Present company excepted, of course."

"No one's sure whether I'm a mammal or not," said Malena, far too cheerfully.

(She was right, though. Chupacabra looked human in their bipedal form. They had hair, presumably they had bones in their inner ears, and females had what looked like mammary glands, although that could have been a case of Batesian mimicry. No one had ever worked up the nerve to ask a female chupacabra whether she lactated. On the other hand, they transformed into terrifying lizard-wolves from the dawn of time, and were known to be egg layers. Maybe they were mammals. Maybe they were reptiles. Or maybe they were something old and ostensibly extinct—the most common theory held that they were therapsids, and should have died out millennia ago. But that was an argument for another time.)

Brenna blinked at Malena, looking momentarily nonplussed. Then she shrugged, turned back to the door, and pulled it open to reveal the cavernous depths of the dragon's Nest.

Dragon Nests are like human homes: every one is unique, even if they began from the same original floor plan. At the same time, just as all human homes will include features like "kitchens," "bathrooms," and "beds," all Nests contain certain points of similarity. Chief among them is the gold.

The dragons of Los Angeles had made their home in an artificial cave created by gutting the interior of what looked like a hospital building. I glanced to Brenna for confirmation.

"The Shady Oaks Mental Institution," she said. "Constructed in 1885, abandoned in 1912, following a severe outbreak of tuberculosis among the staff and patients. We were able to buy the property for a song."

"And, of course, you're immune to tuberculosis, so there was no need to be concerned," I said. "Clever."

Brenna smiled. "We try to be."

The building may have started as a place of human suffering, but it had been reforged since then, becoming something wonderful and new. The windows had been boarded over; I could see the ghosts of those structures beneath the layers of gold leaf that covered them. Heaps of gold covered the floor, coins and chains and random bits of cutlery, like the world's most expensive thrift shop had been emptied out for everyone to walk on. Brenna reached down and removed her heels before stepping, barefoot, into the nearest pile of golden rings and wiggling her toes in evident delight.

Malena was staring around herself, eyes wide. "This is all real?" she asked.

"And quite pure," said Brenna. "We have a few Cash for Gold franchises scattered around the city. We melt the cheaper pieces, clean out the impurities, and make them into coins before we bring them here. It keeps the atmosphere nicely balanced."

Alice was narrow-eyed as she looked around. I paused, realizing what had to be wrong.

"Betty isn't here, Grandma," I said quietly. "She was in New York. She's dead."

Alice cast me a startled look, eyes going back to normal. Then she nodded, and said nothing.

Betty was a dragon—a dragon princess, according to what we'd known when we'd first encountered her—and she'd hated my family for reasons I still didn't understand, but which had originated when Grandma and Grandpa Thomas had been active. There was clearly some history there. If I was going to keep working with the dragons, I was going to need to find out what it was. And this was not the time.

"Actually, it looks like nobody's here," said Malena. She looked to Brenna, shoulders suddenly tight with tension. "Is this a trap?"

"No, it's a safety precaution," said Brenna. She cupped her hands around her mouth and called, "All's clear! It's me, with Verity and her friends. We need to talk to Osana."

There was a moment of silence, broken only by the ghost of Brenna's voice echoing in the high, gold-coated rafters. Then doors began slamming open, and piles of gold leaf and gold chain began to explode with little golden-haired girls who climbed out and swarmed toward us in a sea of prepubescent pseudo-mammalian excitement.

"Verity?"

"*The* Verity?"

"We watch the show every week! I voted for you!"

"I voted for you *twice*!"

"Don't listen to her, she forgot and slept through the whole thing!"

Brenna put her hands up, laughing despite herself, and said, "Girls, girls! There will be no swarming of our guests! We want them to see how respectable and dignified we are!"

Her words had an electric effect on the younger dragons. They skidded to an immediate halt before shuffling themselves around into a configuration that would have looked perfectly natural at a finishing school for young ladies. Their clothing broke the illusion: they were dressed in patched hand-me-downs and thrift store finds, as well as a wide assortment of clearly homemade sundresses, some of which had started life as sheets, curtains, and pillowcases.

"We're sorry, Auntie Brenna," chorused the girls.

"I know you are," she said. "Now go on. I need to take Verity to see Osana, and I don't want any of you making our guests feel like they're being spied on."

The girls nodded and scattered, running past the adult dragons who were closing, more sedately, on our location. It was hard to determine exact numbers, but going by the number who were awake and in the Nest, I was placing this group as slightly larger than the Manhattan group. They clearly had the space, the resources, and the cover story necessary to keep expanding for a while yet before they'd need to talk about creating a new Nest. That was good. Male dragons were essentially solitary creatures, due to their size, functional immobility, and the resources needed to keep them healthy, but female dragons did better when they lived in higher numbers. They were social creatures, even if they were fairly antisocial toward most non-dragons.

The first of the adults reached us and stopped at a polite distance, although the way they looked us up and down was anything *but* polite. Alice looked calmly back. Malena squirmed. I smiled my brightest stage smile, and waved.

"Hi," I said. "I'm Verity Price. It's a pleasure to meet you all."

"So, the famous Verity finally came to see what she'd

be bringing our new husband into." The other dragons parted, allowing the speaker to walk toward me. I blinked.

Brenna was unusually tall for a dragon; this woman, on the other hand, was unusually short, even shorter than me. Her hair wasn't blonde, which was normal for the European exemplars of the species; it was red-gold, almost matching the freckles on her nose and cheeks.

She smiled. "Laidly worm," she said.

I blinked again. "I beg your pardon?"

"I said, laidly worm," she said.

"I thought you were extinct," said Alice.

The woman—Osana—turned to my grandmother and said, "No offense, but that's what we wanted you to think. Those of us who survived have been living with the dragons for centuries. We make good administrators, and the dragons have been happy to accept us as full members of their Nests. That'll change if we can find a husband of our own, of course. Our species are similar, but not *that* similar. I don't suppose you've heard tell of any great worms sleeping in the earth, have you?"

"Not yet, but I'm starting to feel like I'll have a lot of spelunking in my future," I said. "Osana, I presume?"

"The very same," she said. "My family's been here since the Nest was founded. Since my mother was the former Nest-mother, I took over when she passed on. It usually goes to the eldest, but Catherine is a little slow these days. It was better to let her have her space."

I tilted my head. "I hadn't heard about dragons having senility issues."

"We've been cloning ourselves for hundreds of years, with no new genetic material," said Osana. "I did go to college. I read a lot on parthenogenesis. It seemed relevant to my life. If you're a member of a species that has both sexual and asexual reproduction—"

"You need both to remain healthy," I said. "Got it."

Osana nodded. "Now you see why we were willing to empower Brenna to approach you, and why we haven't set an upper limit on what's to be paid. Finding a husband for the girls here won't save me or my sisters, or our daughters, but it will save our family. That makes it worth whatever it costs. We're even willing to send them one of our own to act as a financial adviser, if that would sweeten the pot. We're even better with money than most of our kind."

The more I learned about the damage the Covenant had done in their blind rush to protect humanity above all else, the more convinced I became that the real monsters had won. But that was a conversation for another time. "We're here because Brenna wanted us to tell you what's been going on at the theater."

"Oh?" Osana's attention shifted from me to Brenna, going hard and cold at the same time. It was suddenly easy to see how this tiny woman had been able to convince a whole Nest to let her be in charge. She had a way about her that was pure Nest-mother, ruthless where the protection of her people was concerned. "What's been going on, Brenna?" *What haven't you been telling us?* floated behind the question, as clear as if it had been spoken aloud.

"I just found out tonight," said Brenna, shooting a pleading glance at me and Malena. We were the ones she knew: Alice was the terrifying new factor.

Having mercy on Brenna wasn't hard. She'd been my friend for a long time, and she'd always been kind to the dancers, even when they had nothing to offer her but their good regard. "There's a snake cult operating out of the theater," I said. "They've been killing the eliminated dancers every week, using them to fuel a summoning ritual. They've killed at least eight people so far."

"At least?" asked Malena, giving me a sharp look.

"At least," I repeated. "They only have the dancers in their summoning configuration, but there's no way of knowing whether they've also killed audience members or local residents and not added those bodies to the circle. It's unlikely. It's not impossible." Had I noticed any absences among the crew? No, but until recently, I hadn't exactly been looking.

"How is it that this has been going on under your nose without your noticing, Brenna?" asked Osana.

"They have confusion charms all over the theater," said Alice. "Strong ones, too. I have anti-telepathy sigils and anti-compulsion runes in my current suite of tattoos, and I was still led astray by the charms. I'm going to need to talk to my artist about that."

"We didn't realize our friends were leaving and then disappearing, because the snake cult was making us forget they'd ever existed unless we were actually confronted with the evidence," I said. "We're still trying to find them. There are a lot of tunnels under the theater, and these people seem to know how to use all of them."

"Charming," said Osana. She looked from Brenna to me, raising an eyebrow. "Is this where you tell me that there are strings attached to your offer to negotiate us a husband?"

"No," I said. "I mean, I'd like your help. It's not connected to your request. Brenna mentioned using dragons to bulk out the audience, which would also give us a lot more eyes on the ground. We know the snake cult won't be killing anyone before next week's show—at least not if they stick to their current pattern—but that just means we have a deadline, and we're going to need to keep eyes on all nine of the remaining dancers in danger."

"Nine?" said Osana.

"I'm a chupacabra," said Malena.

"I can keep an eye on myself, and one of the other dancers is an Ukupani," I said. "That leaves us with nine humans who don't know what a snake cult is and don't know they're in danger. We need to keep them safe, we need to find the people who are killing them, and we need to put an end to this."

"But you're not going to make negotiating on our behalf conditional?" asked Osana.

I shook my head. "No, I'm not. I mean, technically my negotiating on your behalf is already conditional: if this snake cult kills me, I'm not going to be able to help you. But I'm not going to stand here and say that you have to risk yourselves before I'll help you. We're talking about the survival of a species here, not loaning me a pair of earrings."

"Humans." Osana chuckled wryly. "Sometimes I think I could have a wend's lifespan and not have the time to understand you. The show's Thursday night, correct?"

"Yes," said Brenna.

"We'll be there. I'll flood the audience if that's what I have to do. Brenna, you'll be helping me get the tickets. We'll pay for as many as we need to in order to avoid raising suspicion." Osana turned back to me, looking me square in the eye. "You didn't try to blackmail me, and I respect that. It doesn't mean I won't happily blackmail *you*. We need that male. I want you to remember, when the time comes, that we were willing to step up."

"I will," I said, and smiled. "Thanks."

"Don't thank me yet," said Osana. "We still need to find this snake cult."

"And I need to get you lot back to the apartments before midnight," said Brenna, glancing at her watch. "You'll need your beauty sleep if you're going to dance your best tomorrow."

"I always dance my best," said Malena.

I didn't say anything. I just took a deep breath and reveled in the fact that for once, I felt like we might actually get through this in one piece. It was a nice feeling. It wasn't going to last, and that made it all the more important that I enjoy it while I could.

Sometimes it's all about the little things.

Nineteen

"Complacency is more dangerous than cowardice. The coward sees danger around every corner. The complacent sees danger and laughs it away."

—Enid Healy

The Crier Theater, bright and early the next day

BRENNA WAS TRUE TO HER WORD, and dropped us off at the apartments almost half an hour before midnight. The party in the courtyard was still going strong, with everyone celebrating the first day of a new rehearsal week by eating, drinking, and boogieing on the tables. The noise provided good cover as Malena and I smuggled Alice back into her apartment. We looked at each other, nodded, and vanished back to our own lodgings.

Pax was asleep on the couch when I came in. Either Anders was snoring again, or he'd been trying to wait up for me. It was as sweet as it was unnecessary, no matter what the cause, and I stopped to look at him, smiling just a little.

"I'll keep you safe," I said, taking the blanket from the back of the couch and drawing it over him. He made a small grumbling noise and nestled deeper into the cushions. I left him there, walking to my own bed and collapsing.

The rest of the night passed without incident, as did the early stages of the morning. Lyra wasn't speaking to me. Pax and I sat next to each other on the drive to the theater. I put a hand on his arm, signaling him to wait as the others flowed inside. As soon as we were alone I asked, "Everything okay?"

"Yeah," he said. "I just felt bad about letting you go off on your own like that. I should have been there."

"Sweetie, it's nice how you think you're the muscle, but I promise, we were fine," I said. "Between me and Malena, we could take most comers, and Alice and Dominic were with us, too. It would have been nice to have you there, for the sake of keeping everyone on the same page, but we were okay. I promise."

"I still feel bad," said Pax.

"Then make sure you're ready to fight after this week's show," I said. "We're going to need all hands on deck to make sure no one else gets hurt. Between you and the rest of us, we'll have five people to cover the nine remaining dancers. We should be able to do this."

"Only if we remember that we're supposed to be watching them," he said.

"Grandma's on it," I said. "There's a Saturday flea market in Chino. She's heading down there to look for her friend the routewitch and see about those counter-charms. We should be protected before the eliminations."

Pax smiled. "You think of everything."

"I wish." I sighed. "Now wish me luck. I have to go convince Anders my head is still in the competition before he calls for an intervention or something."

"Good luck," said Pax. He punched me lightly in the shoulder before turning and heading for the studio where Lyra and their choreographer would be waiting. Anders was waiting for me in a similar room. I reached up to check the pins in my wig before continuing down the hall. It was time to get to work.

With a plan in place, Alice off arranging for the counter-charms, and everyone I cared about safe—for the moment—it was a relief to let go of my worries and *dance*. Valerie had been clawing at the walls of my psyche, reminding me in every pause and pose that this was supposed to be *her* space, *her* time. She wasn't real; she was an idea I sometimes embraced, when it was convenient, when it was safe enough to let that part of me out into the world. But sometimes that part of me could be awfully loud.

"Good!" called Marisol, clapping her hands together for emphasis. "See how easy this is when you let yourself go? See how much nicer it is? Anders, let her to her feet."

Anders, who had been holding me in a deep backbend when Marisol called for us to stop, smirked as he pulled me back into a standing position. "See, Val?" he said. "All you have to do is stop worrying about whatever it is you were worrying about, and remember how much you want me."

"In your dreams," I said. Inwardly, I was scowling. Anders was there when I'd told Marisol my grandmother was sick; he'd heard the genuine concern in my voice. To have him dismissing it as not worth worrying about was frustrating in the extreme. There was a time when he and I and Lyra had been a united front, taking on all comers and making poor Pax feel like he was slightly outside the joke, even as Lyra flung herself at him. Now . . .

I'd come back on the show to let Valerie have one last moment in the spotlight before I put her away forever. I was starting to realize that it was already too late for her. I'd moved past the people I'd loved so dearly when my life was Valerie's, and now they were just shadows in the memory of the girl I might have been. We had nothing in common. They didn't *want* to have anything in common with me. That hurt.

I could channel the pain into my dancing. I forced a feral grin, wiping the sweat from my brow, and asked, "Can we do the pot-stirs again? I think I'm finally ready to hit them the way they're supposed to be hit."

Anders blanched. He was a tapper before anything

else. The pace Marisol and I had been setting since the start of rehearsal was starting to wear on him.

Sadly, I wasn't the only one who saw it. "No, no, no, you'll break the poor boy," said Marisol. "We're going to take twenty. Get some fluids in you, maybe eat a thing, and then get back here. It's time to start *working*." She beamed before heading for the door at the back of the room. The two cameramen who'd been filming our rehearsal turned off their cameras. Twenty minutes for us meant twenty minutes for them. More importantly, it meant they had time to sneak a cigarette out behind the theater.

(Adrian hated smoking, and regularly reminded his dancers that cigarettes were tools of the devil—not that we needed much reminding, since our careers depended on having clear lungs and the ability to keep moving for hours without running out of air. This didn't stop most of the crew from smoking, which made sense once I stopped to consider the fact that they had to work for Adrian *all the time*. I probably would have started smoking also, or at least drinking heavily, if that had been my lot in life.)

Anders waited until we were alone before giving me a sidelong look and saying, "Something's up with you, and I want to know what it is."

I blinked as guilelessly as I could manage. "I don't know what you're talking about."

"Last time we were on this show, you were first in and last out any time there was a chance we were going to party. This time, I've barely seen you in the courtyard at all. The dancers from like, *all* the other seasons think you're unfriendly and uppity. They think you think you're too good for us, which is weird, because you didn't used to be that way, and I *know* you haven't been working." Anders glared at me. "Everyone who knew you in New York says you vanished off the scene months ago. So what's going on? What's the deal with you?"

"There is no deal, Anders, honestly," I said. "I just ... I've been reevaluating my priorities since the show. I probably wouldn't have come back at all, except that I missed everybody, and I knew I wouldn't be taking a slot away from anyone else. I'm an All-Star. I earned this. So I came back to do it, but it's made me realize that this isn't what I want anymore. I've changed."

"So what, you're trying to screw me over? Some of us still want this, Val. Some of us would kill for this, and you're willing to throw it away." His glare intensified, and I realized what this was really about. I hadn't danced well enough the week before. We were probably going to be in the bottom six, and we might be eliminated—and here I'd just admitted that dance was no longer my life.

"My grandmother was sick," I said, as levelly as I could. "I'm sorry I didn't dance as well as you wanted me to, but as long as I'm here, I'm here to win. I did not intentionally hurt your chances. I wouldn't do that to you."

"You were dancing for crap yesterday, too," he said.

"My grandmother was still sick yesterday," I replied. "I got the call that she was out of the woods last night, and I got my head back in the game. I don't know what you want from me, Anders. I apologized. I'm doing better. We're going to tango so well that we'll set the stage on fire, and there's no way the judges will send us home after that. Have a little faith in me, why don't you. I got you to the finale last time."

Anders' eyes widened. My stomach sank. That had been the exact wrong thing for me to say.

"Is that what you think?" he asked, voice suddenly low and tight. "You carried me? Because I didn't earn my place on the show by myself."

"Anders, I didn't—"

"No, you did. You've always been good about saying what you meant, even when you probably shouldn't have. This was one of those 'probably shouldn't have' times, in case you were wondering." He shook his head. "I really thought we were friends."

"Anders, I'm sorry."

"You should be." He turned on his heel and stalked out of the rehearsal room, leaving me alone with the mirrored walls. My reflection looked back at me—my reflection, and not, because I didn't have red hair, and I didn't wear clothing that exposed me so completely to the elements. I was alone with Valerie.

I didn't want to be.

She was everything my sister had ever accused me of being: the sort of person who'd keep dancing above a vault filled with dead bodies. It didn't matter that I was doing it so we wouldn't be thrown out of the theater; I would have wanted to do it anyway. I might have allowed Dominic and Alice to drag me away . . . but I might not have. This was my second chance at the dance career I'd believed I was leaving behind, and the temptation had been huge from the beginning. The temptation was still huge, if I was being honest with myself. I wanted this.

And at the same time, I didn't. My wig had never slipped during my original season, not once. I'd kept it pinned so tightly that it might as well have been epoxy-bonded to my scalp. This time, it had slipped so often that it was a miracle no one had seen. I'd allowed my personal feelings to get in the way of my dancing. I'd brought Dominic to Los Angeles in the first place. Sure he was my husband, and I loved him, but I could have left him behind. Before we'd known about the snake cult, it would even have made sense. The Be-Well was cheap. It still cost money. I'd brought him with me anyway. Why?

Was it because I had already known that I'd outgrown Valerie? Had I come here to try again for the spotlight, or had I come to bury her?

Someone knocked on the ceiling. I looked up. Malena's head was protruding from a hole that hadn't been there before. She'd moved a tile aside to make room, and was watching me with a dubious expression on her face.

"How much of that did you see?" I asked.

"Most of it," she said. She paused before admitting, "All of it. Damn, girl, you know how to say the wrong thing at the right time. You're going to be lucky if he doesn't drop you on your ass during the next show."

"He wants this too much to do that," I said. I

understood her concern. The Argentine tango was all about connection between the people dancing it. We had to sell the idea that we were hopelessly in love with each other, and that wasn't going to be easy when Anders didn't even want to be in the room with me.

Every time I started to feel like I had a handle on *something*, however insignificant, it got pulled right out from underneath me. There was probably a moral in that somewhere. If I ever found out what it was, I was going to knock its teeth right down its metaphorical throat.

"Anyway, your grandmother's outside, and she said I should tell you she has the you-know-whats."

I raised an eyebrow. "Malena. You're in the *ceiling*. You're dangling from the ceiling like some sort of weird bat. Do you really think this is the time to get coy about saying the words 'counter-charm' out loud?"

Malena responded by wrinkling her nose. "Well excuse me, Miss Knows-Everything. She's in the alley. She said to tell you."

"Right, and thank you for that." I paused. "Why are you in the ceiling? You could have come in the door."

"I wanted to wait until I could get you alone. Troy and I are doing a contemporary thing this week, and our choreographer wanted some time to work with him one-on-one, so she told me to go eat some ice chips and really try to embody my character."

Contemporary dance routines were the most likely to come with weird, depressing, and outright morbid backstories. "Cancer dance?" I guessed.

"Thankfully not this time. It's about eating disorders." Malena smirked. "Troy has to pick me up like eight times, and catch me six more, and pretend I'm completely weightless for the whole routine. I figure that counts as payback for him being a total tool earlier this week."

"Revenge is a dish best served with trust falls," I said. "Did Grandma give you a charm?"

"She did," said Malena. "Dominic has his, too. So it's down to you, party girl."

"On my way," I said, and started for the door.

When I looked back at the ceiling, Malena was gone. Nothing lingered for long in places like this one. There wasn't time.

Slipping out of the theater during the day was easier than I'd expected, thanks to the absence of both my choreographer and my partner. There were supposed to be security guards around, but since they were mostly to keep overeager fans from getting into the theater, they didn't really pay much attention to dancers who were trying to get out.

The alley behind the theater was empty. I let the door swing shut behind me as I took a careful step away from it. "Olly olly oxen free," I called softly.

A shadow peeled away from the wall behind the dumpster, stepping into the light and resolving into my grandmother. "Malena said you were having a fight with your partner," she said.

I sighed. "Okay, wow, are we trying to set the land speed record for gossip out here or what? I said some things I didn't mean, Anders took them in the worst way possible, everything is awful, I'm going to try to fix it tonight. I don't want him getting eliminated if there's anything I can do about it."

"Just keep your focus and keep the faith, baby girl. I don't want him getting eliminated, but I'm a little more focused on keeping *you* among the living." Alice dipped a hand into the pocket of her motorcycle jacket and withdrew a long silver chain. "Catch."

The metal was a glimmer in the air as she flung it in my direction. I reached up and snatched it, opening my hand to reveal a small silver disk engraved with a spiral of runes I didn't recognize and couldn't read. "What do I do with this, and what do I owe you? I thought these weren't going to be ready for *days*."

"You don't owe me anything: you're family," said Alice. "And apparently, she had a feeling someone was going to need this sort of thing, so she had them waiting. I traded her my old hiking boots for the six charms. Nothing expensive. I've already replaced them." She raised a foot, showing off the heavy black leather boots that had taken the place of her brown ones. "As for what you do with it, you keep it with you. Always, period. I don't care if you have to tape it to the underside of your boob, you keep it with you."

"Got it." I tucked the charm into my bra, securing it against my skin. "You okay?"

"I'm good." Alice slid her thumbs through her belt loops. "Bon and I had a nice chat about what it would take to chuck someone like me through the walls of the world when I didn't want to go. We also had cake. I'm pretty happy when people want to feed me cake."

"Cake and chaos, that's your modus operandi," I said. The twenty minutes Marisol had given us had to be almost up. I glanced at the theater door behind me, and then back to Alice. "You have a plan for the rest of today?"

"Watch the theater. Watch you. Make sure nobody else gets chucked into a dimension they don't plan on visiting without a passport." Alice shrugged broadly. That worried me. The harder she tried to seem unconcerned, the more concerned she probably was. "Dominic will be here in an hour. He's going to relieve me. You, missy, are going to go back in there and shake your tail feathers like there's nothing wrong."

"But—"

"But nothing." Alice fixed me with a bright-eyed, unforgiving stare. "We're here because you wanted to dance. Turns out that was a good thing: this snake cult would have been killing people whether you were on the scene or not. Having you on the inside gives us a better shot at stopping them. A big part of that shot depends on you continuing to *be* on the inside. You have to dance,

and you have to make it believable. You're not just selling yourself to the audience at home. You're selling
yourself to the people in that building. If they don't believe you're one of them, you're never going to close the
deal, and we're all going to wind up in a world of trouble."

I sighed. "I don't know if I can. It's getting harder and
harder to pretend that dancing matters more than saving
lives."

"That's because it doesn't." Alice's tone was matter-
of-fact and left no room for argument. "Saving lives matters more than just about anything else you can think of.
That's why we do whatever we have to. That's why you're
going back in there."

"But, Grandma—"

"Don't you 'but, Grandma' me. Get back in there,
keep an eye on your people, and tell me if you notice
anything different now that those confusion charms
aren't clouding your vision." Alice shook her head. Her
mouth was a hard line. I knew that expression very well:
I had been seeing it on my father's face since I was a
little girl.

Sadly, that meant I also knew there was no further
point in arguing. Once that face came out, I had lost. "I
have my phone. Call me if you find *anything*. I'll find a
way to get out of rehearsal if I need to."

"You won't need to," said Alice, and pointed to the
door.

I sighed, and went.

The hallway was still empty, and for the first time, it
occurred to me how odd that was. There should have
been production assistants and security guards everywhere, even during rehearsals. One of the unexpected
truths of reality television was that no one was ever
alone. There was always someone there, watching, monitoring, making notes on an endless series of clipboards.
Hollywood was a self-perpetuating machine, creating
jobs for people who wanted to move up the food chain,

while it moved the cousins and nieces and nephews of the elite up in place of the people who fetched the coffee. So where were they?

Maybe this snake cult was taking the employees after all.

I prowled through the halls back to the rehearsal room, not even trying to walk like Valerie. She was a pampered creature, designed for controlled environments and safe spaces, and this wasn't a safe space anymore. Maybe this had never been a safe space in the first place. Maybe I'd just been imagining it.

The door to the rehearsal room opened before I could grasp the knob, and there was Anders, a hangdog expression on his face. "I'm sorry, Val," he said. "I shouldn't have yelled, but when I came back to apologize, you were gone."

He sounded genuinely anguished. Even if I'd been angry with him, and not disappointed in myself, I would have forgiven him then. "It's okay. I just needed to take a walk and clear my head. I shouldn't have said that. You know I didn't carry you."

"Yeah, just like I know that without you, I would never have made it to week four in our original season. I'm the only tapper who's ever made it to the top ten, because the rest haven't been lucky enough to have partners who'll prop them up until they get their stage legs." He offered his hands. "Forgive me?"

"Forgiven," I said, taking them.

We were still standing there, smiling at each other, when Marisol pushed through the door behind me and reentered the studio. "Good, you're both here," she said. "We're going to take it from the top. I want to believe you're going to leave the stage and head straight for the nearest broom closet to conceive your love child."

Broom closet. "Marisol, did we cut way down on the janitorial staff for this season?"

The choreographer turned and frowned at me. "What do you mean?"

"I didn't see as many people in the hall as I was

expecting when I went down to craft services for a cup of water."

"We have the same staffing levels as always," said Marisol. "You must have been lost in your own little world. Hopefully, it was the world of dance. Now come. Show me what you've learned."

We assumed our starting positions. Marisol hit "play" on our backing music, and for a little while, I did what my grandmother had told me to do: I danced, and I trusted my friends and allies to keep an eye on the situation.

This was almost over.

Twenty

"There ain't no drug in the world like the siren song of the stage. Once you've tasted it, you'll always want more, even when you know it's killing you."

—Frances Brown

The Crier Theater, the following Thursday afternoon

DANCERS RACED DOWN THE HALL, glistening with sweat and smelling of hairspray. The army of makeup assistants that had wiped away our vampiric pallor and fake blood after the opening number was behind us, getting ready for the rush that would follow the requisite introduction sequence. Sometimes it felt like *Dance or Die* was a series of sprints disguised as a dance show.

Anders beat me to the stage entrance by a few seconds. He stopped there, waiting for me to catch up. Then he grinned. "Season two for the win, right?"

"Season two for the win," I agreed, looking over my shoulder to where Pax and Lyra were getting into position. Pax flashed me a thumbs-up. I could see the pale metallic gleam of the counter-charm around his neck. We'd done everything we could to make this safe. It was all down to chance now.

"Jessica and Reggie!" announced Brenna, from the stage. The last two dancers from season one ran out to take their places under the lights. Jessica raised one leg in a high, perfectly vertical extension, showing off her muscle control, while Reggie executed a series of standing flips that would have taken my breath away if I hadn't seen him do it a hundred times before.

They ran for the back of the stage, beginning the lineup, as Brenna called, "Valerie and Anders!"

We ran to center stage, where Anders executed a quick tap step before grabbing my hands and allowing me to go into a series of fast, supported turns, ending with my weight on my right foot and my left leg shifted to the side in the classic "I am a sexy tango dancer" pose. We let go and joined Jessica and Reggie at the back as Brenna announced Lyra and Pax.

"Nice turn," said Jessica, sotto voce, as we clapped for my season-mates. "What, you couldn't figure out how to stage a wardrobe malfunction?"

"Says the girl who starts every show by announcing the color of her panties to America," I replied. Lyra ran up next to me. Malena and Troy took the stage.

"Shut up, Jessica," said Lyra automatically.

Jessica glared daggers.

Emily—the third remaining dancer from season three—took the stage with Ivan from season four. He'd originally been partnered with Raisa, whose body was lying in a circle below the theater, alongside all the other dancers who'd left us. Seeing Ivan sent a chill down my spine. This wasn't over. This was nowhere *near* over, and if it didn't end tonight, two more people were going to die. Two more people I *knew* would die—and it was going to be my fault.

Ivan danced like he had no idea his former partner was dead, and when he ran back to join the rest of the male dancers at the rear, leaving Emily to fall into line with the girls, they were replaced by Lo and Will, who had been dancing together since the beginning of season four. She was elegance personified; he was strength and languid grace. It was lovely to watch them, but it was also terrible, because it drove home the fact that they were the last: all four dancers from season five were already gone and waiting for their graves.

"These are your girls, America," called Brenna, as the music signaled us to strut to the front of the stage. The lights were near-blinding, but I squinted through them, smile firmly in place, as I scanned the audience for dragons. Blonde heads were dotted throughout the rows. It was hard to tell whether that meant Brenna's Nest was in attendance, or whether there had been a run on bleach at the local salons.

I hoped for the former. I hoped I was surrounded by saurian cryptids wearing human disguises. Because we needed all the backup we could get.

"And here are your boys!" The male dancers joined us in the strut for the front of the stage. We interwove, finding our partners and striking our poses as the music ended and Brenna's jubilant voice announced, "It's your top twelve!"

The crowd went wild. Malena, frozen in a dip next to me, whispered, "You got a plan?"

"Try not to die," I whispered back. Then the lights were on Brenna, who was introducing the judges to the audience, and it was time to form our line across the back of the stage, falling into position and waiting to hear our fates.

It was the usual three judges tonight: Adrian, Lindy, and Clint, waving and smiling while they were facing the audience, but reverting to all business as they turned back to Brenna. She was saying something about how the cut from top twelve to top ten was always one of the hardest, because we'd all worked so hard and come so far, and didn't the judges agree that it would be better if we could all stay forever? It was a spiel I'd heard from her before, and only the fact that she was genuinely sorry to see any of us go saved it from becoming saccharine.

Malena's hand found mine and squeezed. I glanced her way without moving my head. None of us were smiling now. Silence and solemnity were the order of the night when it was time to learn who was in danger and who was guaranteed another week on the dance floor.

Brenna finished talking to the judges and drifted

back, accompanied by the spotlights, to speak to the
dancers. "Hello, my darlings, hello. Don't you look splendid tonight? What am I saying, you always look splendid.
You know what time it is, don't you? Oh, I hate this
part." She had two small envelopes in the hand not holding her ever-present microphone. They could have wired
the whole stage for sound, but preferred the illusion that
this was a smaller, more intimate sort of show. I'd never
had a problem with that. We wouldn't have been able to
whisper among ourselves if the place had been fully
wired.

"Last week, America voted, and now three girls and
three guys are in danger of elimination. Remember that
this week is the last time the judges will be able to save
any of you: after this, it will be purely about the audience
votes."

The judges haven't saved any of us, I thought, looking
straight ahead as Malena squeezed my right hand and
Anders squeezed my left. Pax had his arms around Lyra's waist, using her almost like a human shield against
what Brenna was going to say next.

"Let's get this over with," said Brenna, and opened
her first envelope. "Troy, step forward. Ivan, step forward. Anders, step forward."

The look Anders shot me as he let go of my hand and
stepped forward was pure anguish, overlaid with a layer
of resigned betrayal. Somehow, that wasn't a contradic-
tion, and I couldn't blame him. It was my fault he was in
the bottom three, after all.

"You are in danger tonight, I'm sorry," said Brenna.
"Will, Pax, Reggie, you may leave the stage."

The music played a descending sting, telegraphing the
disappointment of the dancers on the stage. Brenna
turned her attention to the girls.

"Hello, my girls," she said. That was all she said, but I
caught her flicker-quick glance in my direction, and
steeled myself against what she was going to say next.

The envelope opened with a small tearing sound.
Brenna took a breath.

"Lo, step forward," she said. "Lyra, step forward. Valerie, step forward. The rest of the girls can leave the stage."

Malena grimaced sympathetically as she pulled her hand from mine and let me step into position. Then she was gone, and the six of us were standing, exposed and a little sick, alone with Brenna.

"My darlings, you are in danger. The judges will make their decision at the end of the evening," she said. "One guy and one girl *will* be leaving us tonight. In the meantime, we have six exciting partner dances to come, and will be seeing solos from all six of our dancers in danger. After the break, Jessica and Reggie will be taking you to Broadway, in a Carl Nanson routine. See you in a moment, America!"

The lights flashed, signaling the end of the live broadcast segment. Brenna turned to us, suddenly solemn.

"Dance for your lives, my darlings," she said. "Now go."

We went.

Anders was waiting for me in the hall.

"I knew you'd be in the bottom, but I didn't think you'd drag me down with you," he said, without preamble. "Do you have any idea what this could mean?"

"We need to get ready, we're on third," I said, trying to step around him. He moved to block me.

The color was high in his cheeks; his eyes were narrowed, and he was taking short, sharp breaths, like he was trying to cage his anger. I realized there was a chance he might take a swing at me, and I would have to decide whether to be Valerie and take the hit, or be Verity, and break his goddamn arm.

"I'm *not* getting eliminated because of you," he spat, grabbing my shoulders. "I refuse. Do you understand? We're going to go out there, and we're going to dance like our lives depend on it. We're going to be so amazing that America develops time travel just to go back to last week and pick up the phones for us. You got me? Dance like I'm going to slit your fucking throat if you let me down."

"Wow, Anders, I had no idea you had such a deep-rooted hatred of women," said Malena, stepping out of the doorway behind him. He whirled. She smiled, as pretty and poisonous as an adder. "Or maybe you're just an asshole. Little bit from column A, little bit from column B, I guess. You want to take your hands off my girl before I take them off your body?"

"Dyke," said Anders, taking a step away from her.

Malena raised an eyebrow. "Was he this bad during your season, Val, or has he been taking asshole lessons?"

"Search me," I said. I stepped around Anders to stand next to Malena. He glared at me. I looked back as impassively as I could, trying to conceal the fact that I was shaken and confused. I thought we'd made up during rehearsal. He wasn't supposed to be like this. He was supposed to be my *partner*, and if I hadn't been completely committed to that partnership this season, I still hadn't done anything to deserve this sort of treatment.

Could the confusion charms have been doing this? I'd never heard of that sort of magic making someone violent, but then, what I didn't know about magic could fill a university.

I took a steadying breath before I said, "I'll see you backstage, Anders. And remember, even if the dance says you need to touch me, that doesn't mean you get to do it ever again when the lights aren't on us. Do you follow me? I'll break you."

"Don't fuck with the ballroom girls," said Malena. She hooked her arm through mine and led me away down the hall.

I let her. At the moment, anything more complicated than putting one foot in front of the other felt like it would have been too much for me—and I still had to get changed for my partner routine, and swap my wig for something wilder, more suited to the tango. I just kept seeing Anders, shouting those horrible things I'd never heard from his mouth before, and nothing made sense.

Malena waited until we were almost to the dressing room before she murmured, "You okay?"

"Yeah." I forced myself to smile. "I didn't . . . he surprised me, that's all. It won't happen again."

"Yeah, because maybe he meets one of us in a dark alley and gets reminded why you don't talk to a lady like that." Malena cast a dark look back along the hall. "Or maybe I tell your dangerous boy what he said to you, and his body is never found."

"We're supposed to be saving the other dancers, not digging new graves for them." Still, I couldn't quite deny the appeal of her unmarked grave proposal. There was something to be said for burying the people who pissed you off.

"We can revisit this after we've won." She let go of my arm. "Get changed, be amazing, and don't get eliminated. You get ganked, I am out of here so fast I'll leave claw marks all along the walls. I'm not sticking around to be somebody else's sacrifice."

"I'll be amazing," I said solemnly. "And Malena?"

"Yeah?"

"Thanks."

She grinned, showing the pointed tips of her incisors. "Don't mention it. I'm still going to beat your ass for the title once we take care of this stupid snake cult."

"Of course," I said, and slipped inside.

There were dancers and costume assistants everywhere. The room still felt jarringly empty compared to the beginning of the season, and it seemed like there were ghosts everywhere I looked, dancers who'd died for their art and would never be taking the stage again. I wondered whether Aunt Mary would be able to find any of them haunting the theater, if I called her and asked her to come and have a look. Maybe I would do that, after this was all over. The dead dancers deserved the chance to rest in peace.

Lyra waved from where she was having her face

painted, keeping her expression neutral to avoid messing up the beautician's careful chart of colors and designs. From the look of her, she was going to be doing some sort of incredibly complex jazz number for her solo. I realized with a pang that I didn't know. I'd never asked. We were sharing the same apartment, we were sleeping in the same *room*, and I didn't know what she was going to be dancing this week.

"Hey," I said, dropping into my designated seat. My own makeup assistant was there almost immediately, clipping my hair back with two banana clips before reaching for her palette. They never asked me to pull it back myself, and they never made any attempt to actually style it. They *had* to know I wore a wig, which meant the producers probably knew—which meant Adrian probably knew. He just didn't care enough to say anything about it.

This wasn't my world anymore. Maybe it never had been.

People buzzed around me, getting ready, getting their costumes on, getting their makeup just right, and generally oblivious to the world around them, which didn't matter nearly as much as pointing their toes, shaping their hands, and dancing their way into the hearts of America. I was so envious of them that it physically hurt. My chest ached like I'd bruised my sternum from the inside. I wanted what they had: I wanted the ignorance and the innocence that came with it.

There were things I didn't know about in the world. There were things I didn't *want* to know about. I wasn't being judgmental when I called them ignorant; I was being jealous. They didn't know, and so they didn't have to worry. They could just live their lives, and be happy.

"All done, Val," said the makeup assistant, taking the clips out of my hair. Lyra was still being painted. She flashed me a thumbs up, keeping her face as still as possible.

"Break a leg," I said, and grabbed my bag off the floor and my costume off the rack as I started for the stalls at the back of the room. They were just heavy fabric sheets that we could pull closed for an illusion of privacy, allowing us to change without the producers worrying about an invasion of privacy civil suit from a disgruntled, eliminated dancer.

The mirror on the back wall showed me smoky eyes, red, red lips, and a wig that desperately needed to be styled. I hung the dress bag on the hook and dropped my duffel on the stool that had been provided for my use. Then I yanked out the pins holding the wig to my head and pulled it off, revealing my spiky, matted blonde hair. Instantly, it was my own reflection looking back at me, and not Valerie's. The bruised feeling in my chest remained, but it diminished, becoming easier to overlook. This was her world. She wasn't accustomed to feeling like an outsider when she was in it. But it wasn't mine.

If what I had to do tonight meant I got eliminated, or even banned from the theater, that wouldn't matter. I wouldn't be losing the world I belonged in. Valerie . . . there was every chance she was about to have her last dance. I owed it to her—and to the part of my life she represented—to make it as memorable as possible.

It only took a few minutes to get dressed. I'd been slipping in and out of competition costumes for my entire adult life, and that process had always included putting on and properly affixing my wig. I'd be wearing this one for the rest of the night; it would see me through my solo, and through elimination, whatever the outcome of that happened to be. It was long enough to frame my face, with careful curls running down my back, while still being believably the hair I'd had since the start of the season. The audience would accept a certain number of extensions and styling tricks, but it was important to keep them limited enough to be believable.

The dress was less realistic. Bright red and mostly consisting of fringe, with no modesty panels to cover the wide expanses of bare skin at my right shoulder and left hip, it was the kind of thing my father used to call a "maybe." As in "maybe you'll get a knife under that, but I wouldn't want to know how you managed it." I gave my hips an experimental shake. The dress continued moving for almost two full seconds after I had stopped.

Strapping on the matching heels added four inches to my height. I stomped, making sure they were firmly on my feet, and gave myself one last, assessing look in the mirror. Valerie looked back, red-haired, red-garbed, and ready to dance with the Devil himself for the chance to own the spotlight. I smiled.

"I'm going to miss you," I said.

Someone rapped on the wall outside my little cubby. "Five minutes, Miss Pryor," called a voice—a wonderfully, frustratingly familiar voice.

I stuck my head out through the opening between the curtain and the wall. Dominic, who was holding a clipboard and wearing a headset, smirked at me. It was the slow expression of a man who is profoundly amused by what he sees, and it didn't waver one bit as my eyes widened and my eyebrows climbed toward my artificial hairline.

"Five minutes," he repeated.

"You're here," I said, pushing the curtain open and stepping into the changing room. It was still a bustle of activity, but none of those people were paying any attention to us: they all had their own roles to play, their own tasks to accomplish before they could take their turns upon the stage.

"I am," he agreed, allowing his eyes to travel the length of my body. I've never been a tall person, but the amount of time he took made me feel longer than the Mississippi River. I blushed. His smirk widened in answer as he reached up and tapped his headset. "It struck me that no one would notice a man who seemed to have a purpose, especially since you've been so beautifully careful to keep me away from their cameras. This way, I'm closer and better prepared to react to whatever might happen."

"Let's hope whatever happens is something that can

be dealt with before it eats anybody." I reached up and touched the lock of hair that fell across my forehead, feeling suddenly self-conscious. "How do I look?"

"Like a thousand fantasies harbored by those unfortunate enough not be married to you," said Dominic. His smirk faded into something almost rueful. "I prefer you blonde, as it happens. But you have no idea how much I want to lead you back into your dressing room and remove that deceptive rumor you enjoy pretending is a dress."

My cheeks reddened, the color mostly hidden by my thick foundation makeup. For once, I was grateful for the pore-clogging necessity of a "game face." "I'll take you up on that later, when I'm not dancing for my life. Right now, I need to hit the stage."

"Break a leg," said Dominic, stepping out of my path.

I paused long enough to shoot him a feral grin. "If I do, it won't be mine."

His laughter followed me down the hall to the stage door.

Anders didn't speak as we took our positions at the center of the darkened stage. It might have been awkward under any other circumstances, but here—me in fringe and lace, him shirtless and wearing tight satin pants, my knee pressed to his hip, his hands wrapped around my waist—it seemed only right. This was the dance floor. This was the closest thing I'd ever found to holy ground, and if this was going to be my last dance, I was going to kill it.

The music began, high bell tones warring with a sultry backbeat for dominion over the air. Anders' hands tightened, pulling me closer, and I pressed myself against him as Karissa Noel began to sing.

As a piece, "Corrupt" was about the singer leading her subject astray, wooing him away from the path of righteousness he'd always tried to pursue. It was hard to listen to it without thinking of Dominic, and the way I'd led *him* away from the Covenant. Maybe he would have grown apart from their teachings without me—stranger things have happened—but it would have been disingenuous to pretend I hadn't had anything to do with it. I was the one who'd opened his eyes. If he'd chosen to admit what he saw, that was on him. That didn't mean I hadn't been a part of things.

So I danced. I danced for Anders like I was dancing for my husband, and I knew Dominic was watching me from somewhere offstage, and I knew he would know where the heat in my eyes and the tension in my flexed calves came from. Anders responded to my commitment by matching me beat for beat. When I spun, he was there to jerk me into his arms; when I dropped into a trust fall, he was there to catch me. For the first time since the start of the season, we danced like there were no barriers between us, and all it took was a fight so bad that we might never be able to rebuild our friendship.

There would be time to worry about that after we had both survived tonight's elimination. (In more ways than one. I was still concerned about staying on the show, no matter how much I might wish I weren't: it's hard to break the habits of a lifetime. And if either one of us got cut, I was going to be fighting for our lives in a much more literal sense.)

The dance ended with Anders submitting to me, dropping to his knees at my feet. His chest was heaving, shining with sweat in the lights. I mimed snapping his neck, and his body collapsed to the stage as the music stopped. Smirking, I turned and strutted toward the exit, the riotous applause of the audience putting a little extra wiggle into my step.

Halfway there, Brenna appeared, putting an arm around my shoulders and turning me around as she steered me toward the judging table. She was grinning, holding out her other hand as she beckoned to Anders. The lights shifted, going from performance-bright to something more subdued, and I saw the audience for the

first time since our dance had started. More than half of
them were on their feet, applauding their hearts out.
Marisol was in the second row, her pinky fingers in her
mouth, whistling ecstatically.

My legs were shaky and my heart was pounding from
the combination of adrenaline and exertion, but with
that much applause ringing in my ears, it was easy to
square my shoulders, raise my chin, and walk confidently
beside Brenna to the marks on the stage that showed us
where to stand while we faced the judges.

. . . the judges, who were also on their feet. My eyes
widened, my mouth going dry at the sight of Lindy
standing, Lindy applauding like she wanted to transcend
the limitations of flesh striking flesh and become a whole
drum corps all by herself. She dropped back into her
seat, talking fast, like she wanted to be absolutely sure
no one else was going to get a word in before she had her
say.

"Valerie, I have always, always been hard on you, and
I know you've hated me for it. No, don't deny it—I know
what it means when a girl smiles at you with eyes like ice.
Well, honey, this, tonight, was the reason why. You were
transcendent. For the first time in all the times I've seen
you dance, you moved that body of yours the way I've
always known you could."

Lindy was known for yelling. Sometimes she got so
close to the microphone when she did it that the feed-
back became physically painful. Not this time. Her voice
was low, earnest, and utterly without bullshit. She
sounded like she meant every word.

"I pulled for you to be in the top twenty of your original season, because I knew you had the potential to be
amazing. And I've ridden you as hard as I could, because
I knew you weren't living up to that potential. Tonight, I
saw that potential become reality. It was worth waiting
for. Don't make me wait for it again." She started to sit
back in her chair before apparently remembering Anders was there. Lindy leaned forward again, focus shifting to him. "Anders, you were clean and solid. Your

footwork was good, and if Valerie managed to outshine you, it was only because she finally decided to wake up and start dancing like she should have been dancing from day one. You were both great tonight."

She glanced at me one more time, and her smile was brief but more valuable than diamonds. Lindy approved of me. Maybe the world was coming to an end after all.

Clint said something complimentary and excited. I wasn't really listening. Half my mind was taken up with reviewing what Lindy had just said, while the other half was scanning the theater, looking for signs of danger.

The audience was liberally dotted with heads in various shades of gold: the dragons had kept their word and infiltrated the place. I couldn't see Dominic or Alice, but I knew they were there, sticking to the shadows and ready to move. My counter-charm was cool where it was taped to my inner thigh, despite the fact that I was sweaty and overheated. That was good: it meant it was still working, and I was still sharp . . . or as sharp as it was possible for me to be when I was dizzy from the lack of oxygen and trying to keep my professional smile plastered in place.

Someone was going to get eliminated. Someone was going to get attacked. It was on me to stop it from going any further.

"Valerie, Anders, you have no idea how disappointed I was when last week's show put the two of you in the bottom," said Adrian gravely. He leaned forward, looking between us. "But after seeing this, I have to say you deserved to be there. The fact that you *could* have been dancing like this, and chose not to, is disgraceful. You should be ashamed of yourselves, and you should be aware that if you make it through this week's eliminations, I'm going to expect much, much more from you. I always thought the two of you were brilliant dancers. Now I know that you are artists, and I will not allow you to return to your previous ways. Do we have an understanding?"

"Yes, Adrian," said Anders and I dutifully.

Adrian suddenly grinned. "Then I can forgive you.

You were both brilliant tonight. Be proud of yourselves. America is going to remember why they loved you in the first place."

Brenna hugged us both before going into her spiel about voting and keeping us on the air. I mugged and grinned for the cameras, but I wasn't really listening. Somewhere in this theater there was someone who wanted me hurt, and I had no way of knowing who it was.

Anders took my hand when we were dismissed, and we ran offstage together. I was starting to think that things were going to be okay between us when we passed the dividing line between "public" and "backstage," and he dropped my hand like it had burnt him.

"You made me look like an idiot out there," he spat, whipping around to hit me with the full force of his glare. "All that praise? Was for you finally getting your head out of your ass. Thanks a fucking lot, Valerie."

"What did you want me to do?" I demanded. "I couldn't phone it in. Not with elimination on the line. What the hell do you want from me? First you wanted me to dance like my life depended on it, and now you're mad because I did! Make up your mind."

"Elimination is only on the line because *you* couldn't bring your A-game before you screwed everything up!" Anders shook his head. "I hope you get eliminated anyway. I want a new partner."

He turned and stalked away, leaving me to stare after him.

There was a soft knocking to my left. I turned. Pax and Lyra were behind me, matching looks of concern and confusion on their faces. I sighed.

"Anders isn't happy with being in the bottom," I said.

"You think?" asked Lyra. "We watched you on the monitors. You were amazing."

"Thanks," I said. "You up next?"

She nodded, a nervous smile tugging at the corners of her mouth. I realized with a pang that I might have made her situation a lot more difficult. I'd already decided I was going to have to walk away from this life again—and this time, it would have to stick. I couldn't be Valerie and Verity; one of me had to give, and when you got right down to it, I liked Verity more. She had a family. She had a husband she loved, and who loved her in return. She had a colony of talking mice that would remember her forever. She had everything, and Valerie only had the dance floor. It wasn't a hard choice to make ... but Lyra didn't have it.

Lyra was real. Lyra belonged here. And by dancing as well as I had, I'd put her in even more danger of elimination.

"You're going to be amazing," I said, putting every ounce of conviction I could into the words. "You always are, I mean. There's a reason you beat me the first time, and you're probably going to beat me again."

"You really think so?" she asked. There was a pleading note in her voice that seemed almost alien when stacked against her usual unshakeable confidence.

"I absolutely do," I said. "You're one of the best dancers I've ever met. You can dance rings around anyone who thinks they can beat you. Now get out there and show America how much they screwed up last week."

"You're a good friend, Valerie," said Lyra. She stepped forward, hugged me, and then was gone, letting Pax pull her toward the stage.

I watched them pass through the curtain that kept stage and backstage separate. I'd have to hurry if I wanted to get to the monitors in time to see them dance. I didn't move.

A light scuff from behind me alerted me to the person approaching. I didn't turn. Dancers walk softly, but they don't walk *that* softly. I was about to meet either an ally or an enemy, and either way, I was staying where I was.

"Hey," said Alice. "The halls below are deserted. No one's gone in or out."

"They wouldn't need to before they had a sacrifice," I said, finally turning to look at her.

My grandmother was in her usual gear—tank top, khaki shorts, boots that looked like they could wade through rivers of acid without being seriously damaged—and the moth-eaten tattoos on her arm and shoulder just drove home how much trouble we were in. Her arsenal of unusual weapons was all but depleted.

"I know," she said. "How long before the end of the show?"

"About an hour."

She nodded. "All right. Let's see if we can get through it alive."

Twenty-One

"Everything's better with a little extra boom."
— Alice Healy

The Crier Theater, about an hour later

WE STOOD IN A RAGGED LINE across the stage, me between Lo and Lyra, each clinging to one of my
hands with the bone-crushing strength of people who
had everything to lose. Our heads were bowed, eyes half-
closed against the glare of the stage lights and the tension in the air. Even the audience seemed to be holding
its collective breath as we waited to hear from the judges.
We'd changed back into the costumes we'd worn for our
solos, putting our most iconic finery on display. The stage
lights were hot, but I was freezing in my sequins and
fringe.

"Well, Adrian? Have the judges come to a decision?"
Brenna's voice was as warm and professional as always,
but I could hear the quiver underneath her carefully rehearsed question. If I got eliminated tonight—if I died—
I would be taking the hopes of her entire Nest to the
grave with me.

"We have. Valerie, step forward."

Heart hammering in my chest, I let go of Lo and Lyra
and moved into position, lifting my head high. I would
not cry. I would not flinch. I wasn't going to give them the
satisfaction. Instead, I was going to prepare for the fight
of my life.

"Tonight you danced the way we've always known you could: with grace, power, and *passion*. You've been a remarkable, consistent technician from the beginning, but there have been times when it seemed as if technique was all you had. If you remain on the program after tonight, we're going to expect this level of performance every week — and so is America. Honestly, we can't be sure you have the stamina to deliver on our expectations. Valerie, step back."

I stepped back.

"Lyra, step forward."

The whites of her eyes were showing all the way around her irises as she stepped into position. Adrian's face softened.

"The judges have discussed this, and I'm afraid we're unanimous, darling. You've always been one of our favorites. You are an incredibly skilled, accurate, daring dancer, and your journey through this season ends tonight. It's been a pleasure having you, but Lyra, you have been eliminated."

Lyra's eyes began to fill with tears, glittering like diamonds in the stage lights.

"Valerie and Lo, you are safe for another week and may leave the stage."

Adrian's voice sounded tinny and distant, filtered through the ringing in my ears. On automatic, I moved to hug Lyra. She wrapped her arms around me and clung as tightly as a limpet. She wasn't crying yet, but it was coming; those tears were going to fall.

"I'm sorry, I'm so sorry," I whispered.

Lyra didn't say anything. She just nodded, and let me go.

Lo was there, waiting to grab my hand and pull me from the stage before we could get in trouble for lingering too long and screwing up the schedule. Together, we walked down the stairs to the space in front of the judges' podium, joining the rest of the safe dancers. Lo pulled her hand out of mine and threw her arms around her partner, Will, who gathered her close.

My partner wasn't there to gather me close, even if

he'd been willing to consider it—or I'd been willing to let him. Anders was still on stage, waiting to hear his fate proclaimed by the implacable force of the judging panel. I turned to watch, lacing my fingers together and tucking my joined hands up under my chin, where I could take some small comfort from the pressure.

"Well, Adrian?" said Brenna. "We still have three dancers in danger here. Can you let us know who else will be leaving?"

"Anders, step forward," said Adrian, and my heart soared. If I'd danced well enough to save myself, maybe I'd danced well enough to save us both. I'd follow Lyra, catch whoever had been killing dancers, and then bow out of the competition, leaving an open field for my friends to exploit. Maybe they'd even let her come back.

"Anders, you danced beautifully tonight, but I'm afraid it wasn't enough to justify your remaining in this competition, and you will be leaving us."

"Troy and Ivan, you are safe, and can leave the stage," said Brenna. "Anders—"

"Shut up!" Anders whirled on her, suddenly scowling, brows drawing toward his nose and mouth twisting into a sneer. Brenna took a half-step backward, looking as stunned as I felt. "You stupid bitch, shut up! You always liked Valerie! You probably told the judges to save her! But what, you couldn't be bothered to save me at the same time?"

"Anders, calm down," said Adrian. "We know you're upset, but that's no call for that sort of language."

"Yeah, because we're live on the air," murmured Malena. She had appeared at my elbow, working her way through the crowd of stunned and staring dancers. Her eyes were fixed, like everyone else's, on the stage. "Swearing gets us big FCC fines, and too much could get us put on a tape delay. Not good. Not the sort of thing that makes the sponsors happy. Did you hit him in the head backstage or something? Boy's having some sort of meltdown."

"Chernobyl is a go," I whispered, turning back to the stage.

Anders switched the target of his rage from Brenna to Adrian, glaring daggers at the head judge. "I'm a better dancer than either of those assholes you just saved and you know it. You're trying to cover your asses because you don't want a tapper to win—you don't want *me* to win. Good thing it doesn't matter, huh? This show is *nothing*. You people are *nothing*."

"Anders—" began Adrian.

"Shut *up*, Dad!" shouted Anders.

Silence descended over the theater, broken a split second later by Lindy's hushed exclamation of, "Holy shit."

Anders wasn't finished. "You know, I let you convince me to pretend we weren't related, because it 'wouldn't be fair' if people knew I was your kid. No one would believe I was as good as I am, even though they'd see me dancing with their own eyes. You didn't stick around to raise me, but you stuck your dick in my mom once, so I guess that means there's no way I could have gotten here on my own merits. Right? I let you ignore me and talk down to me and treat me like garbage, and for what? So you can eliminate me when we're right on the edge of getting everything we ever wanted? I was going to save your show once I had unspeakable power, you asshole. Your ratings have been sliding for the last two years. I was going to *make* you. But now you're going to die with the rest."

"Adrian, is this true?" demanded Brenna. "Is he really your son?"

"Way to focus on the scandal and not the implication of mass murder," I said. I didn't have a gun. My dress was too skimpy to conceal one, and the tango had required me to kick my legs around too much for me to have strapped anything big enough to matter to my legs. I reached behind myself and drew one of the throwing knives from under my bra.

Malena looked at me with a mixture of disbelief and amazement. "Do you go *anywhere* unarmed?"

"The bathroom sometimes, if I know I'm on a secure property," I said. The knife was small enough to conceal in the palm of my hand. I held it there, tense and waiting for the moment when I'd need to let it go.

"Fuck you," snarled Anders. He grabbed Lyra, who'd been standing in stunned silence throughout his outburst. She squeaked as he jerked her against his chest. "Fuck you all."

"That is quite enough," snapped Adrian. "You will stop that, right now. You will be silent, and you will get off of my stage. I am ashamed to call you my son. I *refuse* to call you my son. You're never going to work in this town again."

"Wow, Dad, way to embrace the cliché." Anders slid a hand between Lyra and his chest. The gesture was surprisingly familiar. I knew it. Why did I know it? Why—

He pulled his hand back into the open. He was holding a knife, a wickedly curved thing that looked like it had been designed for use in a butcher's shop.

Oh. That was why.

"Didn't have to go this way," said Anders, and jerked the knife across Lyra's throat in a hard arc, severing her jugular and carotid veins in one continuous motion. Blood sprayed everywhere, splattering the stage. Lyra jerked like she'd been shocked, her hands going to the wound. There was nothing she could have done: the blood was coming too fast, and she couldn't possibly stop it. She didn't even have the chance to scream.

I screamed for her. I was already moving, my heels finding little purchase on the blood-slick stairs to the stage as I thundered toward Anders. My knife flew straight and true, catching him in the wrist. He swore and dropped his own knife. It landed in a pool of Lyra's blood.

Lyra fell a heartbeat later.

She hit the stage like a sack of wet cement, limbs splayed and open eyes staring at the ceiling. Anders jerked my knife out of his wrist and dropped to his knees next to her, rolling her onto her stomach before dragging his hands through her blood. He started painting symbols on her back, smearing the careful makeup provided by our costumers. Lyra would *hate* that. She hated looking anything less than perfect.

"He's our cultist!" shouted a voice, and I turned to see Alice running from the wings, onto the stage.

But there are cameras here, I thought dazedly. She'd be caught on film. If this was going out live, the Covenant would see her—and while they might believe she was dead and buried, there was no way they didn't have her picture in their files. She was virtually Covenant Public Enemy Number One, thanks to what she'd done to my grandfather. The Covenant didn't look kindly on traitors. They looked even less kindly on those who led their people astray. And none of that mattered, because we had lives to save.

Alice was running. I was running. She had a gun in her hand, a complicated, old-fashioned pistol. I was still trying to draw a second knife from under the tight nylon strap of my dress.

Then the center of the stage exploded, and we had bigger things to worry about than a few cameras.

The snake that came bursting into the light was something like a king cobra, something like a python, and something like a SyFy Channel Saturday night special. Its head was the size of an SUV and its body was sized to match, flowing out of the hole it had created in a seemingly endless river of scales and heavy musculature. The stage lights glinted off its side, making its reality all-too-concrete. This was real. This was happening.

Alice and I had both pulled to a stop as soon as the wood began to splinter, recognizing that we were charging straight into something a little too big for us to handle without a plan. Its body was between us now, blocking easy access. That wasn't good.

"Aw, shit," I said. "He finished the ritual." Lyra's death had been the tipping point.

The first screams from the audience sounded almost hesitant, like the screamers were afraid this was a hoax and didn't want to be the only ones who fell for it. The snake kept coming, until its terrible head brushed the ceiling. Then it turned, tongue flickering, and looked at the people behind it.

"Holy *shit*," said Adrian.

The snake opened its mouth and hissed. It was a sound from the dawn of time, one that hit my simian hindbrain like a jolt of electricity, reminding me that I was something snakes might enjoy eating, if they were large enough. *This* snake could swallow a Guernsey cow if it wanted to. Eating me would be no big deal.

Lindy's scream was high and shrill, and would have been ear-piercing even without the microphone to amplify it. As it was, I could feel it all the way down to my bones. I wasn't the only one. The snake's head whipped around, homing in on the source of the irritation. Then it struck.

I caught a glimpse of its teeth as it shot past me, enough to know that they were long and sharp and far too plentiful. It moved like a freight train, mouth closing around Lindy and cutting her off in mid-shriek. The rest of the audience picked up the slack, screaming and rising from their seats as they stampeded for the doors. Most of the audience, anyway. The blonde women who'd been scattered through their ranks remained where they were, going so still that it felt like a joke to think anyone could mistake them for mammals. Nothing hot and fast could ever be that still.

"Thought snakes didn't have ears," said Malena. She was at my elbow again. I glanced at her long enough to see that she was in her human form before focusing my attention back on the snake.

"They don't," I said tightly. Anders was laughing and capering around Lyra's body, the hole in his wrist apparently forgotten. He was one of our snake cultists, absolutely. But he hadn't acted alone. I *knew* he hadn't acted alone. "The vibrations from the noise must have been enough to catch its attention, and that was all it took."

Poor Lindy. She hadn't been my biggest fan, but she'd deserved better.

"How the fuck do we kill it?"

Hearing her say "we" was like a shock to my system. Here I was, just standing there, staring at the giant snake as if it was someone else's problem. Well, it wasn't. It was my problem, because I was in the building, and if there's one thing I've learned from my family history, it's that sometimes responsibility and proximity are the same damn thing.

"Get to my grandmother," I snapped. "I need a gun."

"On it." Malena took off at a run, seeming to turn inside out as soon as she reached full speed. She hit the stage on all fours, slick black-and-orange hide gleaming like oil in the light. Some more people screamed. It was hard to know whether that was due to her, or due to the giant monster snake. Sometimes "why" doesn't matter as much as we might want it to.

The snake was back in a holding pattern, swaying as it reared back to its original height. I needed more help. The edge of the stage was only about ten yards behind me. Careful to move slowly enough that I wouldn't attract unwanted attention, I took a half-step backward and turned.

Pax met my eyes without hesitation, like he'd been waiting for my cue. I nodded. He stepped onto the stage.

Jessica grabbed his arm.

"I don't think so, shark-boy," she said. There was a gun in her free hand. Where did Jessica get a gun? More importantly, why was she holding it on Pax? He stopped staring at her.

I started to take a step. Jessica turned her head, smiling sweetly.

"Move, and I'll blow his head off," she said. "He's not human—did you know that? He's some sort of monster. But even monsters need skulls. They get squishy and sad without them."

"You're one of the snake cultists," I said. It made so much sense that I was almost ashamed of myself for not seeing it sooner—and actually ashamed of the snake cult for recruiting someone so *obvious*.

Then a gun cocked behind me, and I turned again to

find Clint holding a pistol only a few feet away. The snake was still swaying behind him, although it seemed to have lost interest in wreaking havoc on the theater. Anders was down on his hands and knees, using Lyra's blood to paint more runes on the stage.

"Oh," I said. "You, too."

"We don't like the term 'snake cult,'" said Clint. "It's pejorative and retrograde. We prefer 'dimensional capitalists.' We're going to be kings when this thing settles down and realizes who's in charge."

"No one's in charge of a snake god," I said. "That's where you people always screw up." There were a few drops of blood on the collar of his shirt. It was Lindy's, it had to be. She'd had time to bleed before the giant snake swallowed her. "God, Clint, why? I liked you."

"Why did you have to be a nosy parker who stuck her nose where it didn't belong? I liked you, too, Val. You're a good dancer. You've got a great ass. But you can't just go hiring inter-dimensional bounty hunters because you want to get an edge in the competition."

I blinked. Clint smirked.

Everything suddenly made a hell of a lot of sense.

Alice had a reputation in certain circles: she was, after all, an apparently ageless, extremely violent woman who traveled from dimension to dimension with a large supply of knives, grenades, and chocolate chip cookies. Clint had only ever seen me as Valerie. He'd have no reason to think Alice had a granddaughter, much less suspect the granddaughter was me. If Alice was here, and keeping company with me—something Jessica and Anders would both have reported to him by now—I must have hired her. If I was hiring muscle with dimension-traveling capabilities, I must be trying to cheat.

The fact that a *snake cultist* was passing judgment on my ethics would have been funny, if not for the part where he was holding a gun to my head. "You know, if you have a problem with my hiring decisions, you should also have a problem with murder and summoning giant snakes through the stage floor."

"It's the cost of doing business, sweetie," said Clint. He adjusted his aim, keeping the muzzle trained on my heart.

Costuming is going to be pissed, I thought nonsensically. Aloud, I said, "Now would be nice."

Clint blinked. "I thought you'd beg for your life, not for a bullet."

I smiled. "Who said I was talking to you?"

There was a scream from behind me, high, shrill, and feminine. Clint's eyes darted in that direction. It was a natural response: anyone human would have had trouble not looking in the direction of that scream, which was filled with pain and terror.

Well. Anyone human who didn't know that it was caused by an Ukupani biting off the hand that threatened him. Knowing Pax wasn't human and seeing him suddenly twist and distort into an eight-foot-tall bipedal shark-beast was probably pretty damn surprising.

Judging by the look on Clint's face half a heartbeat later, it wasn't as surprising as my kicking the gun out of his hand. It flew across the stage, landing out of reach of either one of us.

"I'm a *tango dancer*, you *asshole*," I snarled, and kicked him in the face. I was wearing four-inch heels. Blood spurted from his nose in a hot red gush that reminded me too clearly of the flood from Lyra's slit throat, so I kicked him again, harder. We generally make it a rule not to kill humans, but if a few bone slivers found their way into this dick's brain, I wasn't going to lose any sleep over it.

Jessica was still screaming. I started to turn, to order Pax to shut her up—through whatever means necessary, which sure, could mean decapitation, but I was out of fucks to give—when I saw the snake moving out of the corner of my eye, drawing back to strike.

There was only a second for me to make my decision, and I chose the path most likely to end with my survival. "Pax! *Move!*" I shouted, diving to the side. The snake slammed down on the stage a second later, striking unerringly for the sound of screaming and the smell of blood.

Jessica stopped screaming. That was a mercy. My shout had given Clint time to move out of the way; when the snake pulled back again, he was still standing, glaring at me with blood on his face and shirtfront and hatred in his eyes.

"Catch!" Malena's voice came from above. I stuck my hand out, and the gun dropped into it. The weight was a great comfort. The feeling of the safety clicking off was an even greater comfort.

"Thanks!" I called. "Any eyes on Dominic?"

"Other side of the stage," said Malena.

The snake was rising back into position, head moving back and forth with increasing speed as it took in the situation. It was recovering from whatever disorientation accompanied its passage through the wall between worlds; soon, it would be back to whatever served as normal for a massive fucking snake, and then we were going to have to deal with it.

I was fast. The striking snake was faster. Once I started moving, I was going to have to keep on going. "Pax, I need you," I called.

The Ukupani's footsteps sounded like flippers slapping against the wood. I turned to the massive shark/human hybrid as soon as he was close enough, and said, "I need you to throw me at the snake."

Pax no longer had eyebrows, or the sort of face that transmitted human emotions well, but he didn't need them for his dismay to show. I found myself grateful that he couldn't talk, either. If I had to explain myself to him, he might try to stop me, and I didn't see another way through this—not without risking a hell of a lot of people who hadn't had any idea this was going on. It had only been a few minutes since the snake broke through the stage, and two people were dead. Sure, Jessica may have deserved it, but not Lindy. I had to move. I had to act. And as soon as I did, I trusted my family to have my back.

"Seriously," I said. "Throw me."

Pax shook his head in pantomime disbelief. Then he knelt, forming a basket with his hands. I shoved the gun into the back of my dress, anchoring it as best I could, before running at him, my heels like gunshots on the polished stage floor.

My foot hit his hand and I was in the air, launched by all the force an eight-foot, four-hundred-pound Ukupani could generate.

Please realize what I'm doing, I thought. *Please follow this lead.*

I couldn't blame them if they didn't. I *wouldn't* blame them if they didn't, because I would be dead, and dead women aren't usually big on slinging blame around—well, except for a few of my relatives.

The sound of me hitting the side of a giant snake from another dimension was surprisingly mundane, the same dry slap I used to hear when my father dropped a leg of lamb on the counter. I'd expected something more exciting. There wasn't time to dwell on it: I had to scramble to get a handhold on its rough-edged scales, cutting up my fingers in the process. Another thing to worry about later. Right now, I had a giant snake to worry about.

Gunfire from the other side of the snake told me Alice had seen me move, and was reacting accordingly. Dominic was more of a knife man—a fact that was reinforced a few seconds later when the snake suddenly hissed and whipped its head around, so fast that I was sent flying.

This is it, I thought, as my body inscribed an arc through the air. *This is how I die.*

Malena dropped from the ceiling above me, wrapping her arms around my waist as she fell. The sudden added weight dragged me down, and we both landed, with a thump and a grunt, on the judges' table. It collapsed underneath us, dropping us at the feet of a stunned Adrian.

"What the fuck is wrong with you?" I demanded, pulling away from Malena and staggering upright. "*Run!*" I

kicked off my heels and followed my own advice—
although sadly, I was going in the wrong direction. If
Adrian was smart, he'd be heading for the door as fast as
his legs could carry him. I was heading for the giant fucking snake.

At least I wasn't doing it alone. My fall had put me on
the side of the stage with Dominic and Alice. They'd
pulled back to the wings, out of the snake's direct line of
sight, and they beckoned Malena and me forward as we
ran.

Dominic broke cover when we got close, grabbing my
wrist and dragging me the rest of the way to temporary
safety. "Are you hurt?" he demanded.

"Later," I said, pulling my hand away and drawing my
gun for a second time. "We need to stop this thing."

"How?" asked Brenna. She was farther back in the
shadows, where I hadn't noticed her at first. She looked
terrified, and there was blood on the front of her previously spotless dress. It was the first time I'd seen her look
anything less than perfectly groomed.

Oddly, seeing her shaken made me think of something. "Does Osana have a cellphone?"

Brenna blinked. "Yes."

"Good. Call her. Tell her Clint's our magic-user, and he
needs to be stopped. There are so many dragons in this
place, there shouldn't be any problem restraining him."

"Anders was the one who finished the ritual," said
Malena.

"Anyone could have finished it once it was that far
along," I said, unable to suppress the stab of betrayal
accompanying the words. "Anders spends too much time
dancing to have done the necessary research. Clint recruited him. Both of them." Had he been trying to re-
cruit me? I sort of thought he might have been.

"I'll call her, but she's not going to risk my sisters for
this," said Brenna.

"Tell her if she does, I will move heaven and earth to
get you that baby." It felt like I was bargaining with
things that weren't mine to give, and I'd feel bad about

that later, when this was over and we were still alive. Right here, right now, I needed everything I could get.

Brenna's eyes widened. "Got it," she said, and retreated, presumably to make her call.

I turned to the others. "We have to stop it."

Alice nodded grimly. Dominic just looked at me. Then, with no warning, he grabbed me by the shoulders, pulled me close, and kissed me.

Maybe it was the mortal peril, and maybe it was the adrenaline, but that might have been the best kiss I'd ever had.

When Dominic pulled away, his eyes were bright and his breath was coming a little too fast. "Do not die," he said, and his words were a plea and a command, all at the same time. "Do whatever must be done, but do not die."

"Same to you," I whispered.

"This is fun and all, but let's go see where on a giant snake we can stuff a grenade," said Alice.

We turned.

The snake was still swaying, tongue flicking constantly. Anders had stopped painting with Lyra's blood and moved to Clint's side, both staring at the snake with expressions of proprietary satisfaction. This was their terror, their great accomplishment, and they were planning to enjoy it.

I still didn't know if they could control it, and I wasn't waiting around to find out. "The scales were rough but graspable; I think I could climb it, if nobody stabbed it while I was on the way up."

"Gunshots seem to hurt it less, maybe because it's so damn armored," said Alice. "I can distract it without making it thrash. Then you see about feeding it something it won't like." She held out a grenade.

I took it and stuffed it down the front of my dress. It wasn't like I had anyplace else to put it. "Great, let's do that. Malena, think you can make it up with me?"

Malena stared at me like I'd just grown a second head. "Are all humans this suicidal, or are you a fringe case?"

"My mother always said I was special. Dominic—"

"I will help your grandmother. *Do not die.*"

I couldn't keep the bitterness out of my voice as I said, "Enough people are dead already. Now move."

We moved.

I ran for the snake like I was being timed, leaping at the last moment and grabbing hold of the rough scales on the side of its body. Malena didn't jump. She just slipped back into her quadruped form and swarmed up the snake, talons finding grips where I would have sworn there were none. I struggled to hold on, before realizing there was a better way.

"Malena!"

She knew. Immediately, she knew, and climbed back down, moving to cling to the snake next to me. I swung over to cling to her back, locking my left arm around her neck while I dug the grenade out with my right hand. Malena climbed.

I looked behind me. Dominic and Alice were on the stage, shooting at the great snake's body as they ran around it. They were fast. It was faster. It tensed to strike, and then recoiled, nearly knocking us off. I twisted. There was Pax, still in his half-and-half form, burying his teeth in the snake's side. It hissed like a steam engine getting ready to explode and tensed again. Alice and Dominic resumed their shooting. It was like a terrible game of whack-a-mole, and I found myself feeling almost bad for the snake. It hadn't asked to come here. It was just an animal, doing what animals do, and we were doing our best to kill it.

At the same time, there was one thing the Covenant of St. George got right, all those years ago. When your choice was kill or die, kill was the only answer worth giving.

Malena climbed higher, moving from side to side to avoid the worst of the thrashing. I leaned close to her ear.

"When we get to the head, I'm going to climb off, and you're going to run," I said. "I'll try to feed it the grenade."

Malena grunted. Whether it was from exertion or because her face was currently too distorted to allow for human speech, I couldn't tell.

"I'll find my own way down," I assured her. "It'll be fine."

This time, I didn't need a translation for her grunts. Profanity is the universal language.

The snake thrashed and squirmed beneath us, presenting a difficult climb as only a living thing truly could. I held on for dear life, until we had reached the head, and it was time to put my terrible, awful, no-good plan into effect.

Letting go of Malena was harder than I expected. I rolled onto the top of the snake's skull, and it hissed, irritated by the fact that something was touching its head. It pulled back, nearly knocking me off. I grabbed the ridge over its left eye at the last second, anchoring myself.

If it started shaking, I was going to fly. That couldn't happen.

"Hey, big guy," I said, pulling the pin from my borrowed grenade. "How's it hanging?"

The snake hissed. I let go of the eye, letting gravity pull me down the length of its nose. I was going to get one shot at this. If I missed, well. It wasn't going to matter much to me, after that. It would matter to my family, and to everyone else the giant snake killed before someone took it down.

I fell.

The natural urge of the falling human is to claw at empty air, looking for purchase, some miraculous rescue from the force of gravity. I've been falling recreationally for most of my adult life. I did no such thing. Instead, I pulled my arm back and chucked the grenade into the snake's open mouth before balling myself up to minimize my area of impact and giving myself over to the inevitable.

Fifteen feet was enough of a drop that I'd break an ankle if I tried for a normal landing. It was still short enough that I might be okay, if I got lucky about where I landed. I clung to that thought. I might be okay.

There was an explosion above me as the grenade

went off, and warm wetness splattered over the world, marking the giant snake's demise. That was a good thing. I had succeeded.

Then I hit the edge of the stage, and stopped thinking about anything but pain, even as the stage shook from the impact of the snake's body, which fell beside me and mercifully *not* on top of me.

"Verity!" Dominic's shout was loud and terrified.

I opened my eyes and pushed myself up on one hand, trying not to look as sick and disoriented as I felt. "Anybody get the number of that freight train?"

"You're alive!" Dominic dropped to his knees, wrapping his arms around me and setting off a whole new cascade of exciting agony.

"Your ex-partner isn't," said Malena. I turned toward the sound of her voice. Her dress was shredded, but she was relatively clean, presumably because she'd been outside the blast radius when the grenade went off. She wrinkled her nose before continuing, "Snake landed on him. Asshole deserved it."

"Clint!" I pulled away from Dominic, scrambling to my feet. Everything hurt. I had never let that stop me before. "Where is he?"

"Here."

Alice sounded pleased with herself. As well she should have; she was standing over Clint's body, tying his hands behind his back. She beamed when she saw me looking her way. "Hi, baby girl. I'm going to take this back to my home base with me, if that's okay. I have some friends who have strong opinions about pulling endangered super-snakes through the walls of the world."

I blinked. "Oh. Okay."

Pax came trotting up. "We have a problem."

"Of course we have a problem. Is there ever a time when we *don't* have a problem?" I looked at him. "What's the problem?"

His face was a grim mask, streaked with blood and lacerated where he'd been sliced by the snake's scales. "We've been on the air this whole time."

Slowly, I turned to the nearest camera. The red light was on. The red light had never gone off.

"Oh," I said.

"We need to get out of here," said Malena.

"Too late," I said. Dominic and Alice had both appeared on camera. Even if the Covenant didn't include any fans, someone would put this on the Internet. Someone would *already* have put this on the Internet. The Covenant would watch. They would see.

They would know we were still out there.

As if in a dream, I walked toward the camera, reaching up with one hand to pull my wig off. It was so sodden with blood that it felt like a dead animal in my hand. I dropped it and kept walking.

Then the red light was right in front of me, and I was looking straight into the lens. I pulled the gun from the back of my dress.

"My name is Verity Price," I said, enunciating each word clearly and distinctly. "This is my continent. Stay the hell out."

The sound of my gunshot was somehow softer than the sound of the lens shattering.

Silence fell.

Epilogue

"Everything changes."

— Frances Brown

A cavern underneath Manhattan, surrounded by dragons

Two weeks later

OSANA AND CANDY WERE LOCKED deep in negotiations, the members of their respective Nests milling around them. The L.A. dragons were trying to act like they weren't awed and speechless in William's presence, while the Manhattan dragons were trying to act like they weren't prepared to commit murder to protect their husband. Good times all around. I was sticking close to William, staying out of the way and observing the chaos without involving myself in matters that didn't involve me.

"This is really okay with you?" I asked, for what must have been the tenth time.

William chuckled. "Yes," he said, in a cultured English accent that would have sounded perfectly reasonable coming out of a human man, but was a little weird coming from a lizard the size of a Greyhound bus. "This is as it has always been for us. I was sold shortly after I was hatched, to a Nest capable of sustaining me. Our ways may seem odd to you, but I assure you, they've worked for a long time."

"I believe you," I said. I was leaning against the cavern wall, trying to look casual and hide how much the descent had taken out of me. I was still healing after my fall from the giant snake. I'd managed to crack my pelvis when I hit, in addition to leaving bruises along the length of my legs and hips. It was a good thing the rest of the season had been canceled after our little "special effects display." There was no way I would have been able to dance.

Adrian was in a *lot* of trouble with the network, since we'd violated more than a few FCC rules during the fight—but the show's ratings had been spectacular, and he was going to be all right. He was a human cockroach. He always found a way to come out ahead.

"Are you well, Miss Price?"

"As well as I'm going to get." I closed my eyes.

Malena and Pax had gone home to their respective families, melting back into the therianthrope communities they belonged to. Pax would be fine. He could live in the water until all this blew over. I was more concerned about Malena, but she'd assured me she'd be okay, and I was choosing to believe her. She had my number if things got bad.

As for Clint . . . Alice had taken him with her when she went back to whatever dimension she called "home" in between trips, and something in her eyes had told me that I didn't want to ask for any details about what was going to happen to him there.

I had my own problems. My parents had been understanding about my spur of the moment decision to essentially declare war on the Covenant. That didn't mean they knew what was going to happen next. Dominic and I were in New York to make introductions between the two groups of dragons, and so we could check in with my contacts, warning them that trouble might be coming, and setting up a network for notifications in case the Covenant came looking.

My Valerie ID was well and truly blown. I hadn't even been able to go to Lyra's funeral, since she'd never officially met "Verity Price," and my showing my face in public could have brought the Covenant down on my head. I'd had to leave her to be buried without me, and could only hope she was at peace. Aunt Mary hadn't been able to find any ghosts in the theater, so there was that. Maybe Lyra had been able to move on.

Maybe.

As for Dominic . . . a hand touched my shoulder. I opened my eyes and offered him a weary smile. "Sorry," I said. "I didn't know it would take this long."

"It will take as long as it takes," he said. "Kitty sends her regards, and has agreed to host a meeting tonight at her club. I told her we'd be there."

"Of course we will." I pushed myself away from the wall, only wincing a little. "This is our job."

I'd warned the Covenant to stay out of North America, and I'd meant every word. I glanced at the sea of dragons around us, intelligent cryptids who only wanted to be allowed to live their lives in peace. Humans were a much greater danger. Humans summoned snake gods and killed their own kind. Cryptids just wanted to go a little longer without becoming extinct.

If the Covenant came here, if they pushed the issue, we'd fight. And we'd win. That was the only acceptable outcome for this particular competition.

Dominic smiled at me wryly as he slipped an arm around my waist.

"Yes," he said. "I suppose it is."

Price Family Field Guide to the Cryptids of North America
Updated and Expanded Edition

Aeslin mice (Apodemus sapiens). Sapient, rodentlike cryptids which present as near-identical to noncryptid field mice. Aeslin mice crave religion, and will attach themselves to "divine figures" selected virtually at random when a new colony is created. They possess perfect recall; each colony maintains a detailed oral history going back to its inception. Origins unknown.

Basilisk (Procompsognathus basilisk). Venomous, feathered saurians approximately the size of a large chicken. This would be bad enough, but thanks to a quirk of evolution, the gaze of a basilisk causes petrification, turning living flesh to stone. Basilisks are not native to North America, but were imported as game animals. By idiots.

Bogeyman (Vestiarium sapiens). The thing in your closet is probably a very pleasant individual who simply has issues with direct sunlight. Probably. Bogeymen are close relatives of the human race; they just happen to be almost purely nocturnal, with excellent night vision, and a fondness for enclosed spaces. They rarely grab the ankles of small children, unless it's funny.

Chupacabra (Chupacabra sapiens). True to folklore, chupacabra are bloodsuckers, with stomachs that do not handle solids well. They are also therianthrope shape-shifters, capable of transforming themselves into human form, which explains why they have never been captured. When cornered, most chupacabra will assume their bipedal shape in self-defense. A surprising number of chupacabra are involved in ballroom dance.

Dragon (Draconem sapiens). Dragons are essentially winged, fire-breathing dinosaurs the size of Greyhound buses. At least, the males are. The females are attractive humanoids who can blend seamlessly in a crowd of supermodels, and outnumber the males twenty to one. Females are capable of parthenogenic reproduction and can sustain their population for centuries without outside help. All dragons, male and female, require gold to live, and collect it constantly.

Ghoul (Herophilus sapiens). The ghoul is an obligate carnivore, incapable of digesting any but the simplest vegetable solids, and prefers humans because of their wide selection of dietary nutrients. Most ghouls are carrion eaters. Ghouls can be easily identified by their teeth, which will be shed and replaced repeatedly over the course of a lifetime.

Hidebehind (Aphanes apokryphos). We don't really know much about the hidebehinds: no one's ever seen them. They're excellent illusionists, and we think they're bipeds, which means they're probably mammals. Probably.

Jackalope (Parcervus antelope). Essentially large jackrabbits with antelope antlers, the jackalope is a staple of the American West, and stuffed examples can be found in junk shops and kitschy restaurants all across the country. Most of the taxidermy is fake. Some, however, is not. The jackalope was once extremely common, and has been shot, stuffed, and harried to near-extinction. They're relatively harmless, and they taste great.

Johrlac (Johrlac psychidolos). Colloquially known as "cuckoos," the Johrlac are telepathic ambush predators. They appear human, but are internally very different, being cold-blooded and possessing a decentralized circulatory system. This quirk of biology means they can be shot repeatedly in the chest without being killed. Extremely dangerous. All Johrlac are interested in mathematics, sometimes to the point of obsession. Origins unknown; possibly insect in nature.

Laidly worm (Draconem laidly). Very little is known about these close relatives of the dragons. They present similar but presumably not identical sexual dimorphism; no currently living males have been located.

Lamia (Python lamia). Semi-hominid cryptids with the upper bodies of humans and the lower bodies of snakes. Lamia are members of order synapsedia, the mammal-like reptiles, and are considered responsible for many of the "great snake" sightings of legend. The sightings not attributed to actual great snakes, that is.

Lesser gorgon (Gorgos euryale). One of three known subspecies of gorgon, the lesser gorgon's gaze causes short-term paralysis followed by death in anything under five pounds. The bite of the snakes atop their heads will cause paralysis followed by death in anything smaller than an elephant if not treated with the appropriate antivenin. Lesser gorgons tend to be very polite, especially to people who like snakes.

Lilu (Lilu sapiens). Due to the striking dissimilarity of their abilities, male and female Lilu are often treated as two individual species: incubi and succubi. Incubi are empathic; succubi are persuasive telepaths. Both exude strong pheromones inspiring feelings of attraction and lust in the opposite sex. This can be a problem for incubi like our cousin Artie, who mostly wants to be left alone, or succubi like our cousin Elsie, who gets very tired of men hitting on her while she's trying to flirt with their girlfriends.

Madhura (Homo madhurata). Humanoid cryptids with an affinity for sugar in all forms. Vegetarian. Their presence slows the decay of organic matter, and is usually viewed as lucky by everyone except the local dentist. Madhura are very family-oriented, and are rarely found living on their own. Originally from the Indian subcontinent.

Manananggal (Tanggal geminus). If the manananggal is proof of anything, it is that Nature abhors a logical classification system. We're reasonably sure the manananggal are mammals; everything else is anyone's guess. They're hermaphroditic and capable of splitting their upper and lower bodies, although they are a single entity, and killing the lower half kills the upper half as well. They prefer fetal tissue, or the flesh of newborn infants. They are also venomous, as we have recently discovered. Do not engage if you can help it.

Oread (Nymphae silica). Humanoid cryptids with the approximate skin density of granite. Their actual biological composition is unknown, as no one has ever been able to successfully dissect one. Oreads are extremely strong, and can be dangerous when angered. They seem to have evolved independently across the globe; their common name is from the Greek.

Sasquatch (Gigantopithecus sesquac). These massive native denizens of North America have learned to embrace depilatories and mail-order shoe catalogs. A surprising number make their living as Bigfoot hunters (Bigfeet and Sasquatches are close relatives, and enjoy tormenting each other). They are predominantly vegetarian, and enjoy Canadian television.

Tanuki (Nyctereutes sapiens). Therianthrope shapeshifters from Japan, the Tanuki are critically endangered due to the efforts of the Covenant. Despite this, they remain friendly, helpful people, with a naturally gregarious nature which makes it virtually impossible for them to avoid human settlements. Tanuki possess three primary forms—human, raccoon dog, and big-ass scary monster. Pray you never see the third form of the Tanuki.

Ukupani (Ukupani sapiens). Aquatic therianthropes native to the warm waters of the Pacific Islands, the Ukupani were believed for centuries to be an all-male species, until Thomas Price sat down with several local fishermen and determined that the abnormally large Great White sharks that were often found near Ukupani males were, in actuality, Ukupani females. Female Ukupani can't shapeshift, but can eat people. Happily. They are as intelligent as their shapeshifting mates, because smart sharks is exactly what the ocean needed.

Wadjet (Naja wadjet). Once worshipped as gods, the male wadjet resembles an enormous cobra, capable of reaching seventeen feet in length when fully mature, while the female wadjet resembles an attractive human female. Wadjet pair-bond young, and must spend extended amounts of time together before puberty in order to become immune to one another's venom and be able to successfully mate as adults.

Waheela (Waheela sapiens). Therianthrope shapeshifters from the upper portion of North America, the waheela are a solitary race, usually claiming large swaths of territory and defending it to the death from others of their species. Waheela mating season is best described with the term "bloodbath." Waheela transform into something that looks like a dire bear on steroids. They're usually not hostile, but it's best not to push it.

PLAYLIST:

Here are a few songs to rock you through Verity's adventures.

"All the Right Moves" . . . . OneRepublic
"The Spine Song" . . . . Cake Bake Betty
"Second Chance" . . . . Liam Finn
"Shake It Off" . . . . Taylor Swift
"Society Song" . . . . Sarah Slean
"Born To" . . . . Jesca Hoop
"Disturbia" . . . . Rihanna
"Toxic" . . . . Yael Naim
"Candyman" . . . . Christina Aguilera
"Only Prettier" . . . . Miranda Lambert
"Phonecall" . . . . Emm Gryner
"Road Buddy" . . . . Dar Williams
"L.A. Song" . . . . Christian Kane
"Paint the Silence" . . . . South
"Better Sorry Than Safe" . . . . Halestorm
"Goodnight L.A." . . . . Counting Crows
"El Tango de Roxanne" . . the *Moulin Rouge* soundtrack
"Get It Get It" . . . . Scissor Sisters
"Dragula" . . . . Rob Zombie
"Jerusalem" . . . . Mirah
"Corrupt" . . . . Karissa Noel
"Valerie" . . . . Amy Winehouse
"Hunter" . . . . Dido

ACKNOWLEDGMENTS:

Ladies and gentlemen, Valerie Pryor. *Chaos Choreography* is Verity's third adventure and the fifth book in the series overall, and I don't mind admitting that I've been looking forward to this little turn around the dance floor since page one. Verity has always been a dancer. It just took a while for me to be in a position to show everyone what that really means.

As always, my greatest thanks go to Phil Ames, whose fault this series really is. My tireless machete squad provided proofreading and editorial services, spearheaded by Michelle Dockrey, without whom I would be genuinely lost. Big thanks to Amy Mebberson for putting up with my ongoing quest to have pictures of all the In-Cryptid girls on my walls, and to Aly Fell, whose covers never fail to delight. Meanwhile, back on the ranch, Chris Mangum and Tara O'Shea kept my website and graphic design needs rolling right along. These people make so many things possible.

My agent and personal superhero, Diana Fox, remains my rock, while Sheila Gilbert and the entire team at DAW worked to make this book a thousand times better than it was to start. It's good to have people like this in your corner.

Thanks to Michelle Dockrey for accompanying me on endless trips to Disneyland, to Amy McNally for being infinitely patient, to Brooke Abbey for being infinitely impatient, and to Shawn Connelly, who helps me keep body and soul together. Any errors in this book are entirely my own. The errors that aren't here are the ones that all these people helped me fix.